Wolf Blood

Lycanthropic Book 1

Steve Morris

This novel is a work of fiction and any resemblance to actual persons living or dead, places, names or events is purely coincidental.

Steve Morris asserts the right under the Copyright, Designs and Patents Act 1988 to be identified as the author of this work.

Published by Landmark Media, a division of Landmark Internet Ltd.

Copyright © 2017 by Steve Morris.
All rights reserved.

stevemorrisbooks.com

ISBN-10: 1976021251
ISBN-13: 978-1976021251

The Lycanthropic Series

Acknowledgements

Huge thanks are due to Margarita Morris, Michael Smith and James Pailly for their valuable comments and help in proof-reading this book.

Chapter One

The mountains of Romania, midwinter, full moon

Professor Norman Wiseman poured himself another shot of whisky and tried to ignore the distant howling of the wolves. He wondered how many glasses he'd need to drink to block out the noise completely.

'Six so far,' he muttered to himself. 'Nowhere near enough.' He knocked back the crystal glass of golden-brown liquid and poured another.

A wolf howled again from somewhere outside the log cabin. It sounded closer than before, but the winter wind blew so violently at this altitude he couldn't be certain. The heavy snow played tricks with sounds too, muffling some while seeming to amplify others. A man couldn't trust his own senses in this place. Not human senses, at any rate.

What was he doing up this mountain in the middle of winter anyway? He had come chasing wolves. Now they chased him. There was a certain justice to that, he supposed. Wolves had always ruled the Carpathian Mountains. Humans had driven them out of the lowlands and civilized lands. But here, among the rugged peaks and thick forests of Romania, nothing much had changed since humans had first come. Wolves, bears and lynxes went about their business as they always had. It wasn't just ordinary wolves he feared now though. If only it were just wolves.

The wind gusted again outside the cabin, twitching the flames of the candles on the table, making shadows dance across the wooden walls. He had killed the electric lights earlier that evening when the full moon rose above the densely-packed trees. No point drawing attention to himself, although he doubted that would make any difference. They knew exactly where he was. But the ambience of candle flame and moonlight soothed his nerves and quenched the worst of his fears. Or perhaps that was just the alcohol.

He drank the eighth whisky more slowly than the seventh. If it was going to be his last, he might as well try to enjoy it.

'A twenty-year-old single malt doesn't come cheap,' he reminded himself.

His grad students had clubbed together to buy it for him on his fiftieth birthday. No need to waste a good malt.

Professor Wiseman, his students had called him. He had been Professor of Emerging Diseases at the London School of Hygiene and Tropical Medicine once. He still would have been, if his paper hadn't been leaked to journalists. He'd sent it in confidence to the *International Journal of Virology, Epidemiology and Communicable Diseases*. It was the most important scientific paper he'd ever worked on, with content that would have rocked the field of epidemiology. And some idiot had given it to the popular press. He had a pretty good idea who'd done it. The academic world was small, and full of petty rivalries and bitterness.

Now they called him *Professor Wolfman*, or worse. *Professor Wolfman predicts Werewolf Outbreak. Doctor Werewolf's Evil Experiments.* He forgot some of the most absurd headlines now. The whisky was starting to do its job.

What stung him most was the way his former colleagues had treated him. They should have defended him from ridicule. They should have recognized the significance of his discoveries. But they were just as bad as the newspaper journalists. Oh, they dressed it up in academic language so they could claim the moral high ground, but most of what they wrote was just vindictive.

Completely unsubstantiated speculations. Groundless scaremongering. Preposterous and dangerous theories and poorly-designed experimental protocols. He knew what they really meant. *This doesn't fit our pre-conceived models. Conventional theories cannot account for your rogue ideas. You've gone off the rails, Professor.*

In a way, he hoped they were right. He had uncovered something so horrifying that he had questioned his own sanity at times. He had double-checked his calculations, repeated his experiments under different control conditions. His conclusions were robust. The journal editors should have seen that. He had handed over every last piece of data and all his notes from the past two years. Photographs even. All the evidence, documented, analyzed and repeated. But once the story had leaked to the newspapers, they had rushed to denounce him and dismiss his results.

'One day it will all come back to bite them.' Wiseman chuckled. That was a good joke. It was a pity he had no one to tell it to.

Unless …

No, he mustn't even think about that.

He sipped the whisky and tried not to think any more about biting. How much of the bottle would he need to drink so that when they came for him he would no longer care? He intended to find out. There was no point saving the whisky for another night. This would be his last.

A faint rapping came from inside the cabin. Not outside, this time. Not the howl of a wolf, or the scratching of icy pine needles against the cabin wall. A muffled rhythmic drumming, from inside. Metal against wood. He knew what it was and where it came from. He glanced quickly at the bedroom door, then looked away. The door was firmly locked. He patted his shirt pocket to check. Yes, the key was still there. He had locked the door himself. Firmly.

'Don't open it, Wiseman. Don't even think about it.'

He picked up the bottle to pour again, then thought better of it. Easier just to drink straight from the bottle. He preferred his whisky neat anyway. He stood up, slightly unsteady, and walked the short distance to the window of the log cabin. White. All was white out there. Snow thick on the ground, icicles hanging from the trees. Above everything, the moon. A beautiful night. And black too, of course. Black of night. Black of shadow. Black of the unknown.

The beauty hadn't struck him quite so forcefully before. A fierce beauty. Untamed nature in its purest state. Mile upon mile of pine trees standing tall, or bending under the weight of the snow. Unchanged for ten thousand years. And beneath the trees, wild beasts roaming freely, indifferent to human concerns. If only they could have remained as beasts.

The snow was deepening. Perhaps it would fall all night and bury the cabin. Maybe he would survive then, hidden beneath a layer of white. He would emerge in the morning and the nightmare would have passed. But that was crazy thinking. There could never be that much snow, not even in this desolate wilderness. And there was no time now. They were close, not more than a mile away he guessed.

The tapping sound started up again from inside the other room, louder this time. 'Dammit!' It was impossible to ignore. He turned away from the winter wonderland outside and paced the wooden floor of the cabin. Twelve feet by ten. That was the size of his world now. Outside no longer mattered. You could get cabin fever, living here. And yet that was the least of his worries. He wished that cabin fever was the worst thing he'd discovered in these mountains.

He wondered again at the events that had conspired to bring him to this godforsaken cabin for his last night on earth. He could discern no rational reason for it. He had done nothing to deserve this fate. No good would come of it. His discoveries had been pushed aside and ignored. One day they might be unearthed by some researcher somewhere, but by then it would be too late. His thoughts were turning maudlin again. He could blame the whisky. Either that, or the clarity of knowing he had less than an hour to live.

He paused at the locked door and listened carefully. No knocking now. He reached for the handle and pulled it slowly. It turned just so far and then stopped. Locked. He felt for the key in his pocket again. What if …?

No, that was dangerous thinking. And yet … what difference did it make now? The two outside were coming for him, and they were fully turned. Stage Three of the condition already. No longer a shred of humanity left. Whereas the girl was still human. Just … different.

Leanna. She had been a promising student once. The other two had been too. But Leanna had always been the best. Smart girl, straight A grades, a promising academic or clinical career ahead of her. He'd been delighted when she volunteered to come with him to the mountains. A three-year project, isolated from other people. It was a lot to ask from a young student with the world at her feet. And yet she'd had faith in him. All three of them had. They'd followed him to this wilderness, and he had let them down. He'd failed in his basic duty of care. Poetic justice then. He deserved what he got.

A wolf howled again outside, quickly followed by a second. Not wolves, though. Creatures.

They were very close now. As if in reply, the knocking started up again, louder and more violent. Wiseman tipped the bottle and swallowed a big mouthful of whisky, slopping half of it down his front. He'd lost count of how much he'd drunk. What the hell, he would open the door. He drew the key from his shirt pocket and inserted it into the lock. Slowly he turned it, until the lock clicked softly. He tried the handle again. This time it turned all the way. He pushed the door open a few inches and peered inside.

Chapter Two

Moonlight from the window threw a stark strip of white into the darkened room beyond. Careful now. He mustn't let the moonlight reach her. If it did, everything would be over. Moonlight was the catalyst for Stage Three.

The bedroom was even smaller than the main room of the cabin, and sparsely furnished. It was incredible that they'd all lived together for so long in such primitive conditions. A combined kitchen diner and living space, four tiny bedrooms and a basic bathroom. Leanna's room had few items of furniture, but still felt cramped. A wardrobe against one wooden wall, a locker just visible opposite. He pushed the door to the room open a little more. The moonbeam crept further across the floor, reaching almost to the bedside locker. He mustn't open it any more.

He grabbed one of the candles from the kitchen table

and held it before him as he slid through the half-open door. The candle flashed monstrous shadows on the back wall as it swayed in his hand. Once inside he put it on top of the locker, keeping the bottle of whisky in his other hand. He was going to need that.

Leanna lay on the bed where he had secured her, arms and legs tied tightly to the metal bed-frame with thick ropes. Congealed blood covered her wrists and ankles where she had struggled with the knots. The bedsheets beneath were stained red and brown. He felt a pang of guilt, but quickly fought it away. Those knots were all that had kept him alive.

The stench from the room made him want to gag. She had been lying in her own filth for days now, strapped to the bed. He hadn't been to see her since Stage Two had taken hold. There had been no point after that. She had stopped accepting food and water, so what could he have done for her in any case? No cure existed. Nothing could slow the onset of the next stage. And she had been unconscious for much of the time.

Wiseman pulled up a wooden chair and sat next to the bed. The chair rocked slightly from leg to leg on the uneven floorboards as he tipped back the whisky bottle, swallowing another mouthful. She hardly seemed to be aware of him at first. Her eyes remained closed, almost as if she were sleeping, but then she arched her back and thrashed at the ropes that bound her, making the bed frame rattle and thud against the back wall of the cabin again. She was still fully human to look at, but her face was horribly gaunt and pale, her cheeks like hollows, the skin stretched taut across her forehead. You could see the skull outlined beneath the translucent flesh. It was hardly surprising she looked so thin and pinched, given that she had refused all fluids for over a week now. A normal human would be dead already.

That was how he knew she had entered Stage Two of the condition. The refusal to eat or drink. The disgust she showed when offered food. The acute sensitivity to sunshine or electric light. Symptoms he had meticulously catalogued and sent to the journal, only to be met with ridicule and disbelief.

Her fingernails had become unnaturally long, and he could see that the shape of her jaw had changed to accommodate the extended teeth. Her nose had changed shape too, becoming more animal-like as her wolf senses developed. And her golden hair, always beautiful, had grown even longer and thicker than before. It shined lustrously in the orange flicker of the candle. She was ready to make the transition to Stage Three.

Her eyes snapped open as he looked at her. Bright yellow eyes.

It startled him to see that. It was the most inhuman aspect of the transformation. Her eyes had been blue before. The purest blue. Now they burned yellow like the fires of hell.

She struggled when she noticed him, thrashing from side to side, trying to break free of the ropes that bit into her flesh.

'Calm down, Leanna,' he said soothingly. 'You're just hurting yourself.' He reached out a hand to touch her, but she snarled at him, wolf noises, growls and stifled yells. He was thankful for the ball of cloth he had stuffed in her mouth to gag her. She shook her head violently from side to side in frustration, trying to shake the gag free, but he had tied it too firmly.

'Leanna,' he tried again. 'You know I had to tie you. It was for your own sake.' There was truth in that. She would have battered herself to death when the fever took her. Before the calm set in, she had been like a rabid dog, thrashing her limbs, hurling herself to the ground as the disease spread through her body, squeezing the last vestige of humanity out of her very bones. It had been horrible to watch, and just as bad to listen to. The gag had been for his own benefit, there was no point denying that, least of all to himself. Least of all now.

She stopped shaking her head and lay still, seemingly exhausted. Then she fixed him with those yellow eyes and started to make a new sound. It sounded like speech, but he couldn't be sure.

He bent his head closer to her face. 'Leanna? Are you trying to say something?'

She gave him a quick nod of her head, then fell silent again, beseeching him with her wide eyes.

Wiseman took another swig of whisky. He might as well remove the gag. What harm could it do now? The worst of the animal noises had ceased at least a day ago. Since then she had stayed mostly silent. And now perhaps she wanted to talk. Why not? He had little to fear from her now. The two outside were the true threat.

'Leanna?' He spoke quietly to her, pronouncing the words carefully so that the wolf brain would understand. 'I'm going to remove the gag, but you have to promise not to scream or howl. Do you understand?'

After a brief pause she nodded.

'Okay.' He put the bottle down on the floor next to the bed and reached his fingers around the back of her head, taking care to keep his arms and hands well away from her mouth. The knot had pulled taut from the strain of holding her for so long. The cloth had been soaked in sweat and grime and had become so knotted he couldn't unpick it.

He kept a Swiss Army knife in his back pocket and he drew it out, flipping one of the blades open. He tried the gag again, this time sawing at the cloth until it split. He folded the knife closed and pulled the material away from her head. The cloth wad was still in her mouth though. 'Can you spit it out?' he asked.

She shook her head.

'I'm not going to put my hand in your mouth. You have to remove it yourself.' He was drunk now, but he wasn't going to make a rookie mistake like that.

She threw her head from side to side, trying to dislodge the gag, but it seemed to be stuck fast. She may have partly swallowed it.

'Use your tongue to push it out.'

He watched as she pushed the cloth slowly out of her mouth, saliva drooling from her lips as she regurgitated it out. Briefly he glimpsed the sharp canine teeth that had appeared during the past few days. Astonishing. How could such rapid transformation occur? There were precedents for it in other parts of the animal kingdom. Cats could extend and retract their claws at will; pufferfish and certain types of frogs could produce spikes on previously smooth skin. Octopi had the ability to change the hue and texture of their skin as camouflage, and cuttlefish could even change shape to evade predators or when hunting. He suspected that regenerative stem cells were at work – the same process that enabled crocodiles to quickly regrow lost teeth.

He wished he had more time to study the development of the condition, to track its progress, maybe even develop a cure. That was all a pipe dream now.

The last of the gag came away from her mouth and she licked her teeth slowly and smiled up at him. The smile was that of a beast. It chilled him as much as the yellow eyes that shone brightly in the semi-light.

The candle was burning low but was still bright enough to light the room. He knew that electric lights would cause her pain, and in any case his own eyes had become accustomed to the dark. The moon had swung around slightly since he last checked and its light now crept to the edge of the bed. If it touched her skin, she would change. But he would remember to keep an eye on it. If the moonlight came too close to her, he needed only to close the door.

'Professor Wiseman,' she said, her voice hoarse, but still recognizably hers. They were the first words she had spoken in almost two weeks. Once he had thought he would never hear her speak again. 'Thanks for coming to see me. I missed your company.'

He had attended to her almost constantly when the condition had first taken hold. He had nursed her, brought her water, mopped her brow when the fever began, administered painkillers and basic medication. He had tended to the other two just the same. But nothing he did slowed the onset of the condition. It always progressed in the same way. Flu symptoms at first, followed by fevers and uncontrolled shaking. The subject might well die without medical attention in those early days. But as the condition took hold, less could be done. The patients became disgusted by any food he offered, and eventually even water would cause them to vomit. At that point they became violent and had to be restrained, for their own safety as well as his. They looked close to death, but somehow they were actually gaining in strength, undergoing some kind of metamorphosis from man to beast. He couldn't be certain when they ceased to be human, but Leanna had certainly passed that point.

The face regarding him now was no longer that of the girl he once knew. Still he found that he needed to talk to her. 'I missed you too,' he admitted. 'It's lonely in the cabin by myself.'

'The others?' she asked. 'Adam and Samuel?'

He shook his head. 'I haven't seen them since they ran.'

'How long ago was that? I can't remember how long I've been here.'

'You've been in bed for two weeks. Tied up for most of that time. You know why I had to do that?'

'Sure.' She smiled as she said it. She was a trained scientist. She understood. 'I'd have done the same thing if our roles were reversed.'

'Of course.'

'So how long have the other two been out there?' she asked again.

He didn't need to think about the answer to that. The

full moon outside was all the reminder he needed. 'One month exactly. Since the last full moon.'

'Oh yes.' She turned her head to look at the sliver of silver light coming through the half-open door. It was only a foot away from her now. 'So when the moonlight reaches me, the transition will be complete?'

'You know I can't allow that to happen. I caused two of you to transform. I can't be responsible for you as well.'

Her yellow eyes narrowed, the pupils black within them. 'So what, then? You've come to kill me?'

He shook his head and lifted the whisky bottle off the floor. 'No,' he said quietly. 'Not that. Never that.' He took another slug of liquid from the bottle, swallowed and coughed.

When he finished coughing, she was staring at him intently. 'You can't leave me here like this,' she told him. 'The other two will tear me to pieces if they find me in this state.'

She didn't mention what they would do to him. He was glad of that. She was right though. If she didn't fully complete the transition, the other two would kill her when they came for him. He had seen it happen in other cases. The beasts showed no mercy for anyone but their own kind.

'What then?' he asked, although he already knew what she would say.

'Untie me,' she begged, and a light flickered in her eyes, whether wolf or human he couldn't say. 'Please. I won't hurt you. Just untie me and I'll go. Please, Professor,' she added softly.

It had been a while since anyone had spoken to him like that. She knew it too. There was a wolf cunning about the way she looked at him. Just the right amount of helplessness. A good dose of logic and reason to persuade him. And an appeal to his better nature. Oh, she was cunning all right. Devious and manipulative. He could see that.

But she had a point. He wouldn't survive beyond tonight whatever happened. Surely he owed her this last kindness. He had brought her to this place. He was responsible for all that had happened, even if it hadn't been his fault.

She said nothing, just looked up at him, as if she knew exactly what he was thinking.

'Okay.' He would do it before he had time to reconsider. Don't think, just do it. He grabbed at the bottle again and opened his mouth wide for a last mouthful. He was surprised to find the bottle empty. It had been a good malt, one of the best. He let the bottle fall to the wooden floor.

He reached around to his back pocket and took out the knife again. His movements were becoming clumsy. He guessed he was properly drunk at last. He'd need to be careful with the knife. He didn't want to hurt her any more than she'd already been hurt.

'Thanks, Professor,' she said, as he cut away the rope that bound her ankles. 'You won't regret this, I promise.'

The knife was short and the blade wasn't particularly sharp. He wasn't at his best either, but steadily he cut through the ties that held her. Her legs were free now. She lay still, just as she had promised.

She eyed her right arm, where the rope wrapped around her bloodied wrist. He inserted the blade carefully, trying not to cut her skin. He wriggled the knife back and forth, but the knot stayed firm. God, he had tied it tight. Eventually it came away, leaving one last rope to cut. The moon had nearly reached her fingers. She would turn then, and no rope would be strong enough to hold her.

'You know you were always my favourite student,' he told her. 'Not just because you were so bright, but because …'

'I know,' she said.

'A Professor shouldn't have such thoughts, but I'm only human.'

'Yes,' she nodded. 'Only human.' She licked her lips eagerly, revealing a flash of white teeth.

He could add his inappropriate feelings toward a female student to his list of personal faults. Along with his drinking ... his failure to protect his students from harm ... perhaps his colleagues had been right to dismiss his work out of hand. But no, the proof of his studies was right here before his eyes.

'Hurry, now,' she said.

From outside the wolves howled again. They were very close now, much closer than before.

He cut at the final rope as fast as he could, nicking his hand with the blade as he did. A drop of blood ran down his ring finger. Leanna jerked her head forward and licked the blood away with her long tongue.

Tears stung his eyes as he sliced through the last cords that held her. What had he done? He should have plunged the knife through her heart when he had the chance. But he could never have done that. Never that.

Leanna bounded off the bed when the rope came away and rushed to the door. She moved faster than any human had ever moved. But then, she was no longer human. She flung the door wide open and stood in the glare of the full moon's rays. Bathed in its cold light, her body began to change.

From the side of the bed, Wiseman watched in horrified fascination. He had not seen the transformation this close before. He knew he should run, but he could not.

Over the past days, Leanna had already changed in many subtle ways. Her skin had paled and grown thin, but her hair and nails had become strong and long. Her teeth, her eyes, and her nose had become wolf-like, and her muscles had not wasted from lack of food, but instead had grown lean and taut. Now, with the bright light of the full moon as a catalyst, her final transition to Stage Three began.

At first he thought she was shrivelling up, but rather, her skin was changing. Fine pale hairs sprouted from the back of her hands, her neck, and even her ears. They grew longer and thicker until they completely covered her skin. She kept her face turned away from him but he imagined the hair slowly covering her once beautiful features. She moaned as the golden hair thickened into fur.

Where the ropes had cut her skin, the wounds were healing rapidly, the scratches fading, scabs forming over damaged tissue, shrinking and falling away to the floor, as if in a time-lapse video.

She appeared to be getting shorter, but then he realized she was stooping forward to stand on all fours. Her shoulders broadened and thickened, tight muscle bulging beneath the coat of fur that now covered her entire body. Her clothes tore as she changed, and she ripped them away in shreds, revealing golden fur, not skin, beneath. She paced the small floor of the room impatiently. Her arms and legs had changed, balancing the move from two legs to four, and her feet had transformed into paws, her fingernails into sharpened claws. The transition was complete.

When she turned her head to look back at him, he cried out in fear. A wolf stared at him now, fiery yellow eyes deep-set in a fur-covered face. Her nose had become a snout, and when she parted her lips, a long pink tongue drooled saliva over rows of sharp incisors and carnassial teeth. Perhaps most terrifying of all were the enlarged canines that protruded more than an inch from her upper jaw like fangs. They were the mark of a predator. They were the mark of a beast.

The wolf snarled and paced toward him.

Wiseman backed up against the wall, holding the tiny knife as the beast advanced, trying to keep the bed between himself and the creature. His knife hand trembled violently.

The wolf padded closer, fearlessly. He was shocked

when the creature spoke. 'I'm hungry,' it rasped huskily.

Wiseman stared incredulously at the wolf. He had no idea they could speak once changed. The voice was Leanna's, but deeper, throatier. 'You p-promised you wouldn't hurt me,' he stuttered. The old Leanna would never have hurt anyone. He couldn't have imagined a kinder person.

'No,' growled the wolf angrily. 'Leanna the woman promised that. She is gone. I am Leanna the wolf.'

He realized at that moment that Leanna was no more. No humanity remained, only cruelty. He curled up on the bed, the blade falling from his grasp. His fingers shook uncontrollably.

'But I won't hurt you,' said the wolf slyly. 'Not unless I catch you.'

'What?' Just one word, but what else could he say?

'I'll give you a chance,' said the creature, grinning that hideous wolf grin again, showing him those fangs, those bright eyes shining yellow like torches. 'I'll only hurt you if I catch you. So run.'

He stayed motionless, stupid, rigid with fear.

'Run!' shrieked the wolf.

He stood to run, but where could he go? The cabin was miles from the nearest village, the temperature well below freezing. He wouldn't survive an hour out there. In his condition he would barely make it out of the cabin. Terror made him mute. All he could say was, 'Where?'

'If you can get to the Land Rover, you can drive to the village and ask for help,' said the wolf. 'The snow chains should work, as long as the snow hasn't drifted too deep. If it has, well …'

'That's crazy,' said Wiseman. 'Driving down the mountain in the dark … it's suicide. You know what the road is like in December. I could drive down a gully, or get trapped under ice. It's suicide. You know it is.' He was blabbering now, he knew it.

The wolf snarled again. When it spoke its voice was like

the ice that covered the dark ranks of trees outside. 'I don't care. Now run!'

This time Wiseman didn't hesitate. There was no mistaking the tone of that voice. If he didn't run immediately the wolf would kill him anyway. He lurched toward the open door. The wolf stepped aside to let him pass. It sniffed him as he went, as if he were mere food. That brought him to his senses. He grabbed at his coat, thrusting his arms through the sleeves but not stopping to pull up the zip. He squashed his thick winter hat on his head and pushed out into the freezing night.

Chapter Three

Cold air slapped Wiseman's face as he emerged from the cabin, sobering him up sharply. He slammed the door closed behind him and stood panting on the wooden step, his breath condensing into clouds.

The night held deadly beauty. Snow had drifted up against the outside walls of the cabin, but the steps leading down from the cabin door were still largely clear. A smooth layer of white stretched away before him, untouched by man or beast. No bird moved in the forest, nor stag, nor rabbit, nor dormouse. Only him. And the wolves.

Beyond the clearing the pine trees stood like sentinels, so tall their tops vanished into the black sky above. The earlier wind had dropped, making the forest uncannily still and silent. The snow had stopped too, and the clouds had cleared, revealing a scattering of stars like diamonds against the black velvet of the sky. He wondered if he had dreamed or been overcome by a fit of madness. But no, the dreamlike beauty of the mountains contained a true nightmare. Leanna had turned and he was running for his life.

He looked around the clearing. The Land Rover was parked some way down the slope. It was covered by snow, just another white object amongst the white, but he could make out its mass against the background of dark pine trunks. He'd left it some fifty feet away from the cabin. He hadn't expected he would need to run to it in any hurry. If the snow had drifted too deep, he would die before he reached it.

Wiseman stepped out into the virgin snow and sank up to his knees. He waded in the direction of the vehicle, the snow deepening the further he moved from the cabin, slowing his pace to a crawl.

'Don't fall, Wiseman. Don't fall,' he panted to himself as he lifted first one heavy leg, then the other. 'Don't slip. Don't make a single mistake.'

Clouds of billowing white escaped from his mouth as he dragged his legs through the white drifts, making his way toward the Land Rover. This far from the dimly-lit cabin, the only light was from the moon and its reflection off the smooth mirror of the snow. He could be thankful that the moon was full and bright tonight. He laughed mirthlessly at the irony of that. The moon had always been linked with madness. Now it watched over his own mad flight for life.

He reached the Land Rover after what seemed like an age. He stopped and looked over his shoulder, but Leanna had not yet emerged from the cabin. She was giving him time to run. She must want the thrill of a chase. Well, he would give her that, if he could. The other two had still not shown themselves, although they must be almost here by now. They might even be waiting just beyond the clearing, ready to tear his throat. He could do nothing about that. Instead, he turned his attention to the vehicle.

It was an old model, the type that had served farmers and the military for thirty years or more, not one of those new ones that city types drove to the office. It had done a hundred and fifty thousand miles but was good for another hundred thousand at least. He made a point of keeping the vehicle well maintained. In these mountains, your life could depend on regular oil and filter changes. He just hoped it would start. He hadn't driven it for almost a week, and it had been well below freezing every night, sometimes all day too.

The Land Rover was fitted with high-tensile steel snow chains with an automatic tensioning system. They were designed to operate in sub-zero temperatures and on the steepest slopes, and they had served him well in the two winters he had spent up here in the mountains. This would be their ultimate test.

He fitted the key into the door and tried to turn it, but the lock was frozen solid. Dammit. He gripped the key with both hands and applied as much torque as his cold fingers allowed, but it wasn't enough. Crouching down in the snow he cupped his palms together and breathed out through his mouth, forcing warm, moist air into the lock. Three long breaths and he tried again. This time the key turned.

He took hold of the door handle and pulled hard. The door had frozen too, but after using the key to scrape ice from around the edge, he managed to pull it open using both hands. He climbed inside. As he did so, he heard the sound of the two wolves howling. They had entered the clearing, just next to the log cabin. The sound of the beasts chilled him to the bone.

'Quickly, Wiseman,' he muttered, his hands trembling and teeth chattering from the cold. Back in the warmth of the cabin, the alcohol had dulled his senses nicely, but the shock of the night air and the adrenaline rush of terror had brought him back to reality quick enough. 'Don't drop the key. Don't drop the key,' he chanted as he carefully inserted it into the ignition. He pulled the choke out to the max and twisted the key hard.

The V8 turned over once, twice, three times and died. Damn. If he wasn't careful, he would flood the engine or drain the battery. He let the choke out a little and tried again. The starter motor turned more strongly this time and after the longest ten seconds of his life, the elderly engine spluttered into life. He pressed his foot down, revving it hard, and put the car into gear. The snow lay thick on the windows, but he couldn't get out to clear them. He tried the wipers and they cleared a small patch, just big enough for him to see the space between trees that indicated the direction of the track. He switched on the headlamps and watched their powerful beams cut through the night, turning the dark trunks of trees into pale ghostly fingers.

He could see nothing through the rear or side windows, and his snow-covered mirrors were useless, but these were not his biggest concerns. As long as the wheels gripped the track and he could see the way ahead, he had a chance. He revved the engine once more, feeling emboldened by its throaty roar.

Then another sound assaulted his ears. A third wolf, as distinct from the first two as one human voice from another. It howled as loudly as the other two combined, an eerie wail that carried through the crisp cold air of the clearing, even over the roar of the engine.

Leanna. She had begun to hunt.

Making the sign of the cross and saying a silent prayer, he let out the clutch and felt the Land Rover crawl slowly downhill, the wheels bumping as their chains bit into the powdered snow.

Chapter Four

Leanna leapt down the cabin steps in a single bound and landed in the snow. Wolf blood surged through her veins. Her breath hung heavy in the air before her but she did not feel the cold. Her winter coat kept her warm and snug.

She padded forward slowly at first, enjoying the feel of four-legged movement. How could she ever have walked on hind legs alone? She sped up, travelling with ease, loping forward through the snow, away from the cabin, toward the distant hulk of the Land Rover and its dim red lights. It moved slowly, and she was fast.

What speed she possessed, what power, what grace. She felt strength running through her limbs, an untapped strength, whose full potential she had not yet tasted. Her senses were heightened like never before. She could see clearly by moonlight as if it were as bright as day. Her ears twitched to pick up the smallest sound. She had never guessed that such a rich symphony filled the silent night. But her sense of smell guided her most, giving her a vivid three-dimensional map of her surroundings. She smelled the dirty Land Rover and its nasty exhaust fumes. She smelled the distinct scents of the two other wolves, Samuel and Adam. And over the top of everything else, like a sweet, high note, she smelled man. She smelled her prey.

Leanna's limbs flowed with the pure and simple joy of hunting. She joined the other wolves, and the three of them fanned out in a natural hunting formation, guided by instinct. She howled again as she ran, feeling high with the thrill of the chase. Wiseman had been drunk, but Leanna was intoxicated with blood lust. She had never felt anything like it. She ran faster, moving ahead of the others, the three of them sprinting forward toward the lumbering vehicle. They gained on it quickly.

Chapter Five

Wiseman willed the Land Rover forward inch by inch. The forest track was thick with snow, its edges and the deep ditches to either side invisible beneath the driven white blanket that covered it. He felt the front wheel dip as it strayed from the track, and he turned the steering sharply to keep the vehicle from plunging off the road.

The chains gripped well, but the track was rough with hollows and fallen logs, and the ancient vehicle showed its age with each unexpected lurch. Wiseman urged it onwards, but the track stretched through miles of deserted forest before there would be any hope of help. The engine strained with every new challenge, yet Wiseman kept it going, moving slowly but surely downhill and closer to civilization.

The heater was beginning to pump out hot air, helping to clear his forward view, but he could still see nothing of what lay behind. He could hear nothing either, save for the brutish roar of the engine as he shifted his foot almost continuously from accelerator to brake and back again. His left foot lingered permanently over the clutch pedal. He'd not yet shifted out of first gear. Eight miles at least to go, averaging five to ten miles per hour. Part of his mind began to calculate his journey time but he shut it off before it could complete its estimate.

'Keep your focus, Wiseman,' he told himself. 'Stay on track.'

He was glad he could see nothing of the road behind. Dread followed him, his mind's eye conjuring clearly-imagined monsters. He didn't need to see them for real.

The Land Rover lurched suddenly as a great weight crashed into its side with a bang. He grappled with the steering wheel to keep the vehicle on the road. One wheel shot into space and spun wildly, but he pulled the car back from the brink just in time. He pushed his right foot hard to the floor.

The car dashed ahead, picking up speed. He changed up a gear for the first time. The Land Rover struck a log and he felt the steel chassis scream in protest. The sudden jolt dashed his head against the roof of the vehicle, but he kept his foot to the floor, seeking to escape his hunters. They were on him now, trying to force him off the road.

Another wolf slammed against the Land Rover. Again he struggled to keep it on the road. The car bounced into a pothole and tipped onto two wheels as a third beast crashed against the passenger door. Wiseman gripped the steering wheel with all his might, but he was losing control. The vehicle tipped further, teetering on two wheels. Instinctively he threw his hands over his face as it crashed onto its side and slid toward the gully at the edge of the road.

The car careened into the trees and hit a dark trunk. It came to an abrupt stop and the screen of glass before him caved in, showering him in frozen raindrops that cut his skin. The engine whined noisily as the wheels spun uselessly on their side.

He tried to move, but his left leg was trapped. His right hand pricked sharply and dripped red with blood. He lay against the buckled metal of the door, his eyes closed in terror, too shocked even to unbuckle his seatbelt.

He heard a grating noise and a scratching, followed by the crash of more glass breaking. He sensed a presence in front of him and opened his eyes to see the yellow glare of a wolf looking back, its long snout sniffing hungrily, its sharp teeth bared. Wolf breath steamed into his face.

The wolf had distinctive golden fur and fine features. Close up to the creature, he saw something he had not noticed before. Where at first he had seen only cruelty, now he saw beauty too. The world was filled with beauty, if you only had eyes to see it.

Wiseman tried to smile, although he feared it was more a grimace. 'I'm sorry,' he said to the wolf. 'Please forgive me.'

The wolf moved closer, snarling angrily at his words.

'I forgive you,' continued Wiseman. 'This was all my fault.'

He screamed as the wolf's jaws snapped at his face, rending and tearing. His vision turned red and he screamed again as teeth sunk deep into his throat. His second scream did not last long.

Chapter Six

Leanna hated Wiseman for his final words of conciliation. She didn't want his forgiveness or his pity. Those were the weapons of the weak. She howled with rage and clamped her jaws around his neck, enjoying the iron-rich taste of the blood as it spurted into her mouth and down her throat. She shook her head sharply, shearing the man's spinal column with her teeth. His head lolled loosely from side to side like a doll's.

She gripped his shoulders with her powerful jaws, ripping him from the straps that bound him to his seat, as he had freed her from the ropes that bound her. He was heavier than her, but she was strong. She dragged his lifeless form from the Land Rover and let his limp body collapse onto the snowy ground next to the overturned vehicle, spilling hot red across the frozen white.

The others approached to feed, but she snapped her jaws at them in anger. This was her kill. She stood over her prey, panting breathlessly, daring them to take it from her.

Adam came closer, stepping cautiously through the snow, but she sprang at him, snapping wildly, nipping his flesh and drawing blood. He leapt back sharply, whimpering in pain. She ran to him and made him cower in submission. Samuel too cowered down before her, acknowledging her as leader of the pack. They were both males, but while she lacked their size and strength, she made up for it with ferocity.

She paced around them slowly until satisfied of their acquiescence. Then she returned to her prey, crouching down on all fours to enjoy her spoils. She tore at the flesh greedily, ripping and shearing it with her carnassials, chewing the meat, enjoying the sensation of blood dripping from her long tongue. Not many students got to eat their professor, not even in medical school. Human flesh tasted even better than she had imagined, and she had been imagining little else for many days now. She devoured the meat hungrily, chewing right down to the sweet marrow of the bone. When she had taken her fill, she moved aside to let the others have the remains.

The wolves were ravenous and they wasted nothing. Soon all that remained of Wiseman were bones and memories.

As they feasted, Leanna paced around the clearing's edge, thinking through her next steps. The moon had swung far across the sky now, and dawn could not be far away. The change would come again then, this time in reverse, and they would need to be back inside the warmth of the cabin to survive in human form.

In the days to come they would have their work cut out, disposing of what remained of the corpse and any other evidence. Then they could resume their studies in the laboratory. They would stay here for the remaining winter months, completing their work and making plans. The melting snows of spring would help wash away the last remains of the professor.

When that was done, they could return to London. From there, the whole world would be theirs for the taking.

But before that, another hour remained to enjoy the thrill of being a wolf. When Adam and Samuel had finished eating, Leanna dashed away into the forest, leaping breathlessly around the columns of trees, her paws pounding lightly across the powdery snow. The others followed in her wake. When she reached a rocky outcrop that rose above the snow, she leaped up its craggy face. The tall trees parted around the rock, revealing a circle of dark sky and shining moon above. The moon was setting now, but still bright in the pre-dawn darkness. Leanna had never seen such a beautiful sight.

The moon had given her this gift. From now on, she would worship it in the only way a wolf could. She rose to her hind legs once more and howled. Behind her, and below her, the male wolves lent their deeper voices to her hymn.

Chapter Seven

*Battlefield Road, South London, Halloween,
ten months later*

It was impossible for James to tell how old the man was. He gathered the little kids close around him, well away from the man, and counted them again to make sure they were all still present. Amy, Bethany, Matthew and Henry. Four kids, check.

Aged seventeen, James was the oldest. He was responsible for them.

He wished the man had never opened the door to his home. He looked like a vagrant. His clothes were creased and stained and a size too big. His hair hung lank to his shoulders, unwashed and overgrown. He had clearly not shaved in a week. And he looked sick too – his skin unnaturally pale, his eyes reddened with a yellow sheen to them. Sweat beaded his forehead, and he stooped forward, his back hunched as if in pain.

The man sniffed the air, his nose wrinkling like an

animal. 'What do you want?' he barked unpleasantly.

'Trick or treat!' chorused the kids. They all wore Halloween costumes – Amy a witch, Bethany a fairy, Matthew a skeleton, and Henry some kind of super-hero. James had stuck with black jeans and a sweater.

He willed the little kids to shut up. Couldn't they see what he saw? This was not a man to play trick or treat with. This was a man to keep at a distance.

'Trick or what?' asked the man suspiciously, like he had never heard of it before.

'It's Halloween!' shouted little Amy excitedly. 'Trick or treat!'

The man seemed to understand then. His thin mouth drew slowly into a smile, then a toothy grin. 'Oh, yes,' he said. 'Halloween. I forgot. Silly me. Come on inside.' He stood aside for the children to enter into his grimy home.

'No!' James put out a hand to restrain the children, but Amy and Bethany had already darted inside.

The man leered at James, revealing a row of stained and crooked teeth. 'You'd better all come in.'

It was a ground-floor apartment in a converted Victorian house. James followed the children reluctantly into the narrow hallway. The kids had already run through it into the kitchen at the end. Other doors led off the hallway, but they were closed.

'That's right,' called the man from over his shoulder. 'You go straight through to the kitchen. I'm right behind you.' He shut the front door of the house, sliding a security chain into place.

James could smell him now. He reeked of sweat and urine and God knows what. This was such a bad idea, but how could he get the kids out? Better just to endure it, then leave as quickly as possible.

The kitchen was a pigsty. Mounds of unwashed plates and dishes filled the sink and covered the worktops all around. Partly-eaten meals putrefied in them, days or even weeks old, crawling with flies and maggots. James put his hand to his mouth to block the smell. Even the little kids looked apprehensive now.

The man pushed James roughly into the small kitchen and followed him inside, closing the door behind him. There was barely enough room for them all to fit.

'It smells in here!' said Amy.

'Now, now,' said the man. 'That's no way to talk when someone has invited you into their home, is it, little lady?'

The girl shook her head.

'Now what's this trick or treat you were telling me about? It sounds like fun.' The man winked at James.

James looked around the kitchen. It was cramped, with a small window above the sink, some countertops with storage units above and below, an old gas cooker, and a fridge at the far end. A microwave sat on the counter, its door open, an uneaten ready-meal inside, covered in a fuzzy white film of decay. He moved his gaze along the kitchen countertop, scattered with food debris and other clutter. A column of ants busied themselves in removing some of the smaller crumbs. His attention fixed on a knife. It was about a foot long with a wooden handle and a serrated edge for cutting bread. He moved closer to it and leaned back against the soiled worktop. He could have the knife in his hands in a second if he needed it.

Bethany was telling the man all about trick or treat.

'Is that right? So either I give you a treat or you play a trick on me?' He looked gravely at each of the children in turn, tugging at his wispy beard with thin fingers. 'What kind of trick?' he demanded.

The children bunched together, shaking their heads, silent.

'Stop it!' said James. 'You're frightening them. Come on kids, let's get out of here.'

The man leaned back against the closed door. 'Hey, no need to run. I was just fooling around. Sorry if I scared you. Let me give you a real treat to make up for it. How does that sound?'

The children nodded, still silent, not taking their eyes from the man.

He chuckled. 'Let me see what I've got for you. I'm sure there must be something nice in one of my cupboards. You know, I haven't been very well for a couple of weeks. I haven't eaten a thing in days, so I'm sure there must be plenty of food left over. You won't mind if it's a little past its use-by date will you?'

The children looked uncertain. They still said nothing. Not even six-year-old Amy, who normally never stopped talking.

James reached for the handle of the knife behind his back, hoping the man wouldn't notice. He tried to look casual. His fingers found a plate of something soft and disgusting, and withdrew by reflex. He reached again tentatively, exploring the discarded plates and dishes on the work surface behind him. His fingers found a cup and saucer, and then a spoon, sticky with some nameless ooze. A little further and he found it. His fingers wrapped tightly around the handle of the knife.

The man seemed oblivious to James' movements. He was looking in the cupboards now, making a big show of it. 'Nothing in this one,' he announced. 'Silly me. Oh, what's in here? Half a packet of biscuits. Does anyone like chocolate biscuits? What about mints? You like mints?' He rummaged in some low-level units near the sink. 'I've got a sponge cake here somewhere, I think. It might be a bit stale.'

While he searched for leftover food, James quietly moved over to the kitchen door, clutching the knife in his hand behind his back. His hands felt sweaty despite the cold air in the kitchen. He tried turning the handle of the door. It squeaked as he turned it, but the door swung open into the hallway that led back to the front door. 'Come on kids,' he whispered. They started to leave the kitchen one at a time.

The man turned around and frowned at James. His

eyes glowed fiercely yellow under the dim light of the single naked bulb overhead. 'You can't go yet,' he said. 'You haven't had your treat.' He stood up.

He seemed taller than before, and stronger. He was standing straight, no longer hunched. He was a good few inches taller than James.

'We're good,' said James. 'Thanks anyway.' The two girls were in the hallway now. James pushed Matthew after them.

The man took a step forward. 'If you don't want a treat, I have to play a trick on you,' he snarled. 'That's the rule.' He reached out suddenly and grabbed Henry by the shoulders. The boy cried out in fright.

James brought the bread knife out into full view and held it between them. He clutched it so tightly his knuckles turned white. He had no idea what he might do with it, but it seemed like the first sensible idea he'd had all evening.

For a moment the man didn't react. Then he started to laugh. He held Henry closer to him, digging into the boy's shoulders with his long fingernails. The little boy's superhero mask slipped from his face, revealing two eyes wide with terror.

The man's laughter dissolved in a fit of coughing. When he spoke again, his voice was filled with menace. 'Thinking to poke me with that, are you, boy?' he demanded, nodding toward the bread knife. 'Think you can stick that in me?'

James gripped the knife as hard as he could, but the tighter he held it, the more the knife shook. 'Amy, Bethany, Matthew, go get help,' he called. He dared not turn around to see where they were. 'Run!' he shouted.

He was relieved to hear the sound of the children running away down the hallway toward the front door of the house.

'Three gone, and only two left,' said the man. 'And I'm so hungry.' He licked his red lips with the tip of his tongue.

James' arms were shaking from hand to shoulder, as if the knife were a huge weight. The trembling started to spread to his knees, but he stood his ground in the kitchen. 'Let the boy go,' he said.

The man shook his head, making his lank hair sweep across his shoulders. 'Didn't you hear me? I told you I haven't eaten for a week. I'm so hungry I could eat a horse.' His tongue darted from between white teeth. 'But it's not horsemeat I want.'

There was a noise from the end of the hallway. The children were pounding against the front door, the door that led to freedom. Amy called out, 'James, we can't open the door, it's locked!'

The man laughed again. 'Oh dear, what a shame. Looks like all five of you are back on the menu.'

'Shut up!' said James. He needed the man to stop talking, so he could think clearly. 'Let go of Henry.' He waved the knife feebly in the air, but his hand shook violently as he did it.

'Or what? Going to have a go at me, are you, boy? I don't think so. I don't think you're going to do anything.'

The children were banging on the door with their fists. They opened the letterbox and shouted for help.

'The police will come soon,' said James. 'Someone outside will hear the noise and break the door down.' He wasn't sure if he was trying to convince himself or the man.

The man shook his head. 'No, I don't think so. Nobody cares what happens round here, least of all the police. Besides, you can scream all you like on Halloween and no one will give a damn. Screaming's all part of the fun.' He chuckled again, shaking Henry by the shoulders. He stopped abruptly, and all the laughter left his face. When he spoke again, his voice was cold and dead. 'By the time the police get here, I'll have eaten every last one of you, I reckon.'

With a sudden movement, he shoved Henry toward

James and lunged at James' knife arm. The little boy tripped and fell on top of James, knocking him sideways into the edge of the door. A sharp pain jarred through James' side. He felt the man twist his arm and grab the blade. The knife was pulled from his grasp.

Tears stung James' eyes, but he had the sense to grab Henry with his free arm and push the boy through the open doorway and out into the hallway. The man slammed him backward into the kitchen wall with a vicious strength, and he doubled over, the wind knocked out of him.

When he lifted his head again, the man was standing right in front of him. He grabbed James by the hair and jerked his head up, banging it back against the wall. The man held the knife now and he pushed it up against James' throat.

In the hallway the children clung tightly together by the locked front door. One of the girls screamed.

The man brought his face up close against James', his stinking breath washing a wave of nausea over him. His yellow eyes glinted and he smiled. 'Oh dear. That didn't go too well, did it? Look who's got the knife now.' He dragged the blade up to James' chin, drawing its serrated edge slowly across his skin. James felt the sting of the knife cutting into his flesh. 'I'll cut your head off, I will. How's that for a treat?' The man laughed coldly. He turned to look at the four children at the other end of the hallway. 'Would you like to see me do that?' he demanded. 'Would you like to see it?'

James didn't think what to do next. Thinking hadn't done him any good so far. Instead he reacted instinctively, bringing his knee sharply up into the man's groin. His opponent shrieked and slashed wildly with the knife, cutting viciously just inches from James' face, but James dodged his head aside. He grabbed at the knife and felt the blade dig into the palm of his hand, pulling beads of blood from his flesh. He let go with a cry.

The man pushed him to the floor and ran toward the

children, huddled by the front door.

James ran after him, but the man moved quickly. By the time James reached the end of the hallway, he already had the knife pressed to Bethany's throat. She screamed. Amy joined her, the two girls shrieking in unison.

'Make them stop!' shouted the man. 'Make them stop or I'll kill them both!'

The girls screamed louder.

The man's eyes held a mad look. He was capable of anything.

Henry and Matthew started wailing too.

'Make them stop!' repeated the man.

Then from outside, a male voice shouted, 'Police! Open up!' A fist banged heavily on the front door.

The man turned to look up.

In that moment, James dived at him, grabbing for the knife. One hand closed around the man's hand on the knife handle, the other grasped the blade itself. A searing pain shot through his hand, but he held on tight.

The man screeched.

James fell on top of him, kicking and twisting as they collapsed together onto the floor. Bethany wriggled free, but continued to scream as loudly as she could. From outside another voice, a woman's, cried, 'Open the door now! This is the police!'

The man let out a roar like a cornered animal, his face contorting in rage. He and James both clung to the knife, the man gripping the handle, James feeling the sharp teeth of the blade biting into his palm. The pain was blinding, but he didn't let go.

He had his weight on the man now and he pinned him down. But the man's grip on the knife was stronger. James felt it slipping from his grasp.

A heavy weight crashed against the door. It sounded like someone was hurling their entire body against it. The man looked up for just a second.

James elbowed him in the face and suddenly the knife

was his. He wrenched it from the other's grasp, ignoring the blood that ran down the blade of the knife, gripping its slick length in his fingers. He twisted it round so he could grip the handle.

The man bared his teeth at James in frustration, then lunged forward, sinking his teeth into his left arm.

Unbelievable pain shot through James' arm. The man bit deep, as if he really did mean to eat his victim alive. James felt sick. He was in danger of passing out from the pain. With a final desperate strength he plunged the bread knife into the man's chest.

The man fell back and James felt a jolt of relief as teeth unclenched and jaws unlocked. Those yellow eyes stared at him with unrestrained hate and the man howled like a kicked dog.

The front door began to splinter and give way as the heavy weight crashed against it repeatedly from the other side.

Still the man struggled, closing his hands around James' neck and squeezing with a desperate strength.

James twisted the knife in the man's chest, pushing it with both hands. The knife went deeper, finding a path between the ribs, and the man howled again. James didn't stop pushing and twisting the blade until the door crashed open behind him and strong hands pulled him away. By then the yellow glow had faded from the man's eyes and he seemed to have found some final peace.

Chapter Eight

Ruskin Park, South London, one day later, full moon

Police Constable Liz Bailey had never seen a wolf.

'What do you mean, you've never bloody seen one?' demanded her colleague, PC David Morgan. Liz called him *Fat Dave*. He was a huge man, six feet six inches tall and weighing at least sixteen stone. *England's answer to Arnold Schwarzenegger*, he boasted. That was wishful thinking. Dave carried too much of his weight around his belly. But he didn't take kindly to anyone who pointed that out. He only allowed Liz to call him Fat Dave because they were such good friends. She would never have permitted him to call her *Short-Arse* otherwise.

'I've never seen one,' repeated Liz. 'It's not like you see a lot of wolves in South London.' She looked out of the window of the patrol car. Streetlights cast an orange glow over the roofs of parked cars. Overhead, the landing lights of an aircraft blinked red and white. She couldn't see any stars in the hazy sky. It was hardly ever dark enough round here to glimpse the heavens, but at least the moon shone full and bright above the old warehouses on the south side.

'Didn't your parents ever take you to the zoo?' insisted Dave, turning the patrol car off the main road and into a slightly more salubrious residential area.

'Can't remember,' lied Liz. Her mum and dad had rarely dragged her beyond the kiddies' playground, or the beer garden in one of the local pubs. She recalled a school trip to London Zoo once, but she and the other kids had run wild and they hadn't got much further than the gift shop before the teachers rounded them up and dragged them back to school. She didn't want to talk about her wasted childhood now. She said, 'I'm guessing wolves look like German shepherd dogs, but meaner.'

Dave gave her a mischievous look. 'Not this one. The report said *as big as a man.*'

'Yeah.' Liz rolled her eyes. Someone had dialled 999 to report seeing a wolf running wild in local parkland. A wolf as big as a man. 'As big as a poodle, more like.'

Dave snorted. 'There are no wolves in London anyway. Probably not since the Dark Ages. Most likely it was just a fox.'

'Or perhaps some weirdo hiding out in the bushes,' suggested Liz. She'd arrested her fair share of those over the years. She hoped it wasn't a weirdo though. She'd had her fill of that after rescuing those kids from that maniac the previous evening. She'd never seen such a severe bite wound before – not from a human bite, at least – and hoped she wouldn't again. If only she and Dave had been a bit quicker breaking down the door, they might have been able to prevent the incident becoming so serious. As it was, that teenage boy had gone to hospital for emergency treatment and the perpetrator had ended up dead with a kitchen knife sticking out of his chest.

Dave pulled the car over to the side of the road and parked it in a space under some oak trees. The trees stood bare, save for a few last heroic leaves and some acorns still clinging to the gnarled branches. 'Let's go take a look,' he said, getting out of the vehicle.

Liz followed. Outside the air held a late November chill, and dried leaves tumbled through the cold night as wind gusted from the open area of parkland next to the road. She was glad of her hat and the thick stab-proof vest she wore over her uniform. The park ran all the way along one side of the street, a black iron fence separating it from the pavement. She peered over the fence into the dark.

Nothing. The park was kept locked at night, and there were no lights within its boundary. Light from the streetlamps penetrated about twenty feet into the park, lending an orange tinge to the trees and shrubs that grew close enough to the fence to be visible. Beyond that, there was nothing to see, save for distant lights on the other side of the park. At least she could see a few pale stars here. The moon was brighter too, casting a silvery reflection on a puddle of water in the wet grass. The whole park couldn't be bigger than forty acres. It was hardly a place for wolves.

'Tell you what,' said Dave. 'Even if there is a wolf in there, we've got a better chance of finding Little Red Riding Hood than catching the bugger.'

Liz walked a little farther along the pavement, staying close to the iron railings. 'Shh!' She had heard something. Maybe a branch cracking underfoot, maybe just the wind snapping twigs off a tree. Her eyes were slowly adjusting to the darkness of the park, and she could see further now. Beyond the iron railings a concrete path ran parallel to the street, bordered by twenty feet or so of well-kept lawn. Beyond that, shrubs and trees loomed tall. A tangle of smaller paths led off from the main walkway, heading deeper into the park. She could see benches at regular intervals along them, and lighter patches of grass.

Nothing moved.

'This is a waste of time,' said Dave. 'Let's get back in

the car and find ourselves a couple of nice hot lattes on the High Street.'

They both heard the sound this time. A howling that touched something primal deep within the human psyche. A sound that no one could fail to recognize, whether they had encountered a wolf before or not. The sound came from close by, piercingly loud, a wild baying that rose and slowly fell away. A cold shiver ran all the way down Liz's back.

'Bloody hell,' said Dave. 'That was no dog.'

Liz saw the creature first. It loped out of the bushes not more than thirty feet from the road. A wolf, with pale, golden fur and yellow eyes that gleamed in the darkness. It was as big as a man too, just like the caller had reported. The wolf ran toward them, covering the distance easily, bounding effortlessly across the grass. As it drew near, Liz noted the way it steadily quickened its pace, its long snout stretching forward keenly.

It was going to jump.

If British police carried guns like their American counterparts, this would have been the moment to use them, thought Liz. Instead she shoved Dave aside, out of the way of the wolf. The big man stumbled and she went down on top of him, her elbow jarring as it hit the cold, hard surface of the pavement.

The wolf leaped at the same time, and she felt the rush of air as it sailed over the metal fence, its jaws snapping on empty space. It landed neatly on the ground behind them and spun round to face them, its bright eyes flashing yellow with anger.

Liz jumped to her feet, but Dave was still lying on the roadside. She pulled at his arm. 'Come on, get up!'

Dave groaned and rolled over onto his back. He sat up slowly, but when he tried to stand his right leg buckled under his weight. 'Damn,' he cursed.

The wolf paced back and forth between two parked cars, its eyes locked on them, assessing, measuring. Liz had never seen an animal that looked more human. The wolf seemed to know their strengths and weaknesses. It was weighing the situation, preparing to make a decision.

Liz made the decision first.

She stepped between Dave and the wolf, pulling her baton from her duty belt. She held the weapon ready and ran at the wolf, shouting for it to flee.

The wolf regarded her coolly, dashing to one side just before she reached it. The creature ducked behind a car and disappeared from view. Liz turned around, looking to see where the wolf had gone. It seemed to have vanished.

She heard another groan from Dave as he lurched to his feet, holding on to the iron fence to take the weight off his injured knee. 'Bugger,' he muttered.

Liz rubbed her elbow and moved cautiously toward him, glancing around for the wolf.

'Where's it gone?' asked Dave.

Liz shrugged. 'It ran behind a car.' Her elbow burned with a sharp pain as if she had damaged a tendon. She rubbed it again, but it did no good. At least she could still use her arm. Dave's leg was a different story.

He tried to put his weight on it, but the knee buckled again and he clutched the fence for support. 'I can't walk,' he complained.

'You stay there,' said Liz. 'I'm going to look for this wolf.' She noticed that she had stopped referring to the creature as a dog.

She moved cautiously around the car and into the road. Nothing. She rounded the car and moved along to the next vehicle. A shout from Dave made her spin round.

The wolf had doubled back on itself somehow and was padding brazenly toward him, stepping sure-footedly over the uneven paving stones beneath the oak. Dave leaned against the park railings and pulled out a can of tear gas.

Liz ran toward him, but she was too slow. She watched as the wolf jumped at his throat.

Dave sprayed the canister in the animal's face as it

leapt. The wolf cried and left off its attack, landing neatly on the ground in front of the police officer. It snarled angrily, shaking its head from side to side, but the gas didn't seem to have had much effect. The creature spun round again, growling menacingly.

'Come on then, you hairy bastard!' Dave let go of the fence and lunged at the animal, wrapping his brawny arms around its middle, using his weight to force it to the ground. The wolf struggled, twisting in his strong grip. Its wet fur made it slippery and it nearly wriggled free of his grasp, but he was too heavy for it. He rolled on top of the creature, pinning it to the ground. 'Call for help!' he shouted.

Liz spoke quickly into her police radio. 'Officer Lima Bravo 295 requesting backup to Ruskin Park area southside. Over.'

The reply came back almost immediately. 'Lima Bravo 295, support vehicle on its way. Should be with you in three minutes.'

From the roadside came a shout, then a scream. The wolf had its jaws clamped to Dave's neck. Liz could see blood spurting from the wound. Dave screamed again and kicked at the wolf with his steel-toe boot.

The wolf whimpered in pain and released its grip on his neck. It sprang back and howled once more. Close up, the sound was deafening. Liz put her hands to her ears.

The wolf ran in a circle around Dave, snapping its jaws in cold fury. It had been hurt. There was no sign of blood, apart from on its muzzle, which was presumably Dave's, but it limped on one of its hind legs. The creature approached Dave again, this time from behind, aiming straight for his head.

'No!' shouted Liz. She let go of the radio and ran forward, waving her arms and screeching. The wolf turned its head to look in her direction. A look of hate filled its yellow eyes and it sprang at her, covering the gap between them in one leap, knocking her backward onto the hard paving slabs. The wolf scratched at her chest with its sharp claws, ripping at the stab-proof vest, but the tough Kevlar fibres of the vest blocked the wolf's claws and saved her from the worst of the attack.

She struggled to reach hold of her baton, but the wolf had her pinned to the ground with its paws. Her elbow hurt like the devil, making her attempts to push the beast away useless.

The wolf raised its enormous head and opened its mouth ready to make a final lunge. She saw a kind of savage laughter in its yellow eyes as it rolled its jaws toward her face.

Then a police siren cut through the night air and the wolf lifted its head with a start. It stood motionless for a moment, then seemed to make a decision. With a last snarl aimed at her, it turned and fled, bounding through a gap in the cars, making its escape down the middle of the road.

Liz rolled onto her side to watch. The wolf turned right at the road junction and disappeared down a side street, almost like it knew where to go. That was strange. Why hadn't it gone back into the park? She turned her attention back to Dave. His neck wound was bleeding heavily and his eyes stared dully at nothing in particular. She recognized the symptoms of shock.

'Hang in there, Dave,' she said, applying pressure to the wound to quench the bleeding. 'Help's on its way.'

The response car was already stopping in the road. The sound of booted feet running toward her had never been so welcome.

Chapter Nine

Department of Genetics, Imperial College, Kensington, London, waning moon

There was a knock, and a pretty young woman stuck her head around the door of Helen Eastgate's office. 'Doctor Eastgate?' she enquired. 'Hi, my name is Leanna. Leanna Lloyd.' She entered the office, limping slightly on her left leg, and closed the door behind her.

Helen rose from her chair and went to welcome her visitor. 'Hi Leanna, come on inside. Let's see if I can find you somewhere to sit. My office is always a bit of a mess, I'm afraid.'

Helen lifted a pile of papers and journals from a chair and dumped them onto the floor next to some books and other piles of work. She moved the chair in front of the wooden desk that squatted in the middle of the room and motioned for Leanna to sit. 'Call me Helen, by the way.' She extended a hand to shake Leanna's hand. The young woman's grip was firm and gave the impression of confidence and self-assurance. It was surprising given all that she had been through.

Helen had been briefed by the university's Admissions Tutor on Leanna's unusual background. A star medical student at the University of Cambridge followed by postgraduate study at the London School of Hygiene and Tropical Medicine under Professor Norman Wiseman, Leanna's prospects had seemed assured. Then it had all gone wrong. After a prolonged research expedition to Romania with Leanna and two other students, Professor Wiseman had gone through some kind of mental breakdown, submitting a research paper that had been universally denounced and ridiculed. He'd taken to the bottle by all accounts, leaving Leanna and the two other students to fend for themselves in the wilds of the Carpathian Mountains. She seemed to have come through her experience remarkably unscathed.

'Is your leg all right?' Helen asked Leanna, noting the way the young woman leaned on the back of the chair for support.

'It's fine. I slipped while out jogging last night.'

Helen carefully navigated her way through the mounds of books and other detritus that covered her office floor and seated herself at the desk, opposite Leanna. She studied the woman in more detail. Leanna was young – twenty-five, according to the Admissions Tutor's notes – and strikingly pretty. Chiselled features and almost hollow cheeks gave her the looks of a catwalk model. Blonde hair tumbled thickly over her shoulders and down her back in flowing waves. She wore a pair of jeans and boots with just a thin strappy top, revealing milky alabaster skin and a small tattoo of a flower on her bare shoulder. As she sat down she removed a pair of dark glasses, showing eyes of striking blue.

'You don't feel the cold, then?' enquired Helen, indicating Leanna's summer-weight clothing.

Leanna shrugged. 'Not really. After you've spent two winters living in the mountains of Romania you realize that it doesn't really get that cold in England.'

'I suppose not,' agreed Helen. 'Personally, I prefer a hotter climate. I'd spend the winters back in Australia if I could.'

Leanna regarded her with cold crystal eyes. 'You're Australian?'

'I was born in Perth. You couldn't tell from my accent?' Helen laughed. 'I guess I must be starting to blend in.'

'I guess.'

'So, I understand you'd like to transfer to Imperial College to continue work on your post-graduate studies. Is that right?' A request to change university mid-course was unusual, but perhaps not so surprising under the circumstances.

'That's right,' said Leanna, nodding. 'But not just to continue at a different university. I want to start again in a new direction.'

'In what way?'

'After all that happened with Professor Wiseman, I want to move to a new field, in a different department. I guess I feel that all the work I did with Professor Wiseman has been discredited. I need a fresh start.'

Helen consulted Leanna's paperwork on her desk. 'According to your application form, you were working in the Epidemiology Department studying under Professor Wiseman but you want to switch your studies into Genetics.'

Leanna nodded again enthusiastically. 'I want to work in molecular genetics. I've read your papers on the genetics of infectious diseases and I can see that you're one of the leaders in the field.'

Helen returned a practised smile. She was used to such flattery from prospective students. Flattery from her colleagues was much scarcer unfortunately. 'Tell me a little about your work under Professor Wiseman. I read the newspaper reports at the time, but nothing that carried any scientific credibility.'

Leanna sighed. 'Professor Wiseman was a bit of a renegade. He had a theory about a new mechanism for disease transmission. In his opinion, a possibility existed for the direct transfer of genetic traits from one subject to another – even from one species to another. He didn't really regard it as disease as such, more like a new approach to evolutionary biology.'

Helen raised her eyebrows. 'That's certainly original. Did he make much progress with his theory?'

'You saw what happened when he tried to publish,' said Leanna. 'Universal scorn. That's why I want to start my research in a new field.'

Helen nodded. 'That makes sense. Tell me, what happened to Professor Wiseman in the end?'

Leanna shrugged indifferently. 'He just disappeared. He went into the mountains one day and never came back. The local police conducted a search, but they never found his body. Nobody was very surprised by that. The Carpathian Mountains are vast and wild. Most likely he jumped into a river or fell into a gulley. He'd been under a lot of stress. He was drinking heavily near the end.'

'I'm sorry.'

'There are wild animals living in the forest,' added Leanna. 'Wolves and bears. His remains are never likely to be found.'

A shiver went down Helen's spine. She scrutinized the young student sitting opposite her carefully. For all her beauty, Leanna had an icy coldness, revealed in her eyes and sometimes in her words. She showed indifference to, or even resentment of her former professor. She didn't even seem to be aware of how much she revealed.

She had ready answers for all of Helen's questions, and everything she said matched the facts as far as Helen understood them. But something didn't quite ring true.

Perhaps it was less what she said, and more the way she said it. Her answers were too polished, too neat. But perhaps Helen was being too harsh. The girl had been through a rough year. She deserved a chance.

'I understand. Well, the university would be happy for you to join as a postgraduate student this term and start work here. You already satisfy our entrance requirements, and I have funding in place for a doctoral student to join my team. We'd waive the normal time constraints, effectively allowing you to make a fresh start. How does that sound?'

Leanna nodded eagerly. 'Perfect.'

'We can talk about a research project soon, but before that, a question I always ask my prospective students is what first drew them into the field of genetics, and into medical research more broadly.'

Leanna sat up straight in her chair, considering the question carefully. 'I think it all goes back to when I was thirteen and my mother died. She'd been ill with the flu. At first it didn't seem too serious, more like a nasty cold, but then it became worse and she developed pneumonia. The doctors treated her with antibiotics, but there were complications. I watched her dying. It was a horrible death. I didn't understand how anyone could die of a disease like that in the modern world. I started to read about the influenza virus and how complex it can be. As a teenager I wanted to be a doctor, to help treat diseases like that. But then as I grew older I realized that my true dream was to work toward the elimination of disease completely, so I decided on a career in medical research.'

'I see,' said Helen levelly. 'It's clear that you're highly motivated, but I must warn you that our work here isn't going to eliminate disease or even cure one type of disease any time soon. At best, it may contribute more to the understanding of how the genetic structure of diseases interacts with other factors.'

Leanna smiled back. 'I understand entirely,' she said.

Helen shuffled through the papers on her desk. 'So can I ask you about practical arrangements? Do you have somewhere to live? What about financial support?'

'Everything's arranged,' replied Leanna. 'I have a place to live near the university, sharing with two other students. And financially, I'm good. You see, my father and my younger brother were both killed in a car accident during the summer, so I inherited the family home and all my father's investments.' She gazed into the distance for a moment, seeming to remember something. A tear formed in one eye, but she blinked it away quickly. 'So financially, I have everything covered,' she finished.

Helen stared at the young woman opposite. To encounter so much tragedy in so short a time. It was almost beyond belief. 'I'm so sorry, Leanna.'

Leanna looked up and caught her eye. 'Oh, yeah, thanks.' Her eyes seemed to redden then, and she bent her head forward, crying softly.

Helen passed her a box of tissues. Leanna took one and blew her nose loudly.

'This must have been such a difficult year for you,' said Helen. 'You've lost your family, and your research supervisor. Are you sure you're ready to start this term? I think it might be better for you to take some time off and make a fresh start next year.'

The girl opposite her froze mid-tears and looked up, her face suddenly hard and determined again. Her momentary display of grief was apparently forgotten. 'No,' she said. 'I want this more than anything.' She returned the box of tissues. 'I've already wasted enough time. I want to start work immediately.'

Helen had never witnessed such a strangely detached display of emotion. She wondered if anything Leanna had said, about losing her mother as a teenager, about wanting to cure disease, was true. The whole performance seemed staged somehow. She wondered briefly if the girl on the other side of her desk was a psychopath.

She had to suppress a strong urge to tell Leanna to get out of her office and find a different supervisor. And yet she had to make allowance for Leanna's state of mind after so many tragedies. Against her better judgement, she replied, 'Let's make a proper start on Monday. Come to my office at ten and we can talk more about the research project you have in mind.'

Chapter Ten

King's College Hospital, Lambeth, South London, new moon

James pushed away the tray of hospital food in disgust. The smell of it made him feel sick. He pressed the button to call the nurse.

'Please can you take the food away?' he asked when she came to his bed. 'It's making me feel queasy.'

The nurse's name was Chanita. She was kinder than the others. Somehow she made time for her patients. She didn't make James feel that looking after him was just another part of her job, like changing the sheets and checking the drip was properly attached. Instead she seemed to really care about people.

She could be strict with her patients too, though. 'You won't get better if you don't eat,' she scolded him, but she removed the tray anyway. 'Is there anything else I can get you? Some fruit perhaps?'

James wrinkled his nose. Fruit and vegetables smelled

the worst. How anyone could eat them was beyond his comprehension. He had liked fruit before, he remembered that. But now the thought of it made him feel nauseous for some reason. He couldn't even face the cooked meals they brought him. He knew that no one ever rated hospital food, but this must be the worst ever. He couldn't face a mouthful of the stuff.

Chanita hovered over the bed, looking concerned. 'You haven't eaten a thing since you arrived,' she said, 'and that was over two weeks ago.'

Two weeks. Had it really been that long? He'd been unconscious or delirious for much of the time at the beginning. The last thing he remembered before waking up in hospital was a police woman pulling him away from the man he'd just killed. Murdered, really. He'd stabbed him through the heart with a bread knife. That made James a murderer. He hadn't meant to do it, though. It had been to protect the children. That man had been totally deranged. He'd had no choice.

If only he could have stopped the little ones from running inside the man's house. If only they had never knocked on the man's door that night. If only he hadn't volunteered to take the little ones out for trick or treat. James pushed the thoughts aside. *If only* led to madness.

He remembered the man's blood too. Crimson blood, bright with life. So much blood, all over his hands, running down the shaft of the knife, smeared over the slippery handle. He remembered the way it pulsed like a living creature as it flooded from the man's chest, the coppery smell rich and tangy. He licked his lips. 'You don't have any uncooked food, do you?' he asked Chanita. 'Like raw meat, I mean.'

Chanita gave him a funny look. 'Of course not.' She turned on her heel and left, carrying the tray and its uneaten food with her.

Raw meat. For some reason, he'd got it into his head that he might enjoy eating uncooked meat. He could taste it in his mind now. Smell it. Even imagine how he would feel ripping hunks of it with his teeth and swallowing it down. A nice bloody steak, perhaps, or even some pork or chicken. You weren't supposed to eat chicken raw, because of the risk of food poisoning. But he had a craving for it. Maybe some raw fish, at a push. Sushi. They might have some of that in the hospital. Yes, when Chanita came back, he would ask her about sushi.

The image of the bloodied knife appeared before him again, his hands twisting the blade ever deeper into the man's heart. If he could hold that knife in his hands right now, he would lick the blood from its blade. Lick it clean.

He hoped the police wouldn't prosecute him for murder. A police woman had visited him in hospital just yesterday, making some enquiries, asking him questions about what had happened exactly. His memory had been a bit fuzzy, and the drugs made it hard to concentrate, so she'd said she would come back when he was feeling stronger.

He was stronger today, even though he hadn't eaten or drunk anything for a couple of weeks. In fact, he felt a lot better, well enough to go home. Maybe they'd let him leave hospital in a day or so, then he'd be able to get himself some real food. Something bloody and raw. The thought of it made him start to drool.

'Hello, James. How do you feel today?' It was the doctor who had been attending him. What was his name? Doctor Kapoor.

James gave him a grin. 'Actually, I feel much better today.'

The doctor was studying some charts and looking concerned. 'That's good, James. Very good. Your temperature is back to normal for the first time. That's a very good sign. And your wound is healing nicely too. You still haven't eaten anything though.'

'I haven't really wanted to,' James told him. 'When do you think I can go home?'

'We'll have to see,' said Doctor Kapoor. 'Let's take it one day at a time. You had a very nasty infection, you know. We kept you in Intensive Care for the first week. Do you remember anything about it?'

'Not really,' said James. 'I only remember the last few days.'

'Well,' said Doctor Kapoor. 'You were in a pretty bad state when you first arrived. The bite wound was relatively superficial, but you were in a state of shock, and suffering from a severe allergic reaction. Do you have any kinds of allergies? Hay fever, food allergies, that kind of thing?'

James shook his head.

'Well, whatever it was, it put you into a state of anaphylaxis. Do you know what that is?'

'No.'

'It's when the whole body responds to some kind of allergen and goes into a state of shock. You were already unconscious when the paramedics reached you. Your throat had swollen up so you couldn't breathe properly and your blood pressure had dropped right away. If they hadn't given you an injection of adrenaline you wouldn't even have made it back to the hospital. You can thank the ambulance crew for that, and the police officer who found you.'

James nodded. The same police woman who had come to interview him yesterday. Liz, her name was.

'After that, an infection set in. We had to pump you with some pretty heavy-duty antibiotics. Even so, it was touch-and-go for a while. You don't remember any of this?'

James shook his head again.

'At one point you woke up and became violent. The nurses had to strap you down with restraints. Your temperature went so high I worried it would cause permanent damage, but you seem to have pulled through all right.' The doctor moved closer and drew an instrument from his pocket. 'Let's just have a quick look at your eyes.

Can you look into this for me?'

James stared at the light in the doctor's device. The bright light hurt his eyes. He could smell the doctor's hot breath on his face. For some reason it made him feel hungry.

'Your pupils are still dilated,' said Doctor Kapoor. 'And your eyes have a yellow tint. There's a kind of mucous covering that must be a residual infection. I've prescribed you some eye drops, and hopefully that will clear up in a day or two. Do you feel any discomfort from the lights?'

James nodded. 'They seem very bright.'

'Let's keep that under review,' said the doctor. 'But all things being well, I think you ought to be ready to go home in a few days. Let's just see if we can persuade you to eat something before you go, okay?'

James thought of asking for some raw meat again, but thought better of it. It wasn't really the doctor's job to bring him food.

Doctor Kapoor flashed James a quick smile. 'By the way, I've told the police it will be all right for them to interview you now. Do you feel up to it?'

'I think so.'

'Good,' said the doctor, and he moved on to his next patient, an elderly man with both legs in plaster.

James lay in bed on his own for a while. His parents had been to see him earlier, and had left him some books and his iPhone, but he didn't feel like reading or playing games. He couldn't concentrate on anything like that. He had too much energy. He really wanted to get up and run around, but that didn't seem what other people expected from him.

He wasn't sure about speaking to the police though. He had stabbed that man. Killed him. Would he be arrested for murder? He didn't think he deserved to go to prison. After all, he had just been trying to protect the children. He'd been so scared, he hadn't been thinking straight. Perhaps they would make allowances for that.

After a while the police woman who had interviewed him the day before came back. She was short and stocky, and waddled a little when she walked. Her skin was freckled and fair, and her button nose and chubby cheeks gave her the appearance of a cute kid. She looked slightly comical in her police uniform, as if she were just wearing a costume. But James remembered how she had dragged him away from that lunatic with her strong arms. She was a lot tougher than her baby face suggested, and her mousy brown hair looked ready to pick a fight with someone.

'Remember me?' she enquired, her mouth a tentative half-smile.

'Sure,' said James nervously. 'Liz. PC Liz Bailey. You came to see me yesterday.' He pushed himself upright in the bed, taking care not to knock the needle that still connected the IV to his arm.

Liz looked concerned. 'Hey, steady. Are you sure you should be sitting up? You were barely able to talk to me yesterday.'

'I'm feeling much better today.' In fact his strength was returning almost minute by minute, despite the lack of food. He felt like superman. He hoped he wasn't heading for some kind of relapse.

'Well, just take it easy,' said Liz. She sat down in a chair next to the bed. 'The doctor told me it would be all right for me to ask you some questions.'

'Yes,' said James. 'I'm sure there are lots of things you need to ask me. I've got some questions for you too. That is, if you don't mind me asking,' he added. There was something reassuring about the police woman. Even though she seemed quite gruff, James felt that he could tell that baby face anything. And it would be a relief to talk to someone about what had happened.

'Of course,' said Liz. 'You can ask me anything. But first, I need to run through my questions. Is that okay?'

James nodded.

'I already know a lot about the sequence of events. I

was first on the scene, along with my colleague. A neighbour reported a disturbance and we broke into the house. Do you remember that?'

'Yes. I remember someone shouting and the door breaking down, and feeling glad that the children would be rescued at last. I wasn't really worried about myself. I think I'd been so frightened that I just wasn't able to feel scared any more. I didn't care about the man either. I didn't feel anything. I just kept twisting the knife. You had to wrench it from my fingers to make me stop. Does that make me a bad person?'

'No, James. It's perfectly understandable. What you describe is a common reaction to severe trauma.'

'And are the children all right?'

'They're safe now. And maybe I can anticipate your next question and put you at ease a little. I want to let you know that you aren't going to be prosecuted for killing Mr Leigh.'

Not prosecuted. It took a moment to fully sink in. He wasn't going to prison after all. He didn't think he would have been able to handle that. But something Liz had said wasn't right. It took a while before he worked it out. 'Mr Leigh. That was his name?' The man had behaved so badly it hardly seemed right he should have a name. He had been more like a beast.

'That's right. And it's clear that there's no case for you to answer. We've already established from speaking to the other children exactly what happened. From what they've told us, Mr Leigh was responsible for the incident, and you were simply protecting them and yourself.'

'Are they really okay?' James asked. He didn't think the man had hurt them, but they must have been traumatized by what happened.

'They're completely unhurt,' Liz reassured him. 'Shaken, but children that age recover quickly.'

'Sure.' He hoped it was true. He wasn't certain he would ever recover from the events of that evening. How could you kill a man and not be deeply affected? 'Do you know why he did it?' asked James. 'Mr Leigh, I mean. Was he just some kind of madman?'

'There'll be an inquest into the death at some point, and the coroner will try to establish the cause of death and the sequence of events leading up to the incident.'

'The cause of death won't be too hard to work out,' said James. A bread knife through the heart, with James' fingerprints all over it. That would be a pretty good clue.

'Right,' agreed Liz. 'So the inquest will focus more on the events that led up to his death. It seems that Mr Leigh had been ill for some time before the incident. He hadn't been to work for several weeks. He'd visited a doctor who told him he could take time off school until he recovered.'

James frowned. 'School?'

'Mr Leigh taught Geography at Manor Road Secondary School.'

'What?' James couldn't process the new information. 'I thought he was some unemployed drug addict or something.' The idea that he'd killed a teacher seemed so much worse. But that kind of thinking made him feel shame. He had killed a man. What right did he have to judge him too?

Liz was consulting her notes. 'We took statements from each of the children, and from neighbours, but I just wanted to check some details with you. Did Mr Leigh at any point indicate why he wanted to harm you and the children?'

'He said he wanted to eat us.'

Now it was Liz's turn to look shocked. 'I wasn't aware of that,' she half-whispered. 'The children didn't say anything about it, just that he had frightened them.'

James carried on. 'He told me he hadn't eaten for days and he wanted to eat us up.' He noticed Liz glance at the bandages that covered the bite wound on his shoulder. 'I guess he decided to start on me.' For some reason, James no longer felt any shock or even disgust at the idea of eating another human being. He could almost begin to understand what had driven Mr Leigh to do it. After two weeks without food, James felt ever more ravenous himself. He wondered what it had tasted like, and whether Mr Leigh had enjoyed it.

'I see.' Liz looked ill.

'Anything else you want to know?' asked James.

'Not for the moment. There will be a report after the post-mortem examination to try to shed some light on the nature of Mr Leigh's illness, and then the coroner's court will be in touch when it's time for you to attend the inquest. You won't be on trial at the inquest. The purpose will be simply to establish the cause of death.'

'I understand,' said James.

'So is there anything else you'd like to tell me?'

'Just one more thing. Thank you.'

'What for?'

'For saving my life. Doctor Kapoor said that if you hadn't arrived when you did and given me first aid, I'd be dead.'

Chapter Eleven

Manor Road Secondary School, South London, new moon

Vijay Singh hurried along the shabby school corridor, worried he'd be late for his Year 10 Geography class. His heavy bag bounced on his shoulders, stuffed with books. Geography was his favourite class. Or at least it had been, before everything had gone wrong.

As Vijay entered the classroom, Drake Cooper jumped out at him from behind the door. 'Gonna eat you, gonna gobble you up!' shouted Drake. The other kids in the class burst into hysterical laughter. 'Mm, tasty kiddy,' said Drake, pretending to chew on a bone. 'Me very hungry.' He rubbed his stomach and patted it with both hands.

Ever since Mr Leigh had attacked those little kids on Halloween, the idea of a teacher eating his class had been all anyone wanted to talk about at school. Vijay didn't think it was funny. He couldn't think of anything less funny.

Mr Leigh had been Vijay's favourite teacher. Vijay had always liked Geography, but the way Mr Leigh taught it really brought the subject to life. Now he was gone and one of the sports teachers, Mr Johnson, had stepped in temporarily. Vijay probably already knew more about Geography than Mr Johnson ever would.

Mr Leigh had been off sick for several weeks before he'd attacked those little kids on Halloween night. No one knew why he'd been sick, or why he'd done what he did. The other teachers refused to talk about it, but that had only fuelled the wildest speculation. Anything from a rare tropical disease to alien mind control had been proposed, but Drake Cooper's theory was probably the most popular. 'Guy just went mental. Ape-shit crazy. So would you if you had to teach at this crap school.'

Vijay couldn't come up with a better explanation himself. Nothing else could explain how a kind and sensitive man could have turned that way. Perhaps teaching at Manor Road School really had pushed him over the edge. Drake was certainly right that the school was crap. Half the kids here didn't want to be taught, and Vijay had the feeling that the teachers didn't want to teach them either. Mr Leigh had been one of the few who seemed to care, but perhaps something had just made him flip. Then again, it might have been some kind of fever that made Mr Leigh act crazy. Vijay guessed he would never find out the truth. All that really mattered was that the best teacher ever was dead, and school would never be the same again.

The other kids in the classroom were still laughing at Vijay. Drake Cooper lunged forward again. 'Gonna bite your head off!' he cried, opening his mouth wide and rolling his eyes.

Drake's sidekick Ash Brown appeared and grabbed hold of Vijay's arm. 'You'll have to pull his turban off first,' he said.

Vijay raised a hand instinctively to his head, shielding the cloth windings that covered his uncut hair. As a Sikh, it was unthinkable that Ash or Drake might pull the turban from his head. He shoved the two boys away from him. 'Get off me, that's sick.'

Mr Johnson, the substitute teacher, sauntered into the classroom with a newspaper tucked under his arm. He glared at the boys. 'Is there a problem, Vijay?' he demanded.

Vijay felt his cheeks flush with shame. 'No, Mr Johnson.'

'Good.'

Everyone scrambled to find a seat.

Mr Johnson started to wipe the whiteboard clean, then thought better of it, clearing just enough space to scrawl the words, *Rainfall Patterns in Western Europe*. 'Okay. Everyone turn to page 52 of your textbook and start reading.' He sat down at his desk and began to read his newspaper from the back.

Vijay heard a loud whisper from his left. 'Hey, Singh, look at this.' He turned to look. Drake flicked a wad of paper straight at him, using his plastic ruler as a catapult. The missile hit him right in the middle of his face, knocking his glasses askew. 'Ow!' he cried.

'Quiet in class,' droned Mr Johnson from behind his newspaper.

Drake and Ash sniggered loudly, but the teacher paid them no attention.

Vijay rubbed his nose where the paper had struck. Sikh scriptures taught that tolerance of adversity was a divine quality, but Vijay had his doubts. At times like this he felt as if the world had no meaning. Nice guys like Mr Leigh lost their mind and tried to eat small children before getting killed themselves. Meanwhile, morons like Drake Cooper and Ash Brown carried on regardless. If there really was a God, he wasn't taking his job very seriously. Rather like Mr Johnson, in fact. Vijay sighed and opened his textbook at page 52. They had already done this chapter with Mr Leigh, but there was no point telling that to Mr Johnson. Instead, he started to read.

After school had finished, Vijay made his way out of the school gates and along Manor Road. Some kids cycled home, and others travelled in their parents' cars or took the bus, but Vijay lived close enough to walk. He hadn't gone far when he heard the sound of footsteps running up behind him. He stepped to the side of the pavement to let the runners pass, but lurched as someone grabbed hold of his school bag and swung him round. Another hand reached out and tugged at the cloth that wrapped his hair. It was Drake and Ash, grinning like a couple of idiots.

'Hey!' he cried, raising his hands to stop them pulling at the turban. 'Stop that!'

'Yo, Vijay,' said Ash. 'Can you lend us some money?'

'What for?' asked Vijay. He knew he'd said the wrong thing immediately.

'So you got some, then,' said Drake. 'Come on, hand it over.'

Vijay shook his head and tried to press past, but Ash blocked his way.

'We'll pay you back next week,' said Drake.

'No,' said Vijay. He looked around for help, but there were no teachers or adults within sight. He knew that none of the other children would help him.

Ash grabbed hold of his school bag and dragged it out of his hands before he could react. 'Is the money in here?' he asked, unzipping the bag and rummaging inside.

'Stop it!' shouted Vijay. He grabbed for the bag, but Ash was bigger than him and held it out of reach.

'Just give us the money, and there'll be no hassle,' said Drake. 'Come on, don't make things nasty.'

Vijay knew they had him beaten. He was the smallest boy in the class. How could he hope to fight back when he was outnumbered two to one? He pulled five pounds out of his pocket and handed the note over to Drake.

'That all you got?' demanded Drake.

Vijay nodded miserably.

'It'll do,' said Ash, dumping the school bag onto the pavement. He and Drake ran off down the road, high-fiving each other as they went.

Vijay picked up his bag and trudged on toward home. Tears pricked at his eyes. A good Sikh should be able to bear pain, suffering and insult without complaint, he reminded himself. But who was he trying to fool? The real reason he had to endure such treatment was because he was too afraid to fight back. Drake and Ash terrified him, and they knew it.

He heard another person coming up behind him and turned sharply in alarm.

It was Rose Hallibury, a girl from his class. Vijay looked away from her, hanging his head in shame. She had seen everything.

Rose walked along beside him for a little while, then she said, 'You live near here don't you? I've seen you walking this way before.'

Vijay was surprised that she had even noticed him. She was much too pretty to be interested in him. He glanced furtively at her, and caught her emerald green eyes watching him closely from beneath a crown of fiery red hair. Her skin was white and her tiny button nose was splashed with freckles. Looking at her face was like staring directly at the sun and he turned his head away, embarrassed. 'West Field Gardens,' he answered timidly.

'You live on the Terrace. I knew the family who used to live in your house.'

'We moved there in the summer,' said Rose. She waited a while, then added, 'I'm sorry about what happened to Mr Leigh.'

Vijay turned his face back to hers in surprise. 'Me too. But why are you telling me?' Rose had never even spoken to him before.

'Because I know he was your favourite teacher,' she

said

How she knew that was a mystery to Vijay. 'Yes, he was. I don't think it's funny that he attacked those children. I just thought it was very sad.'

Rose nodded. 'Me too. Take no notice of what Drake and Ash say.'

'I'll try not to.'

They walked along in silence for a minute, then she said, 'I saw what just happened.'

Vijay felt his cheeks burn. 'It was nothing.'

'It wasn't nothing. And it will get worse if you let it.'

Vijay had no reply to that. She had said aloud what he dreaded himself.

'They pick on you because you look different,' continued Rose. 'That's all. I used to get bullied in my old school because I have red hair.'

Vijay stopped and stared at her shiny copper curls. How could anyone bully a girl with such lovely hair? 'That's stupid,' he said. 'You have beautiful hair.' His cheeks were turning the same shade.

Rose shook her head, her hair flashing sparks of red as it swayed back and forth. 'It doesn't matter. That's how bullying works. It's not important why you're different. It can be anything, something small or stupid. Like having red hair, or glasses, or wearing a turban.' She nodded to indicate the cloth wrapped around his long hair. 'But you have to show them that you're strong, otherwise they'll just get worse and worse.'

Vijay stared at his feet. 'I'm not strong,' he said miserably. 'I'm small and weak, and I wear glasses, and I've never hit anyone in my life.'

'I don't think you're weak,' said Rose 'And hitting people doesn't make you strong. There are different ways to be strong.'

Chapter Twelve

King's College Hospital, Lambeth, South London, new moon

After speaking to James, Liz went to visit her colleague, PC David Morgan. He'd just been moved out of Intensive Care and into the High Dependency unit and this was the first time she'd been allowed to visit him since the night of the wolf attack.

The local newspaper had reported the attack on its front page, and a couple of people had claimed to see the animal roaming around nearby Clapham Common that same night. A local radio station had picked up the story and sensationalized it, calling the animal the *Beast of Clapham Common*. They'd tried to interview Liz about her encounter, but she had refused to speak to them. She didn't think she would mention it to Dave either.

She was shocked at how bad he looked. The big man lay in the hospital bed, wired up to various machines and tubes. His face was deathly pale and beads of sweat stood out on his forehead. At first she thought he was unconscious, but after a minute he stirred and opened his eyes. They glowed with an unhealthy yellow sheen.

She tried to keep her voice calm and casual. 'Hey, Fat Dave. How you doing there, big man?'

'Not so bad,' he replied, his voice hoarse and weak. 'I'd give you a hug if I didn't have so many needles sticking in me.'

'I'd hug you too if you weren't such an ugly bastard.'

Dave made no reply. His breathing was noisy and irregular, as if he'd just run upstairs. The hospital lights seemed to be bothering him and he squinted to look at her. Near the bed a row of machines displayed his vital signs. Liz knew enough to tell that his blood pressure was much lower than it should have been, and that his heart rate was wandering erratically.

She sat down in the chair next to the bed. 'I was going to bring you some grapes, but I thought you might prefer chocolates.' Dave normally guzzled chocolates by the sack load. She showed him the big box she'd picked up on the way.

Dave closed his eyes, murmuring something in reply. It might have been, 'Not hungry,' but she couldn't really tell.

She placed the box on a small pedestal next to the bed. There were some flowers and a bowl of fruit there, but the fruit was still wrapped in cellophane and hadn't been touched. 'I've just been to see that teenager we rescued on Halloween,' she continued. 'The one who stabbed the teacher. Do you remember?'

Liz and Dave had attended the incident with James the evening before Dave had been bitten by the wolf. Dave grunted in response, but gave no indication whether or not he remembered. Liz persisted anyway. 'His name is James Beaumont. He's a nice boy. He seems to be making a good recovery.'

Dave made no reply.

Liz told him, 'I bet you'll be fine in a few days too.' Her

words sounded hollow though. Dave had sustained a much more serious injury than James. A wolf bite, not a human one. He'd been unconscious for almost ten days following the attack. She sat with him for another fifteen minutes, but he said nothing more. Eventually she guessed that he'd drifted off to sleep.

A nurse came over and gave Liz a smile that couldn't completely disguise her weariness. 'How's he doing?' she asked. Her name tag read *Chanita*.

'Sleeping, I think,' said Liz. 'But I was hoping you might tell me how he's getting on?'

The nurse leaned over the bed to take Dave's temperature. She frowned and made a note on a clipboard at the end of the bed. 'Are you family?' she asked.

'Next best thing.' Liz gave the nurse one of her winning smiles, the kind she normally saved for old ladies and small children. 'We've been colleagues for the past five years.'

The nurse looked grim. 'I'm no doctor, but it doesn't look good to me. The bite wound's actually not that serious, although he did lose a lot of blood. It should heal with just some scar tissue left behind. But he's got a nasty infection from where that dog bit him. That's what's making him so weak.'

'Dog?' Liz shook her head, and found herself saying, 'It wasn't a dog.'

The nurse gave her a sceptical look. 'You can't believe everything you read in the newspapers.' She was referring to the *Beast* stories, Liz guessed.

'I don't,' said Liz. 'I was with him when it happened. I'm pretty sure it was a wolf.'

'A wolf in London?'

Liz shrugged her shoulders. 'Stupid, I know.'

'What makes you think it was a wolf?' asked the nurse.

'I'm not an expert of course. But the way it looked, the way it attacked. I've never seen a dog act like that. There was a human intelligence about the way it behaved, as if it knew what we were thinking. There was nothing submissive about it, not like a normal dog. It acted more like a cat, as if it knew it was superior to us.'

'Describe it to me,' said the nurse.

'It looked like a German shepherd dog, but larger, with a longer snout. It was the size of a human, with much longer legs than any dog.'

The nurse was studying her intently. 'Go on.'

Liz visualized the beast in her mind. Picked out in the dark, beneath the street lamps, she remembered the way the creature had stared at her, with those glowing eyes like lanterns in the night, seeming to see right into her soul. 'It had fine fur, very pale, almost a light ash-blonde. Its head was disproportionately large too, like a human head. But perhaps the most startling thing was the bright yellow eyes. I've never seen a dog with eyes like that.' She shuddered.

The nurse continued to study her face. Eventually she spoke in a hushed voice. 'It's not the first.'

'What do you mean?' asked Liz. Now it was her turn to sound disbelieving.

'Normally we get one or two dog attacks a month, but in recent months the number has been rising steadily,' said Chanita. 'They've been much more serious than the usual cases too. The wounds become infected and the patients develop a fever.'

'What kind of dogs were involved?' asked Liz.

'The descriptions vary. Sometimes an animal with light fur, sometimes brown or even black. But the other characteristics are always the same. People always remember the eyes – the bright yellow eyes.'

'But that's crazy,' said Liz. 'One animal running wild in London, I can believe, but several? Were they reported to the police?'

Chanita shrugged. 'I guess so. But if the animals ran off, maybe nothing was done. What happened to the animal that attacked your colleague?'

'It ran away. There was nothing I could do.'

The nurse nodded and turned to leave, but Liz grabbed her arm. 'What happened to the others?' she asked, fixing Chanita with her gaze. 'The patients, I mean. Did they pull through?'

Chanita hesitated. 'Some got better, some worse.' She tailed off, seemingly unwilling to continue.

'Did any die?' asked Liz, not certain she wanted to know.

A bell rang from the other side of the ward and Chanita looked toward it. 'I've got to go,' she said, her eyes pleading with Liz.

'Did any die?' Liz repeated. 'Please, I have to know.'

'About half of them,' said Chanita. She smiled apologetically and walked briskly away, leaving Liz alone with Dave.

Chapter Thirteen

Catholic Boys School, Mayfield Avenue, South London, crescent moon

Doctor Kapoor had wanted to keep James in hospital for another day at least, but he'd begged to be sent home. In the end the doctor had reluctantly agreed. James hadn't eaten anything in the hospital, but at home his mother brought him sushi and watched in amazement as he devoured plate after plate of raw fish.

'You'll make yourself sick,' she warned.

'No,' said James. 'I'm ravenous. I couldn't eat any of the food they gave me in the hospital. But now I could eat a horse.' He wasn't joking either. He really could have eaten a horse, a small one at least. The sushi was okay, but he really craved red meat. Raw steak dripping red with blood. His mum had said no to that, however.

He'd allowed her to keep him home for a day, then he insisted on going into school the next morning. He was bursting with frustrated impatience at having been cooped up indoors for so long. He needed to get out and burn off some energy. And there was something else he desperately wanted to do.

James attended the Catholic Boys School on Mayfield Avenue in a leafy well-to-do part of South London. His father was a stockbroker and could easily afford the cost of living in such an upmarket location. The school was a small Victorian institution attached to the Church of Our Lady on the adjacent plot. While the school wasn't strictly Catholic, many of the boys were, and the priest, Father Mulcahy, sometimes took morning assemblies at the school, and gave religious instruction to boys after classes were finished. The priest was old and quite severe, but James needed to speak to him urgently. He needed to confess his sins.

Coming back to school felt very strange. Although he'd been away for just two weeks, and not much seemed to have happened in his absence, for James himself everything had changed. He struggled to talk to any of his old friends. They all wanted to know about the madman, and how it had felt to stab someone with a knife. James refused to talk about it. The boys he had regarded as his peers now felt like silly schoolboys, emotionally under-developed and with trivial concerns. There was no point trying to tell them anything about what he felt, because they just weren't equipped to understand.

Only God would understand his thoughts and feelings. And the nearest thing to God was Father Mulcahy. After school classes had finished, instead of walking home, James made his way out of the side gate that led to the Church of Our Lady. He crossed the graveyard that bounded the old stone church, stopping halfway to sit on a wooden bench.

At this time of the year, the afternoons quickly turned to dusk and then to night, and James enjoyed watching the day fade. With it came a growing sense of peace.

The horse chestnut trees that screened the church from the school had already been stripped bare by the winter wind, but the churchyard itself was far from bleak. A squirrel darted across the top of a headstone, grey on grey, quick life in the midst of death. The clipped masses of the yew trees remained green all year round, a symbol of Christ's undying love, and James found the churchyard a strangely comforting place.

He sat alone on the bench for a good while, watching the last rays of the sun dip behind the moss-draped stone wall of the church. The whole churchyard seemed to hesitate for a while, as if waiting breathlessly for twilight to slip away to nothingness. He felt calmer than he had done for days. Then a boy walked past on the gravel path that led to the church, and the hunger rose up inside him once more. He wanted to jump at the boy, grapple him to the ground, rend and tear his flesh, and taste the blood and meat.

To his alarm, he found that he had unconsciously risen to his feet and followed the boy several steps before he even knew what he was doing. He had fallen into a natural hunting pattern, probing the boy for weakness, looking for an opportunity to strike.

James turned abruptly away from the boy and covered his face in his hands. The sooner he spoke to the priest the better.

Chapter Fourteen

*Clifton Blood Clinic, North London,
crescent moon*

'Samuel Smalling?' enquired the nurse at the blood clinic. She was petite and pretty, her auburn hair tied back sensibly in a ponytail, her skin rosy, her arms toned and firm beneath her navy-blue tunic. She smelled of blood and antiseptic, and underneath that, the faint but appetizing aroma of living human flesh.

'That's correct,' confirmed Samuel. He nodded and smiled broadly at the nurse – *Dawn*, according to her name tag. She was being very attentive after all. Everyone at the clinic had been very polite and professional.

'Have you given blood before?' she asked him.

He shook his head. 'First time, I'm afraid, Dawn. But I wanted to give something back, to play my part in society, you know?'

She nodded. 'I've got the results of your test here, Mr Smalling, and everything seems to be in order. Your haemoglobin level is nice and high, and we'll be screening your blood for any infections that could be passed to a patient via a blood transfusion. Your blood group is O Negative, which is particularly useful, because it means that we can safely give your blood to patients with any other type of blood group.'

'That's good to know,' said Samuel.

Leanna would be pleased about that. This was her idea after all. She was determined to spread the condition as widely and as quickly as possible. Their research indicated that blood transfusions would be an effective way to transmit it, and this was as good a way as any to get started. It was a lot less risky than running around the Common at night searching for strangers to bite.

'What infections do you test for?' he asked.

Dawn consulted her notes. 'Syphilis, hepatitis B and C, HIV, and human T-lymphotropic virus. We'll write to you if we find any of those infections in your blood sample.'

'Excellent news,' said Samuel. 'So, what happens now?'

'Now we take your blood,' said Dawn, smiling. She took hold of his arm and cleaned it with an antiseptic sponge. 'You don't feel the cold then?' she asked, indicating his T-shirt and lack of any kind of winter jacket.

Samuel shook his head. 'Not at all. I like it. It helps me chill.' This small talk was intended to distract him while she inserted the needle into his arm. But Samuel wasn't bothered by needles. 'The median cubital vein,' he remarked, as she inserted the sharp point of the needle into the wall of the vein with her gloved fingers.

She looked at him in surprise.

'I'm a medical student,' he explained.

'Ah,' said Dawn, knowingly. 'They're usually the worst.' She secured the needle in his arm and began to draw out the bright crimson liquid.

Samuel allowed himself a hearty laugh. The rich smell of the blood had put him in a mellow mood. 'Not me,' he said. 'You won't get any complaints from me. Take as much as you like.'

'Just one pint will be fine,' she said. 'I'm going to leave you now and come back in around five to ten minutes. The machine will draw blood and stop automatically when it reaches its limit. It may beep from time to time, but don't worry, that's normal. If you need any assistance, just raise your other arm.'

'No problem,' said Samuel. 'I'm enjoying everything so far.' He lay back in the plastic chair. It was rather like reclining in a deck chair by the seaside. He had always been comfortable in hospitals and doctors' surgeries. A car crash at the age of twelve had killed his parents and younger brother outright and left him in a critical condition. Doctors had spent two years rebuilding him, carrying out emergency surgery to treat a collapsed lung, repairing more than a dozen broken bones, and grafting skin onto his burned arms and legs. He still had metal rods in his left thigh. The experience had left both physical and mental scars that remained with him to this day, but it had also kindled a strong interest in medicine and a desire to become a doctor himself. It had led him to that fateful expedition to the mountains of Romania.

Samuel had been the first of Professor Wiseman's three students to succumb to the condition. He had only himself to blame for that. He'd been careless with one of the test subjects they'd managed to bring back to their lab. Six months of careful tracking and trapping in the forest to catch a live werewolf, then just a single second to ruin everything. They'd captured a woman from a nearby village. The villagers had told them of a wolf that attacked and killed livestock and had once tried to break into a house. It hadn't taken long for the professor and his team to identify the infected villager – a childless woman in her early thirties, the widow of a man killed by a wolf attack the previous year. Loose talk among the villagers themselves confirmed the conclusion.

Samuel had been working alone in the lab late one

evening, tired and thirsty. He ought to have stopped, but he was close to finishing his tests for the day. Just one momentary lapse of concentration and he'd felt the jaws of the woman lock onto his arm. He'd struggled to free himself, but already he knew it was too late. The condition always took hold after a vein or artery was breeched. There were no exceptions. Every documented werewolf attack had just two possible outcomes – death or infection.

At the time, he'd hoped for death. How foolish that wish had been. Becoming lycanthropic himself had been so much more rewarding than he could ever have imagined.

Since returning to London with Leanna and Adam, he'd been reading up on the history of lycanthropy. The word came from the Greek *lycanthrope*, a synthesis of *lykos* or *wolf*, and *anthropos*, meaning *human*. It was a surprisingly well-researched and documented field of study. Stories of shape-shifters were as old as human civilization, and in late medieval and early modern times, scholars had treated it as seriously as conditions like syphilis. It was only since the late nineteenth century that scepticism had pushed it beyond the accepted field of scientific investigation.

Just like Ebola, HIV and the Zika virus, lycanthropy had existed for thousands of years on the margins of humanity. And just like those diseases, it had persisted quietly, infecting small numbers of victims in localized areas, until conditions were right for it to suddenly explode into a worldwide epidemic. All it needed to take root was a high enough population density.

Medical science had received ample warning of lycanthropy. Gilles Garnier, the infamous *Werewolf of Dole*; Pierre Burgot and Michel Verdun, who confessed to being serial-killing werewolves; the German werewolf, Peter Stumpp, who ate his own son and was caught by villagers while actually in wolf form – the number of documented cases went on and on. In Europe during the sixteenth century alone, dozens of accused or confessed werewolves were put on trial and executed.

Epidemiologists should have spotted the signs a long time ago. But perhaps because of its early associations with witchcraft and superstition, nobody had taken the stories seriously. Scientific orthodoxy had not permitted it. Only Professor Wiseman had been brave or foolish enough to study it scientifically, and he had been ridiculed by the media and betrayed by his colleagues. Well then, people deserved whatever they got.

The machine beeped one last time and the nurse, Dawn, returned to remove the needle and to secure the blood.

'Take care of that,' said Samuel. 'I hope it can be put to good use.'

'I'm sure it will, Mr Smalling.'

He waited patiently while she applied a dressing to his arm.

'Keep the dressing on for at least six hours,' she advised. 'And now go and relax for a little while before you leave. You should drink two cups of tea or another beverage, and help yourself to the complimentary snacks too.'

'Thanks,' said Samuel, standing up. 'But I'm good to go.'

Chapter Fifteen

*Church of Our Lady, Mayfield Avenue,
South London, crescent moon*

James sat on the wooden pew at the back of the church waiting for the other boys to leave. He was scared. Shit scared, if he was honest, although he wouldn't say it out loud. Swearing was a sin, though not a mortal one. A mortal sin was one bad enough to send you to Hell. In the seventeen years of James' life, he had committed a mortal sin only on three occasions. Once, when he had missed Mass on his birthday because he'd wanted to play on his new Nintendo. Once, when he had masturbated, and once when he had looked at porn on the internet. All three of these things were grave offences against God, and sufficient to damn him to Hell unless he repented.

Of course he had confessed, and Father Mulcahy had pardoned him. He'd had to repent his sins and resolve to sin no more, and the priest had given him some stern words and fixed him with a severe gaze. At each new mortal sin, the sternness of the words and the severity of the Father's expression had worsened. James hadn't realized that there was a hierarchy of sin, although it should have been obvious that masturbation was worse than skipping Mass, and that watching porn was worst of all. The fact that it had been gay porn had particularly incensed the silver-haired priest in his black robe and white collar.

Now James had two new sins to confess, and they were far, far worse than anything he had confessed before. He had killed a man. And perhaps even worse than that, he had developed a lust to taste human flesh. He hadn't eaten any. Not yet. But he couldn't get the thought out of his mind. He feared what he might do, if he couldn't put an end to that desire.

So he had no choice. He would go to Father Mulcahy and tell him about his bad deeds and his bad thoughts. The Father would tell him what to do, and he would be forgiven.

While he waited, James made the sign of the cross and said a quiet prayer, asking the Holy Spirit to help him in what lay ahead. Usually this made him feel more relaxed and able to make a good confession, but today his thoughts were too agitated. He could not still his soul to let the Holy Spirit enter, and God remained silent. As he sat staring up at the crucified Christ that looked down upon him from above the altar he found himself becoming more and more scared. He almost fled from the church at one point, but forced himself to stay. If he did not confess his sins now, he would only be making things worse.

When the last of the other boys had left, James entered nervously into the confessional. He crossed himself again at the door and closed it firmly behind him, finding immediate solace in the still, calm gloom and familiar musty smell of the enclosed stall.

'James,' came the priest's voice from the other side of the wooden screen that separated them. 'I am so pleased that you're back from the hospital. Tell me, how do you feel?'

'Bad, Father,' said James nervously. 'Forgive me, for I have sinned.'

'I am sorry to hear that,' came the reply.

'My last confession was eighteen days ago,' began James, intoning the ritual words. 'These are my sins.'

When he fell silent, the priest prompted him gently. 'Yes? Go on. Tell me, how have you sinned? Do not be afraid to say what weighs most heavily on your heart.'

'Father, I killed a man.'

'Ah, yes,' said the Father. 'I have heard all about that, of course. To kill another man is one of the most serious sins against God. Every man is created in God's image and all human life is sacred.' The priest paused. 'But there were mitigating circumstances in your case. The Bible speaks rightly against the murder of the innocent, but from what I have heard the man you killed was not innocent.'

'He attacked me first,' admitted James. 'But still, I killed him.'

'James,' said the priest, 'the Church teaches that under some circumstances it is not only justifiable to kill another man in order to prevent greater harm, but is in fact a duty. We must all stand up for the common good, must we not? Sometimes it is necessary to act as you did in order to protect yourself and others. You saved the lives of four children, I hear. Now that is a brave act, not a sinful one.'

'Yes, Father, but how can it be right to commit a sin even to prevent another one?'

'Well, the Bible says that if a thief is caught breaking into a house and is struck so that he dies, the defender is not guilty of bloodshed.'

James thought about the Father's words for a moment. 'I do not feel brave, Father, only guilty.'

'I understand your wish for atonement, James. I will ask you to make an Act of Contrition, and I will give you your penance. Then God will forgive you. But first, tell me, is there anything else you wish to confess?'

James took a deep breath. 'It is hard for me to say it, Father.'

'I have heard all kinds of confessions in my years as a priest, James. You would be surprised. Say what is on your mind.'

James spoke to the screen. 'I lust for human flesh, Father. I want to know the taste of human meat. I hunger for it.'

The priest was deadly silent. 'I have never heard of such a thing,' said Father Mulcahy eventually. 'I trust that this is merely a thought and that you have not acted on such wicked impulses?'

'Yes,' said James. 'I mean no. I have not acted on it.'

'Unnatural lust is a grave sin indeed. It leads inexorably to ever greater sin. What about that other unnatural wickedness we have spoken of before? Do you still think about that?'

'I'm not sure what you are referring to, Father.'

'I refer to the act of homosexuality,' said the priest gravely.

It seemed that Father Mulcahy would never let it drop. And yet, the more James thought about it, the desire to love another man felt right, not wrong. He thought carefully before answering. 'Is homosexuality worse than eating someone?' he asked finally.

'Do you seek to mock me?' demanded Father Mulcahy.

'No, Father,' cried James. 'I seek your help.'

'Then you must do as I say. Put all such wicked thoughts from your mind at once.'

'I can't,' wailed James. The words were out before he could stop them. 'The desire is too great.'

'The desire to eat flesh or to lie with another man?'

'Both.' It did not matter which path he chose. Eating a man; loving a man. James was damned whichever way he turned. If the priest's words were true, James need not fear being sent to Hell, for he was already there.

Lycanthropic

He sniffed at the air within the confined space. The old priest gave off a terrible stink. His armpits stank of sweat. His breath smelled of menthol sweets. His hair was slick with wax. Stale tobacco lingered on his black cassock. And the dark space of the confessional was filled with the man's fear, like a black liquid. Yet beneath all those offensive smells lurked a more potent scent – living flesh and blood. In such close proximity it was driving James wild.

The old man wasn't the most delectable dish James could imagine, but his hunger had become insatiable. Apart from the sushi, he had not eaten for eighteen days. He had begged the nurse, Chanita, and his mother for red meat, but what he had really wanted all along was human flesh. Now here it was, close by, and his for the taking.

James' heart pumped blood to his limbs. The priest's words had angered him, rousing his passion, rousing his lust. He feared he could not command it any longer.

He heard Father Mulcahy speak again through the slatted wooden screen. 'James, it is important for you to understand that God loves you, but that you can never indulge these wicked lusts. Never. You must turn your back on them and never think of them again.'

'No!' screamed James. 'I cannot do that!'

He punched his fist through the wooden panel that separated him from the priest, and grasped the Father's stout body tightly in an iron grip, anchoring his fingernails in the old man's chest. The priest howled with pain. With his other hand, James swept the battered panel aside like a curtain and hauled the man to him. The priest's face twisted in terror.

James sank his teeth into Father Mulcahy's wrinkled neck, biting deep into the corpulent flesh, rending, biting and chewing. He cut through veins and arteries, seeming to know exactly where and how to bite in order to kill quickly. Hot blood splashed his face and ran down his cheeks. He drank deep and felt the coppery liquid flood his senses, satisfying his craving like oxygen to a drowning man.

After that he hardly remembered anything.

Chapter Sixteen

Manor Road, South London, crescent moon

Chris Crohn would be the first to admit that he got on better with computers than with other people. He'd made his first Myspace page at the age of ten, learned to code HTML at twelve, created his first database application shortly after his thirteenth birthday, and built a Linux server aged fifteen. He'd graduated from university with a degree in Computer Science and had hoped for an exciting job with a cutting-edge tech company. But something had gone wrong. His dream job never happened. Now aged twenty-two, he was back at his childhood school, Manor Road Secondary, working as tech support guy, a job that utilized approximately one percent of his skills and knowledge of computing. Chris thought he knew why, and the reason was *people skills*.

His best friend, Seth, who was basically an idiot, had got a better job than Chris because he had *people skills*. As far as Chris could tell, *people skills* meant the ability to talk to people you didn't like, about things that didn't interest you, at times when you had better things to do. Chris didn't care for that, and he'd said as much at most of his job interviews.

Seth was welcome to his *people skills* and his well-paid job in London's booming financial tech sector. Seth could keep his money, and his swanky Docklands apartment, and the easy way he flirted with girls.

Chris had never had a girlfriend. He didn't know why. He liked girls, they just didn't like him. He had studied girls in the abstract, noting their complex behaviour patterns and subtle social signals. He knew where to go to meet girls, and he had observed what other boys said to girls in order for them to initiate an intimate relationship. He could predict with a high degree of accuracy whether a girl would accept or reject a boy's approach. But reverse-engineering all the protocols didn't seem to help. Girls simply ran from him on sight. He must be doing something really wrong, but he couldn't figure out what.

People skills, Seth would whisper cryptically, as if that meant anything.

Chris didn't really mind too much. If he needed female company, there were plenty of virtual girls available online, and he didn't need to worry about sending them the right social signals, or navigating arbitrary cultural constructions. He just had to click the computer mouse. Besides, not having a girlfriend gave him two key benefits – time and money. Of these, Chris valued time more.

Chris might spend each working day from eight to four performing trivial tasks like keeping the school's anti-virus software up to date, connecting printers, and setting up mail accounts for dummies, but his real work began when he got back to his tiny studio apartment in Manor Road, just around the corner from the school. He'd acquired a lot of hardware over the years – unwanted CPUs, obsolete graphics cards, abandoned disk drives and old motherboards – and had used the kit to rig up quite an impressive server farm in his apartment. It didn't leave a lot of space for cooking, but Chris didn't know how to cook in any case. A few months back, he'd coded an app that could identify and gather intelligence on topics that were trending on social media. The app used a deep-learning neural-network technique developed by NASA for analyzing extra-terrestrial radio signals, but Chris had modified it to search for weird and interesting stuff going around the web. The results had totally surprised him.

His app had picked up a strong reading for the keyword *werewolf*. That was weird, even by internet standards. He'd coded another app to extract geographic data associated with the keyword and had been more than a little alarmed to find a massive concentration of incidents in London. The system had also detected a few occurrences in the north of England, one or two in France and even in Romania of all places, but almost entirely they were located within the M25 orbital motorway that surrounded the capital. The epicentre was uncomfortably close to the school where Chris worked.

He showed the data to Seth when he called round to his apartment that evening after work. 'See? It's happening.'

'What is?' said Seth, flicking his mop of brown hair away from his heavy-rimmed glasses.

Chris spoke slowly to him, the way he explained computer stuff to the dummies at school. 'The apocalypse. Like we always talked about when we were kids. But with werewolves instead of zombies.' He pointed at the computer screen, scrolling through the graphs and correlations, the keywords and geographic references that he'd so carefully compiled. Werewolf sightings in London. He showed Seth the chart he'd plotted showing the steady rise in frequency over the past three months. The conclusion was inescapable.

Seth peered at the screen through his thick glasses and stroked his stupid goatee beard. Chris hated the way he did that. It always preceded some idiotic remark. Right on cue, Seth said, 'Don't be dumb. This is just, like, some new fad.'

'What kind of fad?' demanded Chris. 'How can werewolves be a fad?'

'I dunno. But werewolf can't literally mean werewolf. That's a crazy idea.'

'What else can it mean? Werewolf means werewolf.'

'Yeah, but it might just refer to some new movie or game.'

Chris shook his head vehemently. 'No, this is for real. Look at these tweets.' He pulled up a screen of data and pointed at two of the entries.

Out on the town in Brixton, saw a werewolf in the park #freaky #wtf

Almost attacked at Ealing Broadway by a huge dog #werewolf #beast

'Yeah,' said Seth. 'But maybe this is code for something else. It might be a neo-Nazi thing.'

'How could it be that?'

'You know,' said Seth. 'Adolf Hitler became obsessed with werewolves. He created an inner circle of followers who were called werewolves. This might be like that.'

'No, I don't think so,' said Chris. 'Look at this.' He clicked on a file and opened up an image taken from someone's Facebook feed. The photo was dark and blurry but clearly showed an enormous wolf with yellow eyes lurking behind a parked car. 'That's not code. That's an actual werewolf.'

'Or just a big dog,' said Seth, stroking his beard again.

'One of them attacked a policeman,' continued Chris. 'It was in my news feed. They're calling it the *Beast of Clapham Common*.'

'Bah,' said Seth. 'You shouldn't believe everything you read on the internet.'

Lycanthropic

'There's more,' continued Chris, 'And not just on the internet. One of the teachers at school tried to eat some kid.'

'Ugh,' said Seth. 'Gross.'

Chris glared at him. 'It was Mr Leigh, the Geography teacher. Remember him?'

Seth frowned, a thick crease appearing above his glasses. 'He taught us in Year Nine. Nice guy.'

'Yeah, exactly. And now he's dead.'

'What happened?'

'He went berserk and attacked some kids. One of them stabbed him with a kitchen knife.'

'And now he's dead.'

'I already told you that.'

Seth folded his arms across his chest. 'Proves nothing.'

Chris looked at him in disgust. 'Believe what you want,' he told his old friend. 'I'm going to prepare for the worst.'

And so Chris started prepping himself for survival. He read books written by retired special forces soldiers, he studied survivalist websites, and he made online purchases. A rucksack, an all-weather tent, flashlights, spare batteries, a compass, knives, candles, multi-vitamins, first-aid kit, matches, energy bars, tablets for his hay fever, and a fishing kit.

When the apocalypse came, Chris would meet it head on and prosper. Losers like Seth would find out what happened to those who couldn't be bothered to prepare.

Chapter Seventeen

Royal Park Canal, North London, crescent moon

James ran and ran until he was out of breath. By then the school, the church and the body of Father Mulcahy were miles behind him and he was in a part of London he had never seen before.

He muttered the words of the Act of Contrition, speaking aloud, indifferent to the stares of passing strangers. 'My God, I am sorry for my sins with all my heart. In choosing to do wrong and failing to do good, I have sinned against You, whom I should love above all things. I firmly intend, with the help of Your grace, to sin no more and to avoid whatever leads me to sin. Our Saviour, Jesus Christ, suffered and died for us. In His name, my God, have mercy.'

The familiar words, usually so comforting, seemed to have little effect. He wandered aimlessly, seeking only to keep moving, to put more distance behind him, and found himself on the bank of an old canal. Red-brick warehouse buildings, now converted into trendy urban apartments, backed almost to the water's edge, leaving only a narrow muddy path for him to walk along. He set off along the path, keeping his eyes on the ground before him.

In the time since killing the priest, night had fallen. The overcast sky hid the crescent moon, and the canal path was unlit, but James found that he could see perfectly well in the dark. He preferred the night to the harsh glare of daylight which irritated his eyes.

He stopped at last in a secluded space beneath a low bridge. Discarded bottles and cans littered the path, but there were no people here. It was just as well. James couldn't be with other people now. He was a monster.

He didn't understand how it had happened, but he had become a beast, an outcast. It had all started that awful evening on Halloween. God had punished him for his sin. Not the sin of murdering Father Mulcahy, nor even for killing the teacher, Mr Leigh, but for being gay. Father Mulcahy had warned him, and even though he knew it was a sin, he had been too weak to follow God's path. He could not deny his lust. And that's why he was being punished.

There was no way to redeem himself now. He had killed, not once but twice. There was only one way out of this mess he'd made for himself. He had been weak, but now he had to be strong one last time.

He picked up a big stone from the path and put it in his jacket pocket. He found a brick and dropped it into his school bag. He added a large piece of rusty metal and some glass bottles and another stone. The bag was full and he strapped it to his back. He wasn't sure if it was heavy enough, but it was the best he could do. He stepped to the edge of the canal and sat on the bank, his legs dangling over the side.

He stared into the cold, dark water flowing beneath the bridge. How long would it take to drown? Seconds, minutes? He had fallen into an icy pond once, up to his waist in freezing water. The shock had nearly killed him. If he jumped in this canal in the middle of winter, he might well die of the cold before he drowned. But either way, and however long it took, it would be quicker and better than a lifetime of misery. A lifetime of sin.

Suicide itself was a sin of course, but presumably a lesser one than cannibalism. And it would be a quick one, over in seconds, harming no one else. Maybe he could just stumble and fall into the canal instead of jumping in. Would that excuse him, or would God know his true intention?

A sound startled him. A man descended the steps leading to the canal path and started walking toward him. He should push himself into the water now before the man came. But if he did, and the man saw him, he might try to rescue him. He would wait until he had gone.

The man came closer. He walked confidently, his hands in his pockets, whistling a tune. Tall, with black skin and fine features, he looked to be in his early twenties. He wore jeans and a T-shirt that revealed a slim body and broad chest beneath. Wasn't he cold in this wintry weather? The man smiled at James in a relaxed manner as if they were old friends. James ducked his gaze. He didn't want to attract any attention, not now. He would wait for the man to walk on by.

He didn't walk past, though, but came over to where James was sitting and joined him. He squatted down, then stretched his long legs over the edge of the canal, lifting his strong arms over his head as if he were settling down to watch the sun set on a summer evening. The man said nothing, and James stared down at his feet, willing the stranger to leave him alone.

Something about the man was peculiar, and not just his summer clothes, or his odd manner. He smelled different to other people. Familiar, somehow. Then it hit James. The man smelled of wolf.

Lycanthropic

He glanced sideways, and the man returned his look with a smile of shiny white teeth.

'How are you doing there, kiddo?' The stranger had a deep, resonant voice, a voice of quiet power. 'It's a funny night to be out counting fish.'

James grunted, wishing the man would go.

'I assume you're counting them, since you've not brought any fishing tackle along.' When James made no reply, he continued to talk. 'My old man used to bring me here when I was a kid. He showed me the best spots to fish, where you could avoid being seen by the coppers. They weren't happy with people fishing along the canal for some reason. I think they just liked to find an excuse to harass a couple of black guys, to be honest. But if you could find a quiet spot, like this one, you could expect a good catch. Carp, eels, pike, even trout if you were lucky. You ever been fishing?'

James shook his head.

'It's a good sport to do with your dad. That father and son thing, you know? My dad wasn't much of a talker, not like me, but he liked to fish. Fishing was his way of saying to me, *you're my son*. Know what I mean? Anyway, he used to catch most of the fish, the big ones at least. The perch you can't really eat, you throw them back in and let them swim away. But the eels? Man, they were delicious. You gotta eat them fresh though. My mum used to chop them up and fry them with garlic and spices. Turmeric, chilli, maybe even some coconut.' He stopped and put his big hand on James' shoulder. 'I'm Samuel, by the way. Samuel Smalling. What's your name?'

'James. James Beaumont.'

'So tell me, James, are you gonna jump in this canal, or just sit here counting fish, because if you're gonna jump, I don't think I'll be joining you. I'm happy to sit and count fish though.'

James stayed silent for a minute, staring at the silky black water slipping past. He couldn't see any signs of fish in there. 'I was going to jump,' he said at last. 'I was ready to do it. But I don't think I can now.'

'Too bad,' said Samuel with a grin. 'Sorry if I put you off. Maybe you wanna talk about it instead?'

'I don't think so.'

'It's just that I noticed all this blood down your front, and I wondered if that had anything to do with it.'

James looked at the mess of dried blood over his jacket. 'I just killed a man.'

'Yeah?' said Samuel. 'Did he deserve to die?'

'No,' said James. 'Of course not. No one deserves to die.'

'That's what I used to figure,' said Samuel. 'And yet everyone does, regardless. My dad doesn't catch fish any more. He's dead. My mum too. No more frying fish for her. Even my little bro' died, and he was just a kid. Seems to me like life ain't fair, so I wouldn't worry too much about it.'

'But I killed a priest. I murdered him. That's an unforgivable sin. How can I not worry about it?'

'A priest?' said Samuel with some amusement. 'You really like to do things properly, don't you? I helped to kill a professor once, but never a priest.'

James turned to look directly into Samuel's eyes. 'You killed a professor?'

'Sure I did. That's because I'm a werewolf.'

James stared at the man sitting next to him. 'A werewolf.' He had known it all along. But sometimes you had to hear a thing to truly believe it.

'We are what we are, James. You've never told anyone what you are, have you?'

'I told Father Mulcahy I was a werewolf. Then I killed him.'

Samuel laughed. 'Right. But I didn't mean that. I was talking about you being gay.'

James' face turned hot. 'How did you know? I mean, I'm not gay. It's a sin. I've never been with another boy.'

Samuel put his hand on his. 'Hey, easy. No one's here to judge you. Like I said, we are what we are.'

'Father Mulcahy said that being gay is always a choice, and that we should make the right choice, and choose not to sin.'

'Is that right? This Father Mulcahy seemed to know all the answers. Did he think you chose to become a werewolf too?'

'I ... I don't know.'

'Listen, James. None of us knows all the answers. The world is too complicated, yeah? But we all have to make choices. So choose to be happy, James. Choose love, not hate. Always choose love.'

Chapter Eighteen

University Athletics Park, North London, crescent moon

Bright floodlights illuminated the track of the University Athletics Park on dark winter evenings, and the harsh artificial light made Adam Knight wince. He pulled on a pair of dark glasses to blot out the glare. People had laughed at his glasses the first time he'd raced in them, but he'd shrugged that off easily enough. Small-minded people always betrayed their jealousy in petty ways. Adam had trained at the track as an undergraduate, and had managed respectable times, but since turning lycanthropic he had become undefeatable. Floodlights or no floodlights, he would win this race by a country mile.

As soon as the starting pistol fired it was obvious he was pulling quickly ahead of the other runners. That was no surprise. They were only human, after all. He leaned forward, enjoying the feel of the air rushing past, stretching out first one arm, then the other, powering forward with his strong shoulders, cupping handfuls of air to drag himself ever faster. His enlarged heart pumped wolf blood through his legs as they drove him on, his feet striking the running surface with an unshakeable grip.

He was rounding the first bend already. He leaned into it, straining every muscle to take full advantage of his lead. The modest crowd cheered him on, but he shut them out, turning his focus inward, feeling the wolf power throb through his limbs.

He completed the bend and the next straight almost as if time had ceased to bind him in its worldly passage. He entered the final curve and almost floated around it, every nerve ending tuned to his goal. When he crossed the line, he knew he'd made a new personal best. He'd long since broken the university record. This would put him at Olympic performance levels. And it had been less than a year since he'd changed. Who knew what he might achieve in another twelve months?

He hardly felt tired after the race. While the other runners stumbled across the finishing line and bent over in exhaustion, he jogged another lap in front of the cheering crowd of the University Athletics Club, then went into the changing rooms to shower.

Leanna had warned him not to draw attention to himself. He was supposed to be keeping a low profile. But with Leanna herself having bitten a police officer last full moon, and the newspapers running their stupid *Beast* stories, competing in university-level race events hardly seemed to matter.

He found himself rubbing his nose where Leanna had bitten him, back in Romania. A pink scar served as an unwelcome reminder of his humiliation. He had kowtowed to her then, but the bitch had better watch her back. Adam had never enjoyed being in second place.

'Adam? Can I have a word when you've finished?' The athletics coach, Brian Wooley stood at the entrance to the showers. He'd helped Adam improve his technique when he'd first started running, but he was out of his depth now. He could barely understand Adam's extraordinary performance, let alone offer any useful advice on how to improve. Adam regarded the coach's out-of-condition body with ill-concealed disdain.

'Sure, Coach, whatever,' called Adam. 'With you in five.'

Once he'd changed, he knocked on the door to the coach's dreary office. He entered when Brian responded with a 'Come in.'

Adam stood in the cramped office in preference to sitting. His limbs still felt alive from the race. His exertion had not fatigued him, merely warmed him up. He felt as if he could repeat the race in an even quicker time now. 'What's up, Coach?' he asked.

Brian sat behind an old wooden desk, his silver brows knotted in a furrow. 'You're doing well, Adam, very well. And it's only Michaelmas Term. There are another six months until the inter-university finals in June.'

'Sure,' said Adam lightly. He wondered if the old man was going to tell him anything he didn't already know.

'You're winning, Adam,' said Brian. 'Always winning.' His voice trailed off. There was clearly something on his mind.

'Is there a problem?' Adam demanded.

Brian fixed him with a hard appraising stare. 'I dunno, Adam. No problem with your times, that's for sure. You're winning every race.'

'So?'

'Everyone wants to win. Some people will do anything to become a winner. Anything at all. But I want to make one thing clear. I run a clean team at this university. You understand me? Clean.'

'I understand,' said Adam coolly. 'I understand exactly what you're saying.'

'I don't know what you're using,' said the coach.

Lycanthropic

'Steroids, human growth factor, diuretics. Whatever it is, I'm going to find out. And I'll tell you this, I can't risk the reputation of the club. I've built this club over twenty years. And I can't risk one bad apple ruining its reputation. So I'm going to suspend you, Adam, until I know you're clean. I'll give you some time to fix yourself up, then we'll run some tests. Once I know you're clean, you can run again. You understand?'

Adam felt his rage building as he listened to these words. He approached the desk, putting his fists down and leaning over it toward the coach. 'Oh, I understand all right,' he told the old fool. 'But it seems you don't. I'm already clean. I've never taken any kind of drug or performance-booster. What you see is natural, but you're too much of an idiot to recognize it. So you can test me now, and I'll pass all your tests, just like I intend to win every race.'

The coach shook his head. 'I know you're angry, son, but like I said, a few months off racing will be good for you and good for the club. Now go home and I'll tell you when it's time to come back.'

Adam smashed his fist on the desk. He wished he could transform into wolf form at will, to show the old man his true nature. But even in human form he had the power to destroy. 'No,' he raged, 'I'll tell you what's going to happen. This club needs new blood. People like me. You're from the old world. Soon people like you will be gone, and the world will belong to me and those like me.' He swept his hand across the desk, hurling papers and pencils to the floor. 'You're a lucky old man, Coach. You're going to be one of the first to see.'

Brian pushed his chair away from the desk, his eyes uncertain, thinly disguised fear on his face. 'See what?'

'This!' shouted Adam. He crossed the desk and the space beyond in a single leap, watching as the coach's eyes went wide with surprise. Adam landed on his feet and grasped the old man's shoulders with fingers of steel, burrowing claw-like nails into his flesh. The coach gasped with pain and terror.

Before Brian could move, Adam pushed his head to the man's throat, opening his mouth wide, and clamping down hard. The coach gurgled and began to scream, but Adam crushed his windpipe quickly, killing the scream almost as soon as it had started. He sucked blood from the wound, then withdrew. Too much anger surged through his veins for him to feed.

He drew back his right hand and struck the coach's dead features with his curled fist, enjoying the crack as the nose smashed. He lifted his fist and struck again and again, tearing skin and crushing bone with each new strike.

Some wild instinct had taken over and he lost track of how long he beat the man, and how many bites, blows and kicks he gave him. When the bloodlust finally burned itself away, the body of the coach was unrecognizable.

Adam stood, drawing himself to his full height, gazing down at the broken man with contempt and loathing. He bared his teeth once more and turned away from his work. The age of the werewolf was here now. Anyone who stood in its way would be destroyed.

Chapter Nineteen

Manor Road Secondary School, South London, quarter moon

Something was up, Vijay Singh was sure of it. It had started with Mr Leigh, the Geography teacher, and now it was spreading. Some kind of mystery illness was going around the school, but nobody knew what it was. Several of the teachers had been off sick. Students too. When they came back – if they did – they seemed different. They were cold and distant, even hostile.

Vijay's friend Thomas Murray had been off sick for three weeks. When he returned to school, he refused to tell Vijay why he'd been away. In fact he'd barely spoken a word to Vijay since he got back. There was something wrong about him. His features were pale and drawn. His eyes glittered yellow. The way Thomas looked at him made Vijay afraid.

But it wasn't just that. Children had gone missing.

Jamie Jones and Max Thompson had been given

detention for failing to hand in their English essay last week, but they had never shown up. No one had seen them since, and the school had alerted the police.

Lee Small had got into trouble for flooding the boys' toilets and was sent to the Headmaster's office. He was never seen again.

Now, Mr Harvey the Biology teacher hadn't arrived for the afternoon class, and he was always strictly on time. After Geography, Biology was the subject Vijay enjoyed most. Mr Harvey made it so interesting. Instead of droning on at the front of the class, Mr Harvey always got them to use their hands and study things for themselves. He'd once got the class to build a model of a DNA molecule so they could see for themselves how it worked. The big double helix still stood on the floor in the corner of the classroom. But there would be nothing to learn this afternoon. Mr Harvey was nowhere to be seen. Fifteen minutes without supervision and his class was running riot.

One of the loud girls, Holly Brady, had done a karaoke session with her phone, standing up on top of her desk. Some of the other girls had clapped and sung along. Vijay hoped that would bring a teacher running, but the whole performance had gone unremarked.

Two of the thick-headed kids at the back got into a fight that ended with one of them hurling a chair across the classroom, narrowly missing the DNA molecule. Even that went unnoticed.

Vijay sat quietly at his desk near the front and hoped a teacher would come soon.

'Hey, Singh,' came a voice from behind. It was Drake Cooper. Vijay sat rigid, afraid to do the wrong thing.

'We're talking to you,' said another voice. Ash Brown came to lean against his desk. He jostled it, making Vijay's pencil roll onto the floor.

Vijay didn't dare stoop down to pick it up. 'Get lost,' he said in a quiet voice. 'Mr Harvey will be here any moment.'

Lycanthropic

'No, I don't think so,' said Ash. 'Know what I think? I reckon he's been eaten!'

He jumped at Vijay, his teeth bared, his fingers curled in a comic-book imitation of a monster. Vijay leaped out of his chair in fright. The girls behind him laughed raucously.

'Or perhaps not,' continued Ash, 'Perhaps he's busy eating some kids himself right now. Yum, yum, tasty little kiddies, all chewy and fat.'

'What do you want?' Vijay demanded, trying to sound strong, trying to look Ash in the eye.

A hand reached out from behind and grabbed hold of his school bag. 'We want whatever you got in here,' said Drake. 'Let's take a look, yeah?'

Vijay turned and tried to grab hold of the bag, but Drake dodged away. When Vijay stood to go after him, Drake tossed the bag over his head to Ash.

Ash unzipped it and emptied the contents onto the floor. 'Just boring books in here,' he said, looking at the pile of school books and stationery that had spilled out. 'Where do you keep your money? In your pocket, I expect.'

'I don't have any,' said Vijay defiantly.

'Someone's telling fibs,' said Drake. 'Come on, hand it over.'

'Or else we'll pull your turban off,' said Ash.

'No!' Something snapped in Vijay. It was like Rose Hallibury had said. If he didn't make a stand now it would just get worse. He glanced across the classroom and saw Rose's bright green eyes watching him closely. She nodded at him encouragingly, her ginger curls bouncing on her freckled forehead. Vijay turned to face his tormentors. 'No,' he said again.

'What did you say?' demanded Drake.

Vijay faced him squarely. He realized that Drake was suddenly afraid – he was afraid of losing face in front of the class. 'I said no. You can't have my money.'

Holly Brady and some of the other girls laughed again. Vijay wished they would shut up. He saw something change in Drake's expression. The girls' laughter had put his reputation on the line. Drake nodded at Ash, his mouth straightening into a grim line of resolve.

Vijay felt Ash shove him from behind, and spun round to face him, raising his arm protectively. He looked Ash in the eyes and said, 'Stop that.'

Ash shoved him again and tried to grab the cloth binding of his turban. Vijay repeated what he had said before. Ash looked to Drake for some support. The girls had stopped laughing and were watching intently.

'You're going to give us your money right now, or else,' said Drake.

'No,' Vijay repeated. He wasn't going to fall into the trap of asking what Drake meant by *else*. The classroom had fallen completely silent.

'Well, then, we're gonna have to take it from you.' Drake made a grab for Vijay's jacket. Vijay raised his arms defensively again, but this time Ash punched him from behind. Vijay felt a sharp jab of pain, but shrugged it off. He turned to face both boys and held his arms in front of his chest, blocking against any more blows. 'Hit him again, Ash!' shouted Drake, but before Ash could comply, the classroom door banged open and Mr Johnson the sports teacher strode in.

'What the bloody hell is going on here?'

Drake and Ash jumped clear of Vijay like they'd been burned.

Mr Johnson glared at the room of silent children. Nobody said a word. 'I asked a question,' said Mr Johnson.

'Please, Sir,' said Holly Brady, raising her hand. 'Drake and Ash were fighting with Vijay.'

'Is that true?'

'Yes, Sir,' admitted Vijay. The other two scowled at him.

'Vijay started it, Sir,' said Ash in a high-pitched voice.

Lycanthropic

'I doubt that very much,' said Mr Johnson. 'Frankly, neither do I care. All three of you, come with me to the Headmaster's office at once. You can explain to the Head who did what, not that he will care much either, I expect.'

He marched them along the corridor and down the stairs to the Headmaster's office, Drake and Ash giving him angry looks as they went. Vijay felt humiliated. He had never been in trouble at school before. Mr Johnson should have understood the situation. It ought to be Drake and Ash dragged before the Head, not him as well. He couldn't imagine what his parents would say when they found out.

Mr Johnson rapped hard on the Headmaster's door and stuck his head inside the office. He exchanged a few short words with Mr Canning the Headmaster, and then reappeared. 'You first,' he said to Ash. 'You other two, wait outside quietly.'

The Headmaster was a tall man with steel grey hair swept back from his high forehead. He wore a three-piece suit and a purple-and-gold tie. Vijay found him a forbidding man, and had always been a little scared of him. He dropped his gaze to the floor now under Mr Canning's stern expression. The Headmaster's shoes were polished like mirrors.

Ash showed no such trepidation. He smirked as the Headmaster led him inside his office.

The Headmaster's eye held a strange yellow gleam. The door to his office closed behind him.

Mr Johnson glared angrily one last time at Vijay and Drake, then strode away down the corridor.

The two boys sat opposite each other on plastic chairs, Vijay fiddling nervously with his hands, Drake scowling at him. Vijay had never been summoned to the Headmaster's office before and he had no idea what might happen now. Detention perhaps, or maybe worse. He might be suspended, or even expelled from the school. He felt sick with worry.

Raised voices came from within the office. Through

the thin wall, he could hear the Headmaster, Mr Canning, speaking angrily. Ash said something inaudible in reply.

Opposite him, Drake tried to look nonchalant, but his confidence was clearly draining away rapidly.

Vijay breathed deeply to calm himself. Mr Canning was known to be tough but fair-minded. He had lectured the school often enough about his zero-tolerance policy toward bullying. And Vijay hadn't done anything wrong. He just had to tell Mr Canning exactly what had happened, and the Headmaster would surely take action against Drake and Ash. After all, Vijay was the victim. Now that it had come to this, he realized that he should have gone to the Headmaster sooner. In retrospect the solution appeared obvious.

A shout rang out from the other side of the office door followed by a loud crash.

'What was that?' asked Drake, as if Vijay knew. It had sounded like furniture being broken, but surely ...

Another loud noise, like the splintering of wood, and a boy's scream came from the other side of the door. A banging sound started up, and something crashed heavily against the wall.

Drake shot to his feet. 'What's that? What's happening? It sounds like Mr Canning is attacking Ash!'

Another scream came from the room followed by a sickening thud. Then silence.

Vijay remembered the yellow gleam he'd noticed in Mr Canning's eyes. It was the same inhuman gaze that had so terrified him in his friend Thomas Murray. All the children and teachers who had returned to school after being sick had the same look. He thought again about Mr Leigh trying to eat the little kids on Halloween night. He remembered the students who had gone missing – Jamie Jones, Max Thompson and Lee Small. All three of them had disappeared after being sent to the Headmaster's office. Suddenly he understood.

Wet sounds came from inside the office, the sound of

biting.

Drake had turned as white as a ghost. 'What was that noise? We have to go in and help Ash.'

'No,' said Vijay flatly. 'Ash is already dead. The Headmaster is eating him now.'

Drake stared at him, rigid with horror. He slowly sank back to the chair. 'I don't understand. What's happening?'

They sat in deathly silence, listening to the soft rending sounds coming from the office. Chewing, munching and slobbering noises followed. Drake spilled forward and vomited over his own shoes.

In that moment, Vijay turned his back on fear. He no longer feared Mr Canning, or the monster that Vijay knew the Headmaster had become. He certainly did not fear what his parents would think when he told them what had happened. And as for the quivering boy sitting opposite, he felt only pity. 'There's no time to explain,' he told Drake. 'Either we run now, or we die.'

'Okay,' said Drake, casting one last glance over his shoulder at the closed door to the Headmaster's office. 'Where do we run?'

'Anywhere,' said Vijay, and together they ran.

Chapter Twenty

Greenfield Road, Brixton, South London, quarter moon

James always did his best to be polite and make a good first impression. It cost nothing to smile, and get a new relationship off to a good start. But Adam Knight seemed to have different ideas.

'Who the hell is this?' he demanded, when Samuel brought James back to the house he shared with Adam and Leanna. Adam was a tall and intimidating man. He wore a tight vest, showing off well-muscled arms and a broad frame. He seemed to fill the narrow entrance hall, blocking their way into the house.

Samuel didn't seem to be put out by Adam's attitude. 'This is James,' he said. 'He's a friend. He's going to stay with me here for a while.'

James cleared his throat nervously. 'Hi,' he said. 'Samuel's told me all about you.'

Adam ignored him. 'I don't care what his name is, he

can't stay here.'

'Yes he can,' said Samuel coolly. 'He has nowhere else to go.'

'Not my problem, mate.'

'He's not safe on the streets alone, so he's coming to stay with me. Now step aside.'

Adam stayed exactly where he was. 'We're not a charity, Samuel. We don't take in homeless werewolves.'

'We look after our own kind,' insisted Samuel.

'Our kind ought to be strong enough to look after themselves.'

'He's staying, Adam, and that's the end of this discussion.'

Samuel pushed forward, and to James' surprise, Adam backed off, letting them pass.

'Leanna won't be happy,' he said.

Samuel chuckled, allowing the rich, mellow sound to fill the hallway. 'She never is.'

Adam eyed James coldly as he passed him and headed upstairs to Samuel's room.

When they were inside, Samuel slammed the door shut and locked it. 'Come here,' he said, giving James a quick kiss on the lips. He jumped onto the bed and stretched out languidly, his arms folded behind his head. 'Don't worry about Adam. His bark's worse than his bite.'

James said nothing.

'Hey, that was a joke,' said Samuel with a grin. 'Chill, man.'

'Sure.' James looked nervously around the room. It was about the same size as his bedroom back home. His parents' home, that is. He wondered what they were thinking. They must have been so worried when he didn't return home, especially when they heard about Father Mulcahy. He wondered how long it would be before the police connected him with the murder.

Who was he kidding? They would have already made the connection.

This was his home now. These four walls, and the one bed.

Samuel seemed totally relaxed about everything. 'And don't worry about Leanna, either,' he said. 'At least, just keep out of her way for the time being. Once you've changed, she'll be cool. Adam too.'

The change would come soon, with the next full moon. Samuel had told him all about it. The full moon was just a few days away now, and James was becoming increasingly restless, drawn by the lunar pull. The same force that drew the ocean's great tides was dragging him too, and he couldn't resist. He didn't want to resist, even though a part of him was slowly filling with dread at the prospect. 'Tell me again how the change feels,' he said.

Samuel stretched out on the bed. 'There's no way to really describe it. The only way to understand it is to experience it for yourself. It affects everyone differently.'

'Does it hurt?' James asked, although it wasn't pain that he really feared.

'There's some pain the first time, but not an unpleasant one. It's a kind of fire that burns clean, if that makes any sense. It burns away all that you were, clearing a path for what you will become. There's an intensity, for sure, but I'm not sure that pain is the right word. If there is pain, it's a necessary one.'

James nodded. He understood that. His faith had prepared him for suffering in the name of good.

'The light of the moon is magical,' continued Samuel. 'I mean, not literally magical. I'm a scientist, after all.' He stopped and laughed again, his deep, infectious laughter rumbling in the way that James was growing to love so much. 'During Stage Two of the condition, which is where you're at now, your skin becomes hyper-sensitized, your eyes in a state of permanent dilation. That's why it's so painful to go out in bright sunlight, why you come to prefer the night. All that's to prepare you for the change. The moonlight is the catalyst for the final transition. After the change, your eyes will go back almost to normal, and you won't mind bright lights so much.'

James nodded. That was good to know. He'd become increasingly sensitive to light since leaving the hospital. Even the dimmest electric lights now gave him a searing headache. Going outside in full sun would be impossible.

'Of course, your skin will always be sensitive to moonlight. Every full moon, the change will come again, but it's only painful the first time. Afterwards, it's just like slipping back into a comfortable set of clothes.'

It would be like a baptism. A moonlit baptism. He would immerse himself in its purifying silver rays, and it would burn away his sins, making him anew. Afterwards he would be like Samuel himself, and Leanna, and Adam. He would be one with them. 'How did it feel afterwards?' he asked Samuel. 'I mean, how does it feel now, compared with before?'

Samuel cocked his head to one side, reflecting on that before answering. 'I feel bigger, stronger, more enriched. I've always been an optimist, someone who sees the good in everyone, but the change has amplified that in me. I love the world more than ever. It's like a kind of heavenly light is shining over all of creation and I'm the only one who can see it. You'll probably understand that.' He laughed again, a warm, inclusive laugh. 'But everyone changes differently. Leanna has become cold. She was always a quiet one, an introvert, a big thinker. The change has amplified all that. It's made her cunning too. You can't trust her anymore. She says one thing, but you don't know what she's really thinking. Adam's different again. He's always been a very competitive sportsman, pushing himself with his training, always desperate to win. Now his need to win has become a physical hunger. There's no other way to describe it. If he comes second, he rages and sulks. I believe he has the power to achieve almost any ambition he holds. They're both pretty scary, really, Leanna and Adam. Not like cuddly old me.'

'So it sounds like the change exaggerates whatever qualities you already have?'

'I guess so. Amplifies them ten times, like you've been born into the world a second time. And of course it makes you physically strong. Stronger than you can possibly imagine.'

'I already feel strong,' said James. Despite his photosensitivity and the headaches, despite the weakness in his aching body, he felt an inner core of steel.

'Sure, but what you feel now is just a shadow of what will come.'

James walked over to the bed and sat down next to Samuel. 'I want you to be with me when the change comes. I don't want to be alone.'

Samuel grinned broadly and reached out his hands to grasp James'. 'Don't worry. I wouldn't miss it for the world,' he said.

Chapter Twenty-One

Manor Road, South London, quarter moon

Chris Crohn finished his day's work at Manor Road Secondary School at four o'clock sharp and left immediately. Nothing interesting ever happened at school. Today's highlights had been resetting Miss Jones' forgotten password, and deleting some unauthorized software that Mr Johnson the sports teacher had downloaded from the internet, much to the man's annoyance.

But it could have been worse. At least Chris was the tech support guy and not a teacher. Trying to teach anything to those dumb kids really would have been unbearable.

Back in the cramped quarters of his apartment in Manor Road, he fired up his werewolf tracking app and settled down for some real work. To his surprise and delight he found that today the usual social media tittle-tattle was eclipsed by real werewolf action. A news article from an authoritative source. Even Seth would have to pay attention to this.

Chris read the story with a growing sense of satisfaction. *Priest Brutally Murdered in Own Church*, screamed the sensational headline of the article, before describing as many details of the violent killing as were known. The body of a Catholic priest, Father Mulcahy, had been found in the confessional of his parish church. Or at least what remained of the body. The man had been the victim of a frenzied attack and the body was covered in bite marks. Human bite marks.

Chris rubbed his hands with glee before sending Seth a link to the story, adding the footnote, 'First official victim of werewolf killing.'

Of course, there was no mention of werewolves in the article, so it wasn't really official. Instead the police were remaining *open-minded* about the motive for the attack, and were appealing for information from the public. In particular, they wished to interview a teenager named James Beaumont who was the last person to see the priest alive, and who had apparently gone missing afterwards. The police believed that the witness may have crucial information about the crime, and appealed for him to come forward so that they could eliminate him from their enquiries. At this point in the investigation they did not wish to comment on the nature of the murder weapon, and asked the public not to jump to any conclusions.

Idiots. The conclusions were obvious, as was the nature of the murder weapon. This teenager, James Beaumont, was obviously a werewolf, and he had killed the priest with his own bare hands and teeth.

Chris did a quick search to find the location of the church. Mayfield Avenue in South London. It wasn't far from where Chris lived. His tracking app had already identified the local area as a werewolf hotspot. The new data totally fitted the emerging pattern.

Another news article appeared in his feed and Chris

Lycanthropic

clicked it open enthusiastically. A second murder, this time of an athletics coach in North London. The location was different, but as in the first murder, the body of the man had been badly mutilated, with no attempt made to conceal the body. The police were refusing to confirm a connection between the two murders but there were so many obvious similarities that the newspapers had already made the link. The killings were so gruesome that the headline writers were calling the murderer the *Ripper*.

Chris sent the second article to Seth and waited for a response. The situation was deteriorating even faster than he had thought. In just a few months the incidents had progressed from wolf sightings to bite attacks, and now to a series of savage murders. The apocalypse was surely just around the corner.

A reply from Seth arrived in his mailbox and he clicked it open. 'No mention of werewolves,' Seth had written. 'Police remain open-minded.'

Chris bashed out a contemptuous reply. 'Not open-minded, just empty-headed. Of course they didn't mention werewolves. They are idiots.' He hit the send button angrily. The police had no clue, and neither did Seth. He wondered why he even bothered.

Chapter Twenty-Two

Fifth floor, Ragstone Tower, South London, quarter moon

After his narrow escape from the Headmaster, Vijay desperately wanted to leave Drake behind, but that was proving harder than he'd expected. Drake had insisted on taking Vijay back to the high-rise concrete apartment building he called home.

Vijay stood nervously on the fifth-floor walkway of the building, drawing his collar up against the cold. The walkway was half open to the elements. He wondered how Drake could stand the winter weather with nothing to cover his head except for his closely-cropped fine hair. The wind gusted hard at this height, blowing discarded food packaging and other litter around the grey space, swirling it into a heap near the dark stairwell at the end of the walkway. He peered cautiously over the concrete wall that lined the walkway's edge, and saw the tops of bare trees, and beyond them more identical concrete towers. A mass of grey clouds crawled low across the sky, promising rain.

'Come in here,' said Drake, unlocking the door to his apartment and beckoning Vijay inside.

Vijay followed. Drake led him through another door and into his bedroom. It wasn't a bit like Vijay's own room, which was full of books and old toys, with a desk by the window where he did his homework in the evenings. Drake's room was almost bare, with just some torn posters of rappers and wrestling stars on the wall, and a TV with a games console at the foot of his bed.

'I just need to get some clothes and stuff,' said Drake, grabbing jeans and T-shirts and stuffing them into a duffle bag.

'What for?' asked Vijay suspiciously.

'I can't stay here,' said Drake. 'What if the Headmaster comes looking for me?'

'Where then?' asked Vijay, but the question seemed to have an obvious answer.

'I'll come back to your place.'

'But what if the Headmaster comes looking at my house?' demanded Vijay.

Drake shrugged. 'Your house is safer than here.'

Vijay nodded uncertainly. This really wasn't working out the way he'd expected. 'Are you sure this is a good idea?' he asked. 'Haven't you got any friends you can stay with?'

Drake shook his head. 'Ash is dead now, so you're the only friend I've got.'

Drake Cooper as a friend. That was a bit of a leap. But now that Vijay thought about it, Ash was really the only person Drake had ever talked to. Apart from Vijay of course, if you could call that talking. Vijay had always thought of Drake as a popular kid, but the reality was that he actually had no friends.

'You and me, we're the only ones what know what happened, right?' continued Drake.

'I suppose.'

'So we need to stick together, yeah?'

'But you can't just leave home and not tell anyone,' said Vijay. 'Your parents are going to go out of their minds if you just disappear.'

'Yeah?' said Drake. 'You sure of that?' He pushed past Vijay and into the hallway that led to the other rooms in the dingy apartment. 'My dad's long gone. My mum's got a new boyfriend, who's a complete twat. She don't need me. I don't need her.'

'You've still got to tell her, though. You've got to leave a note or something at least.' Vijay followed Drake into the kitchen, where he seemed to be searching for something.

'I'll leave a note if it makes you happy, yeah? If she wants to speak to me, she can always call me on my phone,' said Drake, rummaging through the kitchen drawers. He pulled out a bulging brown envelope sealed with an elastic band. 'This is what I need.'

'What is it?' asked Vijay, eyeing the envelope with trepidation.

Drake ripped off the elastic band and shook the contents of the envelope onto the worktop. A wad of money fell out. Without bothering to count it, Drake grabbed the money and stuffed it into his jeans pocket.

'Are you stealing that?' asked Vijay with a frown.

Drake gave him a sullen look. 'Not stealing, just claiming it.' When Vijay continued to look unhappy, he explained, 'It's emergency money, yeah? So this is an emergency. I need it more than she does.'

When Vijay said nothing, Drake walked past him back into the hallway. 'Come on. Let's get out of here.'

Vijay trailed after him, leaving the grim concrete building behind. He wondered what Rose Hallibury would think if she could see him and his arch tormentor skipping class and running away from school together. Would her emerald eyes laugh or frown? Would her red hair bob with amusement or would her button nose wrinkle in disapproval?

He could barely work out how all this had happened. One minute he'd been sitting outside the Headmaster's office, ready to tell Mr Canning that Drake and Ash had bullied him. Now, some forty minutes later, Ash was dead and Drake was coming home to live with him. He wondered if this was all just some kind of hallucination.

When they arrived at Vijay's house, things began to feel more real, but even less comprehensible. 'This is my friend, Drake,' he explained to his mum, indicating the boy with ripped jeans and cropped fair hair, his hands thrust into his front pockets. 'He needs to stay with me for a day or so.'

His mother regarded Drake as if he were a puzzle to be solved.

'If it's okay with you, Mrs Singh,' said Drake politely.

'Of course it is, Drake. Only, do your parents know that you are coming to stay?'

'Yeah, sure,' said Drake. 'At least, that is, my mum.'

'I see,' said Vijay's mother. 'I'm afraid we don't have much space in the house, but you can sleep in Vijay's room. We can find an old camp bed and some blankets for you.'

'Thanks.'

'Come on,' said Vijay to Drake. 'Let's go upstairs.'

They went up to Vijay's room and sat down on the bed.

'So this is home,' said Drake, slinging his duffle bag into the corner of the room.

'What are we going to do now?' asked Vijay. 'We need to tell my mum what happened, and yours too. We need to call the police and tell them about Mr Canning. We have to —'

'No,' said Drake, cutting him off. 'There's no point.'

'Why not?'

'No one would believe us.'

Vijay sighed. Drake might well be right. Who would

swallow such a far-fetched story? The police would never accept that the Headmaster of a local school had eaten one of his students. And even if they did investigate, what would they find? Mr Canning sitting in his office, chewing Ash's leg? More likely they would find nothing. Most likely, they wouldn't even bother to look. And where would that leave Vijay and Drake? In deeper trouble than ever.

'But what if Mr Canning comes looking for us?' he asked.

'I don't reckon he will,' said Drake. 'He won't risk it. I reckon he'll keep well away.'

Vijay nodded mutely. He was only just beginning to understand the full horror of what had happened.

'I know some places we can go when we're supposed to be at school,' said Drake. 'It's only a couple of weeks until the end of term. Then we should be safe.'

Drake was probably right. Their best chance was to lie low, stay away from school, and hope that somehow Mr Canning would be discovered soon. Ash's parents would report him missing, or perhaps another teacher would raise the alarm.

'Your mum seems nice,' said Drake.

'Oh? I guess.'

'You got any other family? This is a big house.'

'There's my dad of course,' said Vijay. 'And my older sister, Aasha. They'll both be home later. And my grandmother lives with us too.'

'Happy families,' said Drake.

'Yeah, I guess we are.'

Chapter Twenty-Three

Marsh Lane Kennels, Brixton, South London

Rose Hallibury worked at the Marsh Lane Kennels whenever she wasn't at school, and Saturday was always the busiest day of the week. It was hard work but she loved it, and she loved the dogs too, as if they were her own. Today though, something was wrong. The dogs paced around their kennels nervously. The little dogs like the Terriers and the Cavalier King Charles Spaniel whimpered gently. The big Irish Setter barked and howled. They could sense something. They were frightened.

Rose twisted her copper hair nervously around her slim finger. 'What's wrong with them?' she asked Anna, the kennels manager. 'What are they frightened of?' She patted the dogs and tried to calm them down.

'We haven't got time to worry about that now,' Anna told Rose. Saturday was the day most of the dog owners came to drop off their pets, or to collect them again. Rose had to help Anna get all the dogs ready for collection by ten o'clock and clean out the kennels ready for the new arrivals.

But Rose couldn't help worrying. She had never seen dogs behave like that for no reason. They could hear or smell something bad, or sense it some other way. Something was out there, something dangerous.

'Come on,' said Anna briskly. 'Let's get to work.'

Rose studied the timetable that Anna had drawn up, showing which dogs were due to be collected, so she could wash them and feed them ready for pick-up. She unbolted the door of the Irish Setter and went inside its kennel. The kennel was a good size, almost like a tiny hotel room, with a dog bed and a feeding area. The dogs had an outside space where they could run about too, and in the summer Rose took them out for longer walks.

The Setter bowed its head when Rose entered, and backed into the corner of the room, whimpering. 'It's all right, girl,' said Rose soothingly. 'Your mummy's coming to collect you today. You're going home.'

The dog did not respond to her words.

Then Rose heard it. The sound of engines outside the building. They sounded like motorbikes. She heard a man shouting in the street, and Anna's voice raised in reply.

Rose left the Setter in its kennel, carefully sliding the bolt back on the door. She walked down the corridor to the reception area to check out the disturbance.

Four motorbikes had pulled up in the street outside. They had powerful engines, the kind of bikes that motorcycle gangs drove in movies. The guys riding them wore black leathers, sporting beards and tattoos. One of them, a huge man with a red beard and bulging biceps, had got off his bike and was standing just outside the entrance door. He held a wooden stake, one end tapering to a sharp point. The other men left their bikes and came over to join him. They also carried weapons – knives and baseball bats. Some of the bats were studded with nails. A black

Mercedes van joined the four bikers, pulling up at the curb side, disgorging two more men wearing leather jackets and combat trousers. Behind them came four more bikes.

Anna locked the main door, sliding two security bolts across the top and bottom. 'I don't like this,' she said. 'I'm going to call the police.' She picked up the phone and dialled 999.

Rose watched through the window as the men gathered outside. She had no idea who they were, but they obviously weren't pet owners.

One of the men who had got out of the van seemed to be their leader. He wore wraparound black shades that matched his black beard, and his head was shaven clean. He turned his back to her, and Rose saw a white wolf etched on his black leather jacket. The man strode over to the locked door and rubbed the top of his head with one of his big hands. He kicked at the door, then stepped aside to let the huge guy with the red beard try to break it down with his shoulder.

Rose heard Anna ask for the police, and start to explain what was happening. Behind her, the dogs were going crazy, barking and howling in their kennels.

The door was reinforced with steel struts and redbeard had no luck breaking it down. Instead, two of the other men smashed through a window pane with their baseball bats, knocking away all the glass so they could climb through. One by one, they started to come through the opening, brandishing their weapons and advancing toward Anna.

Rose backed away, but Anna held her ground. 'Get out of here,' she said, the phone still in her hand. 'I've already called the police.'

The bald man who Rose guessed was the leader walked casually up to Anna and struck her on the side of the head with a claw hammer. She didn't even have time to cry out, she just went down.

Rose screamed.

Then the dogs all started barking at once.

There was nowhere for Rose to run or hide. Her first thought was for the dogs. 'Please don't hurt them,' she begged.

The man with the hammer smiled, like nothing had happened, and came over to her. She couldn't stop looking at the hammer. It dripped a trail of red along the ground as he walked.

The man grabbed her chin with his huge hand and lifted her face up to his. 'Hey, little girl,' he said. 'We're here to collect some dogs. You help us out and we'll cause no further trouble. Does that sound good?'

Rose shook her head. 'No. You can't take them. I won't let you.' She risked a glance at Anna. The woman hadn't moved, but she still seemed to be breathing. Her chest rose and fell as blood dribbled from the gash in her head.

The man twisted Rose's face back toward him. 'We're going to take them, with or without you. Now are you going to help us, or shall I give you some of the hammer?' He raised the dripping weapon in his fist.

'Which dogs have you come for?' Rose asked.

'All of them,' said the man, leering at her. 'So open the kennels and let them out.'

'Please don't hurt them,' repeated Rose. She went along the row of kennels, opening each door in turn. The dogs wouldn't come out. They stayed inside, barking fiercely, or retreating into the corner of their kennels, whining or growling.

The men went into the kennels and started sorting the dogs. They grabbed the biggest and fiercest dogs and dragged them out to the van. They took the Irish Setter, a Bulldog, a Doberman Pinscher and a pair of German shepherds. They took a Rottweiler and a Greyhound and a couple of mongrels. Any dogs that were small, or timid, they killed.

Rose screamed as they set about their work. She ran at

them, beating her fists against them, trying to grab their weapons, but the men threw her aside.

They killed the Terriers and the Cavalier King Charles Spaniel. They killed a Toy Poodle and a Chihuahua and a family of Dachshunds. They smashed them with baseball bats, crowbars and sticks. They speared them with stakes. They cut them with knives. After they'd finished, it was like a slaughterhouse.

Rose retched. The enormous man with the red beard shoved her and she fell to the floor, her face in her hands.

Finally the leader came back over to her and smiled again. The bloody hammer still swung at his side. He leaned in close to her before speaking. 'Thanks for your help,' he said, rubbing his thumb back and forth along the top of his bald head. Up close, his scalp was perfectly smooth, like a bowling ball, and when he rubbed it, it squeaked. 'I guess you can go home now. If anyone asks who did this, tell them it was the Wolf Brothers.' Rose watched him go, the big white wolf clearly visible on the back of his leather jacket. He laughed as he walked away, still rubbing the top of his head with his thumb.

Over the sound of her sobs, Rose heard the men leaving the building. Engines roared back to life. The van started up and drove away, the muffled sound of dogs barking inside. Rose curled into a ball and waited. She was still sobbing hysterically when the first police car arrived.

Chapter Twenty-Four

West Field Terrace, South London

When Rose had eventually calmed down, the police took her home.

Anna had already been taken to hospital. The paramedics in the ambulance said that her injuries weren't as bad as they looked, and she stood a good chance of making a full recovery.

The dogs would never recover, however.

A police woman had made Rose a hot cup of tea, and then Rose had answered all their questions as best she could. The police couldn't answer her question though. 'Why?'

The whole thing was senseless. And yet this had clearly been no random attack. Those men had moved with purpose. They had planned it, and executed their plans ruthlessly.

Now the dogs were dead, or taken, and Anna would likely be in hospital for some time. The kennels would close for the foreseeable future.

Rose could do nothing more.

The police woman who drove her home was called Liz. She stood no taller than Rose, but had big arms and the look of a woman who wouldn't flinch from a man twice her size. She made Rose feel weedy and pathetic by comparison. She wondered if the men would have been able to hurt the dogs if Liz had been their guardian, instead of her.

'It's not far,' Rose told her. 'I could easily walk.'

'Absolutely not,' said Liz. 'I can't let you walk around the streets alone in your state. You're in shock. You need to go home and rest. And you need to take care of yourself and stay safe.'

Rose nodded numbly. Safe. She had thought that the dogs were safe in their kennels. She couldn't have been more wrong. 'Do you think those men might come back?' she asked. 'Or come looking for me? I don't think they meant me any harm, or even Anna really. She just got in their way. If they'd wanted to hurt me, they could have done it back at the kennels.'

'At this stage we don't know what they meant to do, or what their motives were. I think you'll be safe enough at home, but you should be on the lookout for anything unusual, and don't hesitate to call us if you have any concerns.'

Rose nodded. Liz had given her the number of Victim Support, and said that someone would call in the next day or so, to see if she needed any help in coming to terms with the attack. Apparently people could suffer delayed shock and need support later, even if they felt okay at the time.

Rose didn't feel okay. She didn't feel anything.

She'd grown up on the streets of South London, and thought she knew how to take care of herself. She'd seen knife attacks and muggings take place in broad daylight. But never had she experienced anything like this.

She was barely aware of the journey home, but suddenly they were outside her house in West Field Terrace. Liz pulled over and neatly maneuvered the patrol car into a tight spot between a rusty Ford Fiesta and a waste skip that had been left on the road. 'Come on,' said Liz. 'I'll come inside with you and explain to your parents what happened.'

'Okay,' said Rose. She was glad that Liz had brought her home. She was like a breath of calm in a storm. 'Thanks for everything.'

Liz gave her a reassuring smile. The police woman's tough exterior melted briefly and Rose caught a glimpse of something softer inside. But Liz didn't let her soft side show for long. 'Just part of the job,' she said.

When Rose got out of the car, she was surprised to find Vijay Singh waiting by the front gate, with Drake Cooper of all people. Vijay was standing tall and seemed to be in charge. Drake's usual swagger had all but drained away.

'We were looking for you,' said Vijay. 'Something bad's happened.'

Rose looked at him in confusion. 'You mean at the kennels?'

'No,' said Vijay. 'At school, on Friday.' He seemed to suddenly notice Rose's dishevelled appearance, and the fact that she was being escorted by a police officer. 'Are you in some kind of trouble?' he asked.

Liz joined her then. 'You'll have to wait, I'm afraid, boys. Rose has been involved in a serious incident and needs to rest.' She took hold of Rose's arm and walked her up to her front door.

'Oh my God,' said Drake. 'Did someone try to eat her?'

Vijay elbowed him into silence.

'What did you say?' demanded Liz.

'Nothing.'

Rose stared at him. 'What did you mean when you said that something bad had happened at school?'

'Nothing,' repeated Drake. 'We didn't mean nothing.'

Lycanthropic

'What happened to you two on Friday?' asked Rose. 'I didn't see you after you went to the Headmaster's office.'

'I think you'd better come in and tell us all about it,' said Liz.

Chapter Twenty-Five

As Liz had expected, Rose's parents were horrified at what had happened, but Liz was experienced at calming people down. 'Your daughter's had a very frightening experience, but she hasn't been harmed. In fact she's coping extremely well, and I'm sure that she'll be just fine in a day or two.'

In fact Rose had shown remarkable self-control under the circumstances, giving a detailed account of the incident, and helping the police understand exactly what had happened. She was clearly still in a state of shock, but Liz felt sure she'd quickly get over it. 'What Rose needs now is some rest, and perhaps a couple of days at home. I'm sure the school will understand.'

Rose's mother nodded, her face still pale. She was a match for Rose, her face like a round, freckled moon, her hair a mass of coppery curls. She had rallied quickly after the initial shock, and had set about that universal response of the British nation to every catastrophe – supplying everyone with a hot mug of tea.

Liz sipped hers now. Milk and two sugars, just how she liked it. She sat in the front room opposite Rose and her parents, Drake and Vijay sitting on the sofa at her side.

It always slightly awed Liz to see a functional family at work, with parents who acted like adults, and children who were so clearly loved. Her own family had been so very different, and so were many of the families that came to her attention through her work.

'What will happen now?' asked Rose's father. 'Will Rose need to give evidence?'

'She's already given us a detailed statement, including a good description of the men and their vehicles,' said Liz. 'She's a very calm and collected young woman. There's a good chance we'll catch the men and recover the dogs safely too.'

'If they're still alive,' said Drake.

Vijay elbowed him again, and Drake shut up.

'And if they're caught?' continued Rose's father. 'Will Rose need to give evidence in court?'

'It's possible,' said Liz. 'Since she's over fourteen, she would be required to give evidence under oath, but if she has any concerns, she can request to give video evidence, or by a live link to the court. From what I've seen of Rose, I don't believe that she would have any problems giving evidence in person.'

Her father nodded.

'Mr and Mrs Hallibury,' said Liz, addressing herself to Rose's parents. 'Would you mind if I spoke to Vijay and Drake alone?'

'Of course not,' said her mother. She stood up to leave. 'Rose, you come with us.'

'If you don't mind, I'd like Rose to stay too,' interrupted Liz. 'It's possible she might be able to help.'

Concern registered on Mrs Hallibury's face briefly, but then she nodded, and she and her husband left, pulling the door to the front room closed behind them.

Vijay and Drake sat huddled together on the sofa, looking anxiously around the room. Drake seemed to have developed a sudden strong interest in the picture hanging above the fireplace. The two boys made an unlikely pair. One a Sikh, sitting quietly, his clothes neat, his hair bound tightly in a turban, his glasses lending him a studious air. One fidgeting nervously, his jeans ripped, his light hair shorn close to his skull, the kind of boy Liz often encountered late at night, pretending to be tough, giving the police some cheek before running away.

She spoke to them gently. 'Now boys, please tell me what you came to say to Rose.'

Vijay cleared his throat and opened his mouth, then closed it again.

Drake gazed at his shoes.

'About what happened at school yesterday,' Liz prompted.

The boys exchanged glances.

'It's going to sound really stupid,' said Vijay at last. 'Especially after what just happened to Rose.'

'That doesn't matter,' said Liz. 'Drake, you asked if someone had tried to eat Rose. Why?'

'Because Mr Canning ate Ash,' blurted Drake.

'What?' said Rose. She looked to Vijay for confirmation.

He nodded miserably. 'It's true, whether you believe it or not. We heard it.'

'Heard it?' asked Liz. 'Okay, you'd better explain everything from the beginning. Who is Ash, and who is this Mr Canning?'

Vijay told most of the story, with Drake interrupting now and again with additional details.

After they had finished, Rose said, 'You've got to be kidding me.'

'It's all true,' said Drake. 'Honest.'

'Tell me again about the eyes,' said Liz. That was the

part of the story that had grabbed her attention. She remembered clearly the yellow film that had formed over PC David Morgan's eyes in hospital. She had noticed the same yellow sheen in James' eyes when she'd visited him. And both had spent a week in Intensive Care with a severe infection after being bitten. Too much of a coincidence to be casually dismissed, even if one had been bitten by a man and the other by a wolf.

'His eyes were bright yellow,' explained Vijay. 'That's how I knew. Everyone who got ill and came back, their eyes were always yellow. The same with Mr Canning. His eyes turned yellow just before he killed Ash.'

'And you didn't see anything of the attack, but you heard biting sounds?'

'Yeah,' said Drake. 'We were waiting in the corridor right outside the office. Either one of us could have gone in first, instead of Ash.' His face had turned white. 'Biting, chewing, … it was gross. I was sick all over my shoes.'

Vijay nodded.

'Tell me,' said Liz. 'You all go to Manor Road Secondary School, don't you?

Rose nodded; the boys too.

'Did you know a teacher called Mr Leigh?'

'He taught us Geography,' said Rose.

'Yeah,' said Drake, 'Until he went mental and …'

'Exactly,' said Vijay. 'Mr Leigh was the first. How do you know him?'

'I was there on Halloween when he attacked the children,' said Liz. 'He bit a boy called James.' She pictured the scene in her mind's eye. The terrified children screaming for help, James holding onto the hilt of the kitchen knife like he was never letting go. And slumped in the doorway, looking for all the world like a meth head passed out in the gutter, Mr Leigh, Head of Geography at Manor Road. An inspirational teacher by all accounts.

'Did he have yellow eyes too?' asked Vijay.

Liz shook her head. 'He had already lost consciousness

when I arrived. His eyes were closed. But I've seen others … they all had yellow eyes.'

'It's some kind of disease, ain't it?' said Drake. 'You gotta believe us now!'

'Had Mr Canning been off school sick before this happened?' she asked.

'Yeah,' said Drake. 'He was away at the same time as Mr Leigh. He came back to school last week.'

Liz studied the boys' faces carefully. Their story was fantastical, unbelievable. A cannibalistic headmaster. Yet they seemed sincere about it. And the yellow eyes tied in with what she had seen herself.

Circumstantial evidence, a lawyer would say to that. *Unreliable witnesses* too, and the case would be laughed out of court. They were probably just telling her what she wanted to hear. But after the so-called Ripper killings she couldn't afford to dismiss their story out of hand.

'Wait here a few minutes,' she said. 'I'm going to the car to make a call. Then I'll be back.'

It didn't take long for her to make the call. The call handler back at the station was quick to confirm that a boy called Ashley Brown had been reported missing by his father that morning. 'It seems that when he didn't come home from school yesterday, his parents just assumed that he was out with friends, or at a sleepover,' the man told her. Liz could practically hear him rolling his eyes in derision.

'Didn't they think of calling him?' asked Liz.

'His phone was turned off. Apparently that didn't overly concern them. Anyway, when he still hadn't returned this morning, they decided to call us. So far that's all we know. You got anything to report?'

'Not yet,' said Liz. 'I'll let you know if I find anything.'

She went back inside the house. The kids looked at her expectantly.

'So what now?' asked Drake. 'Can you arrest Mr Canning?'

Liz shook her head. 'At this stage there's no evidence even that Ash is dead, and certainly nothing to link him to a killer headmaster.'

'But ...' said Drake.

Liz held up her hand. 'Now, here's the thing. If I request a warrant to search your Headmaster's office for evidence that he's eaten one of his students, I'm going to be hauled in front of my boss and given a very hard time. He's going to want to know whether I've been overworking, or if I'm having a laugh. You understand?'

The kids nodded. She'd most likely find herself on sick leave herself, or down at the local job centre.

'But since the first part of your story checks out, and because of certain things I've seen myself, this is what I'm willing to do. If you agree, we'll drive over to the school now and take a look through the window, see if we can see anything unusual in Mr Canning's office. How does that sound?'

'Good,' said Vijay and Drake together.

'Rose, you'd better stay here. The last thing your parents will want is for you to go running off on some hair-brained search.'

'No,' said Rose. 'I want to come.'

'Sorry,' said Liz. 'I'm already going out on a limb. I don't want any more bother from anyone, so you stay here. We'll tell you what we find, if anything.'

'Okay,' said Rose. 'Call me.'

Chapter Twenty-Six

Manor Road Secondary School, South London

Liz drove the patrol car through the open gates of the school and parked it in the visitors' area. She looked out at the school building through the driver's window. A typical red brick building at its heart, with ugly modern extensions bolted on apparently at random, and a large scattering of temporary pre-fabricated additions that looked to have become permanent fixtures. It looked so ordinary, much like Liz's old school. It was hard to imagine that a boy had been murdered here, let alone eaten by his headmaster. Liz wondered what on earth she was doing on this crazy goose chase.

The yellow eyes, she reminded herself.

'That's the window to Mr Canning's office,' said Vijay, pointing. 'The ground floor window on the left.'

Liz ran her gaze along the row of windows, following the line of Vijay's raised finger. The end window looked the same as all the others – flaky paint, slightly dirty, yet uncovered by blinds or other obstructions. All they had to do was look inside.

'Come on. Let's go,' said Drake, opening the door of the car.

Liz followed the boys across the parking area to the window. She glanced around, but they seemed to be alone. It was the weekend, but that didn't mean the school would be completely empty. There might be sporting clubs, or at least a caretaker on duty. She wasn't sure what she would say if someone challenged her to explain what they were doing, other than the fact that a boy had been reported missing.

Drake and Vijay were already peering in through the window.

'Can you see anything?' she asked nervously. If this followed the pattern of the other recent killings, the half-eaten body of Ashley Brown would be lying there for all to see.

'It's a bit dark,' said Vijay.

'Let me see.' She pushed up to the window, treading on some spindly perennial plants that grew close to the wall of the building. The Headmaster's office was dim inside, but she could see well enough to form an overall impression.

An old-fashioned wooden desk commanded the room, its surface neatly organized with papers, reports and letters stacked in a tiered in-tray. A telephone, computer screen and keyboard, and various items of stationery were neatly arranged on its green leather top. The Headmaster's chair was positioned below the window, giving the Head a clear view of the door opposite.

Liz pressed her face to the glass to see what lay beyond the desk. A bookcase stood beside the door, and next to that a small coffee table and chairs. A coat stand completed the furniture.

There was no body on the floor, no blood on the walls, no sign of any struggle or fight.

'I don't understand,' said Vijay. 'We heard him eat Ash.'

Liz stepped away from the window, hoping the plant she'd trodden on would make a recovery. 'Come on, boys. Back to the car.'

They followed in her wake, their protests ringing loudly in her ears.

'We heard it,' repeated Vijay.

'The bastard must have cleaned up the mess,' said Drake. 'Can't you do DNA tests and stuff?'

'Not without a search warrant. And for that we need evidence.' Liz felt as disappointed as the boys, but she couldn't show them that. She'd really expected to find the remains of a half-eaten body in that room. She'd allowed herself to imagine being the police officer who single-handedly solved the Ripper murders. She shook her head, as if to banish the absurd idea that had taken root there. A grown woman of her experience should never have been taken in by such a foolish notion.

Back in the car, she said, 'I'm not saying I don't believe you. You heard something. I don't know what it was, but it wasn't your friend Ash being eaten.'

'No, but –' began Drake.

Liz raised her hand for silence. 'The police have to work with the available evidence. We've all seen the evidence here, or rather the lack of any. You heard something, I don't doubt that. But you were mistaken about what you heard. Ash has gone missing, but perhaps that's just because he got into trouble at school. Let's say he ran away because he was afraid of what his parents would say, or because he was ashamed of what he'd done. Most people who are reported missing turn up again within twenty-four hours. Ash might be sitting at home right now, for all we know.'

'He's not,' said Drake stubbornly. 'Because he's dead.'

'Then where's his body?' asked Liz.

'I dunno. That doesn't mean he's not dead. Mr Canning got rid of the remains, that's all. Why can't you believe us?'

'Because extraordinary claims require firm evidence. And in this case there's no evidence whatsoever. I'm sorry.'

'Thanks for taking a look anyway,' said Vijay.

Liz sighed. 'I'll drive you home,' she said. 'Let me know if anything else happens at school.'

'Ain't no way I'm going back to school,' said Drake. 'Not with a psycho-killer headmaster on the loose.'

Chapter Twenty-Seven

Manor Road, South London

Chris Crohn was naturally slim – Seth called him skinny – but he wasn't fit. His tech support job at the school didn't require him to be, and sitting at a desk in front of a computer screen all day didn't give him much opportunity to exercise. Not that he wanted to. He had never seen the point. He didn't go running, had never lifted weights, and had no knowledge of martial arts. But all that would have to change. The apocalypse was coming and Chris planned to meet it head on.

His werewolf tracking app had flagged the area around Manor Road Secondary School as a danger zone, and he was starting to feel nervous walking to school and back. He found himself glancing over his shoulder whenever he left the safety of his tiny apartment, searching for the tell-tale signs of an unusually large dog, or sharp teeth in a stranger's smile. So far he had noticed nothing out of the ordinary.

At school too, he checked out the teachers and students, peering at them suspiciously, looking for odd behaviour. After all, it was Mr Leigh the Geography teacher who had tried to eat those kids a few weeks back. The Headmaster, Mr Canning, in particular was acting very strangely. Chris had spent an uncomfortable ten minutes in the Headmaster's office on Friday afternoon, installing a new inkjet printer while the Head looked on wolfishly, licking his lips, a peculiar yellow gleam in his eyes. Chris had never completed a job quite so quickly.

The important thing was to be ready for when he eventually encountered a real werewolf. And that meant getting fit. He placed an online order for a set of weights and a home gym kit with next-day delivery. He downloaded some books with titles like *Muscle Boosting for Men* and *Get Ripped Fast* and speed-read them cover to cover before going to bed. According to the books, to have any chance of surviving the apocalypse he would need to increase his muscle mass from his current twenty-five percent of total body weight to at least fifty percent.

On Saturday morning he got up early and went for a run around the block before taking a shower. According to his smartphone, he'd covered a distance of just over half a mile. It had left him exhausted. Tomorrow, he would run a mile. The next day, a mile and a half. He would have to improve quickly. There wasn't much time.

The home gym kit arrived after breakfast and he unpacked it, followed the assembly instructions and installed it in his kitchen. The gym equipment left no room for accessing the sink, but building muscle mattered more than washing dishes now. He would just have to eat his food straight out of its packaging.

Later that morning he went along to the local martial arts centre and enquired about classes.

The instructor looked at him dubiously. 'Have you tried anything like this before?'

'No, but I'm a quick learner. I intend to train hard and

read as much as I can between classes.'

'Which classes are you interested in?' asked the instructor. 'We run courses in Judo, Karate, Brazilian Jiu-Jitsu, and Taekwon-Do.'

'All of them,' replied Chris, staring hard at the man through his thick lenses. 'I need to do them all. Can I start today?'

Chapter Twenty-Eight

Clapham Common, South London

In the seven years PC Liz Bailey had served as a police officer she had never known such a demanding time. The police were under intense pressure both to capture the creature known as the *Beast of Clapham Common* and also to apprehend the serial killer dubbed the *Ripper*. More brutal murders had taken place, and the police were scratching their heads to find a link between the victims, other than the manner of their death.

Liz felt personally connected to both cases. She had seen the Beast for herself, the night it attacked Dave Morgan, and she would have liked nothing better than to track the monster down. Frustratingly, there had been no further sightings of the creature since the night of the attack. Some of her colleagues joked that the whole business had been mere hysteria, but Liz knew otherwise.

Dave Morgan wasn't getting any better. She'd visited him again in hospital a few days previously and had been alarmed to see how weak he'd become. He'd been barely conscious and hadn't responded to anything she'd said. His eyes had flickered open once, and they'd been unmistakably and chillingly yellow, just like the animal that had bitten him.

As for the Ripper, she couldn't stop thinking about the story Vijay and Drake had told her. *Mr Canning ate Ash.* The boys believed it, even though it seemed preposterous. She had checked the missing persons file every morning, hoping for good news, but Ash had still not shown up. She was sick with worry. If the Headmaster really was the Ripper, she needed to tell someone urgently. But no body had been found, unlike the mutilated corpses that the Ripper had left in full view ready to be discovered. More mangled remains had been discovered in parks and by the side of roads, and in each case no attempt had been made to hide the body. Even if Liz took Vijay and Drake at their word, the story they told didn't match the broader pattern. She had made discreet enquiries and discovered that Mr Canning had been in school at the times the various Ripper victims had been murdered, so that seemed to rule him out as a suspect.

The police were still searching for James Beaumont in connection with the murder of the Catholic priest. Apparently the mild-mannered, polite teenager was their top suspect. James, who'd also had yellow eyes, and who had saved those children from being eaten by Mr Leigh, the Geography teacher at Manor Road school.

Connections ... they were everywhere, almost physically tangible, but confusing and contradictory. None of them fitted neatly together. She was driving herself mad turning the facts over and over in her mind.

'You're very quiet this evening,' said her new partner, PC Dean Arnold. A big man with an almost bald head shaped like a bullet, Dean was a man of few words. It was strange for him to be calling Liz quiet. Usually he moaned that she talked too much.

Lycanthropic

They were driving along the edge of Clapham Common, looking out for signs of large animals, or anything out of the ordinary. Unlike the night she and Dave Morgan had encountered the Beast, there was no moon visible, just heavy cloud and light rain. So far they'd seen nothing unusual.

'Just concentrating on my job,' said Liz, looking out at the dark street.

'Yeah? Want to talk to me about it?' Dean scratched at the short, wiry hair that crawled over the sides of his head.

Liz sighed. Dean was no fool. He knew she had something on her mind. 'Suppose you had a hunch that someone was guilty of a crime, but you had no evidence that any crime had even been committed? In fact, the whole story was totally implausible? And you'd been given the idea in the first place by a couple of kids who would never make reliable witnesses in a court of law? What would you do?'

'Hypothetically, right?'

'Hypothetically,' agreed Liz.

'Yet, despite the lack of evidence, and the total implausibility of the story, and the absence of reliable witnesses, you had a feeling in your gut, right?'

'Right.'

Dean was quick to reply. 'I'd tell someone I could trust the reasons for my hunch and see what they thought.'

'Hmm.' It seemed sound advice, and Dean was a man who would tell it to you straight. It would do Liz a lot of good to get it off her chest. And yet she feared what he might say.

'Well, are you going to tell me about it, or shall we play more guessing games?' Dean signalled a left turn, following the road that cut across the western corner of the Common.

So Liz told him, about the wolf that had bitten Dave Morgan, about Mr Leigh biting James, about the yellow eyes, and what Vijay and Drake had said about Ash being eaten. She felt stupid saying it out loud, yet Dean listened carefully and took his time before he gave his reply.

Eventually he said, 'So, here's what I think. These two boys were in trouble at school, they were frightened of the Headmaster, and they'd heard some stories on the news about a serial killer and some half-eaten bodies turning up. They ran off, and then invented a story to cover it.'

Liz had told herself the same thing enough times, but hearing it from Dean felt like a betrayal. 'But the other boy, Ash, really has gone missing.'

'So he ran off too, big deal. I reckon if you want to find Ash, you just need to bring these other two in for questioning, and they'll tell you where he's hiding quick enough.'

He was probably right, of course. Kids like Ash went missing all the time. Ninety-nine percent of them were found safely. And yet ... 'What about the yellow eyes?' she asked, bracing herself for Dean's response.

'Liz, if you value your career prospects, you'll say no more about yellow eyes, not to anyone. You're starting to sound like a bloody nutcase.'

'Gee, thanks,' said Liz. 'I'm glad I told my story to someone so open and sympathetic.'

'Well, what I always say is, if you don't want to be called a nutcase, don't talk like one.'

'Don't you say the nicest things?' said Liz. 'I can't wait until Dave Morgan comes back to work. I never thought I'd miss that grumpy bastard.' She said the words lightly, but they disguised a lump that had appeared in her throat.

'How is Dave?' asked Dean, his voice softer. 'Have you been to see him again?'

'Not for a couple of days. He slipped back into unconsciousness. They've moved him off the High Dependency Unit and back into Intensive Care. They said the infection's getting worse.'

'Poor sod,' said Dean.

Liz felt her eyes sting with tears. 'I'm scared, Dean. I

don't think he's going to make it. The nurse I spoke to reckoned he had a fifty-fifty chance of pulling through.'

'Hey girl, don't give up hope. Fifty-fifty – that's even odds. I'd bet on that. Dave's a tough guy. Isn't he always telling us how tough he is?'

Liz managed a tiny smile at that. 'Yeah. He certainly is.'

'You watch. I bet he'll be out of that hospital bed and back on his feet in no time. Then you won't have to put up with me anymore.'

'Right,' said Liz. 'I'll be glad of that.'

They cruised along in silence for a while, the road deserted on this cold, damp night. Hardly surprising. No right-minded folk would be here on a night like this, especially with news of the Beast and the Ripper splashed across all the front pages. A light rain fell steadily, the car's wiper blades sweeping the drops away, only for more to fall in their place. The Common itself was completely dark. If the Beast was out there lurking in the bushes, or running across its muddy grass, they would never spot it. The search seemed hopeless.

Up ahead, the soft glow of a streetlamp picked out a figure crouching low. 'Slow the car,' said Liz. Something was wrong.

Dean slowed the car to a crawl. As they drew closer, a second figure became visible, lying on the pavement. The first person was crouching over the prone body.

Dean stopped the car about twenty feet from the scene. 'Christ,' he muttered. 'What's this?'

They both knew what it was though. 'The Ripper,' said Liz, almost too afraid to say the word.

Dazzled by the bright beam of the car's headlights, the crouching figure looked up. It was a man, stooped low like an animal, squatting down on his legs, holding some dark object in his hands. He raised one hand to shield his eyes from the glare of the headlights.

The second figure lay completely still. Another man, Liz guessed, his arms splayed out, his clothing torn to shreds, exposing his upper body to the elements. Where his chest should have been, a dark red cavity stared back at Liz, stripped of its vital organs, blood pooled on the ground around the body. The first man huddled over the corpse like a ghoul, and now Liz recognized the object he held in his bloody hands. A human heart.

'Oh, crap,' swore Dean. He called the station on his radio, giving a brief summary of the situation, and requesting immediate backup.

The man by the roadside hadn't moved, except to shield his eyes from the dazzling headlights. In fact, he didn't seem particularly bothered by the arrival of the police car. He continued to chew his bloody mouthful unhurriedly. Liz waited, her hand gripping the door handle, ready to spring.

The car's headlights picked out the man clearly in their twin beams. Liz peered at him through the drizzle on the windscreen, struggling for recognition. The man was dressed in jeans and a dark cotton shirt. His feet were bare. His face was youthful but weather-beaten and browned. He looked like a wild man, his long black hair slick with blood and rain and plastered to the side of his face. More blood dribbled down his straggly beard and soaked into his shirt. Yellow eyes shone brightly under the glare of the headlights.

Liz breathed a deep sigh of relief. It wasn't Mr Canning, the Headmaster. She had already studied his photo on the school's website. This man looked nothing like him, thank God.

The crouching man shuffled out of the white beam of the headlights, moving slowly sideways on all fours. His features dimmed until he was no more than a silhouette under the streetlamp, only his eyes still shining in the darkness. He still gripped the heart in his teeth, and seemed in no hurry to leave the scene.

'The bastard looks like he just doesn't care,' said Dean. 'What should we do? Wait for assistance, or make a move?

I don't want to risk losing him.'

The man squatted down on the wet pavement again, his eyes fixed on the patrol car, chewing hungrily at his gruesome meal.

'I'm damned if I'm going to sit here and watch him do that,' said Liz. 'Let's take him.'

'Right,' agreed Dean, reaching for his Taser.

Liz gripped her baton. 'I'll take his left flank, you go right. On the count of three …'

They flung open the doors and rushed the man together.

He reacted instantly, spitting out the remains of his feast and jumping backward away from the circle of light that ringed the streetlamp.

Liz rushed forward, but the man darted to her right, moving quickly toward the darkness of the Common.

'He's mine!' yelled Dean, diving into the undergrowth to follow him.

'I'm right behind you!' shouted Liz.

She ran as quickly as she could, but her short legs weren't the fastest in the force. Dean sprinted ahead leaving her behind. She stopped for a moment to assess the situation. They were near the northwestern edge of the Common, and the man wouldn't be able to run far before he reached the main road that bounded it. If she headed along the edge of the Common, there was a chance she could cut him off.

She set off in the direction of the road, her progress hampered by the slippery mud of the track and the darkness of the night. It was never truly dark anywhere in the city, but away from the roads, and with thick cloud shielding the moon, visibility was very limited.

She tripped over a branch and went sprawling into the cold wet mud. Dammit. She crawled to her knees, feeling freezing water soak into her trousers, and pushed herself back to her feet. She could see the lights from the road up ahead.

When she reached it, she saw no sign of Dean or the fugitive. The pavement was empty of pedestrians at this time of night, with just a few cars driving along the road itself. A high brick wall ran along the other side of the road, with big houses beyond. Sodium streetlamps cast an orange glow over the area. In this ordinary urban setting, it hardly seemed possible that a man-eating killer was on the loose. She jogged along the edge of the Common, straining her eyes for signs of movement. Beyond the roadside, she could see nothing but trees and bushes.

A noise off to her left was her first warning that someone was coming.

The killer burst out of the darkness, arms and legs pumping furiously. A look of desperate madness filled his eyes and he ran like a man possessed, straight toward her. Dean followed, struggling to keep pace.

The man seemed unaware of Liz's presence. She crouched low and braced herself for impact. He careered straight into her, heedless of where he was going.

She grappled his legs, bringing him down in a tackle. His momentum carried him forward, but she held on tight, rolling with him across the concrete.

The man let out a wild roar like a beast, snarling and gnashing his white teeth. He lashed out at her with his hand, and Liz felt sharp fingernails rake her arm. The man's nails were like claws, overgrown and twisted. They dug into her flesh but she clung on doggedly.

Dean lumbered into view, Taser in hand, approaching from the muddy field of the Common. 'Keep hold of him!' he bellowed.

Liz tightened her hold on the man's legs, but a mania gripped him. He thrashed his limbs and rolled over and over like a lunatic, a shrill scream escaping from his lips. He broke free just before Dean arrived, and leapt to his feet in an instant.

Liz pushed herself up and saw him sprint across the road, dodging one moving car and sliding across the front of another as it sped toward him. Both cars slammed on their brakes and shuddered to a halt in the road. Dean dashed across, weaving between them.

The man reached the other side of the road and ran up the vertical side of the wall, his bare toes somehow finding purchase in the mortared joints between the bricks. He barely slowed as he climbed the ten-foot wall, and sprang lightly atop it.

Liz watched amazed as he sprinted along the top of the wall for some distance before jumping down on the other side and vanishing. She shook her head in disbelief. Response cars were converging on the scene from all sides, tearing the night apart with sirens and flashing lights, but it was already too late. They would never catch him. Not if he could move like that.

Dean bashed his fist against the bricks in frustration, then re-crossed the road to check on Liz. 'You okay?' he grunted, reaching out a hand and pulling her to her feet. 'There's blood on your arm.'

She looked where he was pointing. Her sleeve had ripped away at the shoulder where the man had scratched her. Two red stripes marked the flesh beneath. Small droplets of blood welled up through the broken skin. She wiped them away with her palm. 'It's nothing,' she said. 'Just a scratch.'

Dean gave her a grim look. 'The bastard just slipped out of our hands. Was that a man or a monster?'

Liz shrugged. In her experience, the two were often the same.

They gave their statements to the commanding officer. There'd be a ton of paperwork to complete in the morning no doubt, but for now they could do no more.

On the way home, Liz's phone rang, its shrill ringtone cutting through the shocked numbness of her thoughts. She answered it in a daze. 'Hello?'

'Am I speaking to Police Constable Liz Bailey?' asked a voice. It was a woman's voice, smooth as honey, yet a cold dread seized Liz's heart.

'Yes,' she said. 'Speaking.'

'It's Chanita,' said the woman. 'The nurse from the hospital. I said I would call you about David Morgan, if his situation changed.'

'Yes,' repeated Liz. Her heart was suddenly hammering inside her chest.

'I'm so sorry. He passed away about an hour ago.'

'Thank you,' said Liz. 'Thank you for letting me know.'

Chapter Twenty-Nine

King's College Hospital, Lambeth, South London

Chanita Allen had arrived in Britain as a girl of eighteen, bringing nothing with her except a small suitcase packed with clothes, and a big heart full of dreams. The clothes in her suitcase had consisted mostly of thin summer dresses suitable for the Caribbean island she had called home, and they had quickly been replaced with warmer sweaters, coats and jackets. Over the years she had also swapped girlhood for womanhood, and yet she had never given up on her dreams.

The dreams Chanita brought with her across the ocean had been painted in the vivid hues of the Leeward Islands, and in particular the bright forest green of Montserrat, known as the emerald isle of the Caribbean. The island of Montserrat had once seemed to her like a paradise. With its sunny subtropical climate tempered by fresh trade winds, it had been an easy place to live. Even the occasional cloudbursts that brought rain across the ocean had been refreshing. The island was dense with beauty, from its smooth sandy beaches to the green forested heights of the Soufrière Hills and the Great Alps waterfall. Yet all the while, a malevolent monster had lain concealed within the heart of fair Montserrat. One day, heaven had turned to a fiery hell when the Soufrière Hills volcano erupted, spilling ash and fire across the emerald island, destroying Chanita's home, and the lives of everyone she knew.

Some said that the old island gods had grown angry. At what, they could not say, for the volcano had slumbered peacefully enough for centuries. But whatever their reasons, they had devastated the island and left it almost uninhabitable. Whether they were justified in their anger was not for Chanita to say. Instead she clung to her dreams. For while life had thrown both joys and miseries in Chanita's direction, her dreams endured, built as they were on simplicity and practicality. Her dreams had been nothing more nor less than to help others.

Years of working long hours in London hospitals beneath leaden skies hadn't caused the dreams to fade, for the more misery and suffering Chanita encountered, the more she was able to help. She no longer believed in paradise, whether on an island or elsewhere, and she knew that the direction of her life could change in a heartbeat, but despite that, wherever she found herself, she made the world better by helping others.

Some people described Chanita as a saint, but Chanita didn't believe in saints, and the outbreak of the bite cases had stretched even her patience to breaking point. The ward was as busy as any time she could remember. As soon as a bed was vacated, another patient filled it. Some, like PC David Morgan, passed away. Others, like James Beaumont, were discharged.

The bed occupied by James was now taken by an elderly patient with pneumonia, Mr Lancross. James had been a pleasant, polite boy, who hadn't asked for much. Chanita had heard the story of how he'd saved the lives of a group of children, getting his arm bitten in the process. In contrast, Mr Lancross was a grumpy old man, forever finding reasons to summon Chanita to his bedside. He had called her again just now, probably for some trivial matter.

'Yes, Mr Lancross?' she said wearily, as she arrived at the old man's bedside. The old man waved a weak hand at her and beckoned her close. He was in his eighties and had great difficulty breathing. It wasn't surprising he was grumpy. 'What can I do for you?' Chanita asked him, not unkindly.

'That man in the next bed. He frightens me.'

Chanita glanced sideways at the patient. Jack Clarke, according to his notes. Another bite victim, like James.

Chanita shuddered. She understood how Mr Lancross felt. The bite victims had a sinister quality to them. Even when they recovered, they still seemed damaged in some way.

She didn't know what was going on, but the number of bite attacks had continued to rise in recent weeks. At first she'd wondered if it was a new strain of rabies, but the incubation period was far too short for that. Rabies normally took weeks to produce symptoms after a bite, but with this new condition, a bite could lead to anaphylactic shock within minutes. Most frightening of all was that the latest victims had been bitten not by dogs, or wolves, but by other people.

This man, Jack Clarke, was in his late thirties and had somehow found himself at the wrong end of a set of sharp teeth. He'd been admitted directly to Intensive Care, and had remained unconscious for most of the first week or so, before starting to show signs of improvement. His fever had gone, and he was recovering steadily from his infection. He was asleep now, and had been all morning. He still had an IV drip in his arm, and a breathing tube down his throat, but he was well past the critical stage.

She sympathized with the old man, Mr Lancross, but she didn't have the authority to move patients around. 'Mr Lancross, there really isn't anything I can do. All the beds are full, and I can't move people just because you don't like them.'

'There's something wrong with him,' grumbled the old man. 'He keeps looking at me in a funny way.'

'The man is barely conscious, Mr Lancross.'

The old man shook his head with surprising vigour. 'He wakes up and stares at me. His eyes are bright yellow. I heard him say he wants to eat me.'

'Eat you?' repeated Chanita. A cold feeling gripped her. The old man was half-deaf, but the words sounded chillingly familiar. She glanced over at the sleeping man. His chest rose and fell smoothly. His restraining straps had been removed a few days ago. He didn't look a threat. He probably couldn't even climb out of bed on his own. 'You probably just misheard him, Mr Lancross.'

'The man's a nutcase. He should be in a psychiatric ward. I don't feel safe.'

The old man was right. The bite cases ought to be kept in a separate ward, even the ones that seemed to be recovering well. Until they really knew what was happening, the risk of mixing patients was too great. 'I'll speak to Doctor Kapoor and see if we can get this patient moved.' She squeezed his hand and he gave her a toothless grin.

'Thank you, my dear.' He no longer seemed grumpy at all.

Chanita went in search of Doctor Kapoor and found him examining a patient in a nearby ward. The doctor seemed to have aged in recent weeks. The thin lines around his eyes and mouth had deepened into furrows. She wondered how many hours it had been since he'd last slept. 'Doctor Kapoor? May I have a word?'

The doctor gave her a thin smile of acknowledgment. 'Chanita. Of course.' He finished with his patient and led her into a small staff office. 'Do you mind if we sit down?' He dropped into one of the plastic chairs and removed his glasses, giving his dark eyes a rub. 'What can I do for you?'

Chanita sat opposite him. Without his glasses, the doctor looked vulnerable and all too fragile. 'It's the bite patients, Doctor. I think we need to isolate them from other patients. They're too dangerous.'

Doctor Kapoor frowned, the lines around his eyes deepening further. 'I'm not sure we can do that. We don't have enough beds. It would mean reorganizing the wards, reallocating staff, …'

She cut him off abruptly. 'One of them just threatened to eat another patient.'

The doctor's face crumpled at the news. Chanita realized that he was completely exhausted. 'Which patient made the threat?' he asked.

'Jack Clarke. He was moved onto the ward two days ago, and he's been sleeping most of the time, but …'

'I know Jack Clarke. I moved him out of Intensive Care because another level-one trauma case was admitted and we needed to free a bed. I thought he would be safe to move.' The doctor rubbed his eyes again. 'Jack Clarke was the least sick patient. I didn't know what else to do.'

Chanita hesitated, then took the doctor's hands gently in her own. 'We're becoming overwhelmed, aren't we?'

He smiled at her, suddenly shy and boyish at her touch. 'Not overwhelmed. The official word is *challenged*. The Medical Director told me so himself, just this morning.'

'So you've already spoken to him? Will he provide more resources?'

'No.' The doctor's smile died on his face. 'He's keeping the situation under review. In the meantime, I suggest you keep a close eye on Jack Clarke.'

Chapter Thirty

Leay Street, Battersea, South London

When PC Dean Arnold arrived home, his wife, Samantha, was waiting up for him, an anxious look on her face. He pulled off his coat and shoes and kissed her on the cheek. He was surprised by how hard she hugged him to her.

'Everything okay?' he asked. 'Did Lily get off to sleep all right?' Their two-year-old daughter had been wakeful this past week as the last of her baby teeth painfully emerged from her gums.

Samantha brushed her long hair out of her eyes. 'The teething kept her awake for a long time, but she's gone to sleep now.'

'I wish I could have been here.' Dean checked the time on his watch. A quarter to midnight. Samantha looked exhausted. 'You go to bed,' he told her. 'I'll wait up and listen out for Lily waking. I haven't seen her all day.'

His wife looked at him apprehensively. 'You look dog-tired already, love. What happened?'

He sat down heavily on the sofa, letting the padded leather take the weight off his feet. 'Another killing, up on the Common. The murderer was still at the scene, as bold as brass. Red-handed.' An image of the man's bloody hands clutching his victim's heart flashed into his mind. 'I chased him across the Common, but he climbed over a wall.'

'I saw the story on the news. They said he'd been arrested.'

'Arrested? No, he got away. It was damn frustrating. He was just yards away from me.'

Samantha shook her head. 'They chased him with a helicopter and cars and cornered him by the old sewage works. He's been arrested, love. He was a Romanian man. The police said they'd caught the Ripper.'

Dean let his body sag against the sofa cushions. 'Well, good. I'm glad they got the bastard. I just wish I could have caught him myself.'

Samantha sat next to him, putting her arm around his shoulder. 'You did your best, Dean.'

'I don't know what else I could have done. That man... he was barely human. I've never seen anything like it. He was a savage. When I chased him ... I dunno what happened, Sam, he just ran straight over that damn wall like it wasn't even there. I don't know how.'

Samantha said nothing. It wasn't words he wanted, but her warm touch. She held his big clumsy hands in hers. They were so small and delicate, and so full of tenderness.

He found himself wondering about the man who had been murdered this evening, his body defiled so horribly. Who was he, and was someone waiting anxiously for him to return home? If so, they would never see him alive, never hold his hands in theirs again. His thoughts drifted to the killer with the wild look in his eyes. He, too, could have been anyone. But he'd been caught at last. The world was safe again.

But for some strange reason, Dean didn't feel any comfort from the news of the killer's arrest. Perhaps he'd seen too much tonight. Things that he would never be able to forget. 'I don't know what's happening out there,' he said. 'The Ripper, the Beast ... the world's going mad.'

'You're home now,' said Samantha, leaning in close to kiss him. 'You're safe.'

'I'm going to keep you safe too,' he said. 'Whatever happens. I promise I'll keep you and Lily safe.' Samantha released his hands and he patted her swollen belly. 'And this one too. I'll keep you all safe.'

She kissed him on the lips, then started to undo the buttons of his shirt. She kissed him again, longer this time. 'Let's go upstairs. We can wait up for Lily together.'

Chapter Thirty-One

Park Lane, Mayfair, Central London

Melanie Margolis languished naked in the hotel bed as her latest conquest continued to shower. She could hear the hot water gushing, hear him humming tunelessly as he scrubbed and soaped. She pictured him standing in the shower cubicle, rubbing his body with complimentary products, possibly imagining her hands on his skin again, reliving the experience. He was probably telling himself how lucky he was, or more likely, that he deserved a woman like her, that he was somehow entitled to her.

She would teach him a lesson about entitlement.

She flung the white cotton sheets away and slid out of bed, moving gracefully and silently on her bare feet. Cool winter light filtered through the window blinds and she couldn't resist parting them to peep out. The hotel stood on Park Lane, and from her tenth-floor vantage point she could see right across the green space of Hyde Park, the silvery-blue curve of the Serpentine Lake snaking before her, the elegant lines of Kensington Palace and its royal gardens beyond. She adored this part of London. She could happily look at it for hours, but unfortunately she would have to forego that pleasure today.

Her clothes were still scattered across the floor of the hotel room, where she had allowed him to undress her. She gathered them up and dressed quickly. On the other side of the bathroom door the flow of water stopped, and she heard the glass door of the shower open and close, presumably as he reached for the towel. His humming resumed again.

She was dressed now. She picked through his clothing, also cast aside in passion. She found his wallet easily enough in his jacket pocket. Quality leather, stuffed with crisp bank notes, and a good collection of store and credit cards too. She took them all. She'd already found out his PIN when they checked into the hotel. It would be the same PIN for all the cards. It always was.

She left his phone in his jacket pocket. She had no desire to be mean.

The humming stopped and she heard the shower door open and close again. Quickly now. It would be easier if she were gone before he saw her. She straightened her hair in the wall mirror and crossed the room quietly, her heels leaving tiny indentations in the thick carpet. She slipped the chain off the door.

Behind her, the bathroom door opened and he stepped out, naked as a baby, a big grin plastered across his face. 'Melanie?' The grin quickly turned to disappointment. 'Weren't you going to say goodbye?'

'It's easier this way,' she told him.

'I see.'

He didn't of course. Soon he would, and she would need to be long gone by then.

'Will I see you again?' he asked.

She admired his optimism. She could have laughed in

his face, but there was no need to be cruel. He would discover the truth soon enough. She shook her head, making her long black hair sway from side to side. Nature had been generous with Melanie's hair. It was one of her best assets. That, plus her skin, her figure, and her devious and merciless guile.

He crossed the room toward her. 'Let me give you one last kiss.'

Danger signal. She should run. He was still stark naked. She could be out and away before he had a chance of following. To stay risked discovery, or worse. But she had hesitated, and already he had halved the distance that separated them.

She pasted a smile on her face and stepped into his embrace. 'A goodbye kiss,' she said.

He was in no hurry for her to go. He made the kiss last, and she could feel that he wanted more. She extricated herself from the embrace at last, making it clear that his time was up.

'You sure we can't meet again?' he asked, offering her the most charming smile in his arsenal.

She had to laugh at that. The guy certainly didn't quit easily. 'Best not.' She opened the door and slid through the gap.

The elevators were a little way along the corridor. She swayed over to them and pressed the *Down* button. A green arrow blinked on. She wondered where she would head first. Her favourite department stores were all in easy range. With any luck she'd have at least an hour before he cancelled the cards. In that time, she could clock up a five-figure spend without breaking sweat. She already had an itemized mental shopping list. Start with diamonds, that was the number-one rule.

The number next to the green arrow was slowly counting down. 14, 13, 12 …

The room door opened and he stepped into the corridor. 'Hey!' he shouted. 'My wallet!' He still had no clothes on, not even his underwear. Interesting. She wondered if she'd finally met her match.

The door to the elevator slid open with a ping. She held the wallet up for him to see, noting the look of consternation on his face.

A door to another room opened and a chambermaid emerged, wheeling a trolley stacked high with laundry. Her hand flew to her mouth at the sight of the naked man and she screamed.

Melanie raised an eyebrow and hopped into the elevator, stabbing at the *Lobby* button. It could go either way now. Fifty-fifty. She'd never been this close to getting caught before, and the buzz was quite exhilarating. The soft, quick pad of bare feet on expensive carpet grew steadily louder as she waited for the doors to close.

He was still shouting. The maid was still screaming. Melanie wondered what she would say if caught. There were still plenty of options available to a woman like her.

The doors closed just before he arrived. She heard his muted cry of anguish as the elevator began to descend. She would need to move quickly now. It might be only minutes before he was on the phone to his bank. Maybe she should have taken his phone after all. But he had a lot of cards to cancel. It would take him a while.

When she arrived at the lobby she stepped out casually and headed for the nearest way out. She smiled at a porter and waited patiently while an old lady struggled with the revolving door at the exit.

A breathless shout came from behind her. 'Stop thief!'

No, surely not. But yes, he had followed her down the stairs, still in his birthday suit. The day was turning into more fun than she could possibly have imagined.

She didn't wait to see how far he would get before hotel security stopped him. Running in heels was an entry-level requirement for a woman in Melanie's profession. Five minutes later she was already trying on a diamond necklace with matching earrings.

Chapter Thirty-Two

Manor Road Secondary School, South London

Ben Harvey stood at the front of the classroom, regarding what remained of his Year 10 Biology class with a sense of dismay. The front row of desks was empty, and the back too. Almost half the class was missing for one reason or other. Some mystery illness was doing the rounds of the school, but that alone didn't account for all the empty chairs.

Jamie Jones and Max Thompson were still missing from home. It had been weeks now. Their parents must be worried sick. The same with Lee Small.

Now Ashley Brown had vanished.

It was too much of a coincidence. The wild talk of the Beast and the Ripper had made everyone jump to obvious conclusions, but Ben still took hope from the fact that no bodies had been found. Yet.

And now Vijay Singh and Drake Cooper were off

school too. No one knew why. Apparently they'd been sent to Mr Canning for fighting last week, and nobody had seen them since. He couldn't imagine a boy like Vijay ever getting into a fight.

Teachers were off sick too, and he was having to cover more and more classes. That's why he'd been late getting to his class on Friday, when Vijay, Drake and Ash had been caught fighting. He blamed himself for being late to the class, but such things were almost unavoidable when resources were stretched to breaking point. His evening workload of marking and prep was growing week by week too. He was desperately looking forward to the Christmas break and two weeks to rest and catch up with his workload.

At least Rose Hallibury was back today after her terrifying ordeal at the kennels, although she still seemed traumatized, and had barely spoken a word. It was hardly surprising.

The only upside was that with a smaller class size, and some of the biggest mischief-makers absent, he was starting to make some real progress with the remaining kids. Unlike some of his colleagues, Ben Harvey didn't believe that the kids at Manor Road were unteachable. They just needed the right environment and stimulation. Unfortunately, they mostly had the wrong environment and little or no stimulation or parental support.

He pointed at the image on the whiteboard. 'So, to recap, who can tell me what a gene is?'

Gemma Morley shot up her hand. 'Please, Sir, it's a section of DNA that can be copied and passed from one generation to the next.'

'Good. And what is a chromosome?'

Tom Daniels answered this time. 'Sir, it's a long thread of DNA containing many genes.'

'Excellent. Final question for today. What does epigenetic mean?'

To Ben's surprise and delight it was Holly Brady who

raised her hand to answer. It wasn't that Holly was quiet and shy – quite the opposite – but that her interests normally didn't stray far from TV soap stars and social media gossip. 'Mr Harvey, Sir, it means that genes can be switched on or off by their environment. That means that the environment determines how people and animals behave, not just their genes.'

'Very good, Holly,' he said, and received a beaming smile in return. Unwittingly, Holly had demonstrated the truth of the matter. In the classroom, just as in life, outcomes were never pre-determined. Just because Holly had known almost nothing about Biology when she'd started that term, didn't mean that she couldn't learn if taught in the right way. When nature battled nurture, environment was always the deciding factor, not the raw material of DNA.

The end-of-class bell rang and he watched the kids stampede out through the door.

His own life demonstrated the principle clearly. With a good degree from a top university he could have chosen to do anything. His fellow graduates had gone into well-paid jobs in pharmaceuticals and medical research, or had retrained for finance, law and marketing jobs. He could have done that too. But he'd chosen a more difficult path, opting to teach in a deprived inner-city school. It so often felt like life was determined to see him fail at that. And if all the odds were stacked against him, how could he ever realistically hope to change the course of these young people's lives?

He wondered what advice he would give to his younger self. *Don't fool yourself you can ever make a difference*, perhaps.

Yet on days like this, he knew that he could.

Some better advice for the youthful Ben Harvey then: *hold on to your dreams with all your heart.*

He was tidying away his books and papers for the day when he heard a commotion from the corridor outside. Kids started shouting and screaming, running past the open door of his classroom. 'Hey!' he called, but they took no notice.

Wearily he walked over to the doorway and stepped into the corridor.

It was bedlam.

He had expected to see a few loudmouths causing trouble, but instead dozens of children were surging along the corridor, sweeping past him in obvious distress. Holly Brady came racing toward him, her mouth open in a scream. He caught hold of her arm as she passed. 'Holly, calm down. Tell me what's happening.'

She looked at him in terror, before coming to her senses. 'It's the Headmaster, Sir. He's gone berserk!'

'Mr Canning gone berserk? What do you mean?'

She shook her head mutely and he let her go.

He turned to face the onrushing crowd. They were certainly coming in the direction from the Head's office. But why? It was hard to imagine anyone less berserk than stuffy old Mr Canning.

Mr Johnson, the sports teacher, lumbered into view. Ben grabbed him. 'What the hell's going on?'

The teacher looked as terrified as the children. He tried to pull away but Ben held him firm. 'Pull yourself together! You have a duty of care toward these children.'

Mr Johnson shook his head. 'The Headmaster's gone mad. He's on a rampage. Now let me go!' He struggled in Ben's grip, but Ben clung on.

'You've got to stay and help,' he shouted at the man.

Mr Johnson shook his head again. He swore at Ben and aimed a sharp kick at his shin.

'Ow!' Ben released him with a jolt. 'You coward!' he shouted as the teacher disappeared down the corridor.

The tech support nerd, Chris Crohn, stumbled along the corridor, panic-stricken and out of breath. Ben considered stopping him to get him to help, but the guy looked like he'd be as much use in an emergency as a pre-schooler. Ben let him hurry past.

Another teacher pushed his way through the crowd toward him. It was Brian Lee, who taught Physics. 'Ben, what on earth's happening?'

'It's Mr Canning. I think he's attacked some children.'

'What are we going to do?'

'Come on,' said Ben. 'Let's go and find him.'

Chapter Thirty-Three

*Upper Terrace, Richmond upon Thames,
West London*

Melanie Margolis showed the ill-gotten proceeds of her day's work to her sister, Sarah. Her shopping spree in London's West End had been cut short rather rudely, but Melanie had made sure she'd scored big before the stolen credit cards got cancelled.

'Nice,' said Sarah, running the thread of diamonds through her fingers and watching how the stones split the white light into rainbows. 'What was this one like?'

'The guy? Married, but kind of cute. You won't believe what happened though. He came running after me with no clothes on.'

'Where?'

'All the way down the stairs and into the hotel lobby.'

'Without a stitch on? You're right. I hardly believe anything you tell me.'

Melanie stuck her tongue out at her sister. 'I swear it's

true. He came this close to catching me.' She held up her thumb and forefinger to show how close. 'On days like this I think that you have the easy job.'

'Not easy,' said Sarah. 'But safe. You should lie low for a week. You got a good haul. There's no point taking unnecessary risks.'

'You know I can't help myself. Unnecessary risks are what I live for. And you and Grandpa, of course.' She hugged her sister. 'How has he been today?'

'The same. I don't think he knows who I am anymore.'

'Let's go and see him.'

'He's asleep.'

'I want to see him anyway.'

Sarah led the way down the hallway to Grandpa's room. The house was an old Georgian terrace, big enough for a large family. When they were little, it had been bursting with noise and life. Now just the three of them lived there.

Grandpa had lived in the same house for most of his adult life, watching his children and grandchildren grow up around him. Now the old man was bed-ridden, and never left the one room. His mind was trapped in a single room too, a prisoner of Alzheimer's. The dementia had advanced slowly, slamming shut first one door, then another, until only a tiny corner of his original self remained to him. Where the rest had gone, no one could say.

He lay just as Melanie had seen him that morning, snoring gently, a serene look on his crumpled face. The fear would grip him when he woke.

'Has he eaten today?' Melanie asked her sister.

'A little. I made some vegetable soup for lunch, and he managed a bowl of that.'

'He's getting weaker, though, isn't he?'

'Yes. He sleeps more and more. But I think that's for the best.'

Melanie gave her sister's hand a squeeze. They were

twins, but not alike, neither in looks nor in temperament. Sometimes they fought bitterly, like any sisters. But they were still a team.

The old man's eyelids flickered gently and his left hand stirred.

Melanie leaned closer to him. 'Grandpa? Are you awake?'

The age-mottled hand began to shake and move in agitation. His lips formed soundless words.

'Can you hear me, Grandpa? It's me, Melanie.'

He opened his eyes, and they were filled with terror and confusion. The shake in his hand spread up his arm, and he began to blabber.

She rubbed his arm soothingly with her fingers. 'It's Melanie, Grandpa. Melanie and Sarah.'

'Barbara?' he asked. 'Is Barbara here?'

'No, just Melanie and Sarah.'

'Barbara,' repeated the old man. He seemed to stare right through her. Barbara had been dead for twenty years, but perhaps she lived still, in some walled-off compartment of his mind.

He fell quiet as she stroked his arm, breathing deeply and calmly, his eyes still fixed on some distant vision. His left hand continued to move, as if it had its own private life to lead.

'Are you sure you can manage him on your own?' Melanie asked Sarah. 'I honestly don't know how you do it, day after day.'

Sarah shrugged. 'And I don't know how you do *your* job.'

'One of us needs to earn some money,' said Melanie. 'Besides, what else could I do? Become a nurse, or a teacher? Perhaps an astronaut?'

'You'll have to find something else to do eventually. Looks don't last forever.'

'Thanks for reminding me, darling. But by then, I intend to retire to the beach at Monte Carlo.'

'You'd be better off settling down with someone nice. I don't know what you see in some of these men.'

'I see their credit cards, Sarah,' snapped Melanie. They had talked this over a thousand times. Her sister had never approved of Melanie's way of earning a living. 'What's so hard to understand? I do it for you, you know that. For you and Grandpa. You might show some gratitude.'

Her sister winced. 'You're better than this, Mel. You could have any man you wanted. You ought to have stuck with that nice teacher you dated. What was his name?'

'Ben. Ben Harvey,' admitted Melanie reluctantly. That was all in the past now. Melanie had been horrible to him, something he'd hardly deserved.

'He was cute, wasn't he?'

One of the nicest men she'd known, but Melanie was hardly going to admit that to her sister now. 'Cute doesn't pay the bills, Sarah. He was a Biology teacher at a run-down South London school. What kind of future would we have had together?'

'He really liked you. I liked him too, or at least what you told me about him.'

'You never even met him, Sarah. I wanted to bring him here, but you said no. You never see anyone these days, apart from me and Grandpa. All you know about the outside world is what I tell you. When was the last time you even went out of the house?' It seemed that turning the argument against Sarah was easier than facing up to any hard truths herself. Melanie knew she could be a real bitch at times. She didn't deserve a sister like Sarah, and she hadn't deserved Ben Harvey either.

Her sister looked startled by the question. She began to fidget with her fingers. 'I don't need to go outside,' she protested. 'I manage perfectly well having groceries and things delivered to the house. Anyway, I couldn't possibly go out and leave Grandpa alone. Anything might happen.'

'You know that's just an excuse.' The truth was that Sarah had become too frightened of other people to go outside. It was more than fear, it was a full-blown phobia. She hadn't left the house in months. She refused to let anyone visit. She no longer had any friends. Melanie pointed a finger at her. 'You need to face up to your problem before you start lecturing me about how to live my life.'

'Stop it,' begged Sarah. 'Don't be so mean. You know how strangers scare me.'

Melanie should stop, but she just couldn't help herself. 'Well it's just as well I don't bring any of my men home then. Some of them are quite appalling. Even that nice teacher Ben Harvey would terrify you.'

Sarah said nothing to that, just looked upset. That was how Sarah was. She never fought back.

'I'm sorry,' said Melanie. She hated herself when she picked on her sister. Just as she'd been a bitch to Ben, she always seemed to hurt the people she loved most. Perhaps that was why she spent so much time with people she didn't love at all.

'It's all right,' said Sarah. 'And you're right. I should try to get out.' She nodded her head. 'I'll try,' she promised. 'It's just that ...'

'What?' Melanie could tell something else was bothering her sister. She always could. 'What's wrong?' she asked, more gently. 'What's this all about, really?'

'The police found another body. It was all over the news today.'

'Another one?'

'It was down by the river. Half-eaten, like the others.' Sarah looked her directly in the eyes. 'It's too dangerous for you to carry on. The Ripper's still out there, Mel. Or a copycat killer, some kind of monster. You put yourself at too much risk.'

Melanie laughed it off. 'There are lots of risks in my job, but being eaten by a monster isn't one of them. There's more chance I'll choke to death over a Michelin-star meal, or be battered by a jealous wife's designer handbag in a *crime passionnel.*'

Sarah didn't look satisfied.

'Look, I'll be careful, all right? But don't tell me not to take risks. Taking risks is what lets me know I'm still alive.'

She dropped her gaze again to Grandpa's wasted body. He seemed to have retreated into a world of sleep and memories once more. One thing Melanie knew for certain was that she would never allow herself to live like that.

Chapter Thirty-Four

Manor Road Secondary School, South London

Together, Ben Harvey and Brian Lee strode purposefully down the school corridor toward the Headmaster's office. The crowd of panicked children had dwindled to a few stragglers now and they made good progress.

'What are we going to do when we find him?' asked Mr Lee. 'Do you have a weapon?'

'Of course not,' said Ben.

'Then if talking doesn't work, I guess we're going to have to use our hands.'

They turned down the side corridor that led to Mr Canning's office, questions racing through Ben's mind. He didn't like any of the answers that presented themselves.

As soon as they rounded the corner, it was obvious that talking wasn't going to be the answer. A pool of blood stained the floor of the corridor scarlet. Bloody footprints and a trail of red led from there to the end of the corridor, where the Headmaster crouched outside the door to his office, more blood smeared over his face and hands and dripping from his chin. Ben had never seen so much blood in his life. No one could lose so much and still live.

The body of a girl lay prostrate on the floor beside the Headmaster. There was no doubt in Ben's mind that the girl was dead. The Head was chewing something, and Ben had a horrible idea what it might be.

'Good God,' said Brian Lee. He looked like he was going to be sick.

Ben stared at the scene in horror. *Berserk* didn't even begin to describe Mr Canning's behaviour. Somehow an ordinary day at school had transitioned into a nightmare.

The Head continued to chew on his grisly meal, staring coldly back at the two men with eyes that burned with a strange golden gleam. He made no attempt to flee or otherwise react to their arrival. Instead he behaved like a man whose mid-morning coffee break had been rudely interrupted by subordinates.

Ben tried to make himself think straight. He couldn't be certain about the identity of the girl. She wasn't one of the girls he taught. She was from Year 8 perhaps – Hannah or Harriet, or something like that. They were too late to save her, but they had to do something.

Mr Canning was middle-aged and pot-bellied, and Ben had never thought of him as remotely dangerous. But he'd been a keen sportsman when he first came to the school, and there was a madness in his eyes. It would be folly to underestimate him, especially considering that he'd just murdered this poor girl.

Ben was taller than Mr Canning and much fitter. He ran half-marathons regularly, and sometimes competed in triathlons too. He felt confident that he could handle himself in a fight, although he'd never had to test that hypothesis. Brian Lee was short, but taught after-school Judo classes and looked fit enough. Together, they ought to be able to handle the Headmaster if they had to. Brian Lee looked queasy though, and the Head had an air of calm about him that made him very dangerous. Since the girl was already dead, containment seemed the wisest approach.

'Let's play this quietly,' said Ben. 'We don't want to provoke him.'

Brian Lee nodded in agreement. They separated, blocking the only two exits. Ben moved in front of an outside door, and Mr Lee blocked the way back to the main corridor.

Mr Canning watched them calmly. He seemed to understand what they were doing, but he made no attempt to push past them to escape. Instead he stood up, blood dribbling down his white shirt, and shuffled backward through the open doorway of his office, leaving the mutilated body of the girl in the hallway.

Ben breathed a sigh of relief. If they could just avoid a confrontation until the police arrived, there would be no need for any further violence. And surely even that idiot sports teacher Mr Johnson would have thought of calling for the police by now.

His hopes were dashed by a girl's scream.

The Headmaster emerged from his office again, this time with a second girl. Ben recognized her red hair and freckled face immediately. Rose Hallibury, from the class he had just taught that afternoon. Her face was ashen, her green eyes wide and staring, but she seemed to be uninjured as far as he could tell. Mr Canning gripped her slim neck with one arm, wrapping the other firmly round her middle. Rose walked like she was in a trance. The Head guided her out into the middle of the corridor, then stopped. 'Looks like I've been caught at last,' he said. 'And I haven't even finished eating my dinner.'

The words shocked Ben. The Head had become so monstrous through his actions that he had seemed beyond human speech. The fact that he could speak about his actions in such a casual way seemed utterly chilling. And what did he mean *caught at last*? Ben pushed that thought aside.

'It's very bad manners to watch other people eating,' continued the Head. 'Go away and leave me to finish with Rose.'

Ben opened his mouth to speak, but his throat had dried and he had to swallow before he could form words. 'Let her go, Headmaster,' he said. 'You can't hope to escape.'

Mr Canning squeezed Rose tighter around the neck and she gasped. 'Escape? That wasn't my plan at all. The time for that would seem to be well past. No, I had merely hoped to finish my meal in peace, but you have interrupted me most rudely. Why don't you and Mr Lee just go back to your classrooms and let me finish what I started?'

Ben shook his head disbelievingly. 'Let her go,' he repeated.

'Or what?' demanded the Head. 'If you come near, I'll kill her.' He tightened his grip around Rose's pale neck again. 'I'll kill her anyway,' he laughed. 'Like I killed the others. You can't stop me.'

Others. The word hung sickeningly in the air between them.

Ben measured the distance between himself and Mr Canning. They were at least a dozen paces apart. He took a step forward and saw the Head jerk Rose's neck to one side in response. She cried out and Ben stepped back.

'Release the girl now,' called Mr Lee. 'Unharmed.'

Mr Canning laughed contemptuously. 'Not much of a negotiator, are you, Mr Lee?' he sneered. 'What do you offer me in her place? She's such a pretty little thing.'

Ben took another step forward before he even realized what he was doing. 'Take me instead,' he said. He raised his hands to show that they were empty.

'Hmm,' said Mr Canning. 'You don't look half as tasty as young Rose here.' He bared his teeth and pressed them against the whiteness of her neck.

'No!' Ben stepped forward again, his hands raised high over his head. 'Leave her alone. If you try to hurt her, Mr Lee and I will take you down. But if you release Rose, you can have me.'

Mr Canning paused, his teeth nuzzling against Rose's slender neck. 'To eat?' he inquired.

Ben swallowed hard. 'If that's what it takes.'

'Well, well, aren't you the hero, all of a sudden?' sneered the Head. 'Ben Harvey, hero of Manor Road School. Won't all the ladies be impressed! What a shame he had to die so horribly.'

'No, Ben,' said Mr Lee, putting an arm on his elbow.

Ben put out a hand to silence him. He took another step forward. 'Let her go. I'll give myself up.'

Mr Canning looked at him thoughtfully. 'How can I trust you though? You'll need to tie yourself up. Or better still, get Mr Lee to do it for you. There's some rope in my office. Wait a moment.' He disappeared back through the doorway, shuffling slowly backward, taking Rose with him.

'You've gone mad too,' hissed Brian Lee. 'You can't allow him to take you. It's monstrous.'

'I can't allow him to harm that girl.'

'What if it's a trick?'

'I have to take that risk.'

Mr Canning emerged from his office with Rose once more, kicking a short length of rope in front of him. He slid it across the smooth floor toward Mr Lee. 'There you go. Tie him up. And make it secure. I'll be watching carefully.' He twisted Rose's neck and the girl cried out again. 'Do it now,' he said.

'Go on,' said Ben, turning his back to Mr Lee, his hands crossed over each other behind him.

Mr Lee picked up the rope hesitantly. Slowly he wrapped it around Ben's wrists and tied the ends into a knot.

'Tighter!' yelled Mr Canning.

Lycanthropic

Mr Lee pulled the rope tight. 'Do you have a plan?' he whispered in Ben's ear.

'Just to get the girl away from him. As soon as he releases her, you get her out of here as fast as you can. Don't worry about me.'

Brian Lee nodded, almost imperceptibly. 'Good luck,' he said.

Ben turned to face the Headmaster. 'Okay, release the girl.'

'Not so fast,' said the Head. 'First you come over here and sit on the floor.' He pointed at a place a few paces in front of him.

Ben walked slowly, his eyes fixed on Mr Canning. When he reached the spot the Head had indicated he dropped to one knee, then onto both knees, and sat on the floor. The body of the dead girl lay splayed out nearby, her clothes ripped. Her torso was covered in bite marks.

Mr Canning twitched his mouth into a crude mockery of a smile, revealing a row of sharp teeth, saliva dripping from his tongue. Close up, the veins beneath his skin bulged and pulsed alarmingly. The whites of his eyes were visibly yellow, and his ruby lips seemed engorged with blood. 'Very good, Mr Harvey. Aren't you an obedient little puppy? I wish all my teachers were as tractable as you.'

'Let Rose go now,' said Ben. 'I've done what you asked.'

'Yes,' agreed Mr Canning, but he seemed reluctant to release the girl.

Brian Lee took a step forward. 'Release her now, man! You've got what you wanted.'

'Yes I have, haven't I?' said Mr Canning. A sly look flashed across his face and he spun forward, bringing his leg up.

Ben rose to his knees but the ball of Mr Canning's foot impacted with his forehead, flinging him back against the wall. Pain exploded in his head, and his ears filled with a loud ringing. He collapsed onto his side and sprawled on the floor, unable to move with his arms tied tightly behind him. He looked up at Mr Canning as if through a red mist.

The Headmaster stood tall, an insane glee in his eyes. His mouth opened and closed, but the noise in Ben's head blocked out the words. A smile spread across the Headmaster's face. He pulled Rose's neck toward him and opened his jaws wide to bite.

As Ben watched helplessly from the floor, Brian Lee shouted something. Then everything unfolded in a flash.

Rose kicked her heel backward like a mule, striking the Headmaster in the shin. He roared in fury and relaxed his grip on her long enough for her to twist out of his grasp.

Brian Lee rushed forward to take her, but he was too slow. Rose had already pulled a ball point pen out of her pocket, and before the Headmaster could react she plunged the pen into his left eye.

The Headmaster staggered backward, the pen protruding from his bulging eye, blood spurting from the wound. His arms flailed helplessly in front of him.

Brian Lee dropped his head and barrelled straight into him, sending him crashing to the floor.

The last thing Ben saw before he passed out was the Headmaster writhing like a dying insect, still trying to draw the barrel of the pen out of his empty eye socket.

Chapter Thirty-Five

Manor Road, South London, waxing moon

Chris Crohn knew that he had to get out of the city soon to have any chance of survival. Events were escalating alarmingly and they were worryingly close to home. He'd been right about Mr Canning being a werewolf. He'd been at school today when the Head had attacked that girl. Only some quick thinking and even faster running had saved him from becoming a werewolf snack himself. Even Seth would have to believe him now.

First Mr Leigh the Geography teacher, now Mr Canning the Headmaster. He was certain that other teachers were infected too. Maybe some of the students as well. No way was he ever going back to that school.

It wasn't just at school either. The number of events recorded by his werewolf-tracking app was growing exponentially and they were spreading across the whole of London. He'd identified a few hotspots in the initial stages of the outbreak, mainly south of the River Thames in

Brixton, Croydon and Clapham, and north of the river in Kensington. But now the incidents spread as far as Heathrow Airport in the west and Gravesend to the east. They were appearing in other population centres too, like Birmingham, Leeds and even as far north as Edinburgh all the way up in Scotland. It was safe to say that the werewolf crisis was becoming a national epidemic.

The incidents had steadily stepped up in severity too, from casual sightings and near-misses in the early days, to officially-reported attacks and deaths. And still the authorities hadn't realized what was happening. The Beast, the Ripper, ... why didn't they just say the word? Werewolf.

By Chris' reckoning, London would be overwhelmed with werewolves within months, perhaps even weeks. Other cities and large towns would fall like dominoes soon after. By the time the police and other agencies realized the true nature of the threat it would be too late to stop it.

It was probably already too late. His only hope now was to make it out into the countryside before the werewolves took over.

He spread out a large paper map on his bed. With all the computer equipment and survival gear filling his apartment, there were barely any other flat surfaces left, certainly none big enough to hold the entire expanse of the United Kingdom, including England, Wales, Scotland and Northern Ireland, with every major city, town, road, river and mountain marked in ink.

The printed document was something of a throwback, yet in the short time that he'd owned a real paper map, he had come to appreciate its elegance and beauty. He loved the crisp feel of the paper in his hands, the way that it concertinaed open and closed, and the exquisite detail it presented to the knowledgeable map user. You couldn't pinch or zoom a paper map, and any scrolling involved physically moving your head across its surface. In technological terms it was obsolete, and yet he felt a growing respect for its designers, who had made a two-dimensional model of the real world using such primitive tools and techniques. Plus of course it had the advantage of being always-on, with no need for a wireless network or even electricity.

In idle moments Chris had even begun to wonder if physical media might be the way of the future, and whether he ought to think about replacing his downloaded music collection with vinyl, like Seth had so often argued. But of course the werewolf apocalypse would render such questions irrelevant. There would be no music, downloaded or otherwise, once civilization had collapsed.

In the evenings after school finished and before Jiu-Jitsu class started, he had begun to draw markings on the map, indicating the spread of the epidemic. It was moving out from the capital in all directions, with road and rail links its primary means of propagation. His best bet was to avoid all major transport routes and travel off-grid into the wilderness.

England didn't really have much in the way of wilderness, but there were still pockets of under-development, places where natural beauty, local protesters or a sheer lack of economic impetus had prevented too much building. The county of North Yorkshire had one of the lowest population densities in the country, and so did Herefordshire, close to the Welsh border. Chris' grandparents lived in Herefordshire and he had fond memories of driving past its open pastures and through small market towns. The number of cows living there had always seemed to outnumber the people, and it would be a good place to live off the land after civilization had ended. He drew a large X in red on his 1:1,000,000 scale map of the British Isles and folded it back up carefully.

The main challenge was how to get there. Trains, buses and other means of public transport were no longer safe. A dismembered corpse had been found on a commuter train out of King's Cross station earlier in the week, just another of the unsolved Ripper murders. No way was Chris getting on a train or a bus with werewolves on the loose.

Travelling by private car on minor roads would be by far the best option, but there was one problem. Chris didn't own a car.

Seth did, however.

'You can't be serious,' said Seth, when he came around to the apartment that evening. 'Mr Canning, a werewolf?'

'I saw it with my own eyes. He killed one girl and attacked another. He nearly killed Mr Harvey, the Biology teacher too.'

'No way.'

'I saw it myself, Seth. I nearly died.'

Seth flicked his long unruly hair away from his face. Was that a look of admiration in his eyes, or merely scorn? 'What happened in the end?' he asked.

'Two of the teachers took him down and the police arrested him. They said he'd already eaten one of the girls.'

'Gross,' said Seth. 'And was he actually a wolf?'

'No,' admitted Chris. 'He was still in human form. It's not the full moon until tomorrow night.'

'So how do you know he's really a werewolf? He might just be a sicko.'

'Like Mr Leigh the Geography teacher?' said Chris.

'Yeah.'

'And the Romanian man they said was the Ripper?'

'Yeah.'

Chris glared at his friend. How stupid could someone be? 'What about the Beast?' he demanded.

'There haven't been any Beast sightings for about a month,' said Seth.

'Exactly,' said Chris triumphantly. 'Not since the last full moon.'

Seth flicked the hair away from his glasses. Chris could see that he was thinking it over carefully. Eventually he said, 'Even if you're right, I think it would be best to wait and see what happens.'

Chris shook his head in frustration. 'No. It's already almost too late. Surely you understand how exponential growth works. In the first week there's just a single werewolf, then two in the second week, and four in week three. The increase is almost too small to detect. But after eight weeks there are two hundred and fifty-six, and after twelve weeks the number has exploded to four thousand and ninety-six. Do you know how many there are after twenty-four weeks?'

Seth thought for a minute, his brow furrowed in deep trenches. 'One million, six hundred and seventy-seven thousand, two hundred and sixteen.'

'Right,' agreed Chris. Perhaps Seth wasn't quite as stupid as he seemed. 'Which means that everyone's a werewolf, or else they're dead. Everyone, that is, except us. But only if we get out now.'

'And you want to travel by car?'

'It's the only safe way.'

'And you have supplies and a tent and stuff?'

'Everything we need.'

Seth stroked his beard. 'Well, I suppose it might be prudent. Where did you say we should go?'

'Herefordshire.'

'I've never been there,' said Seth. 'What is there to see?'

'Nothing. That's the whole point.'

'Hmm,' said Seth, after a while. 'Let me think it over.'

Chapter Thirty-Six

*Upper Terrace, Richmond upon Thames,
West London*

Sarah Margolis was perfectly aware that she was watching too much TV, but she had gradually become addicted to it. She'd started recording serious late-night documentaries and watching them the following day when she was home with just Grandpa for company. It was all very educational. But since the old man's company counted for very little and was tending toward zero, she had stepped up her diet, becoming an avid follower of chat shows, reality shows, quizzes, soaps, magazine-style shows and of course the twenty-four-hour news channels. She knew she should stop, but somehow the number of hours spent in front of the screen had grown, steadily becoming the central focus of her life.

All day long now, whenever Grandpa was quiet, she watched.

If only she could get out of the house and meet new

people, she could change. But the idea filled her with dread. It took all her courage to answer the door to delivery men, or exchange a few words with the postman. After signing for a delivery she would have to sit quietly alone in a darkened room for half an hour, watching a game show to recover.

She knew she had a serious problem. She didn't need her sister to point it out to her. Anthropophobia, it was called. Fear of people. She had started reading books about her condition, becoming obsessively interested in self-help and psychology books. But books couldn't cure her phobia. And despite Sarah's pleas, Melanie was spending more and more time out with her men, sometimes leaving Sarah alone for days at a time.

And so, she watched.

The news was pulling her attention more and more. First the creature known as the *Beast of Clapham Common* had drawn her in. The Common was only a few miles from where she lived in Richmond upon Thames. She shuddered to think that a savage monster stalked it after dark. She'd experienced a guilty thrill when that policeman had been attacked by the Beast.

The lunchtime news had been filled with wild speculation, with members of the public calling in with crazy theories about the creature. More sightings of the Beast had been reported in other parts of London too. Commentators wondered aloud how one Beast alone could be responsible for so many different appearances right across the city. 'Does the Beast have a rail pass?' quipped one journalist.

Bizarrely, similar sightings of a Beast had been reported in other cities in other countries – in the Jardin des Tuileries in Paris, and in New York's Central Park – and jerky video footage of strange creatures in those locations also made the headlines for a few days.

But the Beast had been pushed aside once the serial killer known as the Ripper had begun his gruesome work.

Sarah had spent hours watching TV coverage of his murders and following up online, hungry for more details. She'd always had an interest in psychopaths and serial killers. An unhealthy interest, according to Melanie, perhaps even an obsession. The Ripper killings fed that obsession and Sarah had been secretly, guiltily pleased when the Ripper murders continued even after the arrest of the Romanian man.

But this evening, news had broken of two further arrests in the ongoing Ripper search. *Two More Men Arrested in Ripper Hunt* screamed the headline that scrolled continually across the bottom of the screen.

Sarah watched intently as the Police Commissioner gave a press conference to announce the arrests. It seemed that two separate arrests had been made at different locations and times. In both cases, the men arrested had been caught in the act of devouring their victims. Sarah shuddered with a curious mixture of horror and delight. The first man was another Romanian immigrant recently arrived in Britain, the other a respectable headmaster at a school in South London. It seemed that each man had been responsible for several horrific murders.

The police were at a loss to explain why apparently unconnected men should be involved, but the Commissioner eagerly reassured the public that with three men now safely in custody, their reign of terror had ended.

That didn't seem to satisfy the journalists however. Many questions remained unanswered. *Were the three men known to each other? Were they working as a team? Was there a connection to Romania? Were any other people involved? Could the police guarantee that there would be no further killings?* The Police Commissioner declined to answer any of their questions.

Sarah longed for her sister to return home. Much as she had enjoyed the thrill of the Ripper murders, she'd been terrified for Melanie's safety too. And no matter how many times she had begged Melanie to put her 'work' on hold, it had been no use. Her sister needed to be free in a way

Sarah had never quite understood. It wasn't as if they even needed the money any more. Melanie's hauls had put plenty of money into the bank. They had enough. And yet for Melanie it seemed, *enough* was a word that didn't really exist.

Chapter Thirty-Seven

Greenfield Road, Brixton, South London, full moon

When the time for the change finally came, James found that the trepidation and nervousness of the previous week had all but vanished. It was as if he were about to go into an exam where he already knew all the answers. He felt nothing now but anticipation and impatience. He had watched the moon wax steadily over the previous nights, feeling its inexorable pull. The way it dragged at every atom of his being had become almost unbearable. He yearned for its purifying pain, and the fire that cleansed.

Before going out he said a prayer, but as always since he'd been bitten, God's voice remained still. No matter, he knew what he must do. He felt as if he had known it all his life. All that he had lived through, everything he had learned, experienced and felt, had simply been in preparation for this night. All his dreams and yearnings were about to be fulfilled. If God really were listening, he would answer James when the change came.

Leanna and Adam would be going out later. They had already changed so many times that the thrill had become commonplace. But James was eager to taste it as soon as the full moon rose.

Samuel laughed. 'You're like a six-year-old on Christmas Eve, waiting for Santa to come.' But the laughter was just his way of putting James at ease. Samuel understood. He knew how much the change meant.

The two of them went out together, just before sunset, when the sun had lost its power to burn his skin. The sky was clear this evening, perfect conditions for the coming change. Already the moon had risen, but it made a pale face against the light western sky. Not until the fiery sun had relinquished its hold over the day could the cold silver orb begin to bathe them in its pure rays.

They headed out to the park, where Samuel thought they would have the best chance of privacy. The park was locked at four o'clock in the winter months, and no one would be fool enough to climb over its iron fence with the stories of the Ripper and the Beast still circulating. He had never seen any police go into the park after dark either. They ought to have the place to themselves, apart from any other werewolves they might chance upon.

They climbed over the fence together, Samuel giving James a boost up, then leaping over himself in a single bound. James glanced behind at the darkening street, but no one had seen them enter the park.

'Come on,' said Samuel, heading across the clipped grass. 'Let's get into the trees before anyone comes.'

They jogged along together, following the curve of a concrete path that wove between trees and bushes, the canopies of the trees mostly bare now, standing tall like columns in a cathedral, supporting the heavens in their outstretched arms. Above them, the moon rose slowly, becoming brighter as the sun dropped down beyond the horizon and twilight made its entrance. They continued on into the very heart of the park, the light fading as the sun set in a last orange blaze, until the sky began to lighten again as the moon lifted above the trees.

James stopped to look up at it, his eyes narrowing reflexively, but not turning away. The moon smiled back, its mottled face familiar, its bright reflective surface transmuting the steady light of day into a shimmering and magical firelight. As it rose higher, it became blindingly bright, forcing James to look away.

Moonbeams fell against him like the burning rays of the summer sun. His skin and eyes began to prick. 'I think it's beginning,' he said.

Samuel stood beside him, alert and watchful. 'You'll probably feel it before I do,' he said. 'You're fully sensitized.'

'I do,' said James. 'I feel it now.'

With a growing rush the fire took James in its hot embrace. From head to toe his body shuddered as his skin turned first to flame and then to ice, and back to hot, molten lava. Fine hairs erupted from his hands, his chest, his back, legs and face. Even his fingers and toes thickened, first with hair, and then with fur. It wrapped him like a perfectly-fitted glove.

The power coursed through his veins, and his muscles writhed within him like snakes uncoiling. He felt his clothes tear and fall away as his chest and shoulders grew broad, his arms and legs flexing and bending as he stooped forward onto all fours. He pawed the wet grass, enjoying the feel of mud and grass between his fingers and toes. They lengthened as he dug them into the soft ground, and his nails grew thick and sharp like talons. He padded forward purposefully, enjoying the ease of walking on four legs.

Finally he felt a blistering thrill as his teeth pushed through his gums, twisting and sharpening as they readied themselves to kill. A soft growl came from his mouth, turning to a deep-throated roar, and he sprang upright once more, standing tall on hind legs to howl at the moon that watched silently overhead.

He had changed, just as Samuel had promised. The cleansing transformation left him wordless with wonder. Never had he experienced such pure and simple joy.

He remembered Samuel then, and saw that he too had changed. As a wolf he was perhaps even more beautiful than in human form, his fur black, his strong, fine features flowing with fluid grace under the silvery light.

'Ready?' asked Samuel.

'Yes,' said James. The sound of his new voice surprised him. It was his own familiar voice, yet the voice of a wolf.

'Come on,' said Samuel, and he bounded forward away from the path.

The park at night assaulted his wolf senses. Human language simply did not have the words to describe it; it could only be experienced. A thousand distinct scents presented themselves to him, and he instinctively knew the source of each. A fresh, open breeze laced with diesel particulates and petroleum fumes; a decaying mildew tang of dead leaves and rotting vegetation; a lingering trail of smoke from a smouldering bonfire. And beneath it all, faint but rich, the slightly cloying aroma of fresh meat that roused his appetite and made saliva drool from his pink tongue. Their prey was still distant, but they covered ground quickly.

When they reached the black metal fence that girdled the park, they leapt over it without slowing, James now running ahead in his enthusiasm. His nose guided him as much as his eyes. Prey was close, and in some numbers, and his hunger seemed almost boundless.

These streets were familiar, but he saw them differently now. Darkness held no mysteries anymore; it had become his ally. He moved silently from dark space to dark space, clinging to shadows, invisible beneath the shroud of night, Samuel following soundlessly in his wake.

Together they crossed street after street, drawing ever closer to the prey.

James knew their destination. The mainline railway station closest to the park. There would be commuters there, alighting from trains, or waiting to return home after work. Dozens of them, waiting. Waiting for him.

He ran faster, his heart pumping, the fiery blood coursing, the scent growing ever more intense. Blood lust came on him, pushing conscious thoughts aside. He moved purely on instinct. He had no need to think. His teeth, his claws, his jaws thought for him.

They arrived at the station together, leaping easily over the low wall and fence that ringed it, landing on the hard platform concourse out of nowhere. Crowds of people milled about like sheep before him. His wolf eyes delighted at the surprise that turned to horror on those stupid faces.

And they were slow. So slow.

He flew at the nearest, a young man in jeans and hoodie, sinking his canines into his neck, ripping at the throat, and tasting the rich iron blood that gushed into his mouth. The man fell quickly and James wanted to feed on him, but so many others were waiting nearby. He released his prey and turned to the next. This one was smaller, a woman in a smart green raincoat, her eyes wide with terror. James killed her too, taking a hunk of flesh this time, shearing through her neck with his rear carnassial teeth. She didn't even have time to struggle before she dropped to the station platform, her eyes staring sightless and glassy. He stopped to chew, watching the others flee in panic. They rushed in terror, tripping over each other, stumbling, directionless. James watched them, laughing.

After that, he forgot how many he killed or maimed. He didn't stop until Samuel's voice broke through the frenzy that had taken him. 'The police are coming, James. Run! Run for your life!'

Chapter Thirty-Eight

King's College Hospital, Lambeth, South London, full moon

Doctor Kapoor yawned. After working an eighteen-hour shift he was reaching the limit of his endurance. Not since his days as a junior doctor had he been so overworked, and he had been a lot younger then. The number of patients requiring Intensive Care grew almost day by day. Never mind beds – there simply weren't enough doctors to treat them all. Whatever this thing was, it was spreading at epidemic rates.

Chanita was right. The bite cases needed to be kept away from other patients. Doctor Kapoor had already asked the Medical Director for a dedicated ward, but the hospital was stretched to full capacity. He would have to deal with this outbreak with the resources already at his disposal.

He'd begun to make a little progress in treating the condition, mostly by trial and error. Administering intravenous fluids as early as possible was the critical factor. That, and the severity of the wound. Bites were a lot more dangerous than scratches, as far as he could tell.

The patients that survived the critical stage and regained consciousness seemed to make a partial recovery, but he wouldn't say they were completely cured. In the end he had no choice but to discharge them in order to free up beds for new arrivals. The whole situation was just one step away from blowing up.

It had been hard to spot a pattern in the cases at first, because of the high degree of variability of the symptoms. The case reports had confused him too. Dogs, wolves, humans. Sometimes bites, other times just scratches. It was hard to make sense of the data, and he still didn't really know what he was dealing with. He'd had blood samples from his patients tested for viral, parasitic and fungal infections but nothing had shown up. Bacterial infection didn't seem to be a factor either, or at least none of the broad-spectrum antibiotics he'd tried had done much to combat the primary infection.

The white blood cell counts from the affected patients were all severely depressed, so the body's immune system was clearly battling against a pathogen of some type, but the Clinical Pathology lab couldn't identify it. He wondered if it could be some kind of auto-immune condition like Addison's disease or Sjögren's syndrome. These produced similar symptoms, though less severe, and also resulted in a low white blood cell count. But these types of diseases were not known to be transmitted by infection. This new condition had the hallmarks of something completely new to medicine.

He remembered seeing something on the news a year or so previously. Some mad scientist had predicted a werewolf apocalypse, or at least that was how some of the newspapers had reported it. He'd dug out the original articles on the internet, but they were more fevered speculation than journalistic fact. He hadn't been able to locate any actual medical papers. But he'd discovered something else online that had piqued his interest – similar reports of cases from other hospitals, some outside London. He'd even unearthed a few cases overseas, mostly in Romania, dating back nearly a year, close to the time of the newspaper stories. It was starting to look like the professor's predictions contained a grain of truth.

He was examining the progress of one of the bite patients when the screaming started.

They were a man's screams, and not just the usual cry for help you heard on a hospital ward, but something more primal, more desperate. He extricated himself from his task and ran to the source of the cries on the nearby ward.

It was Mr Lancross, the elderly patient Chanita had told him about.

The other patient, Jack Clarke, was leaning over him, lunging at his throat like a maniac. He was still attached to an IV drip by his arm. His skin was deathly white, his eyes covered with the now familiar yellow film, much like a cataract, that was one of the clearest visible symptoms of the condition.

The old man, Mr Lancross, was fending him off with weak arms, but didn't look like he could last much longer. A nurse was trying to help, but was unable to hold the patient back. The younger patient had some mad strength about him, even though he had been close to death just a week earlier.

Doctor Kapoor ran to him and tried to pull him off. 'Mr Clarke, stop that!'

The patient turned to him, a crazed look on his face, his eyes burning yellow. He didn't speak, just snarled like a dog and pushed the doctor to the floor with unnatural strength.

Doctor Kapoor shouted for help, but the nurses close by seemed too scared to intervene.

The man turned back to Mr Lancross, slapping his face and clawing at him, growling as he rained down blows on his victim. The old man writhed in his bed, desperately trying to fend off the attack.

Doctor Kapoor struggled back to his feet. 'Mr Clarke!'

The man had Mr Lancross in a tight grip now, sinking his nails into the age-mottled skin of the old man's arms. Pinning him to the bed, he thrust his mouth to his victim's neck and bit. Mr Lancross shrieked, thrashing from side to side as his own blood spattered across his face.

Doctor Kapoor had no time to think. No one was coming to help. He kicked at the younger man, striking him just behind the knee.

The man's leg crumpled and he collapsed to the floor in a howl of rage and pain. The IV crashed down next to him, the needle still in his arm.

Doctor Kapoor looked on, appalled. He was a medic, here to care for his patients. And yet …

The patient pushed himself up from the floor, his yellow eyes now fixed on Doctor Kapoor.

'Help!' shouted the doctor. 'Some help in here, please!'

The old man, Mr Lancross, was already going into anaphylactic shock.

Chanita arrived, bringing a hospital porter with her. The new arrival grappled with the patient, while Chanita struggled to administer an injection, presumably a sedative to calm him down.

As Doctor Kapoor watched, Mr Clarke threw out an arm and knocked the syringe out of Chanita's hands. With an inhuman shriek, he broke his other arm free from the porter's grip and lashed out, raking the man's face with his sharp, long fingernails.

The porter cried out and staggered back, a red slash drawn from his chin to his ear. His right ear flapped loose where it had been partially severed.

Chanita searched for the dropped syringe, but it had vanished from view. 'I'll get more help,' she cried.

'Mr Clarke, please calm down,' Doctor Kapoor told the patient. 'You're safe here. No one is trying to hurt you.

You're in hospital. But you are very ill. You must calm down.'

The man seemed not to understand the words. He turned his gaze on the doctor, fixing him with a yellow stare that was more animal than human. A deep growl emerged from his mouth, growing louder and turning into a roar of rage.

Doctor Kapoor backed away from the man, trying to draw him away from the other patients on the ward. The man followed him.

The doctor scanned the floor, searching for the syringe that Chanita had dropped. It lay about ten feet to his left. He edged slowly toward it, circling the man until the syringe was just a foot away from him. The man continued to snarl and growl, no human words in those sounds.

The doctor stepped left again and crouched down warily, watching for any sudden movement. The patient clawed the air between them with his bloody fingers, but did not come closer.

Doctor Kapoor reached for the syringe and grasped it with his right hand. He rose steadily to his full height. 'Okay, calm now,' he said in measured tones. 'Stay calm and everything will be all right.' He held the syringe tightly, waiting for his chance.

Chanita returned with three more porters in her wake and Mr Clarke turned to face them.

Doctor Kapoor rushed forward and grabbed the man's arm. He managed to get the needle into his arm and pushed the plunger down hard, watching as the clear liquid disappeared down the barrel of the syringe and into the man's bloodstream.

He stepped back from the patient, waiting for the sedative to take effect, but as he did so the man seemed to find a final surge of strength. He crossed the few feet that separated them and lunged at the doctor, clawing him with his deadly fingernails. The doctor felt pain as the nails ripped into his right arm, drawing out a fountain of blood.

The man came on relentlessly, punching and kicking like a cornered beast. But it was the doctor who was cornered. He pressed himself up against the nearest bed, fending off blows from the madman before him. The sedative should surely have calmed him by now, but the punches and kicks seemed to be getting faster and more furious.

The porters rushed forward to grab him, but as they did so, Mr Clarke lunged forward one last time and sank his teeth deep into the doctor's neck.

The pain was intense, but it lasted just briefly. The man withdrew his jaws, taking a chunk of flesh in his bloody teeth. The doctor watched in a dreamlike state as blood splashed from the open wound, soaking the patient's clothes in crimson stains. A smile spread across the young man's face as he chewed the flesh. All the fight had gone out of him now and he seemed satisfied at last. He didn't struggle when the porters dragged him to the floor and Chanita administered more sedative.

Doctor Kapoor didn't struggle either as his legs gave way beneath him. A feeling of tranquillity had descended over him like a shroud. The rapid blood loss from the severed jugular was like a drug, numbing the pain, quenching any fear. He allowed gravity to do its work, sliding him to the floor, just like his patient. At least he had done his duty to the last, giving himself to his patients. No one would ever be able to take that from him. A smile came to his face then, his last one, and he gave it to Chanita.

Chapter Thirty-Nine

Clapham Common, South London, full moon

The leader of the Wolf Brothers went by the name of Warg Daddy. *Leader of the Pack*, they called him. That had been his idea. He'd always been obsessed with werewolves, so the possibility of becoming one was beyond awesome. Trouble was, it was proving to be harder than he'd expected.

First you had to catch yourself a real live werewolf. Then you had to make it bite you without letting the goddamn motherfucker kill you. Neither step was easy. Kidnapping those dogs from the kennels had been a dummy run. Pretty stupid idea, now he came to think of it. What use was it getting a goddamn dog to bite you? All you got was a nasty flesh wound and a risk of catching some horrible disease. They'd had to get rid of the dogs in the end. That idea was going nowhere.

So now they were trying to catch themselves an actual

werewolf, which was turning out to be difficult. He suspected that half of the Brothers didn't even believe in werewolves. Perhaps more than half. Maybe most of them. But that didn't matter. Warg Daddy was their Leader and they would do what he said. The biggest problem was that the moon was full only one goddamn day a month. How could you work with that? But Warg Daddy was no quitter. The Pack depended on him. He had come up with a plan that seemed workable.

You wanted to catch a fish, you needed bait. Same thing with a werewolf.

Bait.

The trouble was, who? Most of the Pack looked pretty unappetizing to Warg Daddy. Too much facial hair, not enough baths. He wouldn't fancy sinking his teeth into any of them unless he'd downed a good few pints to warm himself up first. No self-respecting werewolf would want to gobble one of the Wolf Brothers in a hurry. They needed a more attractive morsel. That's what they were doing now, trying to find one.

With hindsight, the girl who had been looking after the dogs would have been just perfect for the job. A cute redhead, barely sixteen by Warg Daddy's reckoning. He'd happily have nibbled her himself but the chance was gone. Hindsight was a good thing for sure, but not as helpful as foresight. They'd just have to locate another suitable girl.

In fact, Warg Daddy couldn't believe his luck. One was coming their way right now.

They'd stationed themselves up on Clapham Common in the hope of picking up a tasty late-night jogger. The Common was a good place to hang, big enough to hide in, popular enough to find some innocent passer-by to accost. And it had been where the Beast had first been spotted, exactly one month previously. A Ripper murder had taken place here recently too. Half a naked torso discovered next to a muddy track. The police were still searching for the other half. Good luck with that.

The sky had been clear earlier, but a cold drizzly rain had begun to fall as they left their bikes by the roadside and set out across the Common, the mud sucking noisily at their boots. Warg Daddy worried about Pack morale. The moon was full tonight, but thick cloud covered the London sky and completely hid it from view. He hoped that wouldn't be a problem.

Anyway they'd been here less than half an hour and the perfect bait had already made her appearance. Tall and slim with long blonde hair tied up in a ponytail, she looked like a cheerleader or something. The girl wore shorts, more like hotpants, and a sports vest, and came running right toward them, her long, long legs stretching and flexing as she ran. Droplets of rain sparkled on her hair and face like jewels, but the girl seemed not to care about the cold or the wet.

The Pack watched intently, almost hypnotized by the girl's graceful movements.

Snakebite whistled loudly. 'Now that is serious wolf bait,' he said appreciatively, stroking his long red beard.

Wombat shook his head. 'Too good to waste on a frigging wolf, I say.'

Warg Daddy said nothing, just rubbed the skin on his bald head and watched. He narrowed his eyes as the girl ran right up to the Pack and stopped in front of them. His eyes flicked between her pink shorts and her blue eyes. 'Hey,' he said, trying to keep his cool. This girl was totally hot.

She looked him up and down, her face expressionless, like she was X-raying him with her gaze. He shifted uncomfortably under those clear blue eyes, making his leather jacket squeak. He rubbed the smooth skin on his head more firmly the longer she looked. He relaxed as she shifted her attention to each of the other guys in turn. They shuffled their feet or cleared their throats nervously as she made her round of the Pack.

After she'd given them all the low-down, her red lips broke into a wide smile, although the blue eyes stayed cold. 'Hello boys,' she said. 'Looking for trouble?'

'No,' said Warg Daddy. 'We were looking for you.'

The girl laughed. 'So you found me. Now what?'

'Now we have some fun.'

'I like fun.'

The girl's manner made Warg Daddy nervous. Either she was one dumb-ass chick, or else she knew something he didn't. She didn't look dumb to him. He rubbed his head harder than ever.

Snakebite had something he wanted to say. 'Dude, this chick is hot. Why don't we ... you know ... before we ... you know ...' He trailed off under Warg Daddy's stern gaze.

'No,' said Warg Daddy firmly. If anyone round here was a dumb-ass, it was Snakebite. 'Tonight's our best chance. This chick's a gift. We stay on plan.'

The girl walked right up to him and ran her fingers down his arm, rubbing the black leather of his jacket. 'I like hairy bikers. Is that a tattoo on your neck?'

Warg Daddy showed it to her. 'It's a wolf. A warg in fact. Know what a warg is?'

The girl shook her head innocently, her blonde ponytail swaying.

'Wargs come from Norse mythology,' he told her. 'They were giant wolves with the power of speech.'

Wombat stepped forward and showed her a similar tattoo on his own neck. 'The wargs will kill the old gods in the End Days, the time of Ragnarök,' he intoned.

Warg Daddy glared at him. Wombat was always spouting some shite.

'So the stories say,' added Wombat.

The girl approached him, touching the tattoo on his neck. 'The End Days,' she mused, almost to herself. 'I have a tattoo as well,' she said, showing Wombat a flower on her shoulder. 'And I like wolves too,' she said. 'Do you know why?'

'No,' said Wombat. He tried to draw away, but the girl shot out her hand and grasped his scrawny neck, squeezing it hard and pulling him closer. She seemed surprisingly strong for a girl. Wombat whimpered quietly.

'Some of my best friends are wolves,' she whispered to him. 'In fact, do you want to hear a secret?'

Wombat nodded nervously. The girl parted her lips and drew his head down so that she could whisper in his ear. 'I am a werewolf,' she said. Then she bit him hard, sinking her teeth deep into the side of his neck, severing the carotid artery in a single bite. She released her grip and stepped back to watch.

A fountain of blood gushed from Wombat's neck, spraying fine red drops over the entire Pack. He screamed and clutched at the wound, his eyes turning wildly in search of help. Nobody moved. The blood rushed out in waves, each one less powerful than the one preceding, until finally just a dribble flowed. Wombat shrieked again and fell to the muddy ground. He thrashed his legs and arms for half a minute before settling down to a gentle twitching. Still nobody had moved.

The girl licked her red lips. 'My, that was fun. You guys weren't kidding me. Anyone else like to play?'

Snakebite stepped forward over Wombat's body, pulling a switch blade from his jacket. 'Bitch. You'll die for that.'

Warg Daddy hauled him back. 'You moron. She's a fucking werewolf.'

'I know that,' said Snakebite. 'She just killed Wombat.'

'Never mind that now,' said Warg Daddy. 'Don't you get it? We don't need to use her as bait to catch a werewolf because she is one.'

Comprehension dawned on Snakebite. 'How can we

trust her, though? Look what she did.'

'Yeah, sure,' said Warg Daddy, glancing at the dead man at his feet. Wombat's body lay still now, and he was glad of that. 'But that's because she had surprise. She can't take us all, can she?' He glanced around at the Pack for reassurance. He didn't get much.

Warg Daddy sighed. It was time for him to demonstrate once again why he was Leader of the Pack.

He risked a look up at the night sky. The rain had stopped. Thin clouds scudded quickly above the Common, driven by the winter wind. The moon glowed faintly now behind a thin haze, but it was still covered. If the girl transformed into wolf form under full moonlight, then judging from her performance so far, they would all end up as wolf food. But if he could persuade her to help them, then they still stood a chance.

He would play it carefully though. If he wanted to walk away from here in one piece, he would need to use wolf cunning himself.

He spoke to the girl. 'You've been a lot of fun already, but we're tired of that game now. I've got a better idea.'

The girl smiled her red smile. 'Go on.'

'I'm going to offer you a choice. Either we can cut your throat' – he nodded at Snakebite, who obliged by flicking his knife open – 'or you can bite each one of us on the arm and turn us into werewolves too.'

The girl considered his offer. 'What makes you think I would do that?'

'We're the Wolf Brothers,' said Warg Daddy, hoping that was reason enough. 'We could be good together, you and us.'

The girl paced back and forth, studying the Pack closely. Snakebite snarled as she inspected him. The other guys pulled out their knives and did their best to look mean. Warg Daddy stood back, playing it cool. Eventually she said, 'Well, like I said, I am very fond of hairy bikers.'

Warg Daddy nodded. 'Snakebite,' he said to the man next to him. 'Kneel down.'

'What the fuck, man?' said Snakebite.

'You heard. Get on your knees.'

Snakebite shot daggers at him, but after a moment he did as he was told.

'Do him first,' said Warg Daddy to the girl. 'Then we'll know if you're just shitting us.'

The girl sidled up to Snakebite and grabbed him by his long dirty hair. She dropped to her knees and drew his head close to hers.

'Not my neck, man,' begged Snakebite. 'Bite my arm. That's how it works, yeah? A little bite on the arm won't kill me, will it?'

The girl drew her lips across the ginger hairs on his cheek. 'You'd better take off your jacket, then,' she told him.

Snakebite didn't waste any time doing it. He rolled up his shirt sleeve, revealing a meaty arm brushed with red hair. 'Do it,' he said. 'Do it quick.'

The girl opened her lips wide, rolling them back from her teeth. Her teeth were sharp, like a dog's. She placed them against Snakebite's skin and bit gently, just enough to draw blood. She licked and sucked at the blood for a moment until it ceased to flow. Snakebite watched with a look of horrified fascination. 'There,' said the girl. 'That didn't hurt, did it?'

The man shook his head and stood up. He put his jacket back on. 'Am I a werewolf now?' he asked, a dazed look on his face.

'Soon you will be,' said the girl. 'If you're strong enough to survive the transformation.'

Warg Daddy unzipped his own jacket and dropped it to the ground. 'My turn now.' He kneeled down, rolling up his shirt sleeve as Snakebite had done.

The girl bit into his arm as before, sucking hard to

draw out the blood. Warg Daddy shuddered. The girl's bite felt tender, almost like a caress. He wanted it to last, and felt regret the instant she pulled her lips away. When it was done he looked deep into her eyes, feeling moved in a way he'd never expected. 'You are a Wolf Brother now,' he said with awe. 'You are one of us.'

'No,' said the girl, shaking her head. 'Now you are one of us.'

The moon's rays crept from behind the thin cloud then, and he watched in stunned silence as she transformed into wolf. Her thin clothing ripped to rags as muscles rippled beneath her skin, and golden fur grew to cover her new body from snout to tail. What power she had concealed within her fragile human form. No wonder she had killed Wombat with such ease. The girl had gone, and a monstrous beast paced the ground now, pawing roughly at the grass, snorting thick breath in the cold air. It rose onto its hind legs and howled at the moon, a wailing sound filled with a sadness that Warg Daddy felt as much as heard.

When the creature had finished it dropped back to all fours. 'Who's next?' growled the wolf.

Chapter Forty

Department of Genetics, Imperial College, Kensington, London

Doctor Helen Eastgate looked gloomily out of her office window toward the Imperial College Business School on Exhibition Road, just opposite. The Business School was a recent addition to the Kensington campus, and had an outer wall of sheer glass that allowed her to peer inside and watch the building's occupants go about their business. They scurried along its well-lit corridors, past the giant Christmas tree that had been placed near the building's entrance, climbed its open staircases and sat in its bright lecture theatres like hard-working and attentive insects.

Helen's latest post-grad student, Leanna Lloyd, also applied herself diligently to her studies like a bee or an ant. But in contrast to the transparency of the glass building opposite, Leanna wore an opaque shell of icy professionalism that prevented Helen catching even a glimpse of her interior thoughts or motives.

Leanna refused resolutely to let Helen into her world. She had tried to connect with the girl, but Leanna seemed unable or unwilling to form any kind of emotional attachment. Perhaps she had no emotions. Her steely blue eyes were as cold as ice. If the eyes were a window to the human soul, then Leanna must be soulless.

Helen sighed. Usually her young students had too many emotions on display, all bubbling to the surface and pulling in different directions at once. Helen despaired at some of them. But at least she felt she understood them. Leanna offered no clues to what she was thinking.

Making no headway into Leanna's state of mind with a direct approach, Helen had instead busied herself with some background reading. Her findings disturbed her.

She'd checked out Leanna's story about her father and brother being killed in a car crash. The story was true as far as it went. What Leanna had omitted to mention was that the inquest into their deaths had returned an open verdict, with the coroner being unable to rule out the possibility that their car had been deliberately tampered with. Nobody had been accused of any misdemeanour, but with Leanna being the sole beneficiary, the deaths seemed remarkably convenient.

By pulling some strings she had also managed to uncover the original unpublished material Professor Norman Wiseman had submitted to the *International Journal of Virology, Epidemiology and Communicable Diseases*. The paper was entitled *Horizontal Gene Transfer in Multicellular Organisms: A Small Case Study*. It was hardly a blockbuster title, and the Professor had seemingly gone out of his way to play down his claims. He had couched everything in the ultra-cautious language of an academic who knew that he was playing with fire.

But if his experiments were to be believed, he had uncovered something previously thought to be impossible – a means of transferring genetic material from one living creature to another. The mechanism was already known to occur in bacteria and other single-celled organisms, but Wiseman claimed to have observed it in higher animals. If verified, that would potentially be enough to win a Nobel Prize in Medicine, but Wiseman had gone further. The animals he had studied were none other than human beings. Even more alarming, the genes that he claimed to be transferable via this new pathway could supposedly endow the recipient with super-human strength, agility, sensory perception, and other qualities that were frankly impossible to believe. No wonder he had been ridiculed by his colleagues. No wonder the word *werewolf* had appeared in newspaper articles.

And yet the professor had been highly respected in his field before his fall from grace. He had described his experiments in minute detail in the paper, and at face value his work looked like a careful piece of scientific study. Helen frowned at some of the ethical issues with the way he had conducted his experiments, but Wiseman should never have been treated the way he had. At the very least, an attempt to replicate his results should have been made by the scientific community. But of course the paper had never been published in the scientific journal. Only a misleading and sensationalized account of Wiseman's claims had appeared in the popular newspapers.

The paper had three authors listed in addition to Professor Wiseman – Leanna Lloyd, and two other postgrads, Adam Knight and Samuel Smalling. Helen had made enquiries about Adam and Samuel. Both students had returned to London, and had also switched their research into the genetics of infectious diseases, just like Leanna.

The conclusion was inescapable. Whatever the truth or otherwise of Professor Wiseman's theory, all three students clearly believed in it, despite what Leanna had said about wanting a fresh start. And together they were secretly studying it for some unknown purpose.

Whatever that purpose was, they were working at it with zeal. Leanna could be found in the lab all hours of the day and night, and what she claimed to be doing bore little resemblance to what she was actually doing. She was embarked on some secret research project of her own, and had gone to great lengths to conceal it from Helen. A less attentive supervisor might not have noticed. But not much slipped past Helen Eastgate.

Helen had always thought of herself as a deeply rational person, naturally sceptical and hard to convince. *Show me the evidence,* she was fond of saying. *Stubborn,* her colleagues called her. But science was built on empirical evidence, and she could hardly push aside the weight of evidence that was steadily accumulating before her. She picked up her copy of the morning's newspaper from her desk. The front-page headline read, *Three Killed in New Beast Attack.* The horrific incident had taken place at a railway station the previous evening. The uncanny similarities between the Beast attacks and the description of the disease symptoms so meticulously documented by Professor Wiseman were impossible to ignore.

Much as she wanted to dismiss the notion as ridiculous, she could no longer turn aside from the simple explanation that matched all the available data: there was a werewolf in London, and its name was Leanna Lloyd.

Chapter Forty-One

*Camberwell Cemetery & Crematorium,
South London, waning moon*

A funeral was a tragedy at any time of year, but just before Christmas it seemed doubly so. PC Liz Bailey stood at the back of the crematorium doing her best not to cry. If necessary she would try to cover it up as her cold, or flu, or whatever the damned thing was. She'd been feeling rundown ever since that night on the Common, the night she'd first heard the news of Dave Morgan's death. Her eyes had been inflamed and stinging even before the service started, but she wouldn't have missed this funeral even if she'd had to be carried in on her own death bed.

'You really should go and see a doctor,' PC Dean Arnold told her as she blew hard into her handkerchief. 'That cold's getting worse by the day.'

'Doctors can't cure colds,' whispered Liz. 'Antibiotics don't work against viruses.'

'Well, just go home and lie down for a few days,' insisted Dean. 'Stay in bed with a hot water bottle. I don't want to catch it, whatever you've got.'

'Thanks for your sympathy,' said Liz. 'Just for a moment there, I thought you cared.' She rubbed her upper arm where the madman on the Common had scratched her with his fingernails. The wound wasn't deep, but it had flared up red and angry. She had plastered it with antiseptic cream and taken some aspirins, and it wasn't bothering her so much now. The cold, or flu, was the real nuisance. That had started at the same time, worst luck. Her arms ached, and she'd developed a sore throat and a runny nose. A kind of milky film had appeared over her eyes. She'd got herself an extra-large box of honey-and-lemon lozenges to suck, and they were helping a bit.

'I owe you an apology, actually,' said Dean sheepishly. 'You were right about that headmaster. I should have had more faith in you.'

'Wow,' said Liz. 'I've never heard you apologize to anyone before.'

'Yeah, well. You were right. I was wrong. I'm sorry.'

'It's okay. How could anyone have guessed it? A cannibalistic headmaster. It's not surprising you told me it was a ridiculous idea.'

'I could have been more open-minded. A bit more sensitive.'

'Sensitive? But then you wouldn't be the Dean Arnold we all know and love.'

'S'pose.'

The night after the headmaster had been arrested, Liz had lain awake tormenting herself. If she'd followed up on her hunch, the headmaster might had been arrested sooner. Then he wouldn't have been able to kill that schoolgirl. And yet, what could Liz have done differently? She'd had no real evidence. On the contrary, she'd seen the Romanian man eating his victim on the Common with her own eyes. How could she possibly have known that more than one serial killer was at work?

She wiped her eyes with the last remaining clean corner of her handkerchief. The milkiness that covered them came away, leaving a pale, creamy stain on the cloth.

Police officers were supposed to be tough, but there was no shortage of tears here today, even on the cheeks of the biggest and strongest men. She'd had no idea that Dave Morgan had been so popular. Hundreds of mourners had come to the funeral, most of them from the force, and the Police Commissioner himself had put in an appearance, in full uniform. He stood up now and walked to the front of the room to stand on a podium next to the coffin.

'Police Constable David Morgan was a brave man,' began the Commissioner, speaking in the resonant baritone voice that had surely been a key factor in his appointment. 'He believed in a fair and just world, a world where ordinary people may live out their lives in safety.'

The Commissioner paused to make sure that he had the full attention of his audience. There was no question that he did. 'Our civilization is built on principles of fairness, equality and justice. It protects the weak and the vulnerable against the strong, and ensures that the law applies equally to all, whatever their background, be they young or old, rich or poor, and whatever their race, religion, or gender.

'We cannot and must not take these principles for granted. What we in this country now regard as fundamental human rights were in former times merely dreams and aspirations. Now our liberty and our security are enshrined in law.

'Such a world cannot come about by accident. Each one of us must work each day toward creating the kind of society we wish to live in. Those of us who are strong must do more, and risk more, and sometimes sacrifice more than others to achieve this goal. Society demands that some among us put themselves in danger in order to keep others safe. Dave Morgan was one of those willing to do that, and everyone here today will acknowledge their debt to Dave. What some might call heroism, Dave thought of as duty. He died in the line of that duty, giving his life willingly in the service of those he sought to protect. As such, he serves as an example to us all.'

The Commissioner paused, moving his gaze around all those present, many of them known to him personally, Liz guessed. Finally, he returned his attention to the family on the front row.

'My sincere condolences go to Dave Morgan's widow, Claire, and their two daughters.' He nodded toward the grieving women dressed in black, Claire hugging her two sobbing teenage girls close, torn between their need to express their grief and a desire to retain their dignity.

'I would also like to thank Dave's partner, Police Constable Liz Bailey. Liz was on duty with Dave Morgan the night he was attacked, and did her best to protect him and keep him from harm. I would like to thank Liz, and commend her for her bravery and selflessness.'

Liz felt her face and neck turning beetroot. This should have been all about Dave, not her. And if Liz had been truly brave and fearless, Dave would never have been bitten. She stared down at her feet, feeling eyes turning toward her.

Dean stood implacably by her side, and she suddenly felt very glad of his solid bulk and unflinching bullet head next to her. The big man stood silently, staring straight ahead. *Yet another everyday hero,* thought Liz grimly. This room was full of them and she hoped she would never have to attend any more funerals like this.

The Police Commissioner returned to his seat, and the congregation began a hymn. Liz fought back her tears and tried to sing, but it was no good. She had never been a singer or a crier, but now the tears flowed freely and she sobbed loudly as those around sang *Abide With Me.*

'He didn't mention the Beast,' said Dean after the

service had ended. 'I thought he would say something about it at the funeral.'

The Beast was front page news following the slaughter at the railway station the previous evening, filling acres of newspaper columns and enjoying wall-to-wall TV news coverage. The Police Commissioner had come under intense pressure to 'do something' about the Beast, but so far he had not commented officially. Liz wondered if he was waiting until after the funeral before making an announcement.

'This funeral was Dave's time,' Liz said to Dean. 'It was about him and his family, not some wild animal.' The Police Commissioner had been right to focus on Dave. It had been a time to grieve with dignity, a quiet moment amid the mayhem.

The mayhem resumed as soon as they left the church. Photographers lined the street outside hoping to catch the mourners as they filed away. Questions were shouted, and microphones thrust forward. Liz turned away and drew up the collar of her coat to hide her face as cameras flashed. Dave Morgan's death was just a news story to them. Dave would get his five minutes of fame, and then the journalists would move on to something else. But there would always be a quiet space in Liz's heart for her fallen friend and colleague.

When she returned home that evening, she wasn't surprised to see the face of the Police Commissioner again. This time he was on TV accompanying the Mayor of London. The two men were making a joint statement intended to reassure the public in response to the recent Beast killings.

The Mayor was just finishing his speech. 'And so I would like to reassure the public that we are determined to do everything within our power to make the streets and public spaces of London safe again, and I will now pass you over to the Commissioner of Police to outline the operational details.'

The Commissioner stepped up to the podium, looking much as he had done that afternoon at the funeral. 'Thank you, Mayor,' he said. 'Beginning today, I am pleased to announce the deployment of more armed police on the streets of London. Initially, five hundred specially-trained officers will begin patrolling key sites such as railway stations, public squares, parkland and other designated locations. A reserve force of an additional five hundred officers is available should it prove necessary.

'This new elite force will be equipped with SIG 516 semi-automatic carbines, sniper rifles, and Glock nine-millimetre sidearms. They will be protected by Kevlar suits, reinforced helmets, and riot shields. The force will be mobile, with access to specially-adapted BMW F800 all-terrain motorcycles capable of reaching top speeds of one-hundred-and-twenty miles per hour. In addition, they will have access to rigid inflatable hull vessels and helicopters, enabling them to respond rapidly to incidents anywhere within the city.

'The new force will be highly visible, with a key goal of providing reassurance to the public, and I would urge all citizens to support this initiative by calling the telephone number below with any information that may help us to do our job. Thank you.'

A phone number appeared in the lower part of the screen, and the scene switched to a video showing the new police officers, dressed in distinctive military-style uniforms, carbines in hand, black masks covering their faces. Liz shuddered slightly, whether from the sight of the armed police or from the fever that had still not abated, she couldn't be sure.

After the Commissioner had finished speaking, reporters began calling questions. As well as questions about the Beast, Liz was sure she heard the word Ripper being shouted, but the Mayor and Commissioner left without answering any questions.

Liz shut the TV off. Her limbs felt as heavy as lead, and

the scratch on her arm had flared up again, despite the ointment she'd been applying. Aspirin wasn't really working, she had to admit. She felt like she wanted to lie down and sleep forever, but her alarm was set for six the next morning. As the Commissioner had said at the funeral, those who were strong must do more. Liz wondered how strong she really was, and how much more she still had to do.

Chapter Forty-Two

Greenfield Road, Brixton, South London, waning moon

What James had done at the train station was even worse than killing Father Mulcahy. He and Samuel had attacked dozens of commuters, maiming or killing them mercilessly. He watched the aftermath of their butchery on the news afterwards: terrified people talking about how a beast had savaged their loved ones; victims lying in hospital beds, some with life-changing injuries, some already in the grip of anaphylactic shock from the infection he had given them. Several had died; more would die of their injuries. Some would change and become like him. A monster.

James knew he should feel guilt for what he'd done. Those people had been innocent. Not one of them had deserved to die. He and Samuel hadn't even eaten all their meat. They had killed for the sake of killing itself.

He should feel guilt.

And yet …

All that savagery had seemed as natural as breathing. He couldn't regret it.

Who could blame a predator for killing its prey?

Hurt and suffering afflicted the very core of the world. An earthquake had struck South America just the day before, leaving a hundred people dead in remote villages in the Andes. One reporter said that many of the victims in one village had sought shelter in a church, only for the roof of the building to fall in on their heads. Where was the sense of it?

Did God feel guilty for causing the earthquake? If not, how could James feel guilty about what he had done?

'My God, I am sorry for my sins with all my heart,' he began. He stopped. The words no longer rang true.

Everything he had done last night was wrong. He knew that. He had eaten human flesh and drunk human blood. But it had felt so right. Hadn't Jesus himself commanded his followers to consume the bread of his body and the wine of his blood during the Eucharist?

James had been seeking meaning all of his life, and now, together with Samuel, he seemed to have found some at last. He wasn't going to allow guilt to rob him of that.

He dropped to his knees and prayed again for guidance, but God remained silent.

Whatever.

James had found a new family. He no longer needed the family of the Christian Church.

Father Mulcahy had once told him that Hell was nothing more nor less than separation from God. If that were true, then James was in Hell right now. He'd had no idea it could feel so good.

Chapter Forty-Three

Queen's Road, Harrow on the Hill, North London

'Let me tell you about Jack the Ripper,' said the man.

Melanie Margolis lay sprawled on the bed, her hands and feet bound tightly to the metal bed posts with ropes. She wasn't averse to being tied up now and then, in fact she expected it in her line of work, sometimes even enjoyed it, but this was taking things too far. Much too far. Sarah had warned her that something like this might happen, but of course she never heeded warnings.

She tried to recall the details of what had happened. Details could be vital, especially in a life-or-death situation. But thinking was so hard. Her head throbbed like a train had run across it.

It had been a fancy restaurant, she remembered that. They usually were, but this one had been particularly expensive. The guy obviously liked to impress a girl by

Lycanthropic

flashing his cash. And Melanie had always been a sucker for a good-looking man with money.

The warning signs had been there from the beginning. She should have bailed out after the soup course, certainly before dessert. But she had stupidly stayed to the end, and even gone home with the guy afterwards, so who could she blame but herself?

The man was a talker. Her sister had warned her about talkers. Guys who talked about themselves all the time – it was one of the primary indicators of a psychopath. Sarah read a lot of books about psychology. Or was it psychiatry? Melanie would have to ask her when she got out of this mess. If she ever got out.

Psychopaths didn't scare Melanie. Half the guys she dated displayed strong psychopathic tendencies – glib charm, an inflated sense of self-importance, pathological lying. Sarah liked to point out that Melanie shared many of these attributes herself.

Whatever the psychological theories, Melanie had known there was something wrong with this guy right from the start. He'd spent most of their dinner date telling her about his ex-wife and why that bitch would never get a penny out of him, no matter how many fancy lawyers she hired to do her dirty work. By the time the waiter brought the bill, Melanie had a pretty clear idea why his wife had left him, but she made sure to smile prettily and keep her opinions to herself.

He was still talking now, telling her something about Jack the Ripper, but it was very much a one-way conversation. With a gag in her mouth, she wasn't able to contribute anything beyond the occasional grunt or nod of the head.

They'd driven back in a black taxi cab to somewhere in North London, … that's right, Harrow. Very posh. A smart apartment in a converted Victorian mansion block.

He'd hit her with something. A stick, or a cane, or … yes, that was it, a cricket bat. Sarah would probably have had some insight into what that was all about. Some kind of insecurity going back to his school days, no doubt. She'd blacked out immediately after that. And then he must have tied her to the metal bed posts. He didn't seem to have undressed her, though. So this wasn't about sex. The ropes and the knots must be more of a boy scout thing.

She looked up at him through her stinging eyes, her bound tongue unable to form words. Her left eye had swollen up and was half-closed. That half of her vision was painted red.

Focus, Melanie, listen to what he's saying.

He seemed to be working up to some kind of point at last, after what seemed like hours of disjointed rambling. 'Do you know what Jack the Ripper did to his victims?' demanded the man. 'He eviscerated them.' He articulated the word with care, in five distinct syllables, as if he had been rehearsing it. 'That means he cut their insides out of them,' he explained, just in case she wasn't already familiar with the word.

'Do you know how many women he murdered? Do you?' Melanie moved her head from side to side as much as she could. The movement triggered a fresh bout of intense pain. 'Five. At least five. Maybe eleven. Possibly even more. Nobody knows for certain. It might have been dozens. Dozens of dead women. Eviscerated. Dirty prostitutes, all of them. Just like you.' His eyes flicked over her body, and then around the room.

A prostitute? She didn't recall having entered into any kind of contractual arrangement with this man, nor accepting payment for any services rendered. In fact, no services had been rendered. She was a thief, yes. A liar, certainly. But a prostitute? Technically not. She said nothing however. The gag saw to that.

'They never caught him, though. Do you know why?' Melanie shook her head again. 'He was too clever for them. Too clever by half.'

Lycanthropic

The man produced a knife suddenly and held it up to the light. 'See how it glints,' he said, twisting it one way, then the other.

Melanie watched intently. The knife did indeed glint.

He held it against her throat.

She tried to hold his gaze steadily, but his eyes darted in all directions. She struggled to move, but he had tied her arms and legs brutally tightly to the bed. In an attempt to distract him, she made a gurgling sound in her throat.

'Got something you want to say, have you?' he said, and his face filled with glee. 'Some famous last words? Think I care what you have to say? Think anyone cares? You're just a dirty prostitute. Nobody cares about you. Nobody.'

He removed the knife from her throat and began pacing the room in agitation. She listened hard to catch his words. 'Do it!' he mumbled to himself. 'Just do it!'

After a minute he returned and sat on the edge of the bed. The blade was on her throat again. She could feel its cold edge.

His eyes darted everywhere. 'What about the new Ripper? Have you heard of him? I bet you have. Everyone has. He's all over the news, isn't he? Famous. Can't get away from him.' He laughed. 'They can't catch him either, the police. They keep thinking they've caught him, but he's still out there. Still killing. Do you know what he does to his victims? He doesn't just cut them up, doesn't just eviscerate them, oh no.'

The man leaned in close. The blade pushed hard against her windpipe. Melanie held her breath.

'Eats them, he does. Gobbles them up for his dinner.' He sat back on the bed. The pressure of the blade eased a little. 'You thought you were being taken out for dinner, right? You little slut. Turns out you are dinner.'

The man laughed again and stood up. He waved the knife in front of her, slashing the blade through the air. The activity seemed to please him. 'I'll be back later,' he said and left the room. She heard the key turn in the lock.

She struggled again with the ropes that bound her, but they refused to loosen. She resigned herself to a wait, whether short or long, she couldn't guess. But he would be back at some time, and then who knew what might happen? Sarah might. She knew all about serial killers. She wondered how long it would be before her sister reported her missing, and whether the police would ever find her.

She stared up at the plain white square of the ceiling. A small crack ran along one edge of its elaborate cornice. She followed the line of the crack to the far corner of the room where it ended in one of the alcoves next to the chimney breast. There, a fat black spider busied itself with a captured fly that had become entangled in its web. Eviscerating it, probably.

She couldn't help but think of the look of terror that so often haunted Grandpa's eyes these days. Perhaps this was how he felt.

Chapter Forty-Four

Cambridge Street, South London, quarter moon

When PC Liz Bailey arrived at the centre for asylum seekers, events were already starting to spin out of control. The drop-in centre was a church hall belonging to the adjacent United Reformed Church on Cambridge Street. A large and angry crowd had gathered outside. Liz quickly counted at least forty people as the patrol car pulled up across the street.

The arrest of two Romanian men for the Ripper murders had been followed swiftly by speculation that a sinister gang of illegal immigrants was responsible for the crimes. The fact that a school headmaster had also been arrested seemed to have been forgotten in the rush to find a scapegoat.

The Ripper murders hadn't finished either, despite the three arrests. Another gruesome murder had taken place the previous night. The body of a young woman had been found dumped on waste ground in an area frequented by immigrants from Eastern Europe. The killing had borne all the hallmarks of a particularly violent Ripper murder, the corpse torn to ribbons, limbs ripped from the torso, the body partially eaten. It seemed that one or more murderers was still at large, and the finger was being pointed at the immigrant community.

Now local people had decided to take the law into their own hands.

'Bloody hell,' said Dean Arnold, who was driving the patrol car. 'This looks like a powder keg.'

Liz nodded grimly. Her flu was worse than ever, and the scratch on her arm was hurting like the devil. She had bandaged it up, but the wound kept weeping a yellow liquid. She had stepped up the painkillers from aspirins to ibuprofen, but her headache wasn't getting any better. Dealing with a violent protest was the last thing she needed right now.

The crowd of men, women and children was pushing up against the door of the church hall. The protesters held banners and placards and were shouting abuse at the people holed up inside. One of the banners read, *Romanians go home.* Another read, *Keep murderers out.* A smattering of English flags and Union Jacks waved above the heads of the crowd.

'How many people are in the building?' asked Dean.

'As many as twenty asylum seekers and volunteers. Come on.' Liz pushed open the door of the car and stepped into the throng.

Another two uniformed officers had already arrived and were trying to force their way to the door of the drop-in centre. Dean elbowed his way after them, pushing through the crowd like a bull. Liz decided to start pulling people away from the back.

Before she could get started, a woman came up to her and barred her way. 'You can't stop us from protesting,' said the woman. 'We're entitled to protect our community from these murderers.' She clutched two children close to her side.

Liz raised her voice above the sound of the chanting crowd. 'I'm going to ask you to step away from the community centre, madam. We need to clear a space so that your protest can proceed peacefully and the rights of the people inside the centre are protected too. Now if you'd just step back, we can allow you to continue your protest in peace.'

Two more women and some youths had joined the first woman. One of the youths stepped forward. 'Ain't gonna do that,' he said. 'Not until we've sent these Romanians a firm message.'

'Yeah,' shouted one of the other women, who was carrying a *Romanians go home* placard. 'Everyone knows that's where the murderers are from. They can't stay here. It ain't safe.'

'I'm going to ask you again to step aside peacefully,' said Liz. She was glad to hear the sound of sirens as two more police cars arrived. They were going to need at least a dozen uniforms to get this crowd under control.

'Ain't gonna do that,' repeated the youth. The women nodded in agreement behind him.

'Who's gonna make us?' shouted another youth who had pushed his way to the front. He wore a Union Jack baseball cap and had a scarf wrapped round his face.

'I must warn you that any use of threatening language or behaviour toward a police officer is a criminal offence,' said Liz. She stepped between the two youths and the women, trying to keep her antagonists apart. 'Please step back now and allow me to carry out my job.'

'No way,' said the second youth.

'They can't live here,' said the woman. 'They're murderers and criminals.'

Liz glanced behind her. The new police officers were engaged in stand-offs with protesters across the road. The crowd seemed to be growing as more people came out of side streets. Liz was on her own for now. She turned back to the youth with the scarf over his mouth.

'Stand back now!' she shouted. 'Get back!'

The two youths stepped forward.

Liz grabbed hold of the one with the scarf. 'I am going to arrest you for obstructing a police officer.' She pulled a set of speedcuffs from her duty belt and pushed one arm of the cuffs against the youth's right wrist. The cuffs snapped shut.

'Hey!' shouted the youth. 'What you doing?'

He was fully cuffed before he realized what had happened. Liz grabbed his arm with both hands and dragged him away from the others.

Behind her, she heard shouts from protesters and police alike as the protest started to become violent. A brick sailed over her head and smashed through the window of a parked car as she dragged the youth to a waiting police vehicle. She handed him over to another officer and turned back to the fray.

More police had arrived, but the protesters greatly outnumbered them. The demonstration had turned ugly, with bricks and bottles being thrown overhead. A police officer staggered from the scene with a bloody face. Others followed, bringing their arrests with them, but the crowd had now doubled in size. A large window of the community centre smashed and fell to the ground, scattering splinters of glass both inside and out.

Liz grabbed hold of two of the women carrying *Go home* placards and shouted at them to go home themselves.

'Not until you get rid of those Romanians,' said the woman with the children in tow. 'Yeah,' said her friend, defiantly.

A glass bottle smashed to the ground, scattering glass around the children's feet, making them scream.

'Come on,' said Liz urgently. 'Get out of here before you get hurt.'

The women nodded and left then, a look of fear in

their eyes.

More police cars arrived, and officers dashed out to help. Flashing blue lights reflected off the remaining windows of the building, blazing bright in the late afternoon gloom. The crowd began to break up in panic, with people running everywhere. Liz looked for Dean and found him protecting the main entrance to the centre. He was in a stand-off with two men. She pushed through the crowds toward him.

'Step away from the door!' Dean shouted at the men. 'Get back!' Dean was a burly man, but not as big as these guys. One stood a foot taller than Liz. She grabbed hold of him and pushed him up against the wall. As she did so, the other punched Dean in the face, giving him a bloody nose. Liz twisted the first man's arm behind his back until he cried out, and held him there. 'Help, over here!' she shouted, hoping for some assistance.

She felt a stab of pain in her back and let go of her captive, who ran off. Someone had punched her in the kidney. She clutched at her back and turned to see who had done it. She was just in time to see a hooded and masked youth run forward holding a beer bottle with a burning wick sticking out of the top. The youth hurled the petrol bomb through the shattered window of the drop-in centre, then vanished into the melee.

'Shit!' said Dean. He had subdued his opponent and had him cuffed on the ground. 'Get this bastard out of here. I'll break down the door.'

'No,' shouted Liz, rubbing her back. Adrenaline had pushed her pain into the background. 'I'll go in through the window.'

She stepped up onto the window ledge, avoiding the jagged glass teeth around the edge of the frame, and jumped into the burning building.

Chapter Forty-Five

Inside the drop-in centre, fire had already taken hold. A burning pool of petrol spilled over the floor, and flames ran up curtains and other soft furnishings. A Christmas tree in the corner was a fiery column, hung with blackening decorations. Smoke was starting to fill the air inside the hall. A smoke alarm bleeped frantically overhead.

Liz looked around. A couple of dozen people cowered toward the back of the main hall, away from the windows and door. One woman was seated, clutching a compress to a wound on her forehead. They gazed at Liz in terror.

The back wall of the church hall was windowless. Behind the people a door stood open, but looked to be an internal door leading to another room. There was a fire exit to one side, but the burning petrol had blocked access to it. Liz scanned the space for alternative exits, but the only way out seemed to be the main door behind her, and the broken window by which she had entered. The fire was spreading quickly along shelves of books, leaping from chairs to curtains to piles of cardboard boxes. Flames already reached up to the ceiling, licking it with bright red tongues.

'Quickly!' shouted Liz. 'Over here.' She gestured to the people to cross over to her, but they remained huddled together in a tight group.

She swore under her breath, and crossed the hall toward them, keeping close to the wall and away from the pool of burning petrol that filled much of the floor. The acrid smoke stung her eyes and made her cough. When she reached the group, she went first to the injured woman. 'Can you walk?' she asked.

The woman said nothing for a moment, then nodded.

Liz took hold of her hand. 'Come with me,' she said.

The woman rose to her feet unsteadily. Liz wrapped one arm around her waist and allowed the woman to lean her weight against her.

A second woman came to help. 'I'm the organizer,' she said. 'I'm in charge here.'

'How many people are in the building?' asked Liz.

The woman hesitated. 'Twenty, including me,' she said at last.

Liz realized that the woman was just as terrified as the refugees. 'Is anyone else injured?'

'No.'

'Then help me get her to safety.'

The three women set off, back toward the main entrance of the building. They had to move carefully, hugging the wall closely to avoid the fire. The injured woman was clearly in shock, and Liz half-dragged her along, making painfully slow progress. With each step the fire raged higher.

The smoke alarm had curled into a blackened twist of plastic and had ceased its warning wail. The time for warning was long past. The noise of the flames was now so great that Liz could hardly hear any sounds from outside. The black smoke made it hard to see. She pulled the woman onwards through the smoke and heat until they reached the exit.

The door had been locked from the inside, presumably to keep the protesters at bay. 'I have the key,' said the other woman. She fumbled in her pocket, searching for it.

Liz glanced back at the way they had come. The other people were following in single file, pressing themselves to the wall, away from the heat of the fire.

The woman brought out the key and pushed it toward the lock with trembling hands.

'Here,' said Liz. 'Let me help.' She took the key from the woman and twisted it in the lock. It turned and Liz pulled the handle to open the door.

Fresh air rushed in as she threw the door open, and she gulped it down in welcome lungfuls. But the fire welcomed it just as eagerly. Behind her the flames leaped higher, crackling and roaring, filling the space from floor to ceiling with their wild dance.

Two policemen rushed forward to help the women out of the building.

'Quickly!" shouted Liz, standing at the exit and pushing the people out into safety. She counted them as they went. Ten, ... twelve, ... they emerged one by one from the smoke. Fifteen, sixteen, ... she pushed them out through the door. Seventeen, eighteen, ...

The last one, a teenage girl, staggered through the heat and the smoke, clutching at her throat. She was the nineteenth to emerge. There was no one behind her.

The organizer had said that twenty people were inside.

Liz grabbed at the teenager frantically. 'Are you the last one? Is there anyone else inside?'

The girl nodded. 'One more,' she croaked. 'A boy.' A policeman led her out of the building.

Liz stared back at the raging fire. The noise and heat were overwhelming. She didn't know how anyone could still be alive in there, but if a boy was trapped inside ...

She filled her lungs with fresh air and dived back in, covering her nose with her hand.

Fire filled the entire building now and thick tangles of smoke made it difficult to see more than a few feet ahead. The heat was almost intolerable. She groped her way along the wall, retracing her steps into the furnace. There was no one coming to meet her. She couldn't bear to open her mouth to shout, and in any case the roar of the fire was deafening. Grimly she carried on in silence.

Her hand closest to the wall wrapped around something hard and angular – a black handle. She gripped it tightly. Below the handle was a red cylinder, fixed to the wall. A fire extinguisher. She ripped it from its bracket and pulled out the pin. Squeezing the trigger, she aimed the nozzle at the base of the fire in front of her. Pressurized water gushed from the hose, clearing a narrow path at her feet. She advanced forward, using the extinguisher to sweep out a safe route along the edge of the wall and around the corner to where the people had been waiting. There was no sign of anyone there. She wondered if she had made a mistake in her counting, but the girl had made it perfectly clear. A boy was trapped inside.

The fire extinguisher exhausted itself and she let it drop. The roar of the fire had grown so loud she didn't even hear the clang of the cylinder against the floor.

To her left was the interior door she had seen earlier. Previously it had been ajar. Now it was closed.

She gripped the door handle, but let go instantly. The metal was intensely hot. She pushed it down with her elbow, using her sleeve to protect her from the heat. The door swung open and she almost fell through to the room beyond. She forced the door shut behind her. Immediately she felt the temperature drop several degrees.

She was in a dim room, lit only by the light from a high, narrow window. There were no other exits. Smoke was filling the air, but she could see clearly enough for now. Crouched below the window was a boy, aged about ten. He had wrapped a cloth over his face to keep the smoke at bay. His head was a mop of dark hair and his eyes peeped out at her like big brown berries.

The boy jumped up and ran to her. He seemed to be unhurt.

Liz gripped his hand tightly. She opened the door back to the main hall, but the flames burned fiercer than ever. The safe path she had cleared with the fire extinguisher was completely gone. The fire rose up through the open doorway, seizing the opportunity to follow her inside. She slammed the door shut in its face.

With dismay, she clutched the boy tight. There was no way out of here.

He broke away from her and pointed up.

The window. It was barely large enough for anyone to fit through. And yet, if she could give the boy a chance to escape, she had to try.

She crouched below the window, forming her hands into a step. There was no need to speak; the boy immediately placed one foot onto her clasped hands and gripped her shoulders with his fingers. Liz lifted him up, rising to her full height to power him all the way to the window.

The window was locked. She heard him fiddle with the locking mechanism, and then felt a rush of cold air as the window opened and the fire drew in fresh oxygen. The boy scrabbled to open the window wide and she felt his weight vanish as he pulled himself out.

She looked up and saw his feet disappearing through the open window.

She was alone now. The heat had built to an intensity that made her skin burn. The paint on the door was blistering and peeling away. Smoke seeped around the edges as the door began to fail. She backed away from it, but there was nowhere to run, nowhere to hide.

A shout made her look up. At the open window a

fireman's face appeared. The face vanished and in its place a rope dropped down. She dived for it and began to climb. When she reached the top, strong arms gripped her and drew her through the window opening. It was tight, and she stuck fast for a moment, but suddenly she was free.

Flashing lights from fire engines and police cars dazzled her, but the fresh, cool air was the sweetest she had ever breathed.

Paramedics lifted her onto a stretcher and gave her oxygen. Gradually she felt her breathing returning to normal. The smell of smoke inside her lungs might never leave her again, but at least she was alive and safe. So was the boy. He stayed by her side while the medics ran checks on them both.

'What's your name?' Liz asked him, through her parched throat.

'Mihai,' said the boy. 'Is from Romania.'

'And are your parents here?'

'No. Are all dead,' said the boy, matter-of-factly. 'Is just me now.'

'How old are you, Mihai?'

'Is ten,' he said. 'What happens now?'

That was a very good question. They stayed with the paramedics for a while, but once Liz had recovered from the effects of smoke inhalation, the medical team told her she was free to go home. Mihai could go too, although it wasn't clear that he had a real home to go to any more.

Dean appeared. 'Thank God. I wondered what had happened to you. You didn't come out of the building.'

'I came out the back way,' said Liz. 'Me and Mihai here.'

'Good,' said Dean. 'What happens now?'

The same question again, still looking for an answer. And although she knew nothing about how to look after a ten-year-old boy, Liz surprised herself by offering to take Mihai home with her. Why not? The world was going to hell already.

Chapter Forty-Six

Covent Garden, Westminster, Central London

Chris Crohn sat across the dining table from Seth. He wore his new suit, the one he'd bought that afternoon from an expensive department store on Oxford Street. He flicked a crumb away from his bowl of soup and straightened his tie. This was the best restaurant he'd ever visited, and he was enjoying the lavish setting and delicious food. It made a change from munching microwaved pizza standing in the tiny footprint of his kitchen back in Manor Road.

By contrast, Seth looked like a startled animal on the other side of the table, his eyes drifting nervously around the subdued interior as waiters and waitresses took orders and brought dishes to the well-dressed diners. He flicked his long brown hair back, but it immediately returned to its former position, partly covering his thick glasses.

'Stop that,' hissed Chris in annoyance. 'Try not to look

like you don't belong here.' He stared pointedly at Seth's business-casual attire. A pair of chinos and a checked shirt might be suitable for Seth's office, but looked completely out of place in this environment.

A glob of spinach soup had found its way into Seth's goatee beard. Chris wondered whether he should draw his friend's attention to it, but decided not to bother.

'I don't belong here,' Seth hissed back. 'And neither do you. What are we doing in this place, and why did you waste your money on that ridiculous outfit?' He glared at Chris' tie and cufflinks.

'My suit isn't ridiculous at all. I bought it because it fits the setting. You're the one who looks ridiculous. We have to learn to adapt, Seth. Everything is changing. The Beast, the Ripper, these things are just the beginning. A new world order is unfolding. We have to leave the old ways behind.'

It was funny. Chris had been scared when he'd first discovered the werewolf threat. He remembered how terrified he'd been going to school each day, looking nervously over his shoulder, jumping at the slightest unexpected noise or sudden movement. When Mr Canning had gone berserk, he had almost died from sheer fright. The idea that the world he knew was about to crumble around him had been overwhelming and horrifying.

But he had changed. He'd become fitter and stronger. He'd learned the rudiments of martial arts. He'd prepped and made plans. Now he was ready to face whatever came.

In fact the more that the widening cracks in civilization became apparent, the more confident he grew in his own ability to weather the coming apocalypse. He was almost looking forward to it. In the past Seth had always told him he needed to be more flexible, to embrace change. Now Seth was the one clinging to the past.

'This whole thing is absurd,' said Seth. 'Why are we eating in such an expensive restaurant? Have you seen the prices?'

'Prices are unimportant,' said Chris. 'I am no longer price-sensitive.' He wondered if someone as blinkered as Seth could grasp such a concept. He passed a wrapped gift across the table to his old friend. 'Merry Christmas!'

Seth glared at the package in silence.

'Aren't you going to open it?'

Seth glared at it a little longer, then tore off the wrapping paper reluctantly. But even he couldn't suppress a gasp at what was inside – a rare Japanese origami book that Chris had bought from an online specialist. Seth was crazy about origami, and all things Japanese. 'This must have cost a fortune,' he said.

'I knew you'd like it,' said Chris. 'And in any case, I have far more money than I will ever need.'

Seth put the book on the table unopened and replaced the sudden smile on his face with a sulky frown. 'Well I didn't buy anything for you. Not all of us have imaginary fortunes to spend.' He flicked his mop of hair away from his glasses again. Chris watched it quickly fall back into place.

A waitress came to the table to clear away their soup bowls. She smiled warmly at Chris. He thanked her and smiled back. She didn't seem to have much time for Seth though. It was curious. In the past, Seth had been the one who attracted girls, and they had always ignored Chris, as if he wasn't even there. Some reversal of roles had taken place without him even trying. Perhaps it was the spinach in his best friend's beard, but Chris suspected that other factors were in play, possibly his improved physique after weight training, maybe even some mysterious *people skills.* He filed the information away for future analysis.

'My fortune is not imaginary,' he told Seth. 'My bank account contains enough money to meet all my current needs. In addition I have six credit cards, and I intend to max them out in the next few days. It's important to stock up as much as we can before all the shops close down.'

Seth shook his head in bewilderment. 'The shops aren't going to close down, man. You're acting irrationally. And if you rack up massive debts, think how long you're going to have to work at that crappy school to pay them back.'

'I'll never have to pay them back,' said Chris levelly. 'By next month, the credit companies may not even exist. And in any case, the school has been closed. I'm never going back there.'

'What?' said Seth, as the waitress returned to the table, bringing the main courses.

Chris watched the waitress as she served the food. He had ordered *Saddle of Venison with Caramelized Endives and Celeriac Puree*. He had never eaten any of those things before, but in recent days he had tried many new things, and was enjoying himself very much. He smiled again at the waitress, and she smiled back. He liked the way she continued to ignore Seth.

When she had gone, he said, 'I am not acting irrationally. On the contrary, I have analyzed the situation and am embarking on the most rational course available. Tell me, do you know what happened to the German currency in the aftermath of World War I?'

'No,' said Seth, looking confused by the apparent shift in conversation.

'After the war, goods were in short supply. Costs rose rapidly, and the value of the German Mark fell. After a period of hyper-inflation, the Mark was worth one trillionth of its former value. The same will happen with the apocalypse. First, people will begin panic-buying, and essential goods will become scarce. Then inflation will begin to spiral, and eventually money itself will become worthless. So the debts I am accruing now will be wiped out by inflation, even if the banking system survives in some form, which it almost certainly won't.'

Seth made no reply to that and they ate the rest of their meal in silence. After dessert, Chris continued. 'We need to borrow as much as we can now and spend it all on essential supplies – things that will still have value once money has ceased to exist. I'm talking about fuel, non-perishable food, medicines, camping gear, insect repellent, and weapons.'

'Weapons?'

'Not guns, obviously. Those are illegal in Britain. But we can stockpile knives, then acquire firearms later, once the rule of law has broken down.' He passed his credit card to the waitress and used it to pay for the meal. He tipped her generously. After all, one person could only stockpile so much. 'This card's totally maxed-out now,' he told Seth when she'd gone, snapping it down the middle and leaving its plastic remains on the table.

'You've completely lost it,' muttered Seth. 'You're mad.'

'No,' said Chris angrily. 'You're the one who's mad. I've shown you all the evidence, and explained what's going to happen, but you remain in denial. You're willing to risk your life, but not your credit rating. So who's the irrational one, really?'

Seth said nothing to that. He folded his arms and glared at Chris, the origami book lying on the table between them like a wall.

Chris sighed. Bribing Seth with the book and a lavish meal hadn't changed his mind at all. If anything they'd made him more stubborn. Rational discussion had failed to persuade him too.

Chris made one more effort to reach him. 'Please come with me,' he said. 'I'll go without you if I have to, but I want you to some too.'

'You just want my car,' said Seth sulkily.

'I do want your car, that's true,' admitted Chris. 'But I want you. You're my friend, my best friend.'

'I'm your only friend.'

'Yeah, I know,' said Chris. 'So will you come?'

Chapter Forty-Seven

Brookfield Road, Brixton Hill, South London

The past few weeks had flown and it was the day before Christmas Eve already. Since the funeral, Liz had been working long hours, helping with the hunt for the elusive Beast, which seemed to be lying low again, and also with the ongoing Ripper murders, which showed no sign of slowing. Yesterday's incident at the asylum centre had exhausted her, and yet she'd somehow managed to find the energy to put in another long shift today.

The flu symptoms had ramped up, and she was feeling nauseous now too. She hadn't been able to manage any lunch, and she didn't think she could face anything for dinner.

What had she been thinking of, bringing a Romanian orphan home with her? She had no means of looking after a child, and had simply had no choice but to leave him alone in her apartment all day. Dean had told her she was being stupid and that she should expect to find Mihai long gone, along with anything valuable that was small enough for a ten-year-old boy to carry in his pockets.

Yet Liz trusted her ability to judge character, and in her experience, frightened children weren't likely to suddenly turn into criminals for no good reason. And Mihai seemed resourceful. She hoped he would be able to look after himself.

She unlocked her front door and went inside. The entrance hall was dark, and so was the main living area beyond. Liz sighed. It looked like her trusting streak had got the better of her on this occasion. She flicked the light on and went through all the rooms systematically, looking for Mihai or any note he might have left behind.

Nothing.

At least nothing obvious appeared to be missing, apart from the money she had left for him. Oh, and the spare keys to the apartment. Great.

She sank onto the sofa and put her feet up on the stool. It looked like a night for a bottle of wine and some trashy TV. Either or both might help to distract her from her headache.

She picked up the TV remote and turned it on. A news report was showing the scene of more gruesome killings, this time in the city of Nottingham.

She heard a noise from the hallway and muted the TV. A key turned in the lock. She was on her feet and already in the hall when Mihai pushed open the door and came inside. His brown eyes shone and he grinned impishly when he saw her.

'Where have you been?' she cried. 'I told you not to go out after dark.'

The boy looked crestfallen. He held up some packets of breakfast cereal and cartons of milk. 'Nice lady in shop gave me food,' he said. He handed it to Liz, together with the money she had left for him.

She frowned. 'Did the lady really give this to you? You didn't steal it?'

'Me not thief!' he cried as if she'd slapped his face. 'I never steal. Not ever.'

'I'm sorry,' she said. 'Really, I didn't mean it.' So at least some people were still capable of kindness. She made a mental note to thank the lady when she next visited the shop. She smiled at the boy. 'You shouldn't have gone outside after dark though. It isn't safe with all the trouble at the moment.'

Mihai shrugged. 'Nowhere is safe, ever.'

There was truth in that, although hearing it from this orphaned boy nearly broke her heart. Only ten years old, and already he expected danger and violence. That was why Liz had enrolled in the police in the first place – to make the world a safer place for people like Mihai. It didn't look like she was making much difference though. These last weeks had been terrible. First losing David Morgan. Then the Ripper killings, the Beast attack at the railway station, and the fire-bombing at the community centre. She had never known it quite as bad as this. When terrible things happened to good people it made you wonder if there was any point. But of course that was precisely the point. It was because those things happened that the world needed people like Liz.

At times like this – perhaps only at such times – she missed her father. A grumpy old sod, who had never really grown up, but she had no other family. She hadn't seen him in months, not since they'd had that last bitter argument and major falling-out. He'd been caught smuggling cigarettes into Britain from France, and had asked her to 'pull some strings' to get him off. When she refused, he'd tried to put the blame for his problems on her. She'd promised herself she'd never speak to him again, but she regretted that now. She didn't expect him to change, but if he could just admit he was wrong and apologize …

But that hardly seemed likely. He was a stubborn bastard. She wondered where he was right now, and what he was doing. Out on the road, most likely, although in which country was anyone's guess.

'I miss you, Dad,' she half-whispered to herself, then shook her head incredulously. What was she thinking? The only time she wanted him anywhere near her life was when he was nowhere to be found.

The boy in front of her looked up with a concerned look on his young face. 'Is problem?'

'Shall we open a box of chocolates?' she asked him.

Mihai's eyes went wide as saucers. 'I like chocolate.'

'Me too,' said Liz. She fetched a box from the kitchen cupboard and let him open them.

'How many can I have?' he asked.

'As many as you like.'

He helped himself to three, then passed the box back to her. The smell of the chocolates hit her like a wave of noxious fumes. Suddenly she felt sick. 'Excuse me,' she said, and rushed to the bathroom. She made it just in time.

Chapter Forty-Eight

Sevenoaks, Kent, England

Kevin Bailey would have liked nothing better than to visit his daughter, Liz, as he passed through London. It was almost Christmas, the season for families to come together. But Kevin's family was probably too broken even for Christmas to weave its spell.

Liz was the only living relative he had. His own parents were long dead, almost like they'd lived in another age entirely. His wife – Liz's mum – had taken her own life when Liz was still a teenager. A broken family for certain, and hardly anything left of it now except ruins. Liz was probably still mad at him after his last visit. He'd behaved badly, even worse than usual, and her expectations of him had already been low. It would probably be better if he kept his distance.

He signalled to pull his truck over into the next layby. He'd set off that morning from Nantes in France, stopping briefly *en route* for his mandatory break time and to pick up some illegal immigrants, and he was tired and fed up. He hadn't quite reached London, but this would have to do. He was only a few miles short of where he'd agreed to stop.

There'd been a hell of a row coming from the back of his trailer earlier. Screams and shouts, and who knows what. These asylum seekers were like bloody animals. He'd gladly keep them on the other side of the English Channel, but they paid good money to come across. A grand each. It was as much as he earned in a whole month. How a homeless refugee got his hands on a thousand quid was none of his business. They could sell their own grandmothers for all he cared.

Two Afghans and a Syrian this time. They'd already told him too much, telling him that. They were cargo. He didn't want to hear their sob stories. Just pay the money and he'd get them from Calais to London. Or thereabouts.

He parked the truck by the roadside and checked his mirrors for traffic. It was pretty quiet now that he'd pulled off the motorway. At this time of night all the London commuters had already driven home, and only a few other long-distance drivers still cruised through the night, making the most of the quiet road conditions. It may be the night before Christmas Eve, but freight didn't stop just because of that. Kevin would be out on the road on Christmas Day itself. There was nowhere else for him to go.

He jumped out of the cab and walked round to the back of the trailer, listening for sounds coming from inside the shipping container. All quiet now. They'd finished their bawling, thank God.

He opened up the doors at the back of the container and shone a light inside. 'Oi, you can come out now,' he shouted. 'We've arrived.'

Silence. Had the buggers gone to sleep? He needed to get some kip himself. 'Oi! I said, come out!'

He heard the growl before he saw anything move. A

sound like a wild animal or a dog. Then a flash as a man leapt out of the darkness straight for him. He dodged aside as the man jumped out of the truck, just missing his head. Kevin had been a minor boxing champ in his youth, and he still knew how to move. And just like his daughter, if he lacked for height, he made up for it with ferocity. He landed a hard punch on the man's back as he flew past, and swivelled to face him.

The man landed on the ground and rolled. Now he crouched on all fours, snarling like a lunatic. Kevin didn't wait for him to attack. He lashed out with his foot, catching the man in the jaw. A loud crack was his reward.

The man wailed in pain, blood spilling from his mouth, and lurched toward Kevin, scrabbling at him with his long fingernails. Kevin dodged again and delivered another punch to the man's head. This time the bastard went down and didn't get up. Kevin kicked him, but he was out cold.

'All right, you can come out now,' Kevin shouted into the back of the container. The only response was the echo of his own voice.

The man who'd attacked him was the Syrian. Maybe he'd had some kind of row with the two Afghans. It had been a mistake to put them in the truck together. You never knew if these foreigners might end up fighting each other. They were probably hiding at the back now, too scared to move. He hauled himself up into the container and shone his light into its dark depths.

The container was piled high with crates of aircraft parts. At least that's what the documentation said. Kevin really didn't care what was inside. He stepped along the narrow space by the edge of the wooden crates, holding the flashlight out in front. The bright light cast wavering shadows against the metal walls of the container as he moved.

He slapped the palm of his hand against the metal and shouted again. Still nothing.

He rounded the last of the stacked crates and shone the

flashlight into the back corner of the container. 'Bugger me with a barge pole,' he said. The Afghans were there all right, at least what was left of them. Arms and legs and other spare body parts lay strewn over the crates in a pool of blood. He leaned closer and shone the light to get a better look. Bite marks and scratches covered the dismembered corpses.

Kevin wasn't too fussed by all that. His old dad had been a butcher and Kevin had lived above the shop. He'd seen more gore than most people had inside them. People, animals, they all looked the same from the inside. But what the hell had led the Syrian to do such a thing? Bat-shit crazy, obviously. They said that war did strange things to a man. It didn't get much stranger than this.

The only problem now was what to do with the bodies.

A creak alerted him to danger. He turned quickly and saw the man coming for him again. He raised his arms, but this time he was too slow.

The Syrian grabbed him by the collar and hurled him against the metal wall with a fierce strength. Kevin fell to the floor, winded by the impact. The flashlight flew from his hand and spun away along the floor to cast wild shadows from behind a crate. He looked up and saw the man's foot coming toward him in a kick. He twisted sideways, grabbing at the man's ankle, and brought him down with a crash.

He was back on his knees when the man came for him again, grasping with his claw-like fingers. Kevin gave him a swift uppercut to the jaw, followed by a jab to the man's cheek. The Syrian snarled, scrabbling at Kevin's chest and upper arms, and tearing off a strip of his shirt. Kevin head-butted the man on the bridge of the nose and stood up, facing his opponent head on. He struck him again, this time a double-fisted punch in the middle of the chest.

The man fell backward and hit the side of his head against a crate.

Kevin watched him writhe on the floor for a moment,

then stomped his foot down on the man's chest.

It ought to have been the coup-de-grace, and would have finished off any normal attacker, but the Syrian grabbed hold of Kevin's boot and flipped him off-balance. Kevin fell hard, splitting the side of a crate, and landing on his back on top of the dead Afghans. Wet sounds accompanied him as he struggled to right himself, and he slipped on the bloody mess.

The Syrian sprang forward and landed on top of him with all fours. He was attacking like a beast now, scratching and kneeing, snarling and spitting. The man's bloodshot eyes stared wildly and his forehead was slick with sweat, his matted hair sticking to his skin.

Kevin tried to push him off, but the floor was too slippery. The blood of the dead men completely covered his hands.

The Syrian opened his mouth and forced his jaws down toward Kevin's neck. He was strong, surprisingly so, and Kevin couldn't push him away. The sharp teeth drew closer to Kevin's exposed skin.

So the man was a biter. But Kevin had seen worse than that in his time, and he knew how to fight dirty too. He kneed the man in the groin and followed up with a quick eye gouge.

The man howled and released his grip just long enough for Kevin to roll him over and get back on top. Grabbing the man by the collar he head-butted him again, then finished off with a rabbit punch, pinning the man's head to the floor with his left hand, and chopping his neck at the base of the skull with the side of his right. He felt something snap under the force.

The Syrian's body went limp, his eyes still open but now sightless. His face was bathed in blood, and his head lolled loosely where Kevin had struck him.

Kevin breathed hard, sitting astride the man's chest in case he moved again. When he had regained his breath, he held his fingers to the man's neck, pressing into the soft spot beside the windpipe. Nothing. He counted to thirty. Still nothing.

Damn and bugger, the man was dead.

All three of his human cargo were dead.

He got back to his feet and stared at the scene of carnage before him. What the hell was he going to do now? He could hardly drop off his delivery and hope that no one would notice. Phoning the police didn't seem like a good move either. He'd have a hard job explaining why he had three illegal immigrants in the back of his container, and an even harder one explaining why they were now in pieces.

He could think of only one good option.

Torch the vehicle. Get rid of the evidence. And if he was going to do that, he needed to do it before anyone stopped to see what he was up to.

Chapter Forty-Nine

Department of Genetics, Imperial College, Kensington, London, Christmas Eve

Early on Christmas Eve morning, the lab was empty of both students and staff, but Leanna worked on tirelessly. She'd always been a hard worker, even as a mere human, and lycanthropy had given her almost unlimited endurance.

She studied the image on the scanning electron microscope. One of her own chromosomes was magnified nearly a billion times, certain areas marked in red to highlight the changes to the DNA that had occurred since she had become lycanthropic.

DNA – it was the basis of all life on Earth, a self-replicating nano-scale machine, at once beautifully simple and astonishingly complex. Two polymer strands coiled around each other in the famous double helix form. The spirals were mirrors of each other, ready to divide and create identical copies of the original molecule in a continuous dance that ended only at the moment of death. Each strand was a chain of just four types of base units, and yet with a human chromosome containing approximately three billion base pairs, the number of possible combinations was unimaginably vast. You could hardly design a more exquisite means of encoding information at the molecular level.

Her studies had already isolated the genes that were alien to her original human specification, that were wolf in origin. How wolf genes had mingled with human chromosomes was a mystery lost in the mists of time when early humans and proto-wolves had collided on the Eurasian plains and mountains, countless millennia ago. Maybe it pre-dated even that, originating in some shared ancestry millions of years before the first humans walked in Africa. Leanna had no way of knowing. All she could hope for was to understand the mechanism by which wolf genes passed from one host to another.

Professor Wiseman had uncovered much of the basics of how the condition spread, but there was still a lot to learn. Wiseman had discovered that a virus was responsible for transmitting the wolf genes from one host to another, and Leanna had identified the virus as one that occurred naturally in wolves.

Viruses were broken relics of the molecular world, unable to reproduce on their own. But they were capable of hijacking the cells of their host, tricking them into becoming lethal chemical factories that replicated the virus. But here was the twist. Lycanthropy had reversed this process, enslaving the virus for its own ends, replacing its DNA with wolf genes, and transforming the virus and its molecular machinery into a means of spreading wolf DNA from one host to another. It was a fascinating topic to study, and she was just scratching the surface.

The structure of the virus was even more complicated than HIV and had a capacity to mutate rapidly. It would be almost impossible to find a cure even if she had wanted to.

The DNA payload it carried varied enormously too. Every person infected would receive a different set of genes, and acquire different unique abilities.

Not everyone would survive the transition from human to superhuman. Only the strong would live. But filtering out the weak was all part of the process. Evolution always worked to eliminate weakness, but Leanna's work would accelerate the process a hundred-fold.

Leanna had never doubted her own strength. Her first trial had been as a baby, when a bout of bacterial meningitis had threatened her life. The disease killed more children under the age of five than any other infectious disease in the UK. Many of those who survived were left with severe brain damage or loss of limbs. But Leanna had been strong. She had survived unharmed.

She had survived the onset of lycanthropy too. Many would not, but their deaths would leave the human race stronger and better able to survive and thrive. Everyone had a part to play in Leanna's grand plan, and for some their contribution would be to die.

The new genes would be her gift to the world. She would free humanity from weakness, and replace it with strength, endurance and beauty. And so what better time to work alone in the lab than on the day before Christmas? The season was the time for giving.

Chapter Fifty

J.D.'s Cafe, A312, South West London, Christmas Eve

Kevin Bailey tucked into his steak and kidney pie with relish. Not many places served offal these days, but this greasy-spoon cafe off the A312 cooked it just the way he liked it – the way his mum had done when he was a boy. Happy days, but they were all gone now. Gone far, far away. Life had got worse since Kevin was a boy, a whole lot worse, and just kept lurching downhill. But at least there was still steak and kidney pie to look forward to once in a while.

He'd hitched a lift here with a passing trucker, and that had been an awkward journey if ever there was one. 'I just passed a burned-out trailer by the roadside,' the guy had told him. 'Not yours, was it?' The dark red blood stains all over Kevin's jacket had been a talking point too. 'How did that happen?' the trucker asked nervously.

'Cut myself shaving,' Kevin told him, treating the man

to a cold, dead stare that had kept him quiet for the rest of the trip. Kevin felt bad about that. The man had just been doing him a favour after all. He hadn't deserved the psycho treatment. But when had life ever given anyone what they deserved?

Now that he was alone, he was thinking through his next move. The way it looked to him, there weren't many choices on offer, and none of them held much appeal.

He could have kicked himself in frustration. Running from the scene of a triple murder had been the stupidest idea ever. Torching the vehicle even worse. He might as well have left a note for the police saying, *Call me, I'm guilty*. Now his options were very limited indeed.

He could keep running, heading west out of London, hoping for something to turn up. Or he could turn around and try to get out of the country before the border police got wind of him. But did he really want to spend the rest of his life abroad? He'd never get to see his daughter again if he chose that option. No, he would stay in England, whether it was on the run or in prison.

His best option, though he was loathe to admit it, would be to call on Liz and throw himself on her mercy. Liz always knew what to do. He would tell her what he'd done, endure another lecture about how unbelievably stupid he'd been, and then ask her to decide what to do. If she turned him over to the authorities, so be it. He would face his punishment with dignity.

He crammed the last of the pie and chips into his mouth, mopping up the gravy with a slice of bread, and headed outside into the rain. This cafe served food to a lot of truckers and he might find someone who would drop him off near Liz's place. As long as his serial killer looks didn't frighten them all away.

No matter. He would walk if he had to. The rain didn't bother him. It would help to wash the blood from his clothes.

Chapter Fifty-One

Brookfield Road, Brixton Hill, South London, Christmas Eve

It was pitch dark when the alarm went off. It always was, in the winter. Liz groaned, hit the snooze button and rolled over. She'd felt a little better after throwing up the previous evening, but then she'd woken in the middle of the night with a fever and had hardly slept since. No amount of painkillers seemed to make any difference. Her limbs ached right to her very bones. Sweat bathed her bedclothes, and she could no longer tell whether she was too hot or too cold. She listened to the gurgling and creaking sounds of the central heating swinging into action and wondered what to do.

Go and see a doctor, obviously. Dean had been nagging her all week to go. He was like an unwanted mother hen. But if she phoned this morning it might be days before she could get an appointment. She would probably be better by then. Better to tough it out.

She had proudly maintained a one-hundred-percent attendance record during her whole time in the police force, and she had no intention of taking a day off work now.

Especially not now.

There was so much to do, with the Beast and the Ripper still at large, not to mention incidents like the riot at the refugee centre. Plus, she needed to be strong for Mihai.

The alarm clock beeped noisily again. This time she switched it off properly and sat up, swinging her feet onto the bedroom carpet. Immediately her head swam with dizziness and her vision went black for several seconds, but she gripped the bed tightly until the dizzy spell receded. She stood up carefully and stalked determinedly toward the bathroom.

Once she had showered and made herself presentable she felt a little stronger. A cup of sweet tea and some toast, and she would be as good as ever. Except that the thought of food made the bile rise in her throat again.

She decided to cut her losses and head straight into work.

She was just scrawling a note for Mihai and leaving him some more money when there was a thumping knock at the door.

'All right, all right,' she shouted. 'Don't break the door down.'

She opened the door to a ghost, or the closest thing. Her father stood on the doorstep, his wet hair stuck to his head, two days' worth of grey stubble on his chin, and blood stains down his jacket. His lower lip was swollen and a nasty bruise closed one eye. 'Hey, love, how you doing?' he asked.

Liz stared at him coldly through narrowed slits. The last time they had parted she had told him never to return. 'What the bloody hell happened to you?' she asked.

He shrugged his shoulders. 'Bit of a scrap. Can I come

in?'

'I'm just going out to work.'

'Yeah,' said her father, looking shifty. 'That's why I'm here. It's kind of work-related, you being a copper and all.'

She opened the door wider for him to come in. 'What have you done now?'

He slouched sheepishly into the hallway. 'Any chance of a cuppa?'

She made tea for both of them. If she was going to have to listen to her father's latest stunt, she would at least try to get some hot liquid inside her. She set the tea down on the coffee table in the front room.

Her father had already taken a seat on the sofa. He didn't seem in any hurry to talk however.

'So where have you been?' she prompted.

'Bit of long distance work,' he said. 'Container truck. Mostly France, Spain, Belgium. Sometimes as far as the Czech Republic or even Hungary. I like being on the road, you know? Helps me see things clearly.'

'So what brings you here?'

'I could use some advice. Professional advice, really.'

'You mean you're in trouble and need bailing out?'

He scowled briefly, then his face cleared. 'Listen, love, I know we haven't always seen eye to eye on everything. Last time I left, I was a bit hasty. I said some things.'

Liz waited silently. If this was an apology, it would be the first one ever.

'I shouldn't have said what I said,' he continued after a while. 'It was wrong. I was wrong.'

'Yes?'

He looked around the room, at the pictures on the wall, at the TV in the corner. Anywhere except at her. 'I didn't mean those things,' he said eventually.

Liz reckoned that was the closest her father was ever going to get to the words, *I'm sorry*. 'So, what's up?' she asked.

He still seemed reluctant to talk, knitting his fingers

together like a little boy. 'I had a spot of bother with my vehicle last night. It ended up getting torched.'

'Torched? How?'

He stared at the mug of tea in his hands. 'I set it alight myself.'

'Why on earth would you do that?'

'It seemed like a good idea at the time. But with hindsight, not so much.'

Liz had no idea where this tale was headed. Her father's explanations were often disjointed and rambling, and this one was typical. Then suddenly she remembered. She'd seen the story on the news just before going to bed. 'Oh my God, that was your vehicle. The triple murder. You did that?'

'No, no,' he said hurriedly. 'Only one of them.'

'Only one what? Only one murder?'

'I didn't mean to. I was just defending myself.'

'Jesus Christ, Dad, slow down. Start again from the beginning and tell me everything.'

He told her, in fits and starts. She just about believed his story. It was exactly the kind of stupidity she had learned to expect from him. By the end of it, she didn't know what to do, other than shake her head in bewilderment. A couple of details bothered her, however. 'You said the man tried to bite you, the Syrian?'

'Yeah, but I've no time for that kind of monkey business. Dirty fighting, that is. Below the belt.'

'And he'd bitten the other men too?'

'Bite marks all over them.'

'Did the Syrian have yellow eyes?' she asked. 'Think carefully, it might be important.'

'Can't say I noticed. But he was in a bit of a state. All sweaty, like. Known to you is he, this geezer?'

'No, not exactly. Where did you pick the men up?'

'Just outside Calais. The three of them together, hiding by the roadside. A grand each.' He drained the last of his tea and set the mug back on the table. 'So, what I need to know is, what should I do?'

'You've come to ask me that? You have to hand yourself over to the police, obviously. What the hell did you think I was going to say? I'm a goddamn police officer, Dad. And it might be important – part of something bigger.'

'Okay then,' he said. He held his arms out toward her, his wrists together. 'Cuff me.'

'Goddamn it! Not here. I'm not going to arrest you myself,' said Liz in exasperation. 'You don't get to pin the blame for this on me. This is all your fault, and you can take responsibility yourself, for once. Come with me to the station and hand yourself in at the desk.'

He stood up. 'All right. Now?'

'Yeah,' agreed Liz. 'I was just about to go when you arrived.' She still hadn't touched her mug of tea.

She stood up, and felt the blood drain from her face. She reached out to grab a support, but her fingers clutched at empty space. An uncharacteristic look of concern flickered across her father's face. 'I'm okay,' she heard herself tell him, but her voice seemed to bubble up from the bottom of a deep ocean. Then the room began to spin in a kaleidoscopic swirl, and the floor rushed up to meet her.

Chapter Fifty-Two

*Upper Terrace, Richmond upon Thames,
West London, Christmas Day*

Christmas could be a lonely time for some, and Sarah Margolis had never felt quite so isolated. Melanie had been missing for days now. Sarah had finally plucked up her courage and called the police to report her sister's disappearance. They had tried to reassure her, saying that many people went missing at this time of year. In the UK, someone was reported missing every two minutes, they told her, and the majority were found again safely, sooner or later.

It wasn't the first time Mel had disappeared. Once she'd flown to Rio de Janeiro with some man she'd just met. She hadn't bothered to tell Sarah where she was. It wasn't that Melanie didn't care, just that such practical considerations never even occurred to her. She was impulsive. She lived her entire life on a whim.

She was probably somewhere exotic right now, sipping

a Pina Colada on the beach, while some wealthy older man attended to her every need. Either that, or she was lying dead at the bottom of a ditch, her mutilated body waiting to surprise an early-morning dog-walker.

Whichever it was, Sarah could do nothing about it. Instead, she had Grandpa for company. She always had Grandpa.

He was sitting up in his chair today with a blanket folded across his knees, wearing a party hat out of a Christmas cracker. Sarah wore one too. She had spent some considerable time getting everything nice for the festive season, with a Christmas tree, lights, and even a small turkey, delivered to the house on Christmas Eve. Sarah was a stickler for tradition, and she liked to do Christmas right. In a world that seemed to be falling apart, tradition and ritual was often the only glue that bound things together.

They were watching the Queen's Christmas Day Speech to the nation on TV.

'Is that the Queen?' asked Grandpa. 'She looks so old. Why is she so old, Barbara?'

'We're all getting older, Grandpa. That's just what happens.'

'But the Queen, she shouldn't be as old as that. She never used to be.'

Sarah looked at the familiar, lined face on the television screen. One day, all being well, she would be as old as that herself. Grandpa would be long gone by then. And as for Melanie, who knew? Her sister had a reckless, self-destructive streak that made her court danger. She might be dead already. And even if she turned up again in the New Year, Sarah knew for sure that Melanie would never allow herself to become old and grey. Her sister's life burned hot and bright, and was never destined to endure.

One day sooner or later, Sarah would have to face the world alone, and she had no idea how she might go about it.

Chapter Fifty-Three

Brookfield Road, Brixton Hill, South London, waxing moon

When Liz woke up, the world was yellow. She rubbed the surface of her eyes and a thick mucus clung to her fingers like lemon curd. She wiped the sticky covering away with her thumbs and looked about. She was in her own bed, dressed in some old pyjamas that she didn't normally wear. The curtains were drawn closed, but daylight leaked in around the edges, stinging her eyes. A thermometer lay on her bedside locker, along with a glass of water and a pile of assorted pills and medicine bottles. She had no recollection of taking any medicine. She hardly remembered anything.

She'd had a strange dream, vivid and haunting. She'd been a giant, or a monster, or some kind of beast, roaming through an enchanted forest. The forest folk were elves, and they had run from her in fear of their lives. She had wanted to eat them, she remembered that. She had been so hungry, and they'd looked so tasty. But they had been too fast, scampering away into the undergrowth. She'd tried to follow them but had become tangled in briar roses, the thorns anchoring themselves in her flesh like a hundred tiny knives, twisting into her skin. The thorns had twisted outward, erupting from her skin as a coat of fur that covered her from head to tail. She had stumbled into a clearing where three little pigs huddled inside a house made of straw. The pigs were afraid of the big bad wolf. They were afraid of her.

She had no idea how long she'd been asleep. She felt no hunger now, but her mouth was parched. She reached out to grasp the glass of water by the bedside, but her arm was swollen and puffy. The two red scratches on her skin throbbed angrily. Her clumsy fingers spilled the water, and the glass shattered when it struck the floor. 'Damn it,' she croaked. Her dry tongue scraped against the roof of her mouth like sandpaper.

What had happened to her? Her sickness had started that night on the Common when long fingernails had gouged her flesh. The eyes of the man who had scratched her arm had been filled with yellow, just like hers were now. But he had been a monster, not a man.

'I am not a monster,' she said aloud.

The door to the bedroom opened, and her father peered around. When he saw her awake, he pushed the door wide open and came inside. The bright light from the hallway stabbed Liz's eyes like a knife, and she raised an arm to block it. 'Oh, hey, sorry,' said her father, closing the door behind him. He came over to the bedside, stepping around the broken glass. 'You're awake,' he said. 'How do you feel?'

'Thirsty.'

'I'll get you another glass.' He returned a minute later with some fresh water. 'Here, drink this.'

Liz pushed herself up just enough to take a sip of the drink. It felt harsh against her dry throat, but she swallowed it down.

'I'm not surprised you're thirsty,' said her father. 'You've been out of it for days.'

'Days? What do you mean, days?'

'You were unconscious right through Christmas, love. Do you remember what happened?'

Liz remembered her father arriving on Christmas Eve. She remembered the room swirling around her, the furniture and the floor seeming to turn themselves upside down. Since then, nothing except the dreams. There was something important that she needed to remember though. She couldn't think what it was. 'Have I been unconscious all that time?'

'Pretty much,' said her father. 'You woke up a couple of times, but you were delirious. You seemed to think I was a little pig, or an elf.'

'How long?' asked Liz. She had no idea what day it was.

'About five days. You had me worried. Your temperature was like a rocket.'

'Five days? I've been unconscious for five days? Why didn't you call the doctor?'

'They don't work so much over Christmas. Anyway, I was looking after you. He reached for the thermometer by the bedside. 'Here, stick this under your tongue.'

Liz did as she was told. It was peculiar. She didn't remember her father ever being this attentive when she'd been a child. Was there a chance he was finally growing up? Then she remembered the important thing. 'Dad, you shouldn't be here,' she accused. 'You were supposed to hand yourself over to the police.' The thermometer in her mouth made the words slow and slurred. Dehydration wasn't helping either.

He left the thermometer where it was. 'Yeah, but who would have taken care of you then? And who would have looked after the kid?'

'Mihai! Where is he?' How could she have forgotten him too? Her brain was like a sieve. Hardly surprising since she'd had nothing to drink for five days. By rights she ought to be dead.

He took the thermometer from under her tongue and examined it. 'Temperature's almost normal. And the youngster's doing fine too. In fact, me and him had a mad Christmas together. Pity you weren't around to enjoy it.'

Liz narrowed her eyes suspiciously. 'What did you do?'

'Cooked a turkey and all the trimmings. Stuffing, pudding, mince pies, the lot. When I say cooked, I mean I bought it from the all-day deli round the corner. The kid said he'd never eaten nothing like it. They don't have that kind of thing back in Romania, he says. Poor little blighter, I don't reckon he's had much of anything good in his life.'

'What about work? I should have phoned to tell them I was ill.'

'Don't worry about that. It's sorted.'

'Sorted? How?'

'Some geezer phoned to ask why you hadn't turned up to work on Christmas Eve. Rude bastard, he was. I had to tell him where to get off.'

Liz's heart sank. 'What did you say to him?'

'I told him you was half-dead, and you wouldn't be back at work for at least a week. Oh, and some bloke called Dean Arnold called too. I told him the same thing.'

'I need to phone work as soon as possible and explain.' Liz swung her legs over the side of the bed and sat up. Immediately her head started swimming.

'Whoa. Hold on. There's broken glass down there. And you ain't in no condition to start walking about.' Her father lowered her carefully back onto the bed and swung her legs under the duvet. Don't reckon you'll be going nowhere for a while yet.'

Liz allowed him to manoeuvre her back under the covers. 'I'll just take another day off,' she conceded. 'Then I'll have to get back to work. They're desperate for manpower at the moment.'

After losing PC Dave Morgan, they could hardly afford

for Liz to be off sick too. But should she really be going back to work in her state? She'd seen for herself the effects of the yellow eye sickness. Perhaps she'd be safer locked in a police cell than out on the beat. And yet she felt fine, apart from the dehydration. She was nothing like that headmaster or the madman on the Common. She was not a monster. And if she started getting weird thoughts, she would simply ask a colleague to cuff her and put her in a cell. That reminded her. 'And you'll be coming to the station with me,' she told her father. 'Don't think all this good-guy act has got you off the hook.'

He shrugged. 'If that's what you want, love. I said I would. But you really ought to think about the kid.'

'What about him?'

'He's a nice kid. Only a scrawny little thing, but tough. Don't speak much English, but we've been getting on all right, me and him. While you was, you know, out of the picture. Getting on like a house on fire, in fact.'

Liz shuddered. A vision of the centre for asylum seekers engulfed in flames burst into her mind, but she ignored it.

'Yes? And?'

'I been out to Romania a couple of times, with my driving, to the place he's from. Had to drop off a load of pallets and pick up some crates of ball bearings.'

'Ball bearings?'

'Yeah, they got a factory out there. Turns out ball bearings by the million, it does. Anyway, I seen where he comes from, the kid. Ain't nothing for a youngster out there. Ain't nothing for anyone. Except for ball bearings. Plenty of them, I can tell you.'

'What's your point, Dad?' Liz could feel the conversation wearing her down. Her patience would run out soon, and she'd say or do something she'd regret.

'Just saying that there's nothing for the kid back in Romania. All his folks are dead. We're his family now.'

'We?'

'Well, you, at least. You're his mum now, ain't you? And that must make me his granddad.'

'Oh, don't think you can twist me round your finger like that. Mihai needs a stable family, not someone who's going to run off at the drop of a hat.'

'Yeah, yeah, that's my point, see. How are you gonna look after a kid when you've got a full-time job? With me around to help, it would be much easier. I've been on the road a long time. It's a hard life, you know? And now my vehicle's gone, I don't really have a job anymore. I got some money put away. I could stick around here and help, if you want me to.'

'You must be joking. You barely managed to take care of me when I was a kid. Don't think that I'm going to leave you in charge of Mihai. You're going straight to the police station with me, and you're going to tell them exactly what you did.'

He threw up his hands in submission. 'All right, love. If that's what you want. But I think it'll be tough on the kid.'

'No,' said Liz. 'Stop twisting this. You're trying to make this my fault again. It's what you always do. I won't have it!' She was shouting at him now, and baring her teeth.

The door to the room creaked open again and Mihai appeared, his nut-brown eyes wide in the dim light. When he saw Liz awake, he ran to her and threw his arms around her neck. 'You awake!' he shouted with glee. 'You alive!' He turned to her father and hugged him too. 'She back, Grandpa Kevin!'

'Reckon so, kid,' said her father, ruffling Mihai's mop of dark hair. 'But it looks like I'll be heading off soon. For good.'

Mihai's face fell. 'No! Is not fair!'

'I don't want to, believe me. I'd rather stay here and be with you. But it's up to your mum. I mean, Liz here.'

They both turned to look at her. 'Tell Grandpa Kevin stay!' demanded Mihai.

Grandpa Kevin? Suddenly Liz felt the fight go out of

her. She had no strength for this argument. 'He can stay for now,' she conceded.

Mihai gave a cheer and hugged them both again. There was a brightness in his expression that had been absent before. Somehow, in just a few days her father had managed to lift the boy's spirits and form a real bond with the kid. He'd been a useless father to her. Did he really have what it took to be a grandfather to Mihai? And how would that work if he was sent to prison? She wondered if she could really do a good job of parenting Mihai if left on her own.

One thought bothered her above all others. What would happen to Mihai if she turned into a monster? What then? One thing was certain. She needed her father right now, however much she resented the fact.

Chapter Fifty-Four

Liz tried to get out of bed the next day, but she was still too weak to stand. She tried again the following morning, and this time she found the strength to walk. But she still had no appetite. Her father brought her toast and marmalade in bed, and cups of tea. She drank the tea, but returned the toast untouched. At least the fever had gone, and with it the strange dreams. The daylight poking its way between the curtains still felt uncomfortable, but no longer burned her eyes. Perhaps the yellow eye sickness would vanish as quickly as it had appeared. She dozed the rest of that morning and afternoon, then as evening came she felt strong enough to shower and dress for the first time.

When she emerged from the shower, a smell from her childhood assaulted her senses. Fried liver and onions. It had been over ten years since she had smelled that smell, and it transported her back instantly. The day after her mother had taken the pills, her father had cooked liver and onions. He'd cooked it every day for the following month, washing it down with beer and sometimes whisky. She hated that smell and the memories it disturbed.

And yet …

She followed her nose through to the kitchen, where her father was serving great portions of offal for himself and Mihai at the table. She grabbed a clean plate from the draining board and sat down. 'I'll have some of that, if there's any going spare.' For some bizarre reason, fried liver was just what her stomach suddenly craved.

Her father treated her to a large helping and a grin. 'I bought it from the butcher's shop round the corner,' he said. 'Good bloke, that butcher. Reminds me of my old man.'

Liz tucked into the food eagerly. 'I can't believe I'm eating this. I always hated liver.'

'Good source of iron,' said her father. 'It'll put hairs on your chest. I got some liver sausages and some kidneys in the fridge too. The butcher said he can get me a pig's head if I put in an order.'

Liz tried to think of a retort, but her mouth was too full to speak, and in any case a pig's head sounded surprisingly tempting.

Mihai watched her eat with admiration. 'You are better now?' he asked.

'I think so. If I can keep this down, I'll be ready to go back to work.'

Her father frowned. 'You've been in a bloody coma for nearly a week. Gotta build your strength up before you go back.'

'Hardly a coma,' said Liz, holding her plate out for second helpings. 'And I'll go back to work when I say I will.'

She was right about that, at least. The next day she tucked into a plate of sausages and kidneys, and called the station to say she was fit to work. They told her to report for duty at six o'clock the following evening. It would be New Year's Eve and they needed every officer they could get.

She still hadn't decided what to do about her father though. He seemed to have done a good job looking after Mihai and holding the place together while she'd been ill. It was tempting to say that they were becoming a family of sorts. And yet, her father was wanted for a triple murder. If someone discovered him here, she would lose her job for certain. The situation was impossible.

She was dimly aware that the longer she put off making a decision, the less choice she actually had. But it was hard to think straight.

One step at a time. For now, it was enough to be out of bed and going back to work.

Chapter Fifty-Five

Greenwich, South East London, New Year's Eve, 10am, full moon

Chris Crohn sat in the passenger seat of Seth's car, growing more and more frustrated. Seth had delayed and procrastinated and made excuses, dragging the date of their departure ever later and throwing the whole venture into jeopardy. Christmas had come and gone, and now it was nearly the New Year. At last Chris had snapped, giving his friend a final deadline of leaving by New Year's Eve. They had got as far as loading up Seth's car with all their gear before hitting a new problem. The car simply refused to start. Now they were stuck in the parking space of Seth's apartment building in Greenwich.

Seth turned another page of the car's user manual, scanning the words and diagrams with a hopeful gleam in his eye. He flicked his hair away from his glasses and stroked his goatee beard thoughtfully. After a minute he turned another page. His long hair had already returned to its usual position.

'That's enough,' said Chris. 'Just admit it. You don't know what's wrong.'

'Of course I don't know what's wrong,' snapped Seth. 'That's why I'm looking in the user guide.' He tossed his hair back angrily.

'User guides are for people who don't understand how a thing works.'

'I never claimed I did know,' said Seth. 'I'm not a car mechanic.' He pressed a button on the dashboard and tried the ignition again. The car made a slightly different noise to the one it had made before, but remained resolutely inert. 'If you're so good at fixing things, you tell me what to do.'

'I don't know. I've never driven a car.'

They sat together in uncompanionable silence, the car's windows steadily misting up. The air was freezing without the heater on, despite Chris' all-weather clothing. If he was cold sitting here inside the car, he wondered how cold it would be in the wilderness, if they ever managed to get near to anything resembling wilderness. The back seats of the car were piled high with tents, sleeping bags, sheets, crates of food, bottles of water and boxes of radios, batteries, knives, and assorted electronic equipment that might just mean the difference between life and death. But all their survival gear was as good as useless if the car stayed stuck in Greenwich.

Eventually Seth pulled out his phone. 'I'm going to call the breakdown company and get someone out to look at it.'

'No,' said Chris. 'Call a car rental company instead. In the time it would take to get a mechanic here, we could be driving a brand new rental car. Maybe we could get ourselves an SUV.'

'There's nothing wrong with my car,' said Seth. 'It just needs some attention.' He dialled a number on the phone.

Lycanthropic

The call to the breakdown company seemed to take a very long time. Eventually Seth hung up. 'Right,' he said, avoiding Chris' gaze. 'Good.'

'What?' demanded Chris.

'They're sending a guy,' said Seth.

'Good. How long will that take?'

Seth returned the phone to his pocket. 'It might be a while. Today's their busiest day of the year.'

'How long?' said Chris through gritted teeth.

'Don't know,' admitted Seth. 'Might be hours. I said we'd wait in the car.'

'This is ridiculous. We need to get another car.'

'No,' said Seth. 'I'm not driving a hire car. I want to get my car fixed. We just have to wait.'

'We can't wait too long,' said Chris angrily. 'We have to get away. Tonight is the full moon. The werewolves will come out after dark.'

'If werewolves really exist,' said Seth.

Chris glared at him. Seth glared back.

Chapter Fifty-Six

Queen's Road, Harrow on the Hill, North London, New Year's Eve, 12pm noon, full moon

Melanie surfaced slowly, rising up through tangled layers of sleep, each one seeking to drag her back down into the depths of unconsciousness. She fought against them and pushed upwards. Eventually she broke through and felt daylight brush her eyelids. She opened her heavy eyes and stared at the white ceiling.

The room came gradually into focus. White and cream North London elegance, and the filtered winter light streaming through net curtains. She struggled to fix her attention on details. Her eyes caught the line of the crack in the ceiling cornice and she followed it to where the hairy black spider made its web. The fly it had caught was gone now, and the spider waited patiently for its next victim.

Melanie had learned patience herself these past few

days. Days or weeks, who could tell? Daylight had slipped into the gloom of evening and the dark of night and back again to cold day, and she had lost count of how many times.

She had never been a patient person. As a child she'd been perpetually bored. She had driven her sister Sarah nuts with her constant need for attention and stimulation. Even as an adult she was bored unless she was at a party or with one of her men, or out shopping for some expensive luxury. Sometimes even then. Even sex could be boring with some men. She'd joked with Sarah that if her *job* didn't get her killed, then boredom would finish her instead.

Strangely, being tied up and held prisoner by a lunatic was one of the most stimulating things that had happened to her. And the drugs he was feeding her made time just slip past. Honestly, she had known worse.

He hadn't beaten her again since that first day. The wound where he'd struck her with the cricket bat seemed to have healed somewhat. She'd had a splitting headache for the first few days, or weeks, but the drugs had helped with that too. Now she hardly felt a thing.

The man returned to her regularly, perhaps three or four times a day. Quite attentive really. He let her use the bathroom and even brought her food and drink if he was in a good mood. He kept hold of his knife at all times though, and its evil blade was never far from her throat.

She heard the key turning in the lock. Feeding time again. Unless this time he really was going to kill her.

'Awake are you?' said a familiar voice. 'Time you had something else to drink then.'

He carried a tray with a plastic beaker and a straw, and a bowl of something, probably soup, with a plastic spoon. All mealtimes were the same. He seemed to think she was only capable of eating baby food. Sarah would probably have said that it was some kind of control thing.

'Hungry?' asked the man. 'Thirsty?'

Melanie nodded politely. She'd already learned the hard way that if she didn't, he would take the food and drink away again.

He placed the tray on the floor and untied the gag from her mouth, using the tip of the knife to loosen the cloth. He showed her the blade again in case she'd forgotten. 'Don't say a word or I'll cut out your tongue. Understand?'

Melanie nodded again, feeling her tongue begin to loosen in her dry throat. She moved it up and down, left and right, trying to get some feeling back.

'If you shout or scream, I'll slice you open,' he said. 'Eviscerate you.'

Melanie managed a weak smile. She knew the script by heart now.

The man frowned at her. 'Think that's funny, do you?' He placed the knife against her throat. 'Want me to do it?'

She shook her head a fraction, afraid to move. He breathed heavily, pressing the blade into her soft skin. He held it there a moment longer before removing it. 'Sit up,' he commanded. He stuffed a pillow behind her head to raise her up a little, but left her hands and feet tied to the metal posts of the bed. He reached for the tray and grabbed the beaker first, holding the straw to her parched, cracked lips.

She sucked greedily, feeling the life-giving fluid trickle down her throat. The liquid had a salty tang of dissolved minerals like some kind of hydration drink. The taste probably helped mask the sedatives he was giving her. Whatever was in the drink, she slurped it down until she sucked on air.

The soup came next, some kind of pureed vegetable, and this he spooned into her mouth just like feeding an infant. She was beyond caring about that, and swallowed each mouthful gratefully. He said nothing while he fed her, just watched her through narrowed eyes, as if he expected her to somehow bound free from her restraints. His eyes moved around the room in a disconcerting way.

Lycanthropic

When she'd finished, he wiped her mouth and chin with a damp cloth and put everything back on the tray.

'I need to use the bathroom,' said Melanie. Her voice sounded hoarse and muffled. Everything sounded muffled. That was probably the drugs too.

He looked her over suspiciously, then untied her. He had knotted the ropes so tight he needed the blade of the knife to tease them apart. He waved the knife at her again. 'If you try to escape, you know what will happen.'

Melanie nodded. Eviscerate. She knew it. In any case, her limbs were so numb she could hardly move them. She sat on the edge of the bed for a moment, rubbing the life back into her heavy arms. She couldn't feel her feet at all.

He stood near the door, the blade held aloft. 'Hurry. Don't take so long.'

Melanie put some weight on her right foot and felt her leg cramp. She groaned in agony and saw the knife flash dangerously.

'Silence!'

'It hurts,' she told him. 'I need to get the circulation back.'

'Do it quickly.'

Every time was the same. *Hurry up. Do it quickly. Don't take so long.* What was the urgency? He was probably just as scared of her as she was of him. But that made him even more dangerous.

The blade flashed again. 'Stand up.'

She shifted her weight onto her legs using the metal bedstead as support. A jolt of pain shot through her right leg, but she swung it forward, shuffling across the room to the door. He stood aside to let her past and watched as she hobbled across the hallway to the bathroom opposite.

'Be quick,' he told her. 'And don't lock the door, or I'll break it open. Try to scream and I'll …'

Melanie tuned him out. If she heard the word *eviscerate* one more time she really would scream. She closed the bathroom door behind her, leaving it unlocked like he'd said. The room was tiny, just a toilet and a wash basin. That was all the freedom she knew these days, and she was grateful for a brief moment of privacy.

Her pee was thick and dark, not dissimilar to the soup she'd just eaten. Dehydration, she supposed, and perhaps the drugs too. She used the toilet quickly but left it unflushed. She might have only a minute to spare, and there was work to do.

The bathroom had no window, and no way to signal to the outside world. The cabinet beneath the sink was bare. A search for useful tools had revealed nothing except soap and toilet paper, and no amount of ingenuity could muster an escape plan with just those. But the mirror on the wall held promise.

The reflection of her hollow face stared back at her and she almost recoiled in horror. Her long black hair had lost its shine. The congealed blood from the head wound was gone, but a scar would remain for the rest of her days, whether they numbered few or many. Her red eyes were ringed with black circles, and her whole face seemed to have sunk somehow. The soup-and-sedative diet had taken pounds off her.

A fierce knocking on the door brought her out of her drug-induced reverie. 'Hurry up in there. Be quick!'

Concentrate, Melanie. There really isn't much time.

Four screws fixed the mirror to the wall. She had already succeeded in loosening one, using her fingernail as a screwdriver. She set to work on the second now.

Righty tighty lefty loosey. That's what Grandpa had taught her, in the days when he'd still been able to tell the difference between left and right. She dug the remnants of her thumbnail into the head of the screw and twisted counter-clockwise. It didn't budge, just hurt like hell. *Thank God for the drugs, or it would be even worse.*

The knocking came again. 'Why do women always take so long in the bathroom? I'm going to count to ten.'

She dug in harder and twisted with all her strength. The

screw turned a quarter of a notch. She tried again, applying pressure with both hands. It turned again, but it still had a long way to go. *Patience, Melanie, you can do a little more tomorrow. And then again the next day.*

'Six, five, ...'

To hell with patience. She was done with that. There might not even be a tomorrow. The mirror had loosened from the wall a fraction and she slid her little finger under the free corner. She pushed and wriggled it as far as it would go. If she could just lever the mirror off the wall ...

'Three, two, ...'

She flushed the toilet with her free hand and called out. 'Okay, I'm done. I just need to wash my hands now.'

She held her breath until the answer came. 'All right, but don't take long.'

She turned the water and let it gush into the hand basin. The sound would mask any noise she made removing the mirror. She pushed again, this time with her middle finger. The edge of the glass lifted slightly away from the wall. She strained, forcing two slender fingers behind the mirror.

With a sudden release of pressure the glass broke. It shattered with a loud crack, spraying fragments of glass across the small space of the bathroom. A splinter entered Melanie's finger and she watched in fascination as a tear of blood wept from behind her fingernail, matching the chipped remnants of her red nail varnish. She plucked the glass needle out and dropped it into the sink. The churning water there turned red.

Behind her the door burst open in fury and the man rushed in, blade first, hands shaking and eyes everywhere.

Melanie grabbed a long shard of glass, wincing as it sliced into her palm and fingers, but gripping it tightly. The drugs quenched the pain. The man's knife came at her fast, but she moved faster, despite the fog that filled her head. She plunged the glass into the back of his hand and watched it split the vein that pulsed there so angrily.

The man recoiled with a deafening roar, dropping the knife and snatching his hand away.

She lifted the splinter of glass again, ignoring the pain as it dug into her injured hand, and waved it in his direction. He stepped back, fear on his face. For once, his eyes remained fixed on hers.

'Get back in the bedroom, and close the door behind you,' Melanie ordered him. She waved the glass fragment in front of her. 'Hurry,' she added, when he hesitated, 'or I'll *eviscerate* you.' She pronounced the word carefully, just the way he liked it.

Chapter Fifty-Seven

*Greenfield Road, Brixton, South London,
New Year's Eve, 1pm, full moon*

It was nearly time for the Wolf Brothers to change. Leanna had already explained the process to Warg Daddy in detail. Now the time had come. New Year's Eve. The night of the full moon.

It had been a month since he had first encountered Leanna on Clapham Common. So much had changed since that night. The Brothers had been twelve originally. Now they were nine. Wombat had died on the Common, and two others had succumbed to the fever. Leanna had forbidden the survivors to mourn the fallen. The weak did not deserve it.

Warg Daddy had never doubted his own strength. The fever had proved it once again.

Now they were hungry. Hungry for blood.

They would change tonight, Leanna had promised, when the full moon rose. And then they would hunt, for the first time. Warg Daddy could still hardly dare to believe it. Becoming a werewolf had been a childhood fantasy. As an adult, he had learned that it was an impossible dream. Now it was a reality. If this could be true, then anything could.

But while they waited for moonrise, Leanna had other matters she wished to discuss with him. In private.

Warg Daddy nodded as Leanna briefed him. They sat in comfortable armchairs in the house in Greenfield Road where Leanna lived with her friends. The domestic setting unsettled Warg Daddy. This was no place for a wolf, and he had never felt comfortable in suburban houses. Their dullness constrained him. He longed instead for the freedom of the open road, a powerful engine throbbing beneath him. Dressed in his leathers and helmet, he could imagine himself as a knight of old, an adventurer on a quest. A life without such dreams was not worth living.

Leanna's clipped voice cut through his drifting thoughts. 'So I have two close advisers,' she told him. 'They are smart, but perhaps too smart.'

Warg Daddy listened carefully. She was talking about the friends she shared the house with, Adam and Samuel, both werewolves like her. The three of them were the first of their kind, bringing the condition from the Carpathian Mountains of Romania. Warg Daddy disliked them already. He had never enjoyed being a follower.

'Adam is a power-seeker,' continued Leanna. 'He has a hunger in him that makes him very dangerous. Samuel is loyal, but perhaps a little too metrosexual for my liking. Do you know what I mean?'

Warg Daddy grunted in acknowledgement. He had no idea what a metrosexual werewolf might be like, but he understood Leanna's real problem. It was leadership.

Leadership, and trust.

He had the same issues with the Pack. Snakebite was perhaps like this power-seeker – a strong man with his own agenda. Snakebite could be slow-witted at times, but once he grasped a situation fully, he acted with brutality and a cold ruthlessness. He was Warg Daddy's most valuable ally. But he needed to be watched, to make sure he stayed on plan.

Wombat had been like the other Leanna spoke of, far too clever for his own good. He'd read too many books as well. All that Ragnarök stuff. Norse myths and New Age mumbo-jumbo. Yet despite his brains, he had no street smarts. He'd always had the knack of saying the wrong thing at the wrong time. That's what had got him killed that night on the Common. Leanna had been looking for someone to make an example of, to demonstrate her power, and Wombat had as good as raised his hand to volunteer.

Leanna was still talking, but Warg Daddy had stopped listening. He had already grasped what he needed to know. The details of her two so-called advisers were unimportant. What mattered was that an opportunity existed for them to be replaced. 'I know what you mean,' he told her. 'You need a right-hand man. Someone you can trust.'

She smiled her cold smile at him. 'I need a strong man. A born leader. Can you be that man, Warg Daddy?'

Warg Daddy freed himself from the constraints of the comfy chair, straightening himself to his full height and puffing out his chest. 'I'll be your man.'

Leanna stood too. She was tall, but not as tall as him. She pushed her long, slim body against his. 'I'll be your woman too, if you want me.'

Chapter Fifty-Eight

James could hear voices coming from the front room, a man and a woman deep in conversation. The woman's voice was Leanna's, but he didn't recognize the other. He had seen a stranger arrive at the house earlier – a huge bear of a man, dressed in motorcycle leathers, with a black beard and shaven head, riding the biggest motorbike James had ever seen. He had watched him from the upstairs window, but had not dared show his face. The man scared him.

Leanna scared him too. She didn't like him, even now that he'd fully changed, and she made it clear every time she encountered him. He didn't really like her much either, nor Adam with his sneering disdain. Both were cold, selfish people. Only Samuel made him feel comfortable in the house. He kept his distance from the others.

He slipped quietly down the stairs, taking care to avoid the step near the bottom which creaked loudly. He had become adept at creeping around the house without drawing attention to himself. *Sneaking,* Adam called it. But James was no sneak. He just preferred to avoid confrontation.

The stranger had an almost overpowering smell – a mix of leather, sweat and engine oil. James would not forget it in a hurry. And there was another smell too. The whole house reeked of male and female lust.

He reached the bottom of the stairs and was treading quietly past the room with the voices when the door opened. The strange man stepped into the hallway, blocking his path. He was even bigger than James had realized, almost six and a half feet tall, and built like a bodybuilder. James could smell the wolf in him, although the man wasn't fully wolf. He hadn't yet changed.

The wolf-man regarded him with undisguised hostility. 'Is this the one?' he asked.

Leanna appeared beside the man, her thin frame dwarfed by his bulk, her blonde hair and pale skin contrasting with the stranger's thick black beard and swarthy skin. 'James, this is Warg Daddy. He's a friend of mine.'

'Pleased to meet you, um, Warg Daddy,' said James. He offered a hand, but the man ignored it. Instead he rubbed the back of his head with his thumb.

'Later,' said Warg Daddy. He gave Leanna a kiss on the mouth and turned to leave.

Leanna stopped him. 'James, I want you and Warg Daddy to be friends. We're on the same team, after all. Do you think you can do that?'

'Sure,' said James. 'I want to be friends with everyone.' It was Leanna and Adam, and now this Warg Daddy who were being unfriendly. Why couldn't they just accept him for who he was? He was wolf as much as any of them – more than this biker guy in fact.

Leanna held his gaze with her blue stare. 'Tonight's a very important night. Warg Daddy and the Wolf Brothers will change for the first time. It will be a turning point for all of us. Tonight, the balance of power begins to shift. Can we count on you, James?'

Warg Daddy had turned to stare at him too. James needed all his courage to withstand the combined force of those two hard gazes. 'Of course. We're all wolves, right?'

'Right,' said Leanna, although he sensed her reluctance to admit it. 'This is your chance to prove it.'

Warg Daddy gave him a firm punch on the arm that might have been friendly if it hadn't been quite so hard. 'Right,' he agreed. 'Until tonight, then?'

'Until tonight,' said Leanna.

James watched the man leave the house without another word. He listened to the harsh roar of the motorbike starting up, and waited until the sound of the engine had faded to nothing. Even after Warg Daddy had gone, the smell of engine oil and leather lingered on.

Chapter Fifty-Nine

Queen's Road, Harrow on the Hill, North London, New Year's Eve, 1:30pm, full moon

The man crept backward into the bedroom that had been Melanie's prison cell for so long, and closed the door behind him, just as she had ordered. So far, so good. She stumbled down the hallway, legs moving jerkily, ignoring the searing cramp that hobbled her every step. The shard of glass digging into her palm helped to distract her from the pain of walking. The drug-induced haze that filled her body helped too. That, and the thought of what the man would do once he gathered his wits again.

Eviscerate her. Hadn't he told her enough times?

She was halfway down the hallway when she remembered the key in the bedroom door. The drugs had muddled her head, made her forget. She should go back and turn it. Lock him in. But that would waste time, and time was one thing she didn't have.

Hurry, his voice nagged in her head. *Be quick. Don't take so long about it.* That was damn good advice, and she accepted it with pleasure. Speed was her only hope now. That, and the fragment of broken glass she clutched in her bloody hand. That might be useful too.

Step left, step right, step left again. Ignore the pain. Every move was a monumental struggle, but each step brought her closer to freedom. It was that simple.

She reached the front door of the apartment, and suddenly it wasn't that simple anymore. Metal bolts, a chain, a deadlock and even a padlock sealed the door. Melanie screamed inside.

Keys, there must be keys.

She turned and looked around the hallway. Nothing. No hooks, no shelves, not even a coat stand. An open doorway led off the hall and she rushed through it as quickly as her half-lame feet could carry her.

The room was a lounge or study of some kind, lined with bookcases and filled with clutter. Cardboard boxes were piled high against the walls, even in front of the bookcases. More boxes teetered on a desk, and the table in the middle of the room held a tower of books.

Keys. Where are the keys?

The sedatives that coursed through her bloodstream blurred her thoughts and made her slow. She turned her head at a snail's pace, scanning the room from one corner to the other. Still no keys.

Think, Melanie. Concentrate.

She stumbled forward to the table and collided with it. The mirror fragment in her right hand bit into her palm. She had almost forgotten it, but there was no forgetting now. Fresh blood dripped from her hand. With her other hand she fumbled to open a box. It was packed with more books. She shoved the box onto the floor, watching the books spill out in crazy patterns.

Where are the keys?

Coats, jackets and an umbrella hung on a coat hanger on the wall by the door. She limped over to it and started rifling through the coat pockets. It didn't take her long to strike lucky. Her fingers found a bunch of keys dangling from a large key ring and she pulled it out of the pocket as quickly as she could.

She listened at the door and peeped her head cautiously back into the hallway. There was still no sign of the man. She must have totally terrified him. But he wouldn't stay in the room forever. She hurried to the door and started working through the keys. How many keys did the man own? A crazy number. She couldn't imagine what locks they opened. Lock-up garages, sheds, warehouses. Maybe he had dozens of women locked up all over town. The idea was noxious and helped her focus on her task. The last key she tried unlocked the padlock.

She pulled the heavy padlock out of the chain it secured and dropped it to the floor with a clunk. In her hurry, her still-numb fingers fumbled the keys and the whole bunch crashed to the floor next to the lock. As she stooped to pick it up, she heard the bedroom door open down the hallway.

She slipped the brass chain off its hook and slid open a bolt. A roar of anger erupted from the man. Melanie ignored him and slid open the second bolt. Now only the deadlock remained. But the keys – there were so many of them.

She clutched the fragment of mirror tightly in one hand and started trying keys in the lock. One, two, three, ... there were just so many. Footsteps and heavy breathing drew closer. The fourth key fitted the lock. She was turning it when a hand fell on her shoulder. She spun around in frustration, swinging the sliver of glass upwards. Something flat and heavy knocked it out of her fingers.

The man stood there, eyes wilder than ever, but his bloodied hand held no knife. She wasn't going to be eviscerated after all. Instead he swung the cricket bat a second time and her world exploded in a burst of violet stars.

Chapter Sixty

Battersea, South West London, New Year's Eve, 8:05pm, full moon

PC Dean Arnold had never thought that serial killing could become a fashion, but London's murder rate was escalating sharply as more and more copycat killers joined the frenzy. Bodies were turning up everywhere, their butchered, tangled remains found in ditches, on canal paths, even in residential streets. *Ripper* had become the top internet keyword on search and social media, and it seemed to be the only story the news outlets wanted to talk about. Politicians, celebrities and other news had all but been forgotten.

Even the Beast had faded from the news reports. There had been no Beast sightings for almost a month now, and people were saying that it had all been a hoax, or a mass delusion. But Beast or no Beast, the streets of London were more dangerous than ever, despite the growing number of arrests of suspected or confirmed serial killers.

It wasn't just London, or even England. The serial-killing craze had gone global. Gruesome murders were sweeping the world. The commentators were going wild, wheeling in expert after so-called expert, all with increasingly crazy ideas. There was even speculation about some kind of brain-washing cult or a mind-control drug that turned ordinary people into psychotic murderers.

The authorities had responded with tough talk and pledges to make the streets safe again. Dean found himself out on patrol long hours of the day and night. An additional five hundred armed police had been deployed to bolster police power. More arrests had been made, but still the murders continued like an unstoppable flood.

Vigilante groups had formed in response to the wave of killings. Protests had become violent, immigrants had been attacked, and arrests made in response, but the murders continued unabated.

The long hours were taking their toll. Dean longed to be at home with his wife and daughter instead of out on the streets yet another night. But he understood the reasons for the police presence. The public needed to feel that the authorities still remained in control. Tonight would be an important test, with the New Year's Eve celebrations under way and millions expected to turn out onto the streets of the capital.

He could have used Liz's reassuring company right now, but she hadn't showed up at work since Christmas Eve. He had tried to call her, but had only managed to get a few words out of some shady character who claimed to be her father. He just hoped she was okay.

This evening he was patrolling his home turf of Battersea. Some minor vigilante violence had rocked the district the previous night, and a strong show of force was being mounted to prevent any escalation.

The vigilantes were becoming almost as much of a problem as the killings. Groups of young men had seized the opportunity to protest against immigrants. As far as

Dean was concerned it was just an excuse for violence. While several immigrants had been arrested for murder, not all of the men held were non-British. These so-called vigilantes were largely thugs looking for trouble. He just hoped there wouldn't be any tonight.

While he waited, he thought of Samantha and Lily and his unborn child, and he remembered the promise he had made to keep them safe. Keeping that promise started here, tonight. Order must be maintained on the streets, or they would be safe for no one.

A familiar female voice startled him. 'Hey, Dean. Stop daydreaming. You're supposed to be on duty.'

He turned to greet her. 'Liz! What are you doing here?'

'What does it look like? I'm a police officer. I'm needed on the streets.' She was kitted out in full uniform, ready for work.

At first he felt a strong surge of relief to see her. 'It's good to have you back on board,' he said. But then he paused to study her more closely. To him, she still looked sick. Her inflamed nose and yellow-tinted eyes looked dreadful against her blanched skin. 'You look like you ought to be tucked up in bed with a hot water bottle.'

'I've done enough of that,' she snapped. 'Now tell me what I've missed, and let's get on with the job.'

Chapter Sixty-One

South East London, New Year's Eve, 8:30pm, full moon

Chris Crohn's great escape was underway at last although it had been massively delayed. The car repair guy had taken hours to arrive, and then he'd spent an age fixing Seth's car. It was already dark by the time they were finally ready to leave.

'We should wait until tomorrow,' said Seth. 'Make a fresh start in the morning.'

'No,' said Chris. 'You've been delaying and stalling and pushing back for weeks. If we don't go now, we might never go.'

'What about the werewolves, though?' Seth peered out of the car window through his thick lenses. 'You said that tonight's the night of the full moon.'

'Yes,' said Chris anxiously. 'But that's why we need to escape from London. Highly populated areas are the most dangerous.'

Night had fallen, but the sky over London was covered by a layer of grey cloud.

'I can't see the moon anywhere,' said Seth, gazing about. 'Perhaps we'll be lucky.'

'As long as we stay inside the car, we should be safe,' said Chris. 'Just drive, and don't stop for anything.'

They set off cautiously, Seth using the GPS on his phone for guidance, Chris studying his paper map.

'What have you got that old thing for?' asked Seth. 'Nobody uses paper maps anymore.'

'Just wait until the networks fail,' said Chris darkly. 'Then you'll be glad I brought it.'

The city traffic was heavy, and they made slow progress. The police had cordoned off some of the roads and were redirecting traffic down unfamiliar routes. Traffic reports on the radio suggested widespread gridlock across the capital.

'I don't know this part of the city very well,' moaned Seth, staring out at the run-down warehouse buildings of the industrial area they now found themselves in.

'Just keep heading west and we'll get out of London eventually.'

'I think we should have gone east instead,' said Seth.

'It's too late to turn around,' said Chris. 'Just keep driving.'

After a while the traffic came to a complete halt. 'What now?' asked Seth.

Chris studied his map carefully. He wasn't familiar with this part of London, but he thought he could see the reason for the blockage. 'We should try turning south to avoid the congestion on the roads heading into central London. When the traffic starts moving again, take the next turning on the left. That should get us out of this jam.'

Seth nosed the car down the next side street and put his foot on the accelerator. The road ahead was clear. 'This is better. Nobody's going this way.'

The reason for that soon became apparent.

'Damn, this wasn't supposed to happen,' said Chris.

'Are we lost?' asked Seth.

The road ahead was blocked to cars halfway along its length. A sign read, *Pedestrian access only*. 'This must be new,' said Chris. 'It's not marked on my map.'

'We'll have to turn around,' said Seth.

But that was impossible. Other cars had followed them down the dead end, and the road behind them was now filled with stationary vehicles. The car immediately behind honked its horn loudly, and soon about a dozen drivers were blaring their frustration.

'What now?' demanded Seth.

'Stay in the car,' said Chris. 'Don't unlock the doors for any reason. I'm sure this will all work out okay.'

Chapter Sixty-Two

West Field Gardens, South London, New Year's Eve, 9:15pm, full moon

The Singh family was in the habit of staying home on New Year's Eve. In recent years, Vijay had been allowed to stay up late with his older sister, Aasha, to watch the celebrations on television. He loved to see the fireworks at midnight on the River Thames in front of the Houses of Parliament and the London Eye. It was one of the most impressive firework displays in the world.

This evening there had already been fireworks when Aasha announced that she intended to go out with friends. Her parents had argued with her, saying it wasn't safe, but in the end Aasha had got her way. She always did.

'You can't let her go out on her own,' Drake told Vijay.

'What do you mean? She won't be on her own. She's meeting her friends.'

'Yeah,' said Drake. 'But they're just girls. You're her brother. You should be around to protect her.'

'Protect her from what?'

Drake rolled his eyes. 'Oh, I dunno. Like, cannibals, serial killers, Beasts, all kinds of maniacs.'

'I don't know,' said Vijay. 'Mum and Dad will kill me if I go out too. And Aasha won't want me with them.'

'Never mind that,' said Drake. 'We'll go together, you and me, and follow them at a distance. Just to make sure they're safe.'

Vijay should never have allowed him to talk him into it. The real reason Drake wanted to follow Aasha around was because he fancied her. Although Aasha was two years older than him and ignored him completely, Drake just couldn't take his eyes off her.

Aasha's big dark eyes, long black hair, and smooth milk chocolate skin made her a beauty, for sure. But she was Vijay's sister. Thinking about her in that way was totally gross. And Drake thinking such thoughts – or worse – made him feel ill. If Aasha needed protection from anything, it was from Drake's overactive hormones.

At least Drake had moved back home with his mother and her boyfriend. After Mr Canning had been taken away by the police, the school governors had made the decision to close the school until after Christmas. It meant they'd been given an extra-long Christmas break, and it also took away any reason for Drake to continue staying at Vijay's house – if there had ever been a real reason in the first place.

Thankfully it also meant that Vijay no longer needed to skip school and lie about it to his parents. And best of all it had stopped Drake following Aasha's every move around the house with his stupid puppy-dog eyes.

But now this New Year's Eve thing had kicked off, and Vijay didn't know how to get out of it. 'All right,' he said eventually. I'll give Rose a call, see if she wants to come too.' If Rose was with them, it might make it easier to keep Drake under control. But Vijay knew that wasn't the real reason he wanted Rose to be there. These past few weeks he hadn't been able to stop thinking about her red hair and green eyes. Her pale freckled skin haunted his dreams at night. He couldn't deny it, he was in love, just as Drake had fallen for Aasha. And if following his sister around town meant he could be with Rose, he would do it.

He wondered if Drake suspected the truth, but his friend gave no indication that he knew how Vijay felt about Rose. He was too focused on his own love life to notice anything else. 'I'll meet you at nine o'clock,' Drake told him. 'We'll follow Aasha and her friends into town, and make sure she's safe.'

'Do you know how creepy you sound?' said Vijay. 'Since when did you become a stalker?'

'It's the honourable thing to do,' insisted Drake. 'Any brother who really cared for his sister would do the same.'

As soon as Drake had left, Vijay called Rose. It was good just to hear her voice again.

'You're going to do what?' she asked, once he'd explained why he was calling.

'I know it's creepy, but Drake insisted.'

'Are you really worried that something will happen to your sister?'

'Not really. I'm more worried about what Drake might do. But he made me promise to go with him.' He paused, considering his next words carefully. 'I don't suppose your parents will want you to go out after ... everything that's happened.' He still couldn't get over the fact that Rose had stabbed the Headmaster with the pen. She was so much braver than him. She was amazing.

Rose hesitated before responding. 'If I ask them, they'll probably say no,' she agreed.

'Yeah,' said Vijay, unable to conceal his disappointment. 'That's what I thought.'

'But if I don't ask them, they can't say anything,' she continued brightly.

So now here they were sneaking out into town, the three of them following his sister and her girlfriends as they went from pub to pub along the streets of London. It wouldn't have been Vijay's first choice of activity for a night out with Rose, but she seemed to think it was a great adventure. She giggled loudly and Drake scowled at her, telling her to be quiet. Vijay tried to relax and enjoy himself. He just prayed that Aasha wouldn't spot them, and that Drake wouldn't try anything stupid.

Chapter Sixty-Three

Clifton Blood Clinic, North London, New Year's Eve, 10:10pm, full moon

The nurse at the Blood Clinic was called Dawn. James liked her immediately. She was a tiny woman, but with strong and practised hands, and she pushed a needle into his finger efficiently and almost painlessly. His nostrils flared as he smelled the faint aroma of the blood. After almost a month without feeding, even the scent of his own vital fluid flowing into the syringe had the power to rouse his hunger, making his anticipation of tonight's hunt grow to a new height.

The nurse chatted to him as she took the sample for screening, explaining that the clinic was open later than usual tonight. They expected it to be one of the busiest nights in the capital's hospitals, at least in the Accident & Emergency departments. With all the recent trouble, blood supplies were under unprecedented pressure. Just a single day's supply remained of the rarest blood groups.

James nodded and watched as she withdrew the needle and applied a gauze pad to his finger.

Samuel and the nurse seemed well acquainted with each other already. 'Hello again, Dawn,' he said when he saw her.

'Back again so soon?' she asked.

Samuel grinned. 'I couldn't stay away, Dawn. You stole my heart when you took my blood.'

The nurse raised a sceptical eyebrow. 'Is that so? Well, I'm glad to see you again. O Negative is in urgent demand. This blood will go directly to the operating theatre.'

James had never given blood before and still wasn't sure that he wanted to. 'Won't it weaken us before we go hunting?' he asked Samuel, as they waited for their haemoglobin results.

'Nah,' said Samuel. 'It'll give us a healthy appetite.' He smiled. 'You oughtn't to be afraid of needles after spending all that time in Intensive Care.'

'I'm not afraid. I just haven't done it before.'

'I bet you've tried lots of new things these past few weeks,' teased Samuel. 'Don't tell me you haven't enjoyed them.'

James blushed.

Since becoming a werewolf and meeting Samuel, his life had changed out of all recognition. Everything was new. Everything was bright. Every moment he spent with Samuel stretched out like a blissful eternity. Everything they did together felt like the first time.

They'd been shopping together that afternoon in the New Year sales on Oxford Street, and James had never enjoyed shopping so much. He'd bought clothes he wouldn't have dared choose himself. Samuel had a sharp and adventurous eye for fashion, and by the time they'd finished, James hardly recognized himself.

'What about the money, though?' he'd asked. 'How are we going to pay for all this?'

Samuel had dismissed his concerns with a wave.

'Money's no problem now, James. We have more than enough.'

'But how? Where do you get it from?'

'Leanna. She has enough money for all of us. And in any case, I have a feeling that money isn't going to be important in the future.'

They had talked about that future often enough during the weeks they had spent together. James found it hard to imagine, but Leanna had a vision of a world where all weakness and suffering would be swept aside. Those who inhabited this bright future would be strong and resilient. Samuel also dreamed of a fairer, more equal society, where black and white, gay and straight would live together in harmony. James didn't fully understand either of these dreams, but he hoped with all his heart they would come true.

The meeting with Leanna and Warg Daddy that afternoon had left him anxious though. *Can we count on you, James?* He didn't know what she had meant by that. Count on him for what? He still didn't understand her hostility toward him. He understood Adam's antagonism easily enough. That was all about power. Samuel had defied Adam's authority by bringing James to the house, and Adam hated to be challenged. But Leanna? James had never done anything to make her so antagonistic. Except ... that time he'd first turned, he'd savaged all those people at the railway station, and Leanna had been furious afterwards. It didn't seem to occur to her that she and the others regularly went out killing.

Double standards. James knew all about that. Father Mulcahy had been the same, for all his pious words. *Love thy neighbour,* he had told James. Unless it was the wrong kind of love.

Father Mulcahy had sent him on his journey into the wilderness, and now he had become Leanna's scapegoat. It was a small price to pay to be with Samuel. And he would try to be more careful tonight. When the blood lust came, he would keep it under control.

'Good news,' said Dawn, returning with the test results. You're both cleared to donate. 'Who wants to go first?'

'Me,' said James, standing up. 'I'll go first.'

The procedure wasn't as painful as he'd imagined. As Samuel had said, after all the time he'd spent in hospital, giving blood felt like little more than a pinprick. He didn't even feel weak afterwards. 'Please take more,' he told Dawn. 'I want to help as many people as I can.'

'Hey, easy, there,' she said, swabbing the place on his arm where the needle had been. 'One pint is plenty, thank you very much. You'll end up in hospital yourself if I take any more. You can come back in a few months if you want to donate again.'

'Thanks,' said James. 'I will.'

'I think you've missed the point, James,' said Samuel on the way out. 'Leanna's plan isn't to cure people by donating blood; it's to accelerate the spread of the condition.'

'Oh, I know that,' said James. 'But if we can help people too, shouldn't we try to do that?'

Samuel slung an arm casually over James' shoulder. 'That's what I love about you, James. You're so sentimental. You don't have an uncaring bone in your whole body.'

The New Year's celebrations were already well underway when they left the clinic at eleven o'clock. Party-goers and revellers streamed through the streets, heading south toward the river and the centre of town. They flocked toward the bars, pubs and clubs in search of fun, in anticipation of midnight fireworks. Police in high visibility jackets walked alongside, watching carefully for trouble. There were a few other werewolves too, cloaked in human form, but revealing themselves to James by their scent.

And among them all weaved vigilantes – groups of young men, their heads covered by dark hoods and caps, their faces hidden by masks.

Chapter Sixty-Four

St John's Road, Battersea, South West London, New Year's Eve, 11:10pm, full moon

Vijay, Drake and Rose watched as Aasha and her friends disappeared into one of the noisiest pubs in Battersea. Loud music blared from the pub, and the street outside thronged with people, young and old, many of them the worse for drink. A group of smokers stood immediately outside the entrance to the pub, breathing their poisonous fumes defiantly into the cold night air.

Vijay hesitated as Drake tried to drag him inside. 'I've never been inside a pub before.' He hated the idea that Aasha and her friends had disobeyed their parents' wishes. The pub seemed to contain all the vices he had been taught to avoid – alcohol, tobacco, and idle people who wasted their time smoking and drinking.

'Shut up,' hissed Drake. 'Keep your voice down. It's just a place to hang out and get a drink. Anyway, Aasha's inside, so we have to go in.' He pushed open the door and went inside. Rose went with him.

Reluctantly, Vijay followed.

Crowds of people packed the pub. They were all talking loudly over each other, making the worst din Vijay had ever heard. Everyone seemed to be taller than him, and he only just caught sight of Drake and Rose before they disappeared into the wall of people before him. His glasses were steaming up after coming in from the cold, and he struggled to see clearly. There was no sign of Aasha anywhere. He pushed his way through the crowd, fearing getting lost in here on his own.

A man spilled beer over Vijay's jacket and seemed to think it was his fault. Vijay slipped quickly away from him in case the man became aggressive. The bitter stench of beer on his jacket made him wrinkle his nose in disgust.

He caught up with the others near the bar.

'Let's get a beer,' said Drake.

'What?' shouted Vijay. The noise inside the pub made ordinary speech impossible.

'I said, let's get a beer.'

'No. I don't want anything.'

'Just a coke for me, please,' said Rose.

'Come on, guys, it's New Year's Eve.'

'But we're not eighteen,' insisted Vijay. 'And anyway, Sikhs don't drink alcohol.'

'Live a bit, man. You only live once.'

'That's what you think,' said Vijay stubbornly. All Sikhs believed in reincarnation.

'Come on,' said Drake. 'Watch this.' He pushed his way to the front of the people waiting at the bar. 'Three pints of beer, please, mate,' he shouted at the barman.

'Let's see your ID, then,' said the barman.

'Leave it out, mate. It's New Year's Eve.'

'Yeah,' said the barman, 'That's why I don't have time

to argue. No ID, no beers.'

Drake scowled. 'All right then, just some cokes instead.'

Chapter Sixty-Five

St John's Road, Battersea, South West London, New Year's Eve, 11:17pm, full moon

Warg Daddy had given careful thought to the best location for the Wolf Brother's first hunt. They needed to be cautious. Armed police now patrolled the railway stations and key public spaces, and it would be folly even for a gang of werewolves to risk getting shot, especially the first time they changed. At the same time the public had become wary since the Ripper and Beast killings had begun. Parks and open spaces were deserted at night, with people staying clear between dusk and dawn.

All these factors elevated the risk.

The Pack would have to hunt close to populated areas, but away from the busiest hot spots. Warg Daddy had discussed it with Leanna that afternoon. They had decided to hunt as a single pack, and luck had given them its blessing by making the night of the full moon coincide with the New Year's Eve celebrations. There would be no shortage of revellers on the streets of London tonight, and even a thousand armed police couldn't possibly hope to protect a city of eight million on the busiest night of the year.

Warg Daddy had chosen home ground for this first sortie – Battersea, just south of the Thames, across river from the upmarket bars and restaurants of Chelsea. It was a part of London that hadn't yet been redeveloped. An old inner-city borough, home to a large immigrant population, with a mix of older residential buildings and industrial sites, crisscrossed by nineteenth-century railways, but overlooked by clusters of new and half-built glass towers lining the riverbank.

The area drew a local crowd to its pubs, bars and nightclubs, many of them familiar haunts of the Wolf Brothers, and the nearby green spaces of parks and commons made a perfect getaway route. The streets were wide and open, and as long as they kept away from the major railway stations they ought to be safe.

And there would be people. People in abundance, like lambs waiting to be slaughtered.

The Wolf Brothers set out from their lair just after eleven o'clock. There was no point going earlier, as thick cloud lay heavy over the darkened city. It was forecast to clear in time for the turning of the year at midnight.

What wasn't being predicted was the bloodbath that would follow.

Chapter Sixty-Six

St John's Road, Battersea, South West London, New Year's Eve, 11:45pm, full moon

Vijay heard the noise before the others. Despite the racket inside the pub, sudden shouts intruded from the street outside, even over the loud partying within. The shouting didn't sound like people having fun. It sounded like violence. He grabbed hold of Drake's sleeve. 'What's that noise?'

'Nothing,' said Drake. 'It's nearly midnight. Some people are starting the New Year early.'

'It sounds like fighting.'

'I can hear it too,' said Rose.

Drake cocked his head to one side and listened harder. 'Let's go outside and see.'

'No,' said Vijay. 'If there's trouble we have to stay here and protect Aasha. It's why we came.' He started to push his way through the crowd toward her. Rose and Drake followed.

Close up, Vijay hardly recognized his sister. Aasha wore a low-cut black dress that revealed far more than he wanted to see. She and her three girlfriends had piled makeup onto their faces. Aasha's eyes looked enormous, outlined in fierce black liner, her heavily enhanced lashes flicking dangerously up and down as her anger boiled over. 'Oh my God,' she said when she saw him. 'What are you doing here?'

'Is that your kid brother?' asked one of her friends. The other two giggled loudly.

Aasha was incandescent. 'Did you follow us here? You are such a creep. I am so not speaking to you ever again.'

'There's no time for an argument,' said Vijay. 'Something's happening. That's why we're here. There's some kind of trouble.'

'What trouble?' asked Aasha, looking around.

People were starting to leave the pub now, heading outside to watch the fireworks and sing *Auld Lang Syne* to usher in the New Year at the stroke of midnight.

'The only kind of trouble I see is the trouble you're in,' she said. 'Don't think I'm going to let you off lightly for this. You, or your creep of a friend,' she added, glaring at Drake.

But Drake had his attention elsewhere. 'Shh,' he said. 'Listen.'

'To what?' said Aasha, but they could all hear it now – shouts and screams from outside, car alarms going off, and the tinkle of glass being broken. 'What the hell's that?' she asked.

As if in response to her question, the window of the pub shattered into a thousand pieces as a rock smashed through it from the street. One of Aasha's friends screamed. A young man wearing a baseball cap, his face covered by a ski mask apart from his eyes and mouth, jumped up and scrabbled through the empty window frame into the pub. In his right hand he gripped a baseball bat.

Aasha screamed.

Vijay moved instinctively in front of the others. The man with the mask turned to face him and advanced in his direction, picking his way between the empty chairs and tables of the pub. He paused to kick a table over, spilling drinks and glasses to the floor with a crash. He lashed out at another table, sweeping bottles away with his wooden bat. Beyond him, in the street outside, people rushed past in all directions.

The man came close to Vijay, slapping the thick end of the baseball bat against his open palm. The mask largely hid his face, but he was white and fair-haired, his hair shaved close to his skin. He wore baggy jeans, steel-toe boots and a green jacket.

Aasha and the girls pressed themselves against the back wall of the room.

The masked man stood with his feet apart, his hand gripping the wooden bat firmly. His eyes met Vijay's. 'Time to get this party started,' he said.

Vijay watched the movement of the baseball bat with horror, cringing every time it slapped against the man's palm. He had nothing to defend himself with. He looked around for something that he could use. All he could see were chairs and tables. He moved a chair between himself and the masked man. Laughing, the man kicked it away and onto its side. He stepped into the space where the chair had been, lifting the baseball bat to strike.

Drake stepped in front of him. 'Hey,' he said to the guy in the green jacket. 'Leave them alone. They're just girls.'

'He's not,' said the youth, pointing the bat at Vijay and spitting at the floor next to him. 'What you doing with them, anyway? They ain't your kind. They don't belong in this country.'

Drake grabbed an empty beer bottle from a nearby table and smashed its end against the back of a chair. He held the ragged glass of the makeshift weapon out in front of him, its teeth pointing at the masked youth. 'No,' he said. 'You're the one who don't belong here. Now get out.'

The youth sneered at them and lifted the bat higher. He spat on the floor again, then turned and ran, jumping back through the broken window he had come through.

Vijay's hands were shaking. 'This is mad,' he said. 'We have to get away from here.'

'We can't go outside,' said Aasha. 'Not with people like that out there.'

'But we can't stop them coming in, either,' said Vijay.

Aasha looked around the now-empty pub. 'There must be another way out.'

Rose took hold of Vijay's arm. 'Follow me. I saw another exit near the back.' She set off quickly, the others following close behind.

Chapter Sixty-Seven

St John's Road, Battersea, South West London, New Year's Eve, 11:48pm, full moon

Dean was in the thick of it. There had been isolated incidents all evening, and he'd already made several arrests for various public order offences. His instructions were to crack down hard to prevent an escalation from petty disorder into full-blown riot. At first the strategy worked, but as midnight drew nearer, more and more youngsters flooded onto the streets, many of them clearly looking for trouble.

Dean recognized the type. These men had come prepared for violence, their faces hidden behind scarves or ski-masks, peaked caps pulled low, and carrying weapons too. They chanted racist and anti-immigrant slogans as they marched along, and quickly seized the opportunity to progress to physical violence.

With so many people on the streets, the situation rapidly descended into chaos. Dozens of people filled the street, rocking cars or climbing atop them, picking up missiles to hurl at the police and smashing the windows of cars and shops alike as they went.

A voice over a police loudspeaker tried to calm the crowds, but it was already too late for that.

On one side of the street, the brightly-lit windows of a department store had been broken. Inside, dummies dressed in the latest fashions looked on blankly as looters ran inside the store, searching for valuables that could easily be carried out. Alarms and sirens went unheeded, wailing uselessly over the shouts and cries of the people.

One hooded youth stood on top of a car just a short distance away, throwing a small barrage of stones in Dean's direction. 'Come and have a go!' he jeered. Dean itched to oblige.

Among the rioters, ordinary people were caught up in the trouble, fleeing in panic, and adding to the overall confusion. A car had tried to wind its way through the melee, but had finally got stuck, coming to a halt as people pressed in from all sides. The driver and passengers cowered inside as a group of masked men surrounded them, rocking the car from side to side, laughing and jeering. Dean locked eyes briefly with the driver of the car. It wasn't hard to read the look of terror on his face.

It was time to reclaim the streets.

Dean and his team fanned out across the street in a line, Liz next to him where he could keep a close watch on her. He and the other officers in his squad wore full riot gear, with stab vests, motorcycle-style helmets, circular shields, and batons, but he held no illusion that their protective gear made them invulnerable. He'd seen enough photographs of injuries sustained by riot police to dispel that myth. He looked around at his colleagues and wondered how many of them would end up in hospital by the night's end.

Not Liz, though. Please, not Liz. She was as tough as any officer he'd known, but something was badly wrong with her tonight. She stood with hunched shoulders as if in pain. Bright lights seemed to dazzle her. And her eyes looked more yellow than ever, glowing like candles in the dark. He'd asked her again to go home, but she'd stubbornly refused.

He waited for their sergeant to give the command to advance. A rain of stones and other missiles fell down on them, clattering against their shields and helmets. They would need to act soon, or the situation would spiral out of control entirely. One hooded man ran toward them with a beer bottle and let it fly through the air. The bottle shattered against Dean's shield.

It was enough.

The police began to pound their batons against their shields. They built up a rhythmic pulse that carried its own momentum, becoming faster and louder until it swept aside even the noise of the riot. It tapped into the same primeval bloodlust that drove the rioters themselves. The blood pounded in Dean's head, pushing away all fear, and leaving him with a sense of focus.

'Go!' bellowed the sergeant behind him, and Dean and his fellow officers marched forward eagerly, shields held like a wall before them. The rioters fell back like a wave, and Dean began to run at them, his hand wrapped tightly around his baton.

Chapter Sixty-Eight

Riverside Walk, Battersea, South West London, New Year's Eve, 11:55pm, full moon

James stood with Samuel on the south bank of the River Thames. They were some distance from central London, but with his sharp eyesight he could make out the familiar form of the Houses of Parliament about a mile downriver, its floodlit facade picked out clearly against the darkened sky.

'Look,' said Samuel. He pointed at the tall observation wheel of the London Eye. Lasers began to flicker across its ovoid passenger capsules as the countdown to midnight began.

Enormous crowds had gathered along the banks of the Thames and on the many bridges that spanned it – Westminster Bridge, Waterloo Bridge, Vauxhall Bridge and others. Countless people stood waiting for midnight and the fireworks that would be released from barges stationed along the river.

But James and Samuel had not come for fireworks, or for the turn of the year. They had come to hunt. 'When will the moon come out?' asked James.

'Soon,' said Samuel. 'Very soon now.'

James raised his gaze high above the heads of the crowd, above the London Eye and the other landmarks, up toward the sky where clouds hid the moon. The weather forecasters had predicted the cloud cover would clear by midnight. Well, the hour had almost arrived, and the sky was still overcast, but it was thinning rapidly. It would not be long now.

He was glad they had stayed close to the river. Some kind of trouble was unfolding further south, judging from the number of police cars that had started to converge on the area, and he wanted to stay well away from trouble. 'What do you think is happening?' he asked Samuel.

Samuel shrugged. 'Nothing for us to worry about.'

Another police car sped past, blue lights spinning as it crossed the widely-arched span of Vauxhall Bridge and turned right toward Battersea Park. A fire engine followed, driving past at speed, its siren cutting through the sound of the crowd like a knife. The blaring noise gradually receded as the vehicle drove south, and was replaced by the voice of the people joining together to count down toward midnight.

'... , three, two, one, zero!' chanted the crowd.

Across the water the first chimes of Big Ben rang out. The quarter bells sounded faint at this distance, but James' enhanced hearing picked out the famous *Ding Dong* tune that preceded the striking of the hour. The melody rang out at a stately pace, just as it had every hour for more than a hundred and fifty years.

After it came to an end, the great bell began to slowly chime the arrival of the New Year. Simultaneously, the first fireworks rose into the sky, exploding in a flurry of sparks above the London skyline. All around the crowd cheered.

James looked on impatiently. The fireworks and laser display did nothing to satisfy him. He had not tasted human flesh for a full month. His whole body hungered for it. If the moon did not appear soon, he would not be able to restrain himself. He would be forced to kill, whether in wolf or human form.

Samuel seemed to sense his frustration. He wrapped his huge ebony hand around James' pale fingers. 'Relax, James. There's no hurry. Just stay calm and enjoy the show.'

But James couldn't concentrate on the fireworks. He looked instead at the crowds that lined the river bank. People by the hundred stood nearby. He could taste their flesh on his lips, smell their blood as his nostrils flared, hear the wild pumping of their hearts within their frail bodies.

He turned to the woman closest to him. She stood facing the river, looking into the distance, her bright eyes reflecting the flashes and bursts of the fireworks. She was young – perhaps just eighteen – and her rosy cheeks and smooth skin promised tender flesh beneath. She was wrapped from head to toe in a long, thick coat, but he could easily imagine the pale body beneath the heavy clothing, her arms and legs plump with meat and blood that he yearned to taste.

She was watching the fireworks so intently that she didn't even notice his drooling tongue licking his upper lip.

Chapter Sixty-Nine

*St John's Road, Battersea, South West
London, New Year morning, full moon*

Liz couldn't have chosen a worse night to return to work, but that gave her all the more reason to see it through. She huddled behind her riot shield, facing the crowd, glad for once of her shortness, which made her less of a target for stones and other missiles. The aching in her limbs had returned as badly as before. Her light sensitivity was worsening too, and the bright artificial lights from shop windows almost dazzled her. Thick yellow mucus filled her eyes and she had to keep wiping it away with her thumb.

'I am not a monster,' she whispered to herself.

Dean had twice told her to go home, but that had only made her more determined to stay. Her family needed her, yellow eye sickness or not. Dean, Mihai and her father – they were her family now. She would not let them down, not like her father had let her down.

Hunched over to protect herself from the blinding lights all round, she stood her ground waiting for the order to charge, and when it came, she marched forward with her fellow officers.

'Keep close to me,' said Dean.

The front line of rioters broke and scattered as the police charged, and Liz followed Dean to the stranded car, looking to rescue its trapped passengers as her first objective. There were four people inside including the driver – two men and two women – and they were clearly terrified. Dean reached the car ahead of her and banged on the windscreen. 'Unlock the doors!' he called to the driver, but the man kept the car firmly sealed.

The protesters had fallen back as the police charged, but out of the crowd stepped more youths, hurling stones, bottles and glasses at the police line.

'Get out of the car!' shouted Liz, banging on the car door, but the occupants seemed too scared to move. She and the other police raised their shields to block the hail of missiles from the rioters, but several hit home, smashing against the glass visors of helmets, striking unprotected limbs and shoulders.

A colleague next to her cried out, a red gash across his shoulder.

She grabbed hold of the man, supporting him as he staggered away from the front line. 'Come with me,' she said. She helped him to the safety of a waiting paramedic, then returned to the fray.

Looters were pouring out of shops, leaving with TVs and other goods tucked under their arms. The pavements were already strewn with dropped screens and laptops as well as the detritus of broken glass and stones. The situation was deteriorating further and the police dropped back under a sustained hail of missiles.

'To me!' yelled the sergeant.

Dean and the other police officers regrouped in a line and prepared to charge a second time. Liz took up her place in the formation and readied herself for another assault. For a second time the street quivered to the sound of wooden batons against polycarbonate shields.

She ran forward again toward the car.

A group of masked and hooded young men stood in her path, their faces shadowed, clutching bottles and makeshift weapons in their hands. They put up a show of defiance as Liz and the others ran at them, but quickly turned and fled like rats. Again Dean reached the besieged car before her and pushed away the last stragglers with his shield. He gave one of the youths a glancing blow with his baton as he went.

Again he banged his fist against the windscreen of the car, shouting for the driver and passengers to get out. Still they huddled inside.

Liz lowered her face to the driver's window. 'Open the door!' she cried, but the man inside shook his head. She swore in frustration. The rioters had been driven back, but they were grouping again to attack. The people in the car would be overrun if they didn't get out.

A shout from Dean alerted her to a new danger. 'Liz! Look out!'

At the front of the surging crowd, a young man had appeared, his face wrapped in a black scarf, a bottle in his hand. It flared bright in the night like a candle. A petrol bomb. He took aim at Liz and threw the bottle as hard as he could.

Chapter Seventy

Riverside Walk, Battersea, South West London, New Year morning, full moon

James stood mesmerized by the woman next to him. He could smell her sweet flesh, and hear the blood that rushed through her young body. The hunger that raged within him could not be denied. Every cell of his being strained to be unleashed.

He needed to feed, and soon. It was past midnight, yet still the change had not come.

He dragged his eyes from the woman and looked up, hoping for a glimpse of the moon. The pale milky orb was appearing at the very zenith of the sky, struggling to break free of the clouds that concealed it. James willed them to vanish.

The clouds thinned as he watched, their sparse trails creeping away in retreat. Already a shimmer of light peeked out through the almost transparent haze.

But it was not enough. Still the change did not come.

Suddenly Samuel gripped his arm. 'James, look over there.'

He looked in confusion where Samuel was pointing. Instead of up at the moon, Samuel pointed to his right, further along the river bank.

'They're coming toward us,' said Samuel.

At first James didn't understand what Samuel had seen. People were everywhere, standing and walking, singing and shouting. Over their heads, fireworks exploded in a gaudy wall of red and green against the night sky. Apartment buildings stood proud along the riverside, their residents making the most of their expensive views across the River Thames. And there were police, walking through the crowds toward them. He had seen all this before.

Then in a flash of understanding he realized the danger. These were not regular policemen, but the new elite force of armed police, dressed in their protective suits and helmets, carbines at their sides. He counted four, but they worked in teams and more would be here, hidden by the crowd. If James and Samuel changed now, they would become easy targets, even in wolf form.

James looked up. 'It's too late,' he said.

The last threads of cloud slipped away, revealing the cold, clear stare of the moon. The moonlight struck his face, its silver beams caressing his skin and working their magic. It was too late to run, too late to hide. The change was already happening.

Chapter Seventy-One

St John's Road, Battersea, South West London, New Year morning, full moon

The riot spread like wildfire, but Warg Daddy looked on impassively. This was not his fight. He had not come for this.

Debris lay all around him from looted shops, smashed advertising billboards and broken telephone kiosks. Smoke rose from fires started in the street or in buildings along the road, and alarms and sirens rang out in agitation. Car drivers honked their horns. People shouted at each other and filmed the scene on their phones. None of it mattered. It was all just noise.

'Spread out, Brothers,' he commanded. 'Take your positions.'

Snakebite climbed onto a nearby car to get a better view of the unfolding violence, his black leather jacket, dark glasses and red beard unmistakable amidst the chaos. Some guy ran up onto the car to join him. Snakebite hurled him to the ground, where he lay on his back like a broken doll.

The crowds surged along the street, breaking against the parked and stranded cars like crashing waves. Among them went rioters, police, fleeing party-goers, kids on skateboards. Cyclists rode past, making the most of the breakdown of traffic laws. They were all the same to Warg Daddy. He watched without interest as they passed him by.

A double-decker bus made its way slowly through the crowds as if this were any regular Saturday night and everything would turn out all right. It wouldn't. The bus driver realized that eventually and tried to turn his vehicle in the road. It was too narrow for that however. On board, the passengers stared out fearfully through the glass, or huddled in their seats. Warg Daddy marked them out for attention. When the change came they would be easy meat. That bus would be their tomb.

A shout from Snakebite caught his attention.

Snakebite had turned his gaze toward the sky and Warg Daddy looked up too. A police helicopter drifted overhead, training a blinding searchlight on the anarchy below. The chopping of its blades drowned out the noise on the street as it flew over, and Warg Daddy turned his super-sensitized eyes from the painful beam of light. But the helicopter passed over in vain. The police could do little to contain the violence and it would surely only get worse.

The helicopter flew away and Warg Daddy saw something else. Where previously a thick blanket of grey had hidden the night sky, more and more stars were appearing in his enhanced night vision. They twinkled brightly against a velvet blackness. The clouds retreated swiftly, a strong wind sweeping them away like curtains being drawn aside to reveal the eternal majesty of the heavens above.

Suddenly, as promised, the full moon emerged in all its

majesty. Its clear bright light revealed the street riot as just a petty Saturday-night squabble between police and vigilantes. It would be swept away as easily as the thin clouds overhead had vanished.

Warg Daddy felt the intense light of the moonbeams burn his face and hands. He threw off his leather jacket and peeled away the shirt beneath to bathe fully in the blazing moonlight. His skin writhed as heat broke over him in a lightning surge. Power coursed through his veins and strong black hairs erupted from his arms, chest and face, matting quickly together into a protective coat of thick fur.

A delicious agony rippled through him as his body remade itself from the inside out. His muscles, already strong, bulged larger still, his thighs and triceps pulling taut as the sinews, ligaments and tendons bound themselves like knots. He could feel his very bones growing thicker and pulling like steel rods. His fingers and toes ignited with pain as nails thickened to claws and sharpened into talons. His gums bled as new teeth twisted through, sharp as knives, ready to slice flesh. He swallowed a mouthful of his own blood with pleasure, his tongue drooling with anticipation.

The agony coursed back and forth through every cell of his body, purging weakness, building strength, until all vulnerability had burned to oblivion.

He clawed the ground, feeling the energy that his wolf heart pumped through widened arteries. Power surged through his body. He would explode if he didn't vent it immediately. Rising onto his hind legs, he released it in a howl of ecstasy, saluting the moon that had given him this gift. He would repay that debt with a blood sacrifice to the goddess, Luna.

The police helicopter returned, training its searchlight on the wolves. It did not matter. The Wolf Brothers no longer shunned bright light. Now that they had changed they need not fear light again.

All around him, people had paused in their actions to look. Police, looters and panicked bystanders, they were all just prey, and seemed to know it. Warg Daddy padded into the middle of the street, picking out the weakest. More of the Brothers joined him, pacing in his wake.

A huge red wolf leaped down from the car where Snakebite had stood. Its fiery hackles rose along its back and shoulders like the flames that engulfed the nearby electronics store. The wolf that had been Snakebite rose onto its hind legs and howled at the moon. Fully stretched, the beast stood eight feet tall.

The other Brothers lent their voices to the chorus as well – Slasher, Meathook, Bloodbath and the rest. They wore coats of every colour, from the palest white to the inkiest black. Now all had changed. The hunt could begin.

Warg Daddy studied the people closest to him – a young guy in a hoodie and the policeman he had been about to hurl a bottle at. The terror they radiated was like a drug. He bathed in it luxuriously for a moment. Then he leapt.

Chapter Seventy-Two

Riverside Walk, Battersea, South West London, New Year morning, full moon

The skin along James' arms began to itch. Fine hairs erupted outward, thickening and matting together quickly like a cloak. His gums tingled as sharp teeth pushed through. But as Samuel had said, this second time the change was different.

The first time had felt like a revelation. He had been born again, a new kind of being. The change had gone deep, transforming him from the inside out. He knew exactly what he had experienced that time. The Greek word for it was *anastasis*, or resurrection. It was the rapture promised in the New Testament.

Now he was returning to a familiar state, a condition that was as much a part of him now as his human aspect. The deep change had already taken place and did not need to be repeated. The wolf within him was no longer a stranger. Instead he realized just how much he had missed it. The fur, the enhanced sensory experience, the raw power that surged inside – he craved it as much as he lusted for human flesh and blood.

He turned to the woman he had been drooling over. She saw him now, but like a fool stood still as a statue, her eyes wide. Fear had claimed her, and it would be her undoing. He lunged at her and ripped out her throat. She didn't even have time to scream. Instead, the last sound she made was the gurgle of blood flowing from her open neck.

He ripped at her clothes with his claws and took a bite from her soft flesh. The meat tasted as delectable as he had imagined. He chewed and swallowed it down.

Before he could take another bite, Samuel's wolf face appeared next to his. 'Run, James. They have guns.'

The police. In his rush to feed, he had all but forgotten them.

Samuel leapt forward through the scattering crowd and dashed off on all fours, heading away from the river and the police.

James turned to see the crowd fleeing in panic in all directions away from him. The sight gave him an undeniable thrill. An urge to chase after them flooded his senses. But through the rush of people, the police advanced steadily, carbines and pistols held aloft.

He felt the wolf hatred of guns rise up inside him like bile. His hackles rose. Wolves had survived these thousands of years only by learning a sharp fear of weapons.

Above him came the sudden clattering of helicopter blades. The bright beam of a searchlight swept along the ground toward him. If it picked him out, he would surely die.

With a last snarl at the police, he fled.

Chapter Seventy-Three

St John's Road, Battersea, South West London, New Year morning, full moon

The petrol bomb missed Liz but exploded beneath the car, spreading a sheet of fire across the street. She felt it scorch her legs, and stamped at her clothing, dampening the flames before they took hold. Some of her colleagues were not so fortunate. Fire engulfed the two officers standing nearest the car. Yellow flames clung to them like demons, running up their legs to dance across their backs and shoulders. The officer closest to Liz ducked down, clutching his head as the fire raced across his body, turning him into a human torch.

Inside the car, the men and women looked on in horror. A curtain of flame surrounded their vehicle like a fireball.

Liz froze, torn between her colleagues and the people in the car. Flames raged in all directions. The heat and light from the fire had fuelled a primitive fear inside her. She experienced again the terror of being trapped in the burning building with Mihai, flames closing in on all sides with no way out. Her eyes burned, as much from the bright light of the fire as from its heat. She curled up close to the ground, cowering behind her shield, unable to move forward or back, held captive by fear.

A shout from Dean brought her to her senses. 'Liz!' She felt his strong arms gripping her under the shoulders, hauling her to her feet. 'Come on, let's get you out of here.'

Up ahead, the rioters advanced again, encouraged by the petrol bomb attack. Youths in hoods, scarves and ski masks goaded each other on. Their fists held an assortment of clubs, knives and broken bottles.

Liz snapped out of the terror that had held her in its grip. 'No. Get these men to safety,' she said to Dean, indicating the two officers who had been set ablaze. 'I'll get the people out of the car.'

She didn't pause for a response, but ran to the circle of fire that engulfed the vehicle, searching for a way through the flames. The rear passenger door was clear and she went to it, tugging at the door handle. It held fast. 'Open it!' she shouted at the occupants.

The woman in the rear seat pressed helplessly at the locking mechanism of the door. The door remained sealed.

Black smoke billowed around Liz and hot flames reached out from beneath the car, threatening to catch at her. 'Cover your face,' she shouted at the woman in the car. She took a step back and aimed a blow at the car window with her baton. The baton bounced off uselessly. She struck again, and this time the window caved inward in a shower of glass. The woman inside cowered back.

Liz reached her arm inside and took the woman's hand. 'Climb out!' she yelled over the roar of the fire. 'I'll pull you clear.'

The woman hesitated, then leaned through the gap, pushing herself out of the car with Liz's help. Liz dragged her clear and lowered the woman to her feet.

A hail of stones and bottles fell on them as the rioters pushed forward again. 'Run!' shouted Liz. 'Run to the police line. They'll help you.'

The woman ran as she was told, and Liz turned her attention back to the burning car.

The second passenger in the back, a man, was struggling to push himself through the broken window. 'Help me!' he called. Liz pulled him through and sent him after the woman. The driver and the other passenger remained trapped inside.

Fire had overwhelmed the front of the car, blocking the driver's door with its fiery hand. Liz stuck her head through the broken window of the rear door. 'Grab my hands,' she shouted to the woman in the front passenger seat. 'I'll pull you out.'

The woman had curled up into a ball, hugging her knees, her eyes fixed on the flames that arced across the car's windscreen. 'Come on!' shouted Liz again. Already the flames were reaching around the back of the car. Her eyes were smarting from the smoke and heat.

The woman turned in her seat and struggled into the back of the car. She reached out and clutched Liz's hands tightly, her knuckles as white as her face.

Liz heaved with all her might, dragging the woman through the car window. She stumbled as the woman came out, and crashed to the ground, the woman falling on top of her. Flames leaped around them on every side. Liz pushed herself back onto her knees and hauled the woman to her feet. 'Go!' she shouted. The woman nodded mutely and ran toward safety.

Only the driver remained in the car now. But as Liz stood up, a wall of flame rushed toward her, forcing her away from the broken window. Fire engulfed the whole vehicle and she leapt back from the intense heat.

Inside the driver screamed for help.

A rock struck Liz on the side of her helmet, knocking

her off balance again. The rioters were running toward her, emboldened by the fire. Only Liz's helmet had saved her from serious injury. She looked around for help, but the other officers were engaged in running battles with rioters, or helping wounded colleagues back to the police line.

She ran to the back of the car and raised her baton high. She brought it smashing through the rear windscreen. The glass shattered, making a crawl space just large enough for a man to fit through. She leaned inside and felt two hands clasp hold of hers. With all her strength, she heaved the last man from the car, dragging him from the flames and smoke that filled the vehicle. She dragged him to the ground and rolled him over to smother the flames.

The man was barely conscious. He murmured unintelligibly as Liz lifted him up and staggered toward the police line, the man sprawled in her arms as she carried him.

As Liz half-walked, half-ran up the street, she felt a hand grab her shoulder and yank her back. She spun round and came face to face with a youth wearing a baseball cap and wielding a baseball bat.

'Nice try,' said the youth. 'But you were too slow.' A ski mask hid his face, but there was no mistaking his intentions. The baseball bat slammed into Liz's side, and she reeled backward, still clutching the driver tightly to her chest.

Chapter Seventy-Four

Warg Daddy leapt at his nearest victim, a guy in a hoodie, and tore out his throat, swallowing the blood and gore in a single gulp. His prey flopped to the ground and Warg Daddy stepped over it to lunge at his next victim.

At his right flank, Snakebite attacked the policeman the guy had been fighting. The officer raised his riot shield but Snakebite twitched it out of his hands with his claws. The man turned to flee and Snakebite dragged him to the ground, snapping his neck with his strong jaws.

Warg Daddy and Snakebite ran on together, making for the trapped bus. The doors of the bus were shut, but that was no obstacle to Warg Daddy. He gripped them with his sharp talons and tore them apart, twisting the metal and shattering the glass. The driver of the bus gasped.

Warg Daddy paced slowly up the steps of the bus, savouring the reactions of the driver and his passengers.

The smell of fear inside the bus was delicious. He brought his snout up close to the driver's face and sniffed.

The man was food, nothing more. But Warg Daddy could still play a game with him. 'Do you want to live?' he demanded.

The man gawped at him in speechless terror.

'I asked you a question,' growled Warg Daddy.

The driver nodded.

'Good,' said Warg Daddy, letting the man have a good look at his teeth. 'All you have to do is make a choice. Can you do that?'

The man nodded again.

Warg Daddy licked his lips. 'Here's the choice. If you choose to live, then all these people die.' He indicated the passengers with a jerk of his head. There were about twenty on board the bus, he guessed. 'Or, if you choose to die, these people can walk free. Which is it?'

The man gazed first at him, then at the passengers. He still said nothing. Warg Daddy wondered if he'd lost the power of speech. 'Me,' the man said at last, weakly. 'Let me live, please.'

The people on the bus gasped, or shouted abuse at the man, or just whimpered quietly.

Warg Daddy grinned. Humans were weak, just as Leanna had said. And stupid too. They didn't deserve to live. 'Okay, then,' said Warg Daddy. 'Out you go.'

The man stared in disbelief at the open door of the bus, then back at Warg Daddy. Hesitatingly, he made his way out of the bus, keeping as far from Warg Daddy as he could. Warg Daddy watched him go.

The man stepped outside and there was a flash of red fur. Snakebite took him down, jaws locked around the man's neck. His scream died with him in an instant.

Warg Daddy rushed at the nearest passenger, a young woman, and savaged her to death with his teeth. He sprang to her companion, an older man wearing glasses, and ripped him with his claws. A tall man at the back of the bus reached to open the emergency exit, but Warg Daddy got to him first. Blood sprayed across the windows of the bus. He danced from passenger to passenger, young and old, men and women alike. By the time he had finished, the inside of the bus was painted as red as its shiny exterior. Warg Daddy paused to feed on the corpses.

Outside, the Brothers were killing on a grand scale, cutting down rioters and police alike. It was carnage, just as he had expected.

A sudden sound made him turn away from his feast. A loud crack, or a bang, followed by several more in quick succession. Gunshots.

He ran to the front of the bus and looked out. Three grey vans had pulled up at the end of the road and armed police in grey uniforms were pouring from them. The police carried carbines and rifles and were advancing up the street toward the bus, shooting as they came. A bullet shattered the window next to him, bringing it down in a shower of glass.

He ducked down and ran to the buckled doors of the bus. Corpses and the dying littered the street outside where the Brothers had cut them down. The surviving looters and vigilantes ran for cover as the armed police opened fire. The wolves would need to run too, if they were to survive.

He leapt from the bus and rose up to give his loudest roar. 'Run, Brothers!' he bellowed. 'Save yourselves!' He dropped to all fours and ran himself, dashing from side to side as a storm of bullets followed him up the street.

Chapter Seventy-Five

Liz fell backward under the blow of the wooden bat, still cradling the unconscious driver in her arms. She landed badly, the man's weight forcing her down heavily. She clutched at her side where the youth in the baseball cap had struck her. A sharp pain stabbed at her, and her hand came away from the wound smeared red.

The youth stood over her triumphantly, the wooden bat raised in his hands. He gripped it tightly in his palms and lifted it high, ready to bring it down on her a second time.

Before he could strike, a flying kick from behind knocked him off balance. Dean. He struck the thug again behind his knees, bringing him to the ground. 'Come on,' he said to Liz. 'Let's get you out of here.' He helped her back to her feet, then lifted the body of the unconscious driver in his arms.

She stood uncertainly. The fall had winded her and blood trickled down her face from where the rock had struck her head. More blood continued to flow from the wound at her side. The light from the fire burned brighter than ever, and she had to squint to see through the sticky yellow glue that covered her eyes. 'Where to?' she asked.

Rioters and looters blocked their way to safety, spreading fire and mayhem as they smashed their way along the street. The man with the baseball bat was back on his feet, and three more youths had gathered around him, cutting off any chance of escape. Liz could barely stand, and Dean was struggling to walk with the injured man in his arms. Both had lost their shields and batons in the confusion.

She looked around for a way out. 'Follow me,' she said.

She lurched down a side street, the pain from her head wound and the blow to her side competing to drop her to her knees. But she staggered on, one step after another, Dean carrying the injured man beside her. After a minute she stopped beneath a streetlamp to regain her breath. 'I can't go any further,' she gasped. Dean laid the driver on the pavement while he rested too.

They found themselves in a narrow back alley cut off from their colleagues. 'It's a dead-end,' said Dean. The lane ended with a brick wall. High walls and windowless buildings lined each side. The only way out was back to the burning car and the riot.

The four youths had followed them into the alleyway. Along with the guy wielding the baseball bat were two other thugs wearing hoods and ski masks. Both carried knives. The fourth man wore motorcycle leathers and a helmet with the visor pulled down. A metal pole was slung casually over his shoulder.

It should never have happened this way. Basic training should have prevented them from becoming separated from other officers. But the situation had been desperate. Liz couldn't have left the man to die inside the burning car. She had made a snap decision and she wouldn't regret what she'd done, even if she ended up paying for it with her own life.

But it ain't just your life, her father's voice whispered in her head. *There's the boy to look after now. What will happen to him?*

Dean spoke quickly into his radio. 'Officer Delta Alpha 376 requesting urgent assistance. Location – a side lane off St John's Road.'

'Where the hell are we exactly?' he asked Liz. 'I don't know this alley.'

She looked around for a sign with a street name or another identifier, but there was nothing to fix their location. 'I don't know.' She could have kicked herself in frustration. Without being able to give their exact whereabouts, how could they hope to get help?

The reply from the radio came back immediately. 'Delta Alpha 376, please state precise location.'

'Not known,' blurted Dean. It was hopeless.

Liz turned her attention to the gang in front of her. The guy with the baseball bat seemed to have appointed himself as their leader. He smacked the bat against the meaty palm of his hand as he led them down the alley. The two with the knives were kitted out in almost matching outfits – jeans and dark green jackets, with steel-cap black boots. They spread out across the narrow road like hunters, the blades of their knives clearly visible under the single streetlamp. The biker in his black leathers and helmet waved the steel pole menacingly as they advanced.

'Put the weapons away, boys,' said Liz. 'Don't make more trouble for yourselves.'

Only the eyes of the guy with the baseball bat were visible through his black ski mask. He was little more than a teenager, but that didn't make him any less dangerous. 'We ain't making trouble for ourselves,' he said. 'Reckon you're the ones in trouble now.'

'We have an injured man. He needs urgent medical

treatment. Let us get help for him.'

The youth laughed cruelly. 'He got what was coming to him. You gonna get it too.'

The four rioters came on slowly. Dean kept his position, standing between the advancing youths and the body of the injured man. He was bigger than his opponents but weaponless now.

Liz stood by the brick wall of the alleyway. She strained to breathe, every intake a sharp agony, every outbreath a dull pain. Everything had turned yellow and she shielded her eyes from the light of the streetlamp they had gathered beneath, almost blinded by its glare. She could still hear noise from the rioting on the main street and see people rushing past, but down this deserted side street it was like another world. They would have to face the men alone.

Behind her came a sudden noise. She twisted round, ignoring the fresh stab of pain in her side. More people had entered the alleyway from a back door in one of the buildings. They ran toward her, before stopping as they took in the scene.

The new arrivals were kids – two boys and five girls. None looked older than eighteen, and they were clearly civilians, not rioters. The girls were dressed for a night on the town, in short dresses and high heels. One of the girls screamed when she saw the men blocking the exit.

With a start, Liz realized that she knew some of the teenagers. Vijay Singh, his turban wrapped neatly around his hair, despite the chaos all around him; Drake Cooper, looking very much like one of the rioters with his cropped hair and scruffy jeans; and Rose Hallibury, her pale face and red hair shining radiantly in the dark. They clearly recognized her too. She beckoned to them. 'Stand next to me.' They flocked obediently to her side.

'Well, well,' said the guy with the baseball bat. 'Look who we have here. If it ain't my old friends from the pub.'

'We ain't no friends of yours,' called Drake.

'Let them go,' said Liz, wheezing. 'They're just

children.'

'Sure,' said the guy mockingly. 'We don't want them to get hurt, do we?'

The four thugs moved closer, surrounding Dean and blocking any escape route for the others. Liz leaned against the brick wall for support. The gash in her side continued to bleed steadily. She covered it with her hand, pressing at the wound to staunch the flow of blood.

The guy with the bat spoke directly to one of the girls. 'Come over here, darling, I promise I won't touch you.' He laughed again.

'Everyone stay close behind me,' Dean told the kids. They didn't need telling twice.

The biker with the iron bar kept coming forward, the two men with knives following closely at his heels. Their leader urged them on, slapping his bat against the palm of his hand. They came to within a few yards of Dean.

'Stop,' said Dean. 'Don't come a step closer.'

'Or you'll do what?'

'You don't want to find out.'

The leader gave a signal to the other three. They continued to advance from all sides, knives weaving in their hands, metal bar swinging dangerously, baseball bat raised to strike.

Dean stood his ground as they approached. There was nowhere left to run.

Chapter Seventy-Six

Dean had lost his riot shield and baton during the rescue, but he was trained in unarmed combat. He still wore his helmet, and his Kevlar vest would give him some protection from the knives. But his best defence was perhaps his will to live. He thought again of his wife and daughter, Samantha and Lily, waiting at home for his return. And he thought of his unborn child. A girl or a boy, he didn't yet know, but he was determined to find out. No thug with a crowbar or knife was going to rob him of that.

He had a canister of tear gas too.

He pulled out the can and gave it a quick shake. One of the youths came for him, knife in hand. Dean sprayed his face with the aerosol. The kid screeched as the tear gas covered his eyes, and reeled away, bent over double.

The others hesitated, circling warily.

He aimed the can at the second knife-wielder, but

before he could use it, he saw a blur of movement out of the corner of his eye and felt a sharp blow to the side of his head. He whirled around just in time to see the motorcycle guy lifting his iron bar to strike again. Dean swung the can in his direction, but he was too slow. The cold steel struck him right in the middle of the forehead and he fell backward, arms flailing. The ground crashed against him, squeezing the air from his lungs. Then everything went black.

Chapter Seventy-Seven

Vijay watched in horror as the policeman stumbled backward and collapsed on the ground next to the injured man he'd been trying to protect. His helmet had been knocked aside by the blow from the metal bar, and a crimson stream leaked from a gash in his forehead. He lay motionless, his eyes closed.

The spray can he'd used on one of the thugs rolled over to Vijay's foot. Vijay eyed it uncertainly for a moment.

The guy with the crowbar whooped for victory and spun the iron bar in his hands. He turned toward Vijay. 'You want some too?' he said.

Vijay shook his head.

'Then get out of here,' said the guy. 'But leave the girls behind.'

To either side of the guy with the crowbar was another thug, one armed with a long knife, the other the youth they'd first encountered in the pub, cropped hair, steel-toe boots and baseball bat swinging menacingly. They circled around, trying to separate Vijay from the others. He didn't know what to do. He took a step to the right and his foot brushed against the can of tear gas, sending it spinning.

Drake appeared to his left suddenly, the broken beer bottle still in his hand. The sight of the bottle made the knife-wielder pause. Drake waved the jagged glass weapon in front of him and the guy jumped back.

But the guy in the helmet wasn't fazed. He raised the metal bar and jabbed it at Drake.

Drake dodged to avoid the blow, but the man swept his weapon sideways, catching him on the shoulder. The broken bottle smashed on the ground.

Vijay ducked down and grabbed hold of the spray can. He rose up in front of the man with the knife and pressed down on the spray. A fine jet of aerosol sprayed out of the can, right into the eyes of his attacker. The man fell back, letting go of the knife and putting his hands to his eyes. 'You little runt!'

The guy with the baseball bat didn't wait for Vijay to turn the spray against him. He rushed at him, swinging the bat hard. It hit his arm just below the elbow with a hideous crack. Vijay screamed and stumbled backward, tripping over the body of the prone policeman. The canister of spray fell uselessly to the ground with a clatter.

Drake leaped at the youth, but his injured shoulder had put his right arm out of action. The baseball bat connected with his jaw, and he fell back against the brick wall with a howl.

'Grab hold of the girls,' said the thug to his accomplice.

'No!' Vijay struggled to get up from the ground, but it was impossible. His injured arm dangled helplessly by his side and the slightest movement felt like plunging his arm into fire. He lay still on the ground, watching helplessly as the two remaining thugs seized hold of the girls. The motorbike guy came for Aasha from behind, pressing the metal bar to her throat and gripping it tightly with both hands. 'Aasha!' he shouted.

The ringleader treated him to a twisted smile. 'She your girlfriend?' When Vijay said nothing, he smiled again. 'Your sister maybe?' He laughed and walked over to Aasha, shifting the wooden bat to his left hand. She stared back defiantly as he looked her up and down, but Vijay could see the fear below the defiance.

With his free hand the guy grabbed at her dress, pulling it from the neckline. The thin fabric ripped all the way to her waist.

Aasha struggled in the grip of the man who held her from behind, but the iron bar was still at her throat. She squirmed helplessly as her attacker reached out to her again.

Chapter Seventy-Eight

Liz watched the fight unfold through yellow eyes. The blood still trickled from the wounds on her side and her forehead, and her strength was slowly seeping out of her. She tried to move, but her legs folded beneath her as soon as she let go of the supporting wall. She dropped to all fours, gasping for breath, feeling the last of her energy slipping away. She watched the scene with dismay but was powerless to help as the cropped-haired thugs subdued first Vijay, then Drake, then turned their attention to the girls.

This was the second time she had let down these kids – first when they had told her about the headmaster, and now when they needed her protection the most. She had failed to protect Dave Morgan, and she had failed Dean too. He and the driver she had pulled from the car lay unconscious by her side. She had no idea if either man was still alive. She imagined Mihai at home, and wondered what would happen to him if she died too. Her father couldn't possibly cope with an orphaned child. It was only a matter of time before he was arrested, or ran off, and then Mihai would be orphaned a second time. Liz would fail the boy just as her own father had failed her. And she could do nothing to prevent it.

The action in the alleyway became dim as the life left her. Her eyes were thick with gunk, and everything had become a yellow monochrome, the streetlamp casting a strange golden glow over the scene. Her head lolled back like a heavy weight as she slumped against the wall of the alley. High above, the sky slowly lightened, a colder light adding its silvery sparkle to the lamp's gold. There was beauty there, even amidst the horror. The papery clouds drifted aside to reveal the circle of the full moon looking down on them serenely.

The cool glow bathed her face gently, like a healing balm. Up there, in the heavens, all was at peace. As Liz watched, she felt some of that tranquillity permeate her own thoughts. Unlike the lights that had dazzled her these past days, the cool moonbeams soothed her eyes. The gash on her forehead tingled under the frosty rays, almost as if the moon were healing her wound. A feeling of calm began to fill her, as if she were floating free. Her head slowly cleared and her senses came back into focus. She brushed her forehead and found that the cut had stopped bleeding. She touched her hand to her side, expecting to feel a sharp jarring. Instead, when she removed her hand, her palm was clean. The wound bled no more.

She stood up, tentatively at first, using the wall for balance. But she didn't need it. Strength returned to her limbs; not just normal strength, but a superhuman power. It pulsed through her veins like pure energy. She wiped the yellow film from her eyes and surveyed the scene. Whether because of the light of the moon, or a surge of adrenaline, or some other power, her vision had reached a new level. Every detail was picked out in high relief. Every move and sound came to her amplified.

Two of the thugs lay writhing on the ground, their hands over their faces, the after-effects of the tear gas rendering them immobile for now. The two others were assaulting one of the girls – one holding her from behind, the other tearing her dress.

They moved so slowly, the man's hand reaching out and grasping the dress in his fingers, closing his hand around the material and pulling down, inch by inch, all so slow. He stood back to admire his work, and the girl's face drooped in shame and dismay. So slowly they moved, like a series of freeze frames, every moment dragged out for her to inspect.

Had time slowed, or had she speeded up? She moved before she even knew it, rushing the nearest of the thugs, the one who had torn the dress, a growl rising in her throat unbidden, her fingers reaching out like weapons.

She slashed at the so-called vigilante, grabbing his thick neck from behind, spinning him round to face her, and tearing the smirk from his face with her fingernails. His eyes widened slowly in shock, the blood spurting in dark droplets from his cheeks, the insolent mouth opening and closing in dumb astonishment. She struck him again so hard he dropped straight to the ground. It was like swatting a fly. He lay there, groaning and clutching his head. The girl in the torn dress looked at Liz in awe.

The last of the youths stayed frozen, the metal bar pressed to the girl's throat, his hands gripping the weapon so tightly his knuckles stood out ice-white, just like the cold light of the moon. His face was inscrutable behind the visor of his helmet, but Liz smelled fear leaking from his pores like sweat.

She wrenched the metal bar from his fingers before he could use it, simultaneously raking his exposed neck with her nails. She watched as the metal pole fell spinning harmlessly to the ground, the man also twisting away and stumbling as a fine spray of blood splattered from her nails. She spun on the ball of her foot and kicked him in the chest, sending him reeling backward the entire width of the alleyway. He struck the ground with a satisfying thud.

The girl stood inert, awe turned to terror now.

Liz stopped. The reckless force that had animated her ebbed away as quickly as it had come. Her arms went limp. The march of time caught up with her again as her sight and hearing returned to normal. She gasped for breath and dropped her hands to her hips, suddenly desperate for air, as if she had emerged from beneath the ocean and almost drowned. She panted heavily through her mouth until the urgency for oxygen abated.

The girl she had saved still watched her, but her terror had faded to mere fear. For a moment she'd been more afraid of Liz than of her attackers. 'It's okay,' Liz told her breathlessly. 'Everything's going to be all right now.'

The girl nodded, folding her arms across her chest in modesty. The tattered dress hung in ruins. One of her friends stepped up and helped her sit down on the pavement.

Liz looked around. There were more bodies on the ground than people still standing. Drake and Vijay were both hurt. Dean and the injured driver were unconscious, or worse. The four rioters were all subdued, either from tear gas or Liz's own work. They needed urgent medical attention, but that meant going for help. 'Wait here,' she said. 'I'm going to fetch an ambulance. I'll be back soon.'

But walking was more effort than she had anticipated. Her exertions had left her drained. Her boots felt like lead weights and every step took an enormous act of will. Soon she was shuffling instead of walking, her feet impossible to lift. Halfway back along the alleyway she stopped for breath and leaned against the wall for support. The bricks of the wall were cold, damp and rough, but as good as a feather bed. Liz closed her eyes. Just for a moment. She only wanted a little rest.

Chapter Seventy-Nine

Vijay's arm burned with pain. The baseball bat must have shattered every bone in his lower arm. He could no longer move it below the elbow, and each time he tried, the pain shot through him like a jolt of lightning, bringing tears to his eyes. He feared he would pass out from the torment.

He'd lost his glasses when he fell down and couldn't be certain what he'd seen. The guy with the baseball bat had torn Aasha's dress, he had heard that loudly enough, but after that he couldn't say for sure. The police woman, Liz, had become a blur. Without the help of his glasses, she'd already been hazy, but she had blurred more when she'd attacked the rioters, moving with blinding speed. Impossible speed. But what did Vijay really know? Liz was a trained police officer, and he could barely see past the end of his own nose without his glasses.

He groped around on the ground with his uninjured

hand, his fingers seeking out his dropped glasses, but they were nowhere to be found. Without them he was useless. Tears of frustration welled up in his eyes, and hot pain shot through his injured arm as he fumbled along the cold, hard ground. Then Rose knelt beside him and lifted the glasses from the pavement. 'Thanks,' he said, as she slid them carefully back onto his face. The frame had twisted askew, but miraculously the lenses were intact.

Aasha and the other girls were huddling together under the streetlamp, her friends holding her for support. She looked shocked but safe.

The policeman had been hurt badly though, and lay motionless next to the other injured man.

He looked for Drake, and saw his friend struggling to his feet. Blood trickled from Drake's lips and the skin around his mouth looked broken. Like Vijay, he'd taken a nasty blow from the baseball bat.

A look of cold determination filled Drake's face. He limped to where the baseball bat had been abandoned and picked it up.

'What are you doing, Drake?' Vijay asked. 'Liz said to wait here.'

His friend ignored him. Instead he walked slowly to the prone body of the thug in the ski mask, taking the bat with him. The guy lay in the street, clutching his face. Even without his glasses, Vijay had seen Liz rip into him with her fingernails, splattering blood as she slashed at his face. He was moaning quietly to himself and didn't look like a threat anymore.

'Drake?' said Vijay nervously.

Drake's attention was fixed on the injured youth. 'Not so much fun when it happens to you, is it?' he said.

The youth said nothing, just rolled over, his hands covering his bloodied face.

Drake stepped on him, pushing his shoe against the guy's neck. 'I'm talking to you,' he said. 'But I guess you ain't got so much to say now.'

The guy moaned under the pressure of Drake's shoe.

'This is what happens when you pick on kids younger than yourself,' continued Drake. 'It's what you get when you attack a defenceless girl. Maybe you've learned your lesson now.' He turned to Aasha. 'Do you reckon he's learned his lesson?'

Vijay watched in alarm as his sister slowly shook her head from side to side.

'Shall I teach him properly?' asked Drake. He gripped the handle of the wooden bat firmly in both hands.

'No,' called Vijay. 'Leave him, Drake.'

But Drake was waiting for Aasha. All the fear had gone from her now, replaced by a growing look of admiration toward Drake. She nodded silently but resolutely.

'No!' begged Vijay again, but it was no use.

Rose laid a freckled hand on his good arm, kindly but firmly. 'Sometimes people deserve what they get,' she said.

Drake lifted the baseball bat high and brought it down against the man's right shoulder. It struck home with a loud crack and the guy screamed. 'Bet that hurt,' said Drake. 'That's for what you did to me.' He cracked the bat against the side of a leg, producing another scream. 'That's for what you did to my friend.' He nodded in Vijay's direction. Vijay watched with horror.

Drake tossed the bat on the ground. 'And this is for what you did to Aasha.' He kicked hard, driving his shoe into the youth's side. The dull thud that resulted was somehow worse than the crack of the bat against bone. There was no scream from the youth this time, just a grunt, and a sound like air being squeezed out. Drake kicked again, and again. When the guy stopped making a noise, Drake stopped kicking. He stood in the middle of the alleyway, his fists clenched into tight white balls.

'I reckon that's enough,' he said. 'Didn't no one ever tell you? Bullies always get what they deserve.' His shoulders slumped then and the anger seemed to drain away. Suddenly he was just a skinny kid again. He slipped his small pale hands into the pockets of his baggy jeans, and walked back toward Vijay, looking shamefaced and tired.

Vijay couldn't look at his friend's face. Instead he looked past him to where Liz had stopped. She was leaning against the wall and didn't seem to have noticed what Drake had done. She was no longer moving. He didn't think she would be able to fetch an ambulance.

He was wondering what to do about it when he saw something else. Just beyond her, at the end of the alleyway, a dog appeared and ran toward her. Not a dog though. It was too big to be a dog. The creature was as big as a large man, with thick black fur and a long snout. In the darkness of the alley, its yellow eyes glowed brightly. The beast ran fast, and as it drew near to Liz, Vijay's attention shifted to the whiteness of its sharp teeth.

Chapter Eighty

Liz saw the creature as it rounded the corner and entered the alleyway. It bounded toward her on its four strong legs, closing the distance between them rapidly. She leaned against the wall, watching through heavily-lidded eyes as it drew nearer, readying itself to leap. She'd seen its kind before, that night at Ruskin Park when the Beast had attacked Dave Morgan.

This Beast looked different. The first had been smaller, with lighter fur, almost golden. This one had a pelt as black as coal and an enormous body, its huge head anchored by a thick neck, its muscles pumping like pistons as it ran. It was more like a bear than a wolf. And it carried a strange smell, of engine oil and petrol. Its jaws hung open, showing white teeth like daggers.

It slowed as it approached, trotting forward carefully, its hackles raised. It filled the dim alleyway with a deep throaty growl.

Lycanthropic

Liz pressed herself against the cold, rough wall, every muscle in her body twitching to escape. But she had no strength to run. She needed the wall's help just to stand.

The wolf padded steadily toward her, sniffing the air. Closer it came, baring its teeth, its long pink tongue drooling saliva. Hot breath steamed before it and those yellow eyes glowed like torches. Liz looked on helplessly.

The creature stopped abruptly, sniffing the ground. Then it stepped forward uncertainly. It came right up to her, its long snout twitching. She waited for it to bite her. She was so tired, she could offer no resistance. But the beast paused, its yellow eyes filled with puzzlement. It stared at her face, measuring her, as the first Beast had done – an unsettlingly human gaze behind those alien eyes. She returned its stare calmly. Whatever happened now was up to the wolf.

The creature raised one huge black paw and licked it slowly, almost casually, not once taking its eyes from her face. Then it turned and ran. She watched it continue down the alleyway until it reached the others. Dean, Vijay, Drake, Rose, and the rest. She watched in horror as the monster drew closer to them. When it leaped, she cried out.

Chapter Eighty-One

The wolf ran closer and Vijay couldn't take his eyes off those white teeth. He had never liked dogs. Their sharp canine teeth and loud aggressive barking made them monsters in his eyes, and he always avoided them. Now the Beast itself was coming for him, and there was no way he could avoid it.

The thug that Drake had beaten lay motionless on the ground, but two of the other vigilantes struggled back to their feet and turned to face the oncoming creature. One clutched a knife. The other brandished the long metal pole he had used to knock the policeman unconscious. He turned the iron bar toward the wolf, like a spear against a cavalry charge.

The wolf flew at him, soaring through the air, its tail outstretched. Its huge head seemed almost big enough to swallow the youth whole. It dodged the pole easily, sweeping past the vigilante's outstretched arms, and brushed the bar aside.

The jaws of the monster locked around the man's throat, white teeth slicing savagely. The wolf continued its arc as if nothing had happened, landing gracefully on all fours as the body of the man collapsed to the ground, his neck punctured, head dangling at an impossible angle, blood pumping from severed arteries.

The wolf turned and flew again in a single movement, this time taking the knife wielder. The man barely had enough time to turn his knife arm before he was dead.

The wolf stopped, panting for breath beside its two victims, surveying the survivors with its cold yellow eyes. It circled around them, padding closer and sniffing the ground.

Still Vijay stood mesmerized by its teeth.

'Vijay!' Aasha and her friends huddled together beneath the streetlamp. Drake stood next to them, but a hollow look filled his eyes and he seemed incapable of action. He had no weapon but his clenched fists. Rose stood to one side, her pale beauty like a beacon in the darkness. The sight of her made Vijay suddenly brave, and he turned back to look at the Beast.

Cruel golden eyes returned his gaze. He saw no pity in those eyes, only hunger. Yet Vijay stood his ground. Only he stood between the monster and Rose, and he was going nowhere.

The creature's jaws parted again, and it prepared to leap.

Chapter Eighty-Two

James followed Samuel round a street corner just as another hail of bullets flew past. Brick dust pricked his eyes as the bullets ricocheted off the surrounding buildings and embedded themselves in the brickwork. The armed police followed them relentlessly, their masks and helmets covering their faces, guns in their hands, letting off rounds as they ran. He and Samuel had run all the way from the river seeking to evade their pursuers, but the police came from all directions, more joining from side streets as they ran. Whichever way they turned their path seemed blocked.

'This way,' called Samuel. He dashed down a small side alley off the main shopping street, James following close behind. As soon as they turned, James smelled wolf.

Samuel stopped abruptly and James ran past him, desperate to escape the rain of bullets. The alleyway smelled strongly of wolf and a second later James saw why.

Another werewolf stood in the middle of the dim lane, poised to attack a teenage boy. Behind them huddled a group of girls and another boy. There were bodies strewn along the alleyway, and to his left, a police woman, leaning against a wall. A high brick wall stood at the end of the alleyway, but it was no barrier to a wolf. James could bound it in one leap.

He slowed down and sniffed. The police woman had a strange scent, half-human, half-wolf. She had been bitten or scratched, but had not changed despite the light from the full moon.

He had seen her before. Liz. She had saved his life on Halloween night and been kind to him in the hospital. He padded to her and licked her face, but she didn't react. Whatever had happened to her, she was totally exhausted.

Instead he turned his attention to the big black wolf. A familiar smell rushed over him. Even in wolf form, Warg Daddy stank of engine oil and leather. James padded forward, Samuel following closely.

Warg Daddy paused in his attack and turned to look at the new arrivals. The teenage boy continued to stand stock still in the middle of the alleyway, his face a mask of terror. James walked up to Warg Daddy and stood before him. The big wolf growled at him, a warning snarl.

In his ear, Samuel hissed. 'James, we have to run.'

The huge wolf glared at him angrily and gave another warning growl. 'This prey is mine,' declared Warg Daddy. 'Go!'

One of the teenagers gasped when the wolf spoke. A girl, his own age. Long black hair fell in thick curls around her face. She wore a torn black dress, revealing smooth brown skin that glowed like honey under the streetlamp.

Warg Daddy snarled a third time.

James studied his huge head, jaws parted to reveal white teeth and pink tongue. Yellow eyes shone brightly in black fur. Warg Daddy was a wolf now, like James. He should have felt a bond. They were brothers in blood – he,

James and Samuel. So why did James feel connected to the kids instead?

Can we count on you, James?

These children were human, not werewolf. But they were teenagers, just like him. How could he hurt them without hurting himself?

He thought of the young woman he had just killed. She had been beautiful. Her beauty had drawn him to her. Her skin so rosy, so pure. He had violated that purity. He had destroyed her innocent beauty.

He was a monster.

Everything he touched he defiled. The girl standing beneath the streetlamp was just as beautiful as the woman he'd killed. All his victims were, because life itself was precious and sacred.

Warg Daddy took a step closer, pawing angrily at the ground, fury in those cold yellow eyes. Looking at Warg Daddy was like staring into a black mirror and seeing the worst of himself, the monster he had become.

Can we count on you, James?

He remembered Samuel's dream, his vision of a future where people of all races and religions lived together in harmony, where gay and straight were treated the same. He understood that dream now. And if he killed these children, or permitted Warg Daddy to kill them, he killed that dream. He would not.

'Come on, James.' It was Samuel, by his side. 'Leave Warg Daddy to his kill.'

James shook his head.

Warg Daddy snarled, more menacing than ever. He took a step forward.

James held his ground. 'No,' he said to the big wolf. 'Leave the children. Let them go.'

Warg Daddy scratched at the ground with sharp claws. He flexed his broad shoulders and readied his hind legs, preparing to spring.

James braced himself.

Warg Daddy powered forward, a rush of blackness silhouetted by the bright streetlamp. Two yellow points of light and flashing white teeth closed in on James.

James flew aside, feeling the sweep of air as the great wolf flew past, jaws snapping closed on empty space. He spun round, his tail swishing behind him as Warg Daddy landed and turned to face him again.

Samuel stood to one side, his brow knotted in confusion. 'James! Leave him. We have to get away.'

Warg Daddy prowled forward, unchecked fury contorting his features. He opened his jaws and roared. The noise tore through the enclosed alleyway like a thunderstorm, yet James felt no fear. He had always been part of something bigger than himself. He had lost sight of that vision briefly, but now he saw everything in pin-sharp focus. Right and wrong had revealed themselves, and he had no doubt which side he was on. He positioned himself in front of the children and the injured men and squared up to the wild wolf before him.

Warg Daddy rushed him again, his huge bulk flying out of the darkness, strong jaws and sharp teeth slavering. Again James dodged, but Warg Daddy was ready this time. The beast twisted in mid-air, slashing with his forepaws and raking James' back.

James fell sideways, feeling deadly claws rip clumps of fur from his back and side. He rolled over, avoiding the snap of jaws as Warg Daddy spun around and lunged. Back onto his paws he sprang, turning once again to face his opponent.

Behind Warg Daddy, Samuel gazed on in horror.

James snarled back at Warg Daddy, showing his own teeth in defiance, but the great black creature advanced steadily. The beast lowered his head, protecting his soft flank and underbelly. Step by step the wolf came closer, yellow eyes narrowed. James backed away slowly, never once taking his gaze from those cruel eyes.

Suddenly Warg Daddy charged, forepaws raised, jaws

widening to bite. James met him head on, and they danced together, flanks slick with sweat, jaws and talons locked in a grim pirouette. The black wolf sought to push him over, but James stepped sideways to keep his balance. Again Warg Daddy used his greater strength to wrongfoot him, grappling with locked jaws, twisting James' neck to one side.

James fought back against his larger opponent, but Warg Daddy's powerful head and neck steadily forced him down as they turned and scrabbled beneath the cold silver light of the moon.

Still Samuel watched, unable or unwilling to intervene.

James' head was twisted almost to the ground, and he felt his strength dwindling. Warg Daddy had the upper hand now and pressed home his advantage, forcing James' head to the hard stone. Finally, James' legs gave way and he toppled over, exposing his soft underbelly to Warg Daddy's jaws.

He watched as the huge black snout opened wide, showing teeth like knives ready to cut his flesh. The monster placed his forepaws firmly on James' chest, claws digging into his fur and skin, and drew back his head to bite.

James waited helplessly for the final lunge, but just as the black jaws started to rush toward him, the shape of another wolf appeared behind. Long claws lashed out and caught Warg Daddy's snout full on.

Samuel's attack took Warg Daddy completely by surprise. He squealed and dropped James like a hot coal, springing away and leaving him free again. James righted himself quickly and jumped back onto all fours.

Samuel stood beside him now, wolf by wolf. Before them the black bulk of Warg Daddy spun in confusion and rage, an unearthly roar spilling from his throat. The scratch marks on his snout were clearly visible and he rubbed at them with one paw. The beast paced angrily, continuing to snarl furiously. He drew himself up to his full height, towering even over Samuel, baring his teeth and snorting hot breath like a bull.

But Samuel advanced a step and showed his teeth too. 'Flee!' he growled.

Warg Daddy glared angrily a while longer before speaking. 'You'll pay for this. Both of you.' With that, he turned and ran, sprinting down the alleyway toward the dead end of the wall. With a huge bound he was over it and gone.

James turned to face Samuel, but as he did so, a shout from the opposite end of the lane rang out. An armed policeman stood there, his carbine raised to fire.

'Run!' shouted James.

A shot rang out like a firecracker. Then another. Bullets began to fly past him so close he heard them ping. 'Run!' he shouted again. He powered forward, heading toward the back wall of the alley.

But Samuel did not run with him. Instead his friend lurched to the side and fell.

James ran back to him. 'Samuel?'

His friend lay on the ground, panting loudly, his thick black fur wet with sweat. A slow trickle of blood leaked from a wound on his flank. 'I've been hit. It's over, James. Leave me.'

'No!'

'Save yourself.'

More shouts came from the main road. Bullets whickered past, kicking up dust around them.

'I won't leave you here, Samuel.' James licked at the wound, cleaning away the blood and the dirt. 'Come on.' He butted his friend gently, then forcefully in frustration.

Samuel lay still on the ground, breathing quickly as blood spilled from his wound.

'Come on!' raged James.

Slowly, Samuel began to move. He stood unsteadily, one leg buckled beneath him. 'I can't walk.'

'Yes you can.' James pushed at his friend. 'You didn't

let me throw my life away that night by the river, and I'm not letting you throw yours away now. Now run!'

Samuel staggered forward, uncertainly at first, but picking up speed as they ran together down the alleyway. The kids cowered together, watching them go. A shout came from the distant end of the alley, 'Civilians present! Hold your fire!' The shots ceased and together he and Samuel raced to the back wall. They leapt as one.

Chapter Eighty-Three

Samuel's hind legs clipped the top of the high brick wall as he and James flew over it. He cried out in pain and crashed to the ground, landing awkwardly in the empty street beyond.

'Come on!' said James, 'We have to keep going.'

Samuel limped forward as best he could, but the jump had injured his legs. His face grimaced with every step, and blood flowed steadily from the bullet wound in his side. He staggered as far as a nearby public square before collapsing.

James turned back and licked his face. 'Come on.'

Samuel panted breathlessly. 'No. I can't walk any more. I need to rest.' He lay down in the road, resting his damaged legs.

James nuzzled up to him and licked away the fresh blood from the fur. The blood flowed faster now, but James had no way of binding the wound. He pressed a paw against it, but Samuel winced in agony. 'The bullet's still inside. I can feel it.'

Tears began to fill James' eyes. 'I'm sorry.'

'You've nothing to be sorry for. It wasn't your fault. You did the right thing.'

'Did I? Then why did this happen? How can harm come to good people when they do the right thing?' Anger crept into his voice. He couldn't keep it at bay. If the world was just, how could this have been allowed to happen?

'It doesn't matter if people are good or bad, James. Only whether they are strong or weak, wolf or prey.'

'Then you lied to me,' cried James. 'You said that strong and weak could live together. Black and white, and gay and straight too.'

Samuel was panting hard now, even though he was barely moving. 'I didn't lie to you, James. I've never lied.'

'Then wolf and prey must be able to live together too. They must.'

'How can that happen, James? Wolves eat prey.'

'I don't know. I thought you knew. But if they can't live together, then everything you told me was a lie.'

'I didn't lie, James. Or if I did, I didn't mean to.' Samuel's breath began to ease slightly. His chest rose and fell steadily as he lay there, James nestling against him to keep him warm.

'I'm sorry, Samuel. I didn't mean to call you a liar. You're the only truly honest person I know.'

Samuel's features relaxed as if the pain were slowly melting away. 'What will you do now?' he asked. 'You can't go back to Leanna. She'll rip you to pieces, and I don't mean that as a figure of speech. Even if she doesn't, Warg Daddy and the Wolf Brothers will.'

'Not me, *us,*' said James. 'You and me together. *We* can't go back.'

'No. So what, then?'

'We run. We run together. It doesn't matter where, as

long as you're with me. Will you come?'

'I'll come with you James. Wherever you want to go. I'll stay with you forever. You know I will.' Samuel wheezed softly then and closed his eyes.

James licked Samuel's eyes with his wet tongue. The eyes stayed closed. He licked the wound too, cleaning the blood away from the fur. Samuel didn't speak again, or move. Gradually the flow of blood dwindled until it finally stopped.

In the sky, the moon shone cold and indifferent to the affairs of humans and wolves alike. It had touched James deeply with its silver fingers, changing him forever, yet still it cared nothing for him. Its icy face knew neither justice nor love. Perhaps that was the true lesson here – that justice and love burned only in human hearts.

James turned to tell this to Samuel, but the face of his friend was now as cold and unfeeling as the moon that watched over them. 'Samuel? Samuel!' The tears fell freely as James crouched over his friend, weeping softly. 'Samuel,' he said. 'I love you.'

Samuel, who had saved him from himself, accepted him and loved him despite all his flaws and weaknesses, had been taken from him. James continued to cry quietly for a while. Sadness washed over him like an ocean of pain. Slowly, as he cried, his tears turned to rage. Rage against the policeman who had fired the bullet that killed his friend, rage against Warg Daddy whose lust for violence had forced James to choose sides, but strongest of all, rage against the moon, whose blind eyes stared down with unfeeling coldness.

Rage was all James had now. Everything else had been taken from him.

He stood and rose onto hind legs, howling with anger and hate at the distant moon and the cruel world it looked down on.

Chapter Eighty-Four

South East London, New Year morning, full moon

The sky had cleared and Chris Crohn could see the moon clearly now, shining silvery bright in the sky above Seth's car.

They'd eventually managed to extricate themselves from the dead end, but not before an angry driver had gouged a long scratch in the car's paintwork with his keys.

'My car!' said Seth. 'He scratched my car!'

The man thumped his fist against the side window and made a rude gesture. 'You useless fuckers!' he shouted. 'Now we're all stuck here.' He indicated the dozens of cars that had followed Chris and Seth down this one-way dead-end street and blocked each other from leaving.

'Just keep the doors locked,' said Chris. 'He'll go away soon.'

The man had stalked back to his car eventually, but it had taken a long time for all the cars that had followed them down the wrong turning to reverse out or turn around, and for them to get back onto the main road. By the time they'd managed that, the traffic was crawling along slower than ever and they resigned themselves to a long ride.

Seth had taken over navigation, using his GPS to steer them through the labyrinth of streets that was South East London. Chris caught a good view of Canary Wharf as they crept slowly onward. The bright lights of London's financial sector stood proudly on the opposite side of the river, its high-rise offices picked out against the night sky by rows and columns of bright windows, topped off by high-intensity aircraft warning lights blinking steadily like lighthouses.

Here on the south side of the river, the massed ranks of social housing interspersed with clusters of charity shops, burger and kebab sellers, and rough-looking pubs felt like a world away. Only the shining moon seemed unchanged, staring down indifferently on rich and poor alike.

'I wish we were back in Greenwich,' moaned Seth. 'I wish we'd never come. I should never have listened to you,' he accused.

'Just keep driving,' said Chris sullenly.

But that wasn't easy. Crowds of people surged along the road, pushing between the crawling cars, shouting and jeering as they went. Masked men began to appear among the revellers, marching purposefully in groups, chanting slogans, carrying weapons. Fights broke out, and Chris and Seth finally ground to a complete standstill in the middle of a crowded street.

People filled the road, making any movement impossible, either forward or back. Seth honked the horn in frustration but that proved to be a mistake. A group of youths began to bang the side of the car and a couple of guys hauled themselves up onto the front and sat on it, swigging beer from bottles, throwing insolent stares at

Chris and Seth, as if challenging them to do something about it.

Seth switched off the engine. 'This is hopeless. We're going nowhere. My car's getting wrecked and it's all your fault.'

'It's not my fault,' said Chris. 'If we'd left sooner, like I wanted to, this would never have happened.'

'It only happened because I let you talk me into believing this stupid werewolf idea.'

'Well it could be worse,' said Chris, ignoring a guy who was mooning him through the passenger window.

'How?' demanded Seth.

'At least we haven't seen any werewolves.'

Seth snorted in derision.

A tinkle of breaking glass rang out on Chris' side of the street. He looked out to see masked men climbing through a broken plate glass window to loot a discount store. There was no sign of any police on the ground. Nothing was being done to control the violence.

They sat together in silence for a while, struggling to ignore the crowds of people breaking against the car like human waves. Dozens of people pushed past, breaking the mirrors off the side of the car, snapping the aerial off the roof. Metal scraped along the paintwork and glass bottles smashed on the ground as the crowd made its way past the stranded car.

Suddenly the sea of people began to part in front of them. The crowd was breaking up and starting to run.

'What is it?' asked Seth.

Screams and shouts rang out. A young woman was knocked to the ground next to the car and others ran over her prone body, stumbling blindly as they sought to get away from something. She screamed for help, but total panic had set in and no one paid her any heed.

'Do something!' wailed Seth. 'Help her!'

Chris hesitated, then tried to push the door open. 'I can't open it,' he yelled, struggling to force it open against the onrush. He looked out through the side window, but the woman had vanished beneath the crush.

Seth's face turned white. 'What's happening? What are they running from?'

As if in answer to his question, a huge dark shape appeared from out of the crowd. It bounded down the road and hurled itself against the car windscreen, blocking out the light. It struck the windscreen with a crash that shook the vehicle violently.

Chris gazed in astonishment. A werewolf stood on the front of the car just two feet away from his face, nothing separating them but the glass of the car's windscreen. The beast roared, filling Chris' vision with its huge jaws, dagger-like canine teeth, drooling tongue and the deep hollow of its throat. The roar blocked out all other sound, seemingly loud enough to shatter the glass.

Chris sat as still as a rock in his seat. Beside him, Seth shook and whimpered, all self-control lost.

A space had appeared around the vehicle as people fled, leaving Chris and Seth alone with the monster. The ruined body of the trampled woman lay on the ground where she had fallen, her legs twisted to one side, blood trickling from behind her ear. Broken glass and dropped bottles made a carpet around her.

The beast lifted its massive front paws and lunged at the car windscreen, bringing its full weight to bear against the glass. The car shook again under the impact, and the windscreen began to break, thin cracks stretching out across its surface like a cobweb.

Seth gibbered and wailed, spit flying from his open lips, his long brown hair completely shielding his eyes.

Chris stared at the beast in awe. The werewolf was much more real in the flesh than his graphs and data had ever suggested. It was nothing like the blurry photos he had collected and collated from social media. It was far bigger, stronger and more terrifying than anything he had imagined. The animal raged and howled before him, shaking its great head from side to side as it fought to break into the car. Its power seemed overwhelming.

Yet Chris had trained himself for this. His running, his weight lifting, his martial arts practice had all been for this moment. He knew what must be done.

The knife was in his hand already. He didn't recall having reached for it. He gripped it firmly, readying the blade, waiting for his chance. He might only get one.

The beast roared again, rising up onto its hind legs, filling the air with its rage. It powered forward with all its strength, butting its head against the shattered windscreen. The glass turned white and crumbled like powder, filling Chris' lap with frosty crystals.

Nothing stood between him and the monster now but empty space. Yellow eyes stared at him, radiating hate and violence. The giant jaws opened once more, ready to bite.

Chris lunged with the knife, putting his weight behind the blow, summoning all his strength for this one heroic act.

The knife flew from his grasp and the beast swept it aside with a flick of its jaws. It bounced off the car and fell to the ground out of sight.

Chris stared at his empty hand dumbfounded.

The werewolf had barely paused in its attack. It came on again, more savage than ever, widening its jaws like the mouth of a cavern, sharpened teeth glinting like pearly blades, the dark throat opening up to swallow Chris whole.

A silver blade flashed suddenly in Chris' peripheral vision. It jabbed once at the wolf's paw and the beast howled. The great jaws snapped shut an inch from Chris' face. The wolf jerked its head back and turned, spinning away and dropping back to the ground. It flew, running back down the street and into the night.

Chris turned to look at Seth. The knife was in his friend's hand. Seth's face was white with shock and incomprehension. A single drop of blood clung to the blade. Seth stared at the weapon, seeming not to know why he held it in his grasp. He dropped it onto the dashboard, his hands starting to shake. 'I think I'm going to be sick.' He opened the glovebox and retched into it. When he was finished he closed it again.

The street was quiet now, almost empty save for the still body of the trampled woman, and a sea of dropped litter and glass. Other drivers started to emerge cautiously from their stranded cars, peering around in disbelief at the devastation. In the distance, the wailing sirens of emergency vehicles began to call.

'You did it,' said Chris to his friend. 'You fought off a werewolf.'

'*We* did it,' said Seth breathlessly, flicking long hair away from his thick glasses. 'Awesome.'

Chapter Eighty-Five

St John's Road, Battersea, South West London, New Year morning, full moon

Paramedics lifted Liz carefully onto a stretcher and then into the back of a waiting ambulance. She felt little as they shifted her body. Weariness had washed all feeling away.

'What about Dean?' she asked as they lifted the body of her injured colleague into the ambulance beside her. 'My colleague. Is he alive?'

'Alive and stable,' replied one of the paramedics. 'But unconscious.'

'And the others?'

'Let's get you off to the hospital,' said the man. 'You can worry about the others later.'

A voice from outside the ambulance called to her. Vijay. 'You saved us,' he said. 'Me and Rose and Drake, and my sister and her friends. We're all still alive because of you.'

'Are you hurt?'

'A bit. But I think we'll be all right. That man you rescued from the burning car, he woke up. The medic said he'd be okay too.'

'What about the others? The ones the wolf attacked?'

'You mean the rioters?' Vijay shook his head. 'Dunno. They looked dead to me.'

'Vijay?'

'Yes?'

'Take care.'

The door of the ambulance slammed shut and the vehicle started to move. Its siren blared out as it turned back onto the main street and began to pick its way through the debris of the riot.

The paramedic stayed in the back of the ambulance with Liz, tending to Dean's unconscious form.

'Is the fighting over?' she asked him.

'It's all quiet now in this area,' he said. 'The armed police soon put a stop to the trouble. But the rioting has spread to other parts of the city.'

'What about the wolves?'

'Wolves? You mean the Beast?'

'Not one Beast. Many. Do you know anything about them?'

'Only rumours. But never mind that now. You just try to rest.'

The ambulance drove steadily through the broken city, picking up speed as it moved away from the fires and the carnage of the riot. Beside her, Dean's chest rose and fell irregularly, but he was breathing and that was all she could hope for right now. He was in good hands, and hopefully Mihai and her father were safe together at home. She would have to deal with her problems and face the aftermath of the night's events, but not just yet. Now she should rest.

By the time they reached the hospital, sleep was settling over her. How she could sleep after so much had happened, she didn't really know, but slowly and steadily it wrapped her in its healing cocoon. Even the bright lights of the hospital didn't seem to bother her, and soon she was dreaming sweet dreams.

Chapter Eighty-Six

Upper Terrace, Richmond upon Thames, West London, New Year morning, full moon

Sarah hurried to made a cup of tea for Grandpa. He often woke in the night and asked for a hot drink, and Sarah was usually happy to oblige. But tonight the TV demanded her urgent attention. The news was bad, and with Melanie still missing it couldn't have come at a worse time.

It had been days since she'd reported her sister missing. Mel had never disappeared for so long before without telling her where she was. Sarah had called her repeatedly, but the police said that her phone had been switched off since she'd gone missing. They'd checked their records, and the hospitals too, but had drawn a blank. The situation looked grim, but Sarah hadn't given up hope. Melanie was out there, somewhere, and Sarah knew in her heart that she was still alive. She couldn't say how she knew, but she trusted her intuitions. But where her sister might be was anyone's guess.

And now the rioting had begun. And worse, giant wolves running wild on the streets of London. She could hardly believe it. Neither could the news reporters. *Unprecedented,* they said, but that didn't begin to capture the true horror of the unfolding events. She'd never forgotten where she was when she'd heard about 9/11, and she would certainly never forget tonight. For the first time, wolves had been captured on live TV footage. Beasts. There could be no doubt any more. Wolves in London, and not just ordinary wolves. The experts were at a loss to explain what these creatures really were.

And apart from the horror of the wolves, there were dozens dead from the riots and fires that had swept the capital. Armed police, rioters and wolves in central London. The final death toll might run into hundreds.

She could only hope that Melanie wasn't caught up in the bloodshed.

She glanced out of her kitchen window and saw a red glow on the horizon. Fires, all across the capital. Even here in leafy Richmond, well away from the rioting, she could hear the distant sound of fire engines and police cars racing across the city. Suddenly the events outside felt very real and close.

Grandpa had drifted back to sleep by the time she returned with his tea. She rested it on his bedside locker and turned the TV at the foot of his bed on quietly. Live aerial shots of the capital showed fires still raging out of control in areas south of the river. Then the scene shifted to recorded footage of armed police shooting at running beasts while looters scattered and ran for cover. She'd seen it already, but that didn't diminish the shock.

Grandpa woke up again at the sound of the gunfire. 'Barbara? Is that you, Barbara?'

Sarah gripped his trembling hand tightly. 'Yes, Grandpa, it's me, Barbara.' She would be Barbara if it made him feel any better. They watched the footage together.

Grandpa didn't seem particularly surprised by what he saw on the screen. 'It's war, you see, Barbara. This is what happens during wartime. There'll be millions dead by the end.'

'Yes, Grandpa, here's your tea.'

He held the cup in his hands and watched as police with guns patrolled the streets of London, the fires of burning cars and buildings clearly visible in the background. Shadowy figures moved in the firelight and sometimes the police raised their guns to fire. 'There's no reason for it, you know,' said the old man. 'War, I mean. The enemy soldiers, they were no different to us. We were all young men, just the same. But we had to kill them. It was either them or us.'

'Yes, Grandpa, whatever you say.'

'Sarah,' he said. 'It's Sarah, isn't it?' His expression was suddenly more lucid than she'd seen in months.

She squeezed his hand gently. 'Yes, Grandpa, it's me, Sarah.'

'Sarah,' he repeated. Then he turned his attention back to the scene on the TV. 'You've got to kill the enemy, you see? Before they kill you. It's the only way to survive.'

Chapter Eighty-Seven

Queen's Road, Harrow on the Hill, North London, New Year morning, full moon

Melanie Margolis was still alive. She had thought she was dead, but no, she lived still. Her eyes flickered open, and pain and light rushed in. She closed them again quickly, and darkness returned, but the agony remained undimmed.

Searing pain cut through her head. Her skull ached like it was split in two. So much pain, it was impossible to think of anything else. She let it lance through her skull for a minute, keeping her eyes tightly shut, trying to control it.

She tried to remember why her head hurt so much. After a while fragments of memory returned to her. The man had struck her with the cricket bat. She tried to raise her hand to the wound, but knotted rope cut into her wrist, sending fresh waves of agony down her arm to where the jagged mirror had sliced her palm.

More memories seeped back. She had tried to escape,

had almost succeeded. She would have been out of here now, if it hadn't been for the locked front door with its bolts, chains and padlocks. So many locks. Who knew that a paranoid psychopath would keep that many locks on his front door? She started to giggle at the thought, but the pain sliced through the mirth almost before she began.

Outside, a siren carved a swathe through the night. Beneath its piercing screech the dull thud of a helicopter grew steadily louder. She opened her eyes to see blue flashes outside the bedroom window. A sudden bright white light pierced the night sky like a searchlight.

They were coming for her. At last.

Her sister must have raised the alarm. Of course she had. Sarah would never let her down. A great rescue operation was underway. She struggled with the ropes that bound her to the bed, tried to cry out, but it was futile. The gag in her mouth made any sound louder than a whimper impossible. No worries. They would find her. Soon she would be free.

A cough alerted her to the presence of the man. He was here in the room with her. His dark form stood by the window, studying the activity outside.

The man became agitated. He turned away from the window and paced back and forth across the darkened room, eyes flicking from left to right with each step. She sensed his fear. He must know that they were coming for her, that rescue was near.

She willed herself to remain calm, despite the urge to scream for help, to struggle desperately against her bonds.

The man returned to the window, watching. But now the siren was fading, receding into the distance. The lights came no closer. The helicopter moved away. 'They've gone,' he said at last.

A new wave of realization swept Melanie in its cruel embrace. The lights, the sirens, and the helicopter had not been for her. She was alone, abandoned. The police would never find her and she would never see her sister again.

She might have curled into a ball then in despair, but the ropes kept her arms and legs outstretched, defiant.

The man who had held her prisoner for so long crept over to the bed. 'It's all quiet now,' he muttered. 'All quiet outside.'

He had let himself go these past days. His unwashed hair stuck out at odd angles, and rough stubble crawled over his jaw and neck. Dried blood stained his hand where she had cut him with the broken glass. He still held the dagger he had used to threaten her so many times but he no longer bothered to use it. He simply clutched it to his chest like some kind of comforter.

A new thought seemed to animate him and he waved the knife toward her. 'The end of the world is coming,' he hissed, breathing foul breath in her face. 'The four horsemen ride forth.'

Right, thought Melanie. Just when things didn't seem like they could get any worse, it was time to bring on the apocalypse.

'The signs were there all along,' he cackled. 'Everyone should have seen them. First came the Beast. They even called it the Beast on TV.' He giggled again, waving the knife absent-mindedly before him. The flashing of the blade seemed to absorb all his attention for a while, and she thought he had stopped speaking. Then he started again as if he had never left off. 'The Beast, numbered 666. What else? Seven seals, seven trumpets, seven angels. Or was it eight? Eight angels, perhaps. Seven bowls, a dragon, four horsemen ...' He tailed off, frowning. 'I don't remember all the details. But the earth will burn, I remember that. London is burning now,' he added with glee. 'The people are dying. They deserve it.'

London burning. So that's what the siren had been. A fire engine, not even a police car.

Could it be true? The boundary between reality and fantasy had blurred since he'd started feeding her the drugs, had become even more fluid since he'd struck her with the cricket bat. It was hard to tell what was true. But she was certain that her prison was real, and that her jailer was a nutcase.

'The city will burn,' he proclaimed triumphantly.

The mad emperor Nero had fiddled while Rome burned. And if London was burning, Melanie would have preferred some gentle string music to this insane ranting.

The man leaned back over her, his eyes darting from her feet to the tip of her head and away again. 'I was going to kill you,' he hissed, bringing the point of the knife into her field of vision. 'Eviscerate you. But now I've had a better idea. I'll let you watch the world end. We'll watch it together. First the fires, then the plagues, and then the rivers of blood. We'll die together, you and me. What do you think of that?'

Melanie grunted weakly. The tape that bound her mouth made words impossible, but she had learned that it was best to humour him when he asked his rhetorical questions.

He sat down next to her on the bed, looking at her quizzically. 'Do you know why you're going to die?' he asked. 'Because you're a whore.' He spat the word at her. 'And I've done bad things too. Very bad. It's not surprising that the world is ending. So much wickedness, we all deserve it.' He lifted the knife to her throat and pressed its cold steel against her soft flesh. When he withdrew it, the tip was red. He lifted it to the light, turning it in his fingers, seeming to see some message in the way it moved. A drop of blood ran slowly down the edge of the blade and trickled over the hilt.

He laid the knife on the bed and looked into her eyes, his own eyes steady for once. 'If I allow you to speak, do you promise not to scream?'

Melanie nodded, trying not to show too much eagerness. It was probably just a trick, some twisted game of his.

But it was no trick. He pulled the tape that covered her

mouth. It ripped away violently, leaving her feeling like her lips had been pulled off. 'Open your mouth,' he commanded. She obliged him, and he pulled out the wad of paper he had stuffed inside, discarding the soggy mess on the floor.

He held the knife to her throat again. 'Don't speak unless I ask you a question. Understand?'

'Yes,' said Melanie. It was the first word she had spoken for many hours.

He stood up again and walked back to the window. 'The end of days,' he muttered. 'So it looks like this. Well, well.'

It was still night, but the early light of pre-dawn was turning the sky a lighter shade of grey. The sirens and helicopters had stopped and a sense of calm seemed to be returning to the city. Whatever had happened overnight, the worst of it must surely be over. If she ignored the bindings that tied her hands and legs to the bed, and the throbbing of her head, the day might almost be normal. It was hard to imagine that the world was about to end.

Something new seemed to catch the man's attention outside. He unlatched the sash window and lifted the lower half open. Cold, fresh air rushed inside. 'What's that?' he asked. He stuck his head out, then leaned further, straining to see. He mumbled more words that vanished into the night air before she could decipher them. Then he drew back suddenly, ducking his head inside. His face was white. 'The Beast,' he said, pointing outside with one quivering finger.

The knife was up again in a flash and he ran to the bed, holding it before him. 'The Beast has come for us,' he wailed. 'It knows we're here.' He slashed the knife through the air in wild arcs, his eyes following its path as it danced. 'We will both burn in Hell!'

Melanie screamed.

Chapter Eighty-Eight

West London, New Year morning, full moon

James ran on all fours, iron coursing through his veins, paws pounding against the hard pavement, strong legs pumping like pistons. He ran until sweat poured down his flanks and foam frothed from his loose jaws. The moon followed him relentlessly, low in the sky now, but shining with a bright coldness that seemed to mock him.

The dark streets of the capital were mostly deserted, with just a few late night revellers still out. They fled when they saw him, or pressed themselves against walls or doors as he rushed past, their faces contorted with fear and astonishment, but he paid them no heed. From time to time police helicopters flew overhead, breaking the stillness with a sudden clattering noise, sweeping the streets with searchlights, searching for wolves. He hid from them in gardens, or behind bushes or low walls, a small dark shape amongst shadows, and they passed him by without stopping.

One thought filled his mind, over and over. Samuel was dead. His only friend. His lover. Dead.

It was all James' fault. He had tried to do the right thing, had saved the lives of some children, but Samuel had paid the price with his own life. One life against many. Now James would gladly give any number of lives to get Samuel back. Including his own.

But the choice was made. He could not go back.

So he ran on, hot blood rushing through his limbs as he ran, while Samuel's body lay cold and still and dead.

He ran without knowing where his legs were carrying him. He ran without purpose. He ran without desire, or feeling, or thought. A survival instinct had taken over, and he headed west, away from the cold moon, away from Samuel's body, away from everything he had done. A part of him begged him to turn round and return to where Samuel rested, but that voice was too small and weak to overcome the instinct to flee. And so he ran.

He ran through quiet streets, across empty waste ground, along deserted paths that crisscrossed the city. He dared not cross any of the bridges that spanned the Thames, and so he skirted around the river's snaking coils, sticking to the south bank. The air was cooling rapidly in the clear night and the first crystals of frost glinted like diamonds on the edges of paving stones and on the grass and trees. A vision of Samuel flashed before him, his black skin white with hoar frost, icicles in his hair, his lips frozen blue. His dead friend's eyes opened, accusing him. *I am dead,* they seemed to say, *and yet you live.* Hot tears sprang from his eyes and washed the vision away, just as quickly as it had appeared.

And he ran on, hot in the freezing night.

Gradually, modern apartment blocks gave way to older houses, sports grounds, cycle paths, boat houses and golf courses. The frost grew thicker as he left the urban centre behind. But no matter how far he ran, the moon followed him, reminding him that Samuel was dead.

A bridge beckoned him, and he bounded across it, for no reason he could discern, other than it was there, now, and it led him away from the mocking face of the moon.

Water lapped at the river banks, and the distant hum of city traffic never ceased as he loped across the bridge. Black water slid silently beneath, its surface flapping gently, pulled by the tide, drawn to the moon. Its dark mass slipped past, a reminder of the night he had first met Samuel. He had hidden beneath another bridge that night after murdering the priest, Father Mulcahy. He had wanted to kill himself then, and it would have been better if he had. But Samuel had stopped him, had befriended him, had become his lover. If James had died that night, Samuel would still be alive now. Another choice he had made. He could blame no one else, not even blind fate or destiny. The choices had all been his, whether to live or to die, to kill or to save, to run or to stay, and he had made the wrong one every time.

He bounded across the bridge, soft paws padding silently on stone, a small dark shape under a black sky. Suddenly he froze. From the opposite river bank a police car cut the silence of the night with the blare of its siren.

He squatted down in the middle of the bridge, his eyes alert, his ears pricked, every sense heightened. The siren grew louder with every beat of his heart. Now he saw it. A flickering blue light in the darkness, growing brighter and nearer quickly. The car sped through the deserted streets, heading straight for the bridge.

James squatted uncertainly, poised for flight but not knowing where to run. He had half-crossed the bridge already. The remaining distance was too far to cover before the car reached him. He had come too far to go back. The span of the bridge was open and exposed, leaving nowhere to hide. He ran to the edge, raising his forepaws onto the stone balustrade that flanked the bridge. He leaned over and looked down.

Below him the black water of the river swirled like

boiling oil, eddies spiralling off the arched feet of the bridge. The river surged strongly from recent rainfall and though James was a good swimmer he had never tried to swim in wolf form. The drop was too far, the water too powerful.

Another sound joined the approaching police siren and he looked up. A helicopter, thrumming in the distance, flying low above the river, its searchlights sweeping left to right in wide arcs. It flew toward him quickly, following the curve of the River Thames, and he ducked behind the balustrade, pressing his body against the stone pillars, folding his hind legs beneath him, panting noisily, his breath making clouds in the cold night. The moon hung low over the river, its twin reflected in the flowing water beneath. The two moons watched him together with their cold eyes, gloating, reminding him that Samuel lay still and dead.

The police car grew ever closer, the shrill piercing of its siren drowning even the throbbing of the helicopter. He pushed himself tighter against the grey stone, trying to meld with the pillars at the edge of the bridge. But his hiding place was hopeless. Even if the probing beam of the searchlight failed to spot him, the police in the car easily would.

Part of him had ceased to care. Discovery would be a relief. A bullet to the head and he could be with Samuel, joined together for eternity. That way he could do no more harm. He had betrayed everyone tonight. He had fought against his own wolf kind. He had caused the death of the one he loved most. He had killed the innocent. Every choice he made was wrong. A quick death, and he need make no more choices. He could rest, at last.

The police car was already at the end of the bridge now, and the helicopter was almost overhead. Its bright searchlight shone directly at him, sweeping long shadows across the tarmac.

James stood up.

The beam of the searchlight tracked left as the helicopter flew over the bridge, shining a stark white light across the empty road. He raised his forepaws against his ears to block the deafening noise as it roared overhead, then watched as it banked sharply right across the river, turning a full one hundred and eighty degrees to head back toward the bridge. Toward him. He padded into the centre of the bridge, where he would be easily spotted.

The police car was turning too, but away from the bridge, following the embankment road parallel to the river, the wail of its siren dropping an octave as it headed away from him. He trotted slowly after it, watching in confusion as it roared away.

The beam of the searchlight flickered briefly across his face again, blinding him momentarily, before the helicopter too followed the river east, back toward the centre of the city. He stared after it in disbelief. Somehow they had failed to spot him. They had gone, leaving him alone on the bridge.

He padded forward uncertainly, crossing over to the north side of the bridge, his ears twitching as the noise faded again to silence. Now it was just him and the lapping of the water once more. He peered over the edge at the cold blackness of the river, wondering again what it would be like to drown in that swirling mass. But he didn't stay for long.

Soon he was moving forward again, heading north into fresh territory, keeping to the shadows as best he could. Another police car passed him and this time he lay still, hiding like a thief in the night. Another choice then, and still no one to blame but himself.

He ran through the maze of streets, putting the river far behind him, taking random turns, left, right, straight ahead, doubling back on himself for all he knew or cared. As long as he kept running he wouldn't have to think. Gradually the crowded streets of the city gave way to leafy openness, and the ground rose higher until he could look back at the expanse he had crossed since abandoning Samuel's body. The moon was poised on the horizon now, disappearing below the rise and fall of the land. He felt its pull weakening as it passed slowly out of view. Soon it would be gone.

He slowed at last, walking forward one step at a time along a well-to-do street lined with old terraced houses and trees, their branches bare in the cold of winter. Where was he going? Without Samuel by his side there was no point going anywhere. He might as well stop.

He squatted down in the middle of the road, looking up at the big houses around him. Old Victorian mansion blocks, converted into apartments. A single light shone from one high window. The rest was dark. James rested on his hind legs, panting breathlessly. Now that he had stopped, he could feel the pain in his side where Warg Daddy had ripped the fur with his claws. The wound wasn't serious and he didn't mind the pain. His suffering was small and would help him focus. He turned his mind inward, seeking out the light in the darkness of his soul. There must be a small flicker of light still.

'My God,' he began to pray, 'please forgive me. I have strayed far from your path. Give me courage to continue. Give me a sign.'

He had been asking God for help ever since being bitten, but the voice in his head had remained resolutely silent. He had sinned in so many ways, but surely there was still hope if he repented. 'Help me, God. Give me guidance.'

Nothing. No voice spoke to him. He was beyond redemption, too far gone to save. He had done such terrible things. He had killed a priest, committed sins of lust, and even when he had tried to do the right thing, Samuel had paid for James' choice with his life. James had hurt and betrayed everyone he knew, had done everything wrong. He could not come back.

The moon had dipped behind the houses now, and he

could hardly feel its pull. The night sky darkened as the moon left it, draping the street before him in shadow. A solitary light shone from one high window. Could that light be a sign? James pushed onto all fours and padded toward it.

A man appeared, silhouetted at the window. He opened it, pushing the sash all the way up. James stared, baring his teeth and letting his hot tongue hang out, snorting curls of mist in the pre-dawn cold. The man at the window leaned out over the ledge, almost far enough to fall. James began to trot toward the house more quickly. The man vanished then and seconds later a scream came from the open window. A woman's scream. James bounded forward and ran toward the sound.

Chapter Eighty-Nine

Queen's Road, Harrow on the Hill, North London, New Year morning

Melanie lay on the bed as the man swept his knife in wide arcs just inches from her face. 'The Beast, the Beast!' he cried. 'It's coming!'

She screamed again, louder this time.

'Stop that!' he screeched. 'It will hear us.'

The knife flashed in front of her eyes and pricked her cheek. She struggled again with the knots, trying to pull her wrists free, but they were too tight. The rope bit into her wrists and ankles, chaffing at her skin, rubbing it raw. And every movement triggered a blinding pain in her skull.

'Keep still!' he shouted. 'Stop screaming.' The steel blade jerked before her, his arm dancing wildly and out of control. His eyes flicked around the room, searching for something to fix on.

There was a loud bang from downstairs. Another bang followed, louder than the first, then the muffled sound of wood splintering.

Had Melanie imagined it? Were the noises simply inside her head? The drugs the man had given her, the pain, the constant threats, it had all become too much. This was all a dream, a nightmare.

But no, the man had heard it too. 'What was that?' he screamed.

More sounds followed, the thudding of feet coming up the staircase of the apartment block. They drew nearer and another heavy thud followed from close by. 'It's at the front door!' whimpered the man. 'It's coming!' He sprang from the bed, spinning to face the bedroom door.

Something was pounding heavily against the front door of the apartment. A huge weight, thrown again and again against the timber and the many locks that held it. She heard the door breaking apart, and the pounding of feet coming along the hallway to the bedroom. Many feet, running. Who was coming? She turned her head to look toward the closed bedroom door, half in hope, half in fear, ignoring the fresh pain that the movement induced in her head.

A yellow flash burst through the bedroom door, knocking it flying from its hinges. Some kind of animal had entered the room, a wild animal the size of a man. The creature stood just inside the doorway, filling the space and blocking the exit. An enormous wolf. It had a pointed snout, like a German shepherd dog, and huge jaws hanging open, a pink tongue lolling out, with canine teeth like fangs. The beast breathed heavily, scratching at the carpet with claws like talons.

This was no dog, no wolf. It was a monster from her worst nightmare. It did not belong here in this North London home. Melanie screwed her eyes tightly closed, counted to three, then opened them again. The creature was still there, sweeping its gaze steadily across the room, its bright yellow eyes glowing like lanterns.

The man backed away toward the window, whimpering

quietly, his knife held loosely in hands that shook violently. 'The Beast,' he muttered. 'The Beast.'

For once Melanie had to agree with him. There was most definitely a beast in the room.

The creature padded forward cautiously, studying the room in a most unbeast-like manner. An almost human intelligence seemed to lurk behind those shining eyes. It gazed at the man, watching the knife dart and flash, listening to his deranged ranting. Then the creature's yellow eyes turned to face Melanie. She saw it studying her with interest, its attention shifting from her face to the ropes that bound her to the metal bed frame, and back again to her face. The animal cocked its head to one side. Then, in a single bound it leaped over the bed and flew at the man.

The man shrieked and held his knife aloft, but the beast crashed into him with terrifying force. It opened its jaws wide as it flew, locking them tightly around the man's neck, anchoring its fang-like teeth deep in his flesh. The man shrieked again briefly, then a wave of scarlet flooded the wall behind him and his limbs went limp as life fled from them. The knife fell to the floor where it could do no more harm.

The creature braced its front paws against the wall and ripped through the man's throat so violently that his head came away and flew through the open window. The beast shrugged what remained of the corpse onto the floor. The cream carpet slowly turned red.

Melanie watched in silent astonishment. Her sister, Sarah, claimed that she was never at a loss for words, but for once, she had nothing to say.

The beast panted loudly after its exertions and hung its head, almost as if it were ashamed of what it had done. It licked blood from the man's body, making a wet lapping sound. Then it turned to face Melanie, yellow eyes burning fiercely, its long snout wet from its kill, its canines glinting white against the red.

She faced it unafraid. She had always refused to submit to fear, and after what she'd been through, she didn't know if she could ever feel it again. Anyway, if the whole world really was ending, she had no desire to stay and watch it burn. 'Go on, then,' she said to the beast. 'Do what you've come to do.'

The beast paced around the bed, lifting its head to study her. The yellow eyes swept from her head to her feet, observing the ties that held her. Its hot breath smelled of blood and gore, but she held its gaze without flinching.

The wolf sprang onto the bed, its claws digging into the soft sheets either side of her, tearing the fabric into ribbons. It stood astride her, its enormous mouth hanging open, pink tongue drooling spit on her face, rows of sharp teeth standing tall like white stakes. 'Why should I let you live?' it growled.

Melanie almost laughed in surprise. A talking wolf. So this really was a dream. The result of all the drugs the man had fed her. Yet it felt so real. She could smell the wolf, feel its foul breath on her face.

She struggled to think of a good answer to the wolf's question. 'Well, Mr Wolf,' she began. The question was tricky. Why her, Melanie? With her good looks, easy life and casual approach to other people's happiness, why did she deserve to live, when so many worthy, caring, good people died every day? There were so many more deserving people in the world. Sarah, for example, who gave her life to looking after an old man who could never even understand or appreciate the sacrifice she was making. Ben Harvey, who devoted his life to teaching at a school that others had long since given up on. Why should Melanie live? 'Because I'm not really a bad person,' she said. 'I'm sorry for all the bad things I've done, and I promise to live a good life in the future.'

That's what the dream was about then. The wolf was her own conscience speaking to her. After all these carefree years, the conversation was well overdue.

If she ever escaped from here, she would rethink her life and decide what she really wanted to do. She had talents, after all. She could use them to help others, instead of just herself. 'Let me live, and I'll try to be better, I promise.' Words were easy to say, after all, and no one could fake sincerity better than Melanie, even when it was her own conscience she was trying to fool. All the same, she would think things over. If she got out of here alive.

The wolf stared at her, weighing her words, trying to divine the truth perhaps. She gave it the sweetest smile she could muster. Yellow eyes gazed into hers, seeming to see all her deepest, darkest secrets. Eventually the creature seemed to be satisfied with what it saw. She may even have convinced herself. With a twist of its head it bit through the rope that bound her left arm, brushing it away like a cobweb. A second snap of its jaws and both arms were free. The wolf spun round and she felt the ties that held her legs vanish in two swift bites. She was free.

The wolf jumped down to the floor and brought its huge face to look directly at hers. The bright glow in its eyes dimmed, and the creature hung its head, a look of dejected sadness replacing the fierce anger of earlier.

Melanie reached out with her hand, ignoring the pins and needles that rushed in, and gently patted the animal's muzzle.

Tears welled up in the beast's eyes, splashing to the floor without restraint, and it began to cry, a whimpering, snuffling sound that was uncannily human.

'There, there, Mr Wolf. Please don't cry.' She patted it again, some feeling starting to return to her fingers as she rubbed its snout. Its pelt was strangely smooth and soft, not rough as she had expected. The hairs that covered the creature were spun from fine gold. Under her touch they felt wet from sweat and blood and now tears as the wolf sobbed loudly. She brushed the tears from its eyes.

The creature lifted an enormous paw and placed it gently over her own small hand, taking care not to scratch her skin with its talons. She gave it a reassuring smile. 'You did the right thing,' she told it. 'I will change. I promise.'

But it was the wolf that was slowly changing, even as she watched. The fine hairs that clothed its body were drawing slowly back, leaving bare pink skin as it ebbed away like the ocean tide leaving clean, even sands in its wake. The strong muzzle of the beast was shrinking, flattening itself, while the protruding canine teeth it had put to such devastating effect were receding into the animal's jaw. The creature's broad shoulders and bulging muscles contracted and withered away, leaving behind a slender body so thin she could even see its ribs in places. The great paw that covered her own hand shrunk, the claws receding, the fingers thinning and shortening, until eventually just a small, pink hand, not much larger than her own, gripped her tightly in a sweaty clasp.

Finally, the yellow lights that had burned like beacons behind the inhuman eyes vanished, to be replaced with cool, green orbs nestling in pools of clear white. Tears flowed in rivers from those eyes, and the boy who now crouched naked by her bedside wailed and sobbed in disconsolate despair, his bare shoulders shivering as if the world really had ended.

Chapter Ninety

Imperial College, Kensington, London, New Year morning, full moon

It was almost dawn when Leanna climbed to the top of the roof and looked down with fury at the city beneath her. The moon hung low in the sky, just above the far horizon. It could only be seen now from the rooftops and the tallest buildings. In a matter of minutes, it would be gone and she would revert to human form.

From her rooftop vantage point it was a sheer drop of eight floors to the street below. In her black rage she had to suppress an urge to spring from the roof into thin air. Not even in wolf form would she survive such a fall. She licked her paws instead and sat on the edge of the building, her hind legs bent under her.

The wind gusted across the damp tiles of the roof, making them sing in the cold, but Leanna hardly felt it. She had not felt cold since leaving the Carpathian Mountains. Wolves just didn't feel the cold.

But they felt rage. Warg Daddy's news of James and Samuel's betrayal had filled her with a boiling anger. She had killed, and killed again, but not even that had quelled her wrath. Only vengeance would quiet the fury, but that would take time. While she waited, she would nurture her black hate, cultivate it in her heart. Revenge, when it came, would be sweeter that way.

She turned her gaze from the street below to the buildings opposite and beyond. Lights twinkled from windows, cars and street lamps, keeping the night at bay. Millions upon millions of people lived in this city, huddling together for comfort against the dark, against the cold and the terrors of the unknown, just as their ancestors had gathered around campfires. In the sky, a plane passed overhead, full of people arriving from a distant land. Another followed, about a minute behind. With Leanna's enhanced vision she could see two more approaching in an endless stream of life. People everywhere; a global community that never truly slept.

The midnight fireworks had long since ceased now, and in their place fires burned. The sounds of police sirens and emergency vehicles had replaced the earlier sounds of celebration and festivity. Smoke billowed into the sky, obscuring the stars and sometimes even the bright sphere of the moon itself. It spread across London like a hazy memory of the violence that had engulfed the streets tonight.

This city would soon fall. But before it fell, it would burn.

Wolves had ruled this land once. Ten thousand years ago, at the end of the last Ice Age, after the glaciers had retreated north, the European primeval forest had stretched from the coastline of Ireland in the west to the shores of the Caspian Sea in the east. In that forest, wolves had lived and killed as they pleased. No lights had disturbed the darkness then, save for the cold and distant moon and stars that lit the sky. Then humans had come, bringing weapons and fire. They had burned the forests and hunted the wolves, driving them to the fringes of civilization and into the shadow realm of nightmares.

But the wolves were returning. The hunted had become hunters again.

Now civilization would be their friend. The fires that burned this time would burn for the wolves. Globalization and technology would drive their return to supremacy. Already Leanna had sent servants to the corners of the globe, to seed a new generation of werewolves. New York, Beijing, Sau Paulo, Moscow. By the time the authorities discovered them, it would be too late to stop the global rise of the werewolf.

Werewolf. It came from the Old English word *wer*, meaning *man*. Legends of the werewolf had existed for as long as humans had walked the earth, since the first stories were told around campfires to keep the darkness at bay. But they had never been taken seriously by science, not until Professor Wiseman had begun his experiments in the Carpathian Mountains, hunting and trapping werewolves, studying them, documenting their characteristics and habits. He had brought modern scientific methods to bear on an ancient legend, and like all great scientists had displaced superstition with understanding. Wiseman had taught Leanna everything he knew about the condition.

He'd even named it. *Lycanthropic.*

Wiseman had been a brilliant epidemiologist, but even he hadn't understood the full implications of his work. What he'd discovered wasn't simply a new class of disease, but a superior status to be enjoyed by those strong enough to harness its gift. It was a pathway to super-powers that humans had previously only ever dreamed of.

Ultimately, Wiseman had been too weak to use his knowledge in that way. Humans had always been weak, and nature punished weakness without pity or mercy. It was the cause of all human suffering. Now it was time for weakness to be stamped out.

The days of *Homo sapiens* were coming to an end. *Homo lupinus,* the 'wolf man' had made its debut. The lycanthropic would inherit the earth. And Leanna would be their queen.

She rose up on her haunches and howled at the moon, a sustained call rising and falling in pitch for a full minute before silence closed in again. She dropped back onto all fours and waited, her long ears twitching. A response came back to her, an echo of her own howl, coming from the south of the city. As it died away, another howl began, this one from the east. Then another joined it, and another, from every direction. From across the slate rooftops, from the tops of thrusting steel-and-glass towers, from beyond the ancient steeples and domes and cobbled streets and bustling thoroughfares of the sprawling city, a chorus of howls echoed in reply.

To be continued in Wolf Moon, Book 2 of the Lycanthropic series …

If you enjoyed this book, please leave a short review at Amazon. Thanks!

About the Author

Steve Morris has been a nuclear physicist, a dot com entrepreneur and a real estate investor, and is now the author of the Lycanthropic werewolf apocalypse series. He's a transhumanist and a practitioner of ashtanga yoga. He lives in Oxford, England.

Find out more at: stevemorrisbooks.com

Printed in Great Britain
by Amazon